## WRAPPED IN ZACH

"I came by to apologize for the kiss, for how I handled things."

Sophie could easily have let those words deflate her, but she was stronger than that. Something Zach would do well to remember. Because there was no way in hell a man who kissed like that was sorry that it happened.

"Really? You're going to go that route?" She laughed, knowing how calling him out would irritate him. She was done coddling him and his self-pity. "Don't lie to me. You can't kiss me with so much passion and desire and be sorry for it at the same time."

Those black-as-sin eyes narrowed. "Fine. I'm not sorry I kissed you. I am sorry for the way I treated you."

"Which time?" she countered. "After the kiss or all the years leading up to it?"

Crossing his arms over his wide chest, Zach shifted his feet and continued to glare. A portion of his tat peeked out beneath the hem of his gray T-shirt. Broad muscles stretched the thin material. Zach came by his spectacular frame the old-fashioned, hardworking way, with intense manual labor.

The man exuded sex appeal, but there was so much more to him than physical strength and an impressive exterior. Layers of emotions, some dark and some caring, made up the intriguing man . . .

# BOOK YOUR PLACE ON OUR WEBSITE AND MAKE THE READING CONNECTION!

We've created a customized website just for our very special readers, where you can get the inside scoop on everything that's going on with Zebra, Pinnacle and Kensington books.

When you come online, you'll have the exciting opportunity to:

- View covers of upcoming books
- Read sample chapters
- Learn about our future publishing schedule (listed by publication month and author)
- Find out when your favorite authors will be visiting a city near you
- Search for and order backlist books from our online catalog
- Check out author bios and background information
- Send e-mail to your favorite authors
- Meet the Kensington staff online
- Join us in weekly chats with authors, readers and other guests
- Get writing guidelines
- AND MUCH MORE!

**Visit our website at
http://www.kensingtonbooks.com**

# WRAPPED IN YOU

## JULES BENNETT

## ZEBRA BOOKS
### KENSINGTON PUBLISHING CORP.

http://www.kensingtonbooks.com

ZEBRA BOOKS are published by

Kensington Publishing Corp.
119 West 40th Street
New York, NY 10018

All Kensington titles, imprints, and distributed lines are
available at special quantity discounts for bulk purchases
for sales promotion, premiums, fund-raising, educational
or institutional use.

Special book excerpts or customized printings can also be
created to fit specific needs. For details, write or phone the
office of the Kensington Sales Manager. Attn.: Sales Department. Kensington Publishing Corp., 119 West 40th Street,
New York, NY 10018. Phone: 1-800-221-2647.

Zebra and the Z logo Reg. U.S. Pat. & TM Off.

First Printing: April 2016
ISBN-13: 978-1-4201-3908-2
ISBN-10: 1-4201-3908-8

eISBN-13: 978-1-4201-3909-9
eISBN-10: 1-4201-3909-6

10 9 8 7 6 5 4 3 2 1

Printed in the United States of America

# Acknowledgments

A huge thanks to my awesome agent, Elaine Spencer, for being my cheerleader, my sounding board, and my voice of reason. This series is possible because of you.

To my amazing editor, John Scognamiglio. You are such a joy to work with. Thank you for loving this series and seeing my vision.

To my sister, Angel, for always plotting no matter when my mood strikes. We've done some spur-of-the-moment plotting in strange places!

To Jill, for always having my back and offering advice.

I have to thank God for giving me everything I need and blessing me with this wonderful life.

Lastly, to my husband and girls who are absolutely my world. Every day is brighter because of you.

# Chapter One

On any other day, Zach Monroe would avoid the very tempting, sexy Sophie Allen for several very valid reasons. First, she looked too damn good in her little skirts hugging those round hips. Second, she was dating some prick who didn't deserve her, so Zach had no business lusting.

Most of all, though, he'd ruined her life years ago. He'd been cocky when he should've been responsible.

In a move that shocked him, Sophie had called earlier in the day and asked him to come by her office. Actually she'd called his work line, which rang to his cell. Apparently she wanted to keep this impromptu meeting professional. Whatever. The sooner he figured out what she wanted, the sooner he could leave and get back to his work. A career in construction meant limited time talking to people and plenty of time hammering out frustrations.

Zach tugged on the old oak door of the little town house where Sophie's real estate office was located in Haven, Georgia. A single bell chimed, indicating his arrival.

The second he stepped over the threshold the scent of something floral hit him in the gut.

Sophie. Anytime he'd been around her she'd always smelled like flowers, like freshness and summertime.

Great, now he was sounding like a damn woman describing Sophie's signature scent. He totally lost all control of his thoughts when he was anywhere near her.

A penance for his crime much worse than the year he'd spent in jail.

The small office space with the pale yellow walls, various green plants in colorful pots adorning the waiting area, looked inviting the way he imagined Sophie would want. Sunlight flooded through the wide front window, casting a beam directly into her little space in this world.

The woman he'd once considered a good friend, and possibly something more, rounded the end of the hallway, a document in one hand, pen in the other. She had one of those damn body-hugging skirts that stopped at her knees, this one in dark purple, paired with a simple gray sleeveless sweater and little flats in some animal print. Her golden hair spiraled down around her shoulders in soft curls he'd give anything to feel over his body. She never failed to steal his breath. That instant punch to the gut happened every single time she came near.

Sophie probably just saw him as a scruffy construction worker who drove a beat-up old truck that sounded worse than it looked.

Whereas he saw her as everything his life wasn't: polished, beautiful, and pure. His childhood demons alone were enough to prove how different they truly were.

But it was her limp that got him in a stranglehold and tightened a vise around his chest. Some days her gait was more pronounced than others, but her handicap was always there, always twisting that knife a little deeper into his gut. Visual reminders of his screwups gutted him quicker than anything.

Sophie's bright green eyes came up to meet his. "Zach." Her shoulders stiffened, the grip on her papers tightened. "I'm still waiting on the others, if you want to have a seat in my office."

Attention on her physical beauty and all he'd thrown away held him speechless. Then her words penetrated through the haze. "What others?"

"Liam and Braxton." She turned and disappeared back into what he assumed was her office.

What the hell was this about?

Like the proverbial moth to a flame, Zach followed her. His mood plummeted from intrigued over the meeting to irritation with the impending get-together with his brothers.

Sophie's office was just as inviting as the lobby area. The cheery yellow curtains, the fresh, vibrant floral arrangement in a small vase on her desk, and the picture in a silver frame. Zach's eyes immediately went to the photo of Sophie standing with Zach's late sister, Chelsea.

Chelsea, who was taken from them all too soon. She'd been vibrant, full of energy and life, and always seeking the next adventure. The fact that she'd died in a freak skiing accident was enough to give him some warped sense of peace. She hadn't suffered and she'd been doing what she loved. Still . . .

"Seems unreal, doesn't it?" she asked, her eyes traveling to the photo as she stood behind her desk. "I don't know how many times I've started to text her or I've turned down her street and caught myself. I miss talking to her, miss her laugh."

Zach swallowed hard. Yeah, he'd done the same.

He didn't think he'd ever get used to not having his full-of-life sister around. She was the only one out of all four adopted siblings that ever "got" him.

Pausing at the two chairs in front of Sophie's desk, Zach opted to stand against the wall. No need to get cozy here when he was damn near a panic attack at being so close to Sophie in such a small space.

Zach hadn't seen Sophie since the funeral four months ago, when she'd cried in his arms, clinging to his shirt at the graveside. Zach doubted she'd specifically sought him out for comfort. He just happened to be the one in line behind her when she'd broken. He'd been hesitant to embrace her, but once he had, he'd entered into another level of hell because now he knew how perfect she felt in his arms. He realized what all he'd thrown away.

When she'd pulled herself together, though, she'd released him like she'd been burned and turned on her heels for her car. He hadn't seen her since.

He'd been so caught up in his own grief, he hadn't considered how she was coping. Zach figured her hoity-toity boyfriend with his polished cuff links had probably patted her on the back. While Zach had mascara on his dress shirt, he couldn't imagine Sophie's man letting his suits get ruined.

Seeing her walk away from that graveside had shifted something in him. Something he couldn't define and something he'd had no choice but to ignore.

The bell on the front door chimed again. Zach raked his palm over his face, his whiskers bristling against his palm. Which brother would step through the door next? The one Zach actually still talked to, or the one Zach avoided at all costs?

"We're in here," Sophie called as she crossed her office to greet the new guest.

Folding his arms over his chest, Zach kept his eyes on the floor. Focusing on his scuffed work boots against the pristine white carpeting was far better than seeing Sophie's limp as she left the room.

"Wow. This must be something major for you to show up."

Zach glanced toward the door at his younger brother, Braxton. "I have no idea what we were called in for."

Braxton sank into the chair across from Sophie's desk. "You gonna have a seat?"

"I'm fine."

On his feet, he was one step closer to the exit, right where he preferred.

Looking closer at Sophie's office area gave him an insight into her life, her personality, whether he wanted to learn more or not. She obviously loved the color yellow. She also had an eye for art, if the pencil sketches randomly displayed were any indicator. The sketches of landscapes and old homes and buildings were so detailed.

Before he could study the artwork much more, the bell chimed for a third time. Perfect. The final piece to this missing, awkward puzzle had arrived. Let the party of anger and shouting begin.

Sophie led Liam in. Liam froze as his eyes landed on Zach. "What's going on?"

Zach forced himself not to look away from the scar running down the side of Liam's face. So much pain in this room, pain that none of them would discuss.

"I need to talk to you guys about the property Chelsea left you." Sophie skirted around her desk and took a seat. Lacing her fingers over the rich wood top, she eyed all three men. "I apologize for not telling you all on the phone what was going on. I figured if I told Liam that Zach was coming, or vice versa, you all would find an excuse not to be here, and I needed all three of you in the same room."

"What's so important with the property?" Liam asked, taking the seat by Braxton.

They'd still not decided what to do with that monstrosity of a home on the edge of town. Their sister had bought it at a good price because it needed so much work, but Zach never did know what her true intentions were for the Civil War–era mansion.

Just a month ago he, Braxton, and Liam had been informed they were not only the new owners, per Chelsea's will, they also owed the back taxes Chelsea had failed to pay. Perhaps it was a good thing Sophie called this little meeting, considering the brothers needed to figure out the tax issue and decide what to do with the property.

"The city council is interested in buying the estate," Sophie went on. "They want to turn the main house and the two smaller cottages on the property into a museum and tourist attraction. With being so close to Savannah, and all the historical value of the home, they're positive it will pull in more tourists."

Zach snorted. Whatever his sister had wanted to do with the home was a mystery, but he sure as hell knew she wouldn't want a museum. An old, stuffy museum was the total opposite of his free-spirited, fun sister.

Beyond that, there was no way in hell Zach would sell to anyone associated with the mayor.

He glanced at Braxton, trying to gauge his brother's reaction to this news. Anytime the mayor's name was brought up, Zach cringed for Braxton. Betrayal ran deep in this family.

"We haven't discussed what we're doing with it yet," Braxton said through gritted teeth.

Sophie offered one of her signature sweet smiles. "I understand this is a difficult position. I really am just trying to help you guys get out from under such a burden."

Zach waited for Braxton to say something more, or even for Liam to jump to his defense. When both remained quiet, Zach chimed in. "We need to pay the taxes first."

"Actually, if you sell the home, the taxes would come out of the amount of the sale." Sophie opened a folder and slid a paper out. "This is what the city is willing to pay for the place. It's a good price. The taxes and mortgage would be paid off."

Zach didn't move from his spot against the wall. Hell, he was still grieving. How could he think about facts and figures right now? Facts and figures proposed by a man who had stabbed Braxton in the back only a few short years ago.

"Looks good to me," Liam said after looking at the paper. He settled back into his chair and crossed an ankle over his knee. "I'm fine with selling, but Braxton needs to okay this."

Silent, Braxton still studied the numbers. Whatever emotional turmoil Braxton struggled with, the man was always business first. More than likely Braxton was pushing back that slice of pain and crunching numbers in his head. Zach, on the other hand, didn't need to see the paper.

"I'm not okay with this." The words were out of Zach's mouth before he thought to keep them in. Someone needed to stand up for Braxton and for what Chelsea would've wanted. "We can't decide this second to sell. There's too much to think about and we need to sit down and discuss this privately."

Without turning, Liam snorted. "When the hell have you ever thought about a decision? You rush into everything."

The barb hit home, but Zach wasn't about to dredge up their past here. Or ever, if he could help it.

"Martin has convinced the mayor to offer a very generous amount." Sophie stared at him across the room. Apparently thinking he was crazy. "You don't want to sit on this."

Zach didn't give a shit what her boyfriend, Martin, had done or how generous the mayor's offer was. Both were assholes as far as Zach was concerned.

Even though Zach was currently working on a project for the city, the project he was near completing was all business. This deal that Sophie was proposing on their behalf was crossing into the personal territory.

Beyond Braxton's hatred for Mayor Stevens, Chelsea loved that property and it had been her dream to own it someday. How could they just sell?

The pre–Civil War home had housed slaves in the underground tunnels that led from the main house to two other homes on the estate that overlooked a lake. No boring museum would be going in there. He'd find a way to . . . hell, he didn't know, but he knew he wasn't selling to the assholes in suits.

"You have to pay the taxes somehow," Sophie argued. "This is the best way to pay off the debt and not have to worry about what to do with such a large, empty estate."

Still sitting forward in his seat to look at the paper, Braxton glanced over his shoulder at Zach. He merely stared back, waiting for Braxton's thoughts. Hurt settled in Braxton's eyes, but there was an overlying mask of anger.

Braxton shifted back around and faced Sophie. "We need to discuss this. We can't decide right here."

"And we'll get the damn taxes paid," Zach muttered just as Sophie opened her mouth. "Let us worry about Chelsea's property. You can tell your boyfriend and the mayor we don't want the offer."

Sophie's shoulders stiffened, her eyes narrowing in his direction. "I'm only trying to help everyone here. You don't have to be a jerk."

Yeah, well, he felt like a jerk, so how else was he supposed to act?

"What do you want to do with the property?" Liam asked, turning in his seat just enough to see Zach.

"Pay the taxes and figure it out from there."

"I don't have time to invest in that place," Liam countered. "I understand why Braxton would hesitate, but you have to think about what a liability that property is going to be. I don't want to sink money into something that will have no benefit to me."

Zach uncrossed his arms and stood straight up. "Well, I'm not ready to get rid of that land. Chelsea loved that old house and she had a vision. She used every bit of her savings and her portion of the inheritance from Mom and Dad to buy the place, and you're ready to just give it away for some museum? Or if that's not enough, perhaps you've forgotten about—"

"Enough." Braxton glared from one brother to another. "We'll discuss this once we've all had a chance to think. Bringing up Anna won't solve the problems."

Anna. The woman Braxton had been engaged to until she'd shown her true colors and left Braxton days before the wedding. She'd run straight into Rand Stevens's waiting arms. The two were both shallow, and

Zach hoped they were miserable together for many, many years.

"I've thought of Braxton, but we can't let that situation stop us from using common sense here." Liam came to his feet, hands on his hips and blue eyes blazing. "I'm getting that headache off our hands. We've already paid the mortgage on it this month and still have the taxes due. I'm done."

"Fine. Then be done with it. I'll cover your part." Good thing he had a chunk in savings, but even that would run out if he didn't come up with a plan. "Consider yourself dismissed."

Braxton rose, holding up his hands. "This is a record. You two went five whole minutes without griping at each other. We'll give Sophie a definite answer in a week. Can we all stop and think about what Chelsea would want us to do? Leave my past out of the decision making."

"Chelsea wouldn't want you guys fighting," Sophie muttered.

Zach's eyes cut to her. Her face had paled, showcasing the dark circles beneath her eyes. Damn it. Why did her silent vulnerability always make him feel like a bastard?

"I'll take a week." Zach agreed with Braxton. "But I'm not changing my mind. Selling is a bad idea right now."

He turned to go, when Sophie called his name. Glancing over his shoulder, two sets of eyes were on him. Liam kept his back turned.

Zach raised a brow, waiting for Sophie to say something. Was that moisture in her eyes? She blinked twice, as if willing unshed tears away. Pushing away from her desk, she came to her feet and straightened her shoulders.

"Don't be stubborn about this," she told him, her

voice calm and controlled. "I know Chelsea wanted this house, and I know Braxton has issues with the mayor. The past can't be changed, and Chelsea would understand that you guys have no use for the property."

Zach said nothing as he turned and walked out of her office. He'd barely cleared the door before he heard Braxton say, "That went well."

Exiting the building, Zach actually agreed. He and Liam hadn't thrown punches, as they'd been known to do on the rare occasions they'd been together. And Zach had managed to avoid the giant elephant in the room.

Sliding behind the wheel of his work truck, Zach brought the engine to life. Gripping the steering wheel, he looked down at his hands. The scars criss-crossing his knuckles always reminded him how he'd fought to save those he loved and how he'd severed any bond they'd once shared.

Yeah, that went well in there, considering they were all broken people with very different views of absolutely everything.

Zach was not looking forward to more chitchats with his brothers over this, and he sure as hell wasn't wanting another encounter with Sophie. He couldn't handle being that close, not when he still wanted her despite their past.

Sophie let herself into her cottage, all while juggling four grocery bags full of total crap food that had an insane amount of calories. This day called for ice cream of epic proportions as well as salty chips to follow, for the perfect balanced diet.

Kicking her front door shut, she headed toward the back of the house and into her kitchen, where she dumped her purse and the bags on the center island. Digging through her purchases, she was torn between the chunky chocolate chip and the strawberry with the cheesecake bites.

"Decisions, decisions," she muttered as her cat, Flynn, slithered against the back of her legs.

Choosing the chocolate for now—because chocolate was a staple for emergencies—Sophie put the other ice cream away for later. She didn't have to settle for just one pint tonight, right?

Toeing off her ballet flats, she padded to the living room, where she sank onto her bright red sofa. Having all three Monroe brothers in her office had been quite an experience. They were all so different, but the stubborn trait was one common thread. She'd known calling them all in at the same time would be risky, given the ever-present tension between Zach and Liam, not to mention her own issues with Zach. She'd also known she was taking a big chance with upsetting Braxton, but she knew that of all the brothers, he was the most levelheaded and wouldn't blame her for being the messenger. She really was trying to help, not stir the proverbial pot.

Selling the estate on Sunset Lake was a perfect opportunity for them to get out from under the burden of Chelsea's property.

Sophie and Chelsea had been best friends since grade school when the Monroes adopted Chelsea. When Zach was twelve, the Monroes had taken him in as well, rounding the number of kids to four.

Mr. and Mrs. Monroe were saints. They'd adopted three boys and a girl, none of them biologically related, and had raised them as a united family.

From the beginning Zach had sparked her attention with his quiet, mysterious mannerisms. Since she'd known him he'd been a man of few words. Like today in her office, when he'd propped himself up on one shoulder against the wall and simply stared at her beneath heavy lids. Zach was the type who observed, and it was anyone's guess what went on in that head of his.

Sophie had grown up perfectly proper, with church on Sundays, her parents belonging to the right social groups, and straight A's through school. Yet everything about her life felt boring and stuffy. The moment she'd met Zach, she couldn't help but be drawn to him.

Sophie and Chelsea had instantly clicked when they'd met on the playground. They'd bonded over their schoolgirl crush on Beau Skeens. He'd had a Mohawk. A kid with a Mohawk was beyond cool, and Sophie and Chelsea had both giggled behind the swing set while they watched Beau play basketball. From then on the girls were inseparable.

And when she'd gone home with Chelsea after school one day a couple years later and saw Zach, that infatuation with the bad boy continued. He sat, scowling, at the Monroes' kitchen table until Chelsea punched him in the arm and told him to smile because this house would be the best place he'd ever want to live. Then she'd invited him to walk to the Dairy Dream for a milk shake.

Yeah. Sophie had fallen for the boy who seemed to have a chip on his shoulder, but could be talked into a double chocolate shake by his new perky sister.

While Sophie had been raised to worry what others thought, Zach didn't give a damn. As a teen, she'd wondered how well that would go over with her proper parents, if she just threw caution to the wind and worried about what made her happy and not the rest of the world. Chelsea had hinted more than once that Zach would be good for Sophie, and vice versa.

Nearly a decade had passed since she and Zach had finally stopped dancing around each other. They were heading toward something that could've been remarkable, when all of their lives changed in an instant. Since then, Zach Monroe treated her as if she had the plague, as if he couldn't stand to be in the same room with her. He'd pushed most people away and nearly worked himself to death . . . and all of that was after he'd gotten out of jail.

Swearing off bad boys, silent seducers, and that pull toward the mysterious, no matter how heavy the temptation, Sophie had opted to move on. For a while she'd been afraid to date, afraid for a man to see the scars she had hidden beneath her clothes. Eventually she realized the scars weren't going away and she needed a social life. She'd been dating Martin for six months, and they were quite compatible when they could squeeze in dates between their busy schedules. Well, they weren't so much compatible as they shared similar backgrounds and Sophie's parents loved him.

But lately she'd been wondering if there should be more to a relationship. Shouldn't there be sparks or . . . something?

Flynn jumped onto the sofa and curled up next to Sophie.

"Great, I'm the cat lady," she muttered against the next bite of ice cream. "I'll die old and alone. You'll probably outlive me."

She sighed as she dug in for another spoonful. She needed to call Martin and let him know the guys were going to think about the offer. With the way Zach had left abruptly, and Liam still dead set on selling, she truly had no idea which way this decision would go.

Sophie's cell chimed from her purse she'd left in the kitchen. Normally she'd ignore it, but she had several new listings and she was known for being prompt and professional.

Eyeing the carton of ice cream, she silently promised to return soon. Running as quick as she could allow herself, she pulled the phone from her purse and smiled at the name lighting up her screen.

"Hey, Braxton," she answered.

"Hey, Sophie. Are you busy?"

His rich tone flooded the line. Of all the Monroe boys, Braxton was the peacemaker, the comforter, the "brainy" one. Braxton and Liam had always been like brothers to Sophie. They'd always treated her as family, and their friendship ran deeper than any bond she'd ever had with her own family.

Then there was Zach. Regardless of the anger she held toward him, there was always some nugget of attraction. After all this time, she figured it was just something she'd have to live with.

And her anger didn't stem from the accident. Her years of rage stemmed from him blocking out those who cared for him, those who needed to get through the emotional mess with him. Did he even wonder how she was doing, after all that happened? Did he even care that she'd cried and cursed and broken things when he wouldn't see her?

Gripping the phone, she focused on Braxton and pushed his frustrating brother to the back of her mind.

"Just digging into a dinner of chocolate-chunk ice cream." She made her way back to the couch. "I'm good at multitasking, though."

"I cannot figure out how you live on junk and don't weigh—"

"I'd watch what I said about a woman's weight," she warned with a laugh. "I assume you didn't call to discuss my pounds or my warped version of dinner."

"Yeah." Braxton's sigh came through loud and clear. "I wanted to apologize for everything earlier. I know you're just trying to help."

Propping her feet on the low coffee table, Sophie settled deeper into the corner of her couch. "You may be the most considerate man I know. I put you in an awkward position and you're calling to apologize to me?"

"You were just giving us all the information so we could do what we wanted," he told her. "I actually appreciate that you didn't dance around whatever I would be feeling. It's Zach and Liam's behavior that I'm apologizing for, though."

"I know what I'm getting into with you guys. Liam already texted me and said he was sorry."

"And Zach?"

Sophie laughed. "I think you know the answer to that."

Even though she hadn't expected anything from Zach, his dismissal of her still stung. Did he honestly think he was the only one grieving? Not just Chelsea but years of emotions he held on to were surely going to break him at some point.

Not her problem. She'd moved on.

"I've backed out of playing the middleman with those two," Braxton went on. "They'll have to actually discuss this if they want to come to an agreement."

Sophie cringed. "Without you between them as referee, how will they have a conversation without shouting and one of them storming off?"

"They're adults. They'll figure it out."

"As long as I can tell Martin something by next week, that's fine."

"You'll have an answer," he promised. "One way or another. I need to get to class, so I'll talk to you later. Just wanted to apologize for my asshole brother."

"Can I ask what you're leaning toward?" Silence answered her question, followed by a sigh. "It's okay. Just think about it. I'm not judging you guys either way. I know this is hard for everybody."

"Yeah, it is. That still doesn't give my brothers the right to go at it in your office. It also doesn't give Zach the right to be a jerk just because he can't get a grip on his emotions."

Sophie dropped her spoon into the carton and set it on the table. "No worries. The animosity with Zach isn't new."

"Soph—"

"No." She came to her feet, sending Flynn to the floor. "It's fine. I mean, it's not fine, but it is what it is. Zach has problems he needs to work out on his own. Apparently he's perfectly content to live inside that shell."

"I wish someone would knock some sense into him," Braxton muttered. "I'll call you in a couple days. Gotta run."

Placing her cell on the arm of the couch, Sophie couldn't help but wonder what it would take to get Zach to see that life hadn't ended that night. Yes, mistakes were made, lives were altered. Why did he feel it was okay to hate the world, to push away those who only wanted to help him?

She had hoped the one silver lining to come from Chelsea's death would be Zach waking up and seeing that life was fleeting and he still had people here who cared what happened to him.

Chelsea passed away four months ago, and the man was just as introverted and closed up as ever. How long could one person keep so much locked inside? Not to mention his past, before he ever came to live with the Monroes. Zach was a walking bundle of angst when he'd arrived in Haven, Georgia. Then life happened and added even more.

One of these days his emotions were going to explode. Sophie found herself wondering who would be there to catch him when he broke.

# Chapter Two

Easing his truck up by the curb near the hardware store, Zach pulled out his phone to call Nathan, his right-hand man. They were nearing the end of an outdoor patio and gazebo area at the Community Center. He fully trusted his guys whenever he had to leave the site, but he was itching to get back after that little family reunion. Pounding away with power tools was the best kind of tension reliever.

Okay, sex was the best tension reliever, but that wasn't an option right at this minute.

Before he headed back to the site, he needed a few more materials from Knobs & Knockers, the only hardware store in town. The place had been around for decades and was now run by the third generation.

Zach had just reached the door to the store as he dialed, but before he could hit Send, he spotted Rand Stevens strutting down the sidewalk in a three-piece suit. Who the hell still wore that shit? Especially when the temperatures were flirting with summerlike highs lately. The man probably didn't even sweat.

"Zach." Rand nodded, offering a toothy smile. "I figured you'd be at the site, finishing up."

Zach let the veiled jab roll off his shoulders. "Picking up a few more parts and heading back."

Rand stepped in front of Zach, cutting him off before he could reach for the antique handle to the store. "I heard you spoke with Sophie yesterday."

Obviously this was going to be a game. Zach merely crossed his arms and waited to make his move. Rand prided himself on keeping this town polished and perfectly maintained, all while keeping up appearances. No way would this man cause a scene if Zach opted to tell him what he could do with the offer on the Sunset Lake house.

Zach had more patience than most people, so he'd keep his decision to himself. Rand didn't need to know what went through the minds of Zach and his brothers.

"Our offer was generous," Rand went on. "Selling would benefit the city and help you guys all at the same time."

Zach glanced through the window of the hardware store, then back to the nuisance in the gray suit. He highly doubted Rand was extending any sort of helping hand, but Zach was smart enough to keep his mouth shut.

Just a game, he reminded himself. Zach was fine playing it, considering he was a professional with a good reputation his father had helped him build. Even after the accident and the sentencing, Zach had gotten out of prison. His father had paved the way in the community by not making excuses on Zach's behalf. Zach had paid the price for his crime and once he was freed, it was time to move on. People made mistakes, people deserved second chances.

Zach wasn't about to tarnish his or his father's

hard work by mouthing off, no matter how much he wanted to.

"My sister loved that property," Zach said, stepping aside as a patron headed toward the door. He waited until the person stepped inside before going on. "My brothers and I will decide what's best for our family and you'll hear something by Friday. Now, if you'll excuse me, I have a project I need to get back to."

He didn't wait to hear if Rand had more to say. Zach was done listening. He jerked the door open on the old hardware store—or as he referred to it, his home away from home. He actually spent more time here and on job sites than at his house, which was fine. When he was home and alone, that's when memories started flooding up to the surface and strangling him; one of the main reasons he'd opted to take on the renovations at his house. Being home alone was pure hell, and he needed to stay busy all his waking hours.

Which was why he was so damn good at his job; he lived and breathed work. For the past decade he'd thrown himself into every single project, no matter how small. Letting anything else into his world wasn't an option.

Ed Monroe had nestled the will to work so deep when Zach was a cocky punk. Ed could've, and probably should've, kicked Zach to the curb more than once, but the Monroes had taken Zach in, bad attitude and all.

The scent of freshly mixed paint, metal, and wood hit him as Zach stepped into Knobs & Knockers. Behind the counter, Macy was ringing up a customer. She glanced up and smiled before turning her attention back to the elderly man.

Macy Hayward was the current owner of the bustling little store. She might be young and petite with long, dark hair and wide, expressive eyes, but this woman knew everything from PVC pipe to power tools, and she was actually one person he considered a true friend. Not like someone he'd confide in—he didn't bare his soul to anyone—but he was comfortable around her and they could talk shop.

"Thanks." Macy handed the customer his receipt and a small brown paper bag. "Just call if you need more of those drywall screws. I can always bring them to you after I close to save you another trip out."

Once the man thanked her and left, Zach crossed to the counter and rested his forearms on the scratched, scarred wood surface that had been there from the start of the store.

"Saw you chatting with one of your favorite people."

Zach narrowed his eyes at her smirk. "Funny."

Macy rested her arms on the counter. "Apparently you played nice or you wouldn't be in such a mood now."

"I'm always in a mood."

Her grin widened. "Yes, but now even your eyebrows are drawn in. You must really be pissed." Macy patted his hands and looked him in the eyes. "I promise not to tease you anymore. Now, what can I get ya? I assume you're still working on the Community Center. Or are you picking up something for your house?"

Zach pushed off the counter. "The Community Center. Should be done by next week."

The city council had paid him a nice chunk to add a picturesque patio area that they could rent for receptions or other summer events. His job, to build a large gazebo with curved benches, outdoor seating, and a stone-wall perimeter, was nearly complete. Another reason he wasn't telling the mayor and his cohorts where to shove their offer.

Between the mayor stealing Braxton's fiancée a few years ago and Sophie dating one of the city council members, there was no way in hell Zach would willingly negotiate away a piece of property his sister loved. A piece of property she'd invested her life savings into.

"I'll go find what I need," he told her. "I'll just yell if I need help."

"Heard Liam was in town." Macy smoothed her straight, black hair back and tucked it behind her ears. "Everything okay?"

Was anything ever okay when his oldest brother was mentioned? Not where Zach was concerned.

"Just wrapping up some legal matters from Chelsea's estate."

"She's going to be missed. I know I already feel a void." Her brows dipped as concern filled her eyes. "I'm so sorry you guys are going through this, Zach."

Not wanting any sympathy, Zach shrugged, refusing to discuss such a personal topic in public. "We'll be fine. Chelsea bought that old historic property on the edge of town, and we just have to figure out what to do with it."

"And you three aren't in agreement."

Zach grunted. "You know us all too well."

"You guys never change," she told him with a sigh. "I figure at this point you never will."

The bell chimed again and Macy greeted a customer who came in and headed toward the back where the pipe was stored.

"What do you want to do with it?" she asked, once the customer was out of earshot.

"Keep it," Zach stated. "Chelsea wanted the house and I think we need to hang on to it."

"What do the others say?"

"Liam wants to sell and be done. Braxton hasn't said one way or another."

Macy crossed her arms over her chest. "Must be a difficult position for Braxton."

Zach nodded, shoving his hands into his pockets. "He wouldn't say if this bothers him, but I know it does."

"So what would you do if you kept it?" she asked.

"Still thinking on that one," he replied, rocking back on his heels. "I better get my supplies. Be right back."

She held up a hand and grinned. "I need to ask a favor before you go, if you have the time."

Intrigued, he tilted his head. "What's that?"

"Well, it's more of a business proposition," she corrected, then waved him away. "Go on and get your supplies. We can talk as I'm ringing you up."

Nodding, he headed to the back bins holding various sizes of washers, bolts, screws, and nuts. As he sifted through the items he needed, Zach couldn't help but wonder what it would take to convince Liam that selling wasn't the right decision, at least not now.

Of all the rash decision making Zach had done in his life, for once he was going to think about this property before deciding anything. Sophie surely had to understand that. Or maybe her boyfriend had convinced her selling it to the council would be best. Zach had a hard time wrapping his mind around the fact that Sophie would go against Chelsea's wishes. Sophie was well aware of how much Chelsea loved that house and the land.

More than once Chelsea had snuck over the property

line, ignoring the NO TRESPASSING signs to go sit by the lake or wander around the grounds. She'd had a slight obsession with the historic place, and Zach couldn't let go. Not yet.

Of course, Martin could have convinced Sophie that's what Chelsea would've wanted. Who knows what went on in their relationship? Zach didn't want to know, actually. Sophie had been raised so polished and pure, Zach had no doubt her parents loved that she dated a man with such upstanding social status. A man without a criminal record.

What parents wanted a convicted felon hanging around their daughter? What woman truly wanted a tarnished man in her personal life?

This whole line of thinking was ridiculous, so he didn't even answer his own questions. Zach had no place in Sophie's life. He'd had a narrow window to ease into her life and he'd blown it all to shit. Couldn't fault her for realizing she deserved better.

Damn it, here he was trying to find some simple bolts for the new picnic tables, and his mind had circled back to Sophie again.

He needed to focus. Work came first, leaving no room for foolish, juvenile thoughts.

As he headed back to the counter, Macy was swiping a customer's credit card and chatting about the unseasonal heat with it only being April. Once the man was gone, Zach set his items down on the counter.

Macy knew to put everything on his account. He paid it off monthly, but this way everything he purchased was on one itemized receipt for the month.

"So what was this favor and business proposition?" he asked as she slid his bolts into a small brown sack with the store logo on the front.

"When you built the Clevengers' house, you had designed it too. Right?"

"Yes. They didn't like anything they'd seen in books or online." The bag crinkled as Zach gripped the top. "They liked portions of various ones, so I drew up the plans to their specifications."

"Could I make an appointment with you to discuss some house plans?"

"I wasn't aware you were thinking of building."

"I don't want to live above the store with my dad forever, no matter how state-of-the-art everything is up in that apartment." She shrugged and smoothed her hair behind her ears. "I'm in no rush, but I'd like to get the ball rolling when you have time."

When he had time? That would never happen, but for a friend he would certainly make time.

"Why don't I come by here one evening around closing? We can discuss your ideas then."

A wide smile lit up her face. "That would be great. I know you're busy with so many other things, so don't feel pressured to rush this. Like I said, I'm in no hurry. I've lived upstairs with Dad my whole life. A few more years won't matter."

Stepping back from the counter, Zach gripped his sack and headed for the door. "I'll call you and we can figure out what day works best."

"Thanks, Zach."

He stepped out into the bright midday sun and headed down the wide sidewalk toward his old beat-up work truck. As much as certain people in the town grated on his nerves, Zach supposed he'd be miserable anywhere he lived. Why not live in an area that thrived when so many others were tanking? All of the local shops were bustling at any given time of the day. Cafés, boutiques, downtown loft apartments; Haven had so much to offer.

People took pride in their stores, their homes. All the storefronts still had that vintage feel with the wide windows and displays, bright-colored siding, and little concrete stoops with oversized pots of flowers provided by the city and kept up by the garden club.

Zach jerked the handle on his truck and slid in behind the wheel, pulling his creaky door shut with a *slam*. Braxton still lived in Haven, but Liam had moved to Savannah. Zach had nowhere else to go. This was it for him. The Monroes had given him roots, something no one else had ever done, and in all honesty, he wouldn't have a clue where to go.

Getting all nostalgic was absurd. He fired up the engine and eased out onto the two-lane street, watching for pedestrians. Since Chelsea had passed, he kept running through those deep meanings of life. What was his purpose? Was he meant to just go through the motions of day-to-day living, serving other people while this anger and guilt raged inside of him? Would he ever find peace with himself?

Shit. He cranked up his radio on his favorite heavy metal station and turned onto Vine Street. He had to get his head on straight or he'd drive himself nuts. He planned on finishing his workday so he could head over to Chelsea's old apartment. The landlord had told them to take their time getting Chelsea's things out, but apparently now he had new tenants who were hoping to move in by the end of the month. Now Zach had to fully face that she was gone. Sorting through her things was going to be a difficult task, and he wasn't going to ask Liam or Braxton to help. The last thing he needed was for either of his brothers to see him break down.

Because, of all four siblings, Zach had been closest to Chelsea. She always knew what to say, when to say it. She didn't let him mope or start to slip into self-pity over his past. She'd plunk right down on the window seat in his room and lay it out there. She'd been so wise as a teen, when she'd tell him the greatest days of his life were happening right now. The Monroes were the parents she'd always dreamed of, and if he was going to keep reflecting back on his past, he was stealing the joy from now.

Damn, she'd been right. And after their heart-to-heart talk, which always left him feeling stupid and ungrateful, she would either whip up a batch of cookies or ask if he wanted to head out on the dirt bikes. You just never knew what her mind would think up for fun. Chelsea was certainly not a predictable woman. But she was loyal and she'd loved with her whole heart.

There was no doubt in Zach's mind he'd not be able to get through her apartment without losing it. And with his unstable emotions now, he preferred not to have an audience.

He'd only broken down three times in his life: when each of his parents had passed, and when he turned Sophie away that first time she came to visit him in jail.

With Chelsea gone he was due for another, and he just preferred to be alone . . . like always.

Filtering through the clothes in Chelsea's closet was both painful and amusing. Sophie slid the hangers one after another across the bar, remembering different events with nearly each piece. Like the black halter dress Chelsea had deemed sexy and sure to get her a man. Too bad that when Chelsea set her eyes on the guy lounging at the bar, she'd made her way to him and fallen flat on her face, taking a waiter and a tray of drinks down with her. By the time she'd gotten to her feet, the man was gone and Sophie had nearly doubled over with belly-cramping laughter.

Sophie slid her hand over the shoulder of the purple sweater that she'd bought for Chelsea's last birthday. Seemed so silly now to look at the knitted garment. Sophie knew how much her friend loved purple and had bought the cardigan without hesitation. Had Sophie only known that was going to be Chelsea's last birthday, she would've bought something a hell of a lot more special than a useless, boring sweater.

She carefully slid the sweater from the hanger and folded it on the bed, next to some photos of them as teens and adults, as well as a pencil sketch of the Eiffel Tower Chelsea had framed and hung in her bedroom.

Sophie had been coming here on occasion since Chelsea's death to feel closer to her late friend. She and Chelsea had keys to each other's places because they often shared clothes. Not to mention the fact Chelsea had locked herself out multiple times. On the third time, she'd gotten Sophie a key since Sophie lived closer than Chelsea's brothers.

Today was the first day Sophie opted to start collecting minute items that represented the final thread linking their friendship. She'd make sure Braxton and Liam were okay with the items she wanted to take. If Zach wanted to weigh in, that was fine too, but she wasn't seeking him out for permission.

Refusing to dive back into a Zach memory, Sophie turned back to the closet. There were shoes haphazardly thrown onto the floor, but it was the stack of black binders nestled in the corner that caught her attention.

A part of Sophie felt like an intruder going through all of Chelsea's things. The other part knew Chelsea wouldn't mind one bit. The woman had been so carefree, letting nothing in life really disturb her. Besides, the two were as close as sisters and shared everything. Chelsea would want Sophie to have some things to remember her by.

Shifting the assortment of sneakers, boots, and flip-flops aside, Sophie pulled the binders from the closet. She'd just walked into the main room and set the thick folders on the dining table when keys jingled against the apartment door.

Startled, she cautiously moved toward the couch, where she'd put her purse, which contained pepper spray. Her eyes remained fixed on the knob, which she'd locked, but now it jiggled as an unknown tried to get in.

Did someone know this apartment sat empty and was coming to steal? More than likely she'd just watched too many criminal shows and it was just the landlord or maintenance . . . she had heard keys clanging, after all.

The door opened and the second Sophie saw a thick forearm leading to a wide shoulder, she dove for her purse. Unfortunately, she tripped when her hip gave out on her, and she fell to the floor behind the couch.

"What the hell?"

The familiar male voice only added to her humiliation. The man who let himself in wasn't the landlord, the maintenance man, or even a would-be burglar. Sophie would've rather faced any of those than the man who rounded the sofa and now stared down at her as she struggled to her feet.

"Sophie." He looked worried as his brows drew in. As he crouched down to her, his eyes raked over her body. "Let me help you."

Pushing off the plush carpet, Sophie refused to meet his eyes or even think of the concern she'd seen flash through them. "I'm fine."

"You fell."

"I tripped." Coming to her feet, she placed a hand on the back of the couch until she was steady. The familiar twinge in her hip had escalated to full-on piercing pain, and she needed to remain still until it subsided. "What are you doing here?"

The muscle in his jaw clenched as he came to his full height, towering over her and making her feel so small. He fisted his hands on his narrow hips and said nothing. The way he just stared at her did absolutely nothing to lessen her humiliation. Falling was one thing, but doing so because of an injury that continued to hinder her life at the most inopportune times was degrading.

Knowing Zach had never forgiven himself for her handicap still sent an ache through her that she feared would never go away. Sophie actually hurt for him.

"Zach?"

Dark eyes darted to hers, to her legs, then back up. "You didn't hurt yourself when you tripped, did you?"

"Um . . . no." She'd never admit her pain, especially to him. "I trip all the time."

The muscle ticked even more. "Because of . . ." He trailed off, but pointed to her leg as if he couldn't even say the word "limp."

As embarrassing as this was to make *him* uncomfortable because of *her* injury, she shook her head. "No. I just didn't know who was coming in and I was trying to get to the pepper spray in my purse."

A portion of the truth—that was all he was getting from her.

Zach rubbed his hand across his bearded jaw, and the bristling sound sent shivers through her. She didn't want shivers, had no room in her life for shivers. At least not from this man.

Still, that sound couldn't help but conjure up thoughts as to how the coarse hair would feel against her skin. Unfortunately, she'd never know.

She had to admit Zach Monroe's wide shoulders, scruffy jawline, and menacing, icy eyes were quite mesmerizing. Still, she wasn't looking for a man; she already had one.

Besides, she couldn't fully get over the way Zach had treated her over the past decade. Being dismissed, ignored, or barely given the time of day was damn hurtful, even if he was using it as a defense mechanism.

Still, her body responded to the man each and every time he was near . . . each response stronger than the last. Ignoring that invisible pull was the only option. She had a man in her life, a man she was supposed to meet for dinner very soon.

Sophie was only feeling this thread of attraction for Zach for the same reasons she had as a teen: Zach Monroe was reckless, mysterious in his quiet ways, and sexy as hell. Not boyfriend or relationship material for any woman in her right mind who didn't want to have her heart broken.

But the way he'd looked at her, had instantly gone on alert at the sight of her on the floor. Degrading as the moment was, that was the first honest, raw emotion she'd seen from the man in years.

"You know, you can talk about my condition," she told him, needing him to realize that bringing it out in the open didn't make her upset. "I'm used to it. I rarely notice it, actually."

More lies. Oftentimes after working long hours and showing homes, going up and down flights of stairs, the ache from all the limping got to her, and her other leg actually started hurting from taking up the slack from the injured one. But that was rare. Most of the time there was just an annoying ache she could live with.

"I don't want to discuss that. I just wanted to know if you were hurt from falling just now."

Protective shield back up. His eyes were no longer holding that vulnerable compassion. She'd already taken a mental picture of how he'd looked, and she'd never forget. Why couldn't he just let go? Why had everyone let him close himself off?

Sophie crossed her arms and stared up at him. "Just when would you like to discuss *that*? Because until you and I talk about what happened years ago, you'll never be at peace. I for one am sick of the way you've let this just eat away at you, because it's affected everyone around you."

She hadn't meant to snap; the words just flooded out of her mouth before she could put up her filter. She couldn't say she was sorry, though. A decade was a hell of a long time for any of them to keep all these emotions bottled up.

Zach massaged the back of his neck. "Drop it."

"Drop it? Is that how you cope?"

Those tortured eyes closed for the briefest of moments before his lids lifted and those eyes the color of rich chocolate met hers. "It's the only option I have. That accident . . ."

The low, raspy tone nearly had her reaching for him. The hurt lacing his voice matched that in her heart. They weren't friends anymore, not like they used to be, and she had no right to pry into his life, his emotions. Hadn't she moved on? Purposely guiding her life in another direction, away from anything that resembled the young man she used to love . . . or thought she'd loved.

She waited on him to finish his thought, but he just shook his head and glanced away.

Carefully gauging her words, Sophie took a slight step forward. "No, don't look away. That accident isn't what messed up your life. You messed it up afterward by pushing everyone away and not facing the fact that you're human. Why can't you see that people can't shun you without you allowing it? You're the one who built that invisible wall around yourself, refusing to let people in."

Silence hovered between them. Sophie could hear the steady thumping of her heart. She'd not been alone with Zach since before that night. Chelsea or another family member had always been present the few times they'd been in close proximity over the past several years. Awkwardness was now being pushed aside by long overdue questions.

Zach turned toward the door. "This was a mistake."

Oh no. He wasn't getting off that easy. She struggled to get between him and the door. She made it . . . barely.

"You're not leaving."

His eyes widened as if he hadn't expected such a quick, defiant reaction from her. To be honest, she was pretty proud of herself for being bold where he was concerned. She was sick to death of him running from her, from Liam, from the accident. Someone here needed to grow a set and man up. Apparently that was going to be her.

If she'd learned anything from Chelsea's death, it was that tomorrow wasn't guaranteed and you had to seize the moment or the moment would seize you.

"Move, Sophie."

"No." She forced herself to look into those beautiful, lost eyes. "I won't bring up the car accident, I won't make you talk. But don't run. Chelsea wouldn't want this. She'd want us to be friends again."

"You're right. She would." Zach sighed as he glanced around Chelsea's apartment. "Damn, I miss her."

"We'll miss her forever," Sophie added softly. "Is that why you came by? I do that when I want to feel closer to her. I keep waiting for one of you guys to ask for my key back to give to the landlord."

"I actually came to start going through some things. I can come back."

*Once you're gone.* The unspoken words hovered in the air just as sure as if he'd spoken them aloud.

"No." Sophie headed back to the couch and picked up her purse. "I've been here long enough. I actually already found a few items I'd like to keep. Things I bought for her over the years, and the pictures of us as kids. They're sitting on her bed. Just look through them and let me know if I can have them."

Zach nodded. "You're entitled to whatever you want."

Sophie's cell chimed from her purse. She hesitated answering the text now, but Zach had already moved toward the bedroom. He stopped as he spotted the binders on the dining table.

"Those were in the bottom of her closet," Sophie told him, pulling her phone out. "I haven't looked at them yet."

She glanced down to the text from Martin and sighed. Their dinner date was being put off. Again. Most women would be disappointed, and in a way she was. Sophie realized he was a busy man, with his city job and helping his father run a chain of restaurants. Things came up, life happened. They'd dated for six months, but for the last month they hadn't been on even one date because of their hectic schedules.

Sometimes she wondered if she dated Martin because he was so secure, so safe. Other times she wondered if she was with him because he reminded her of her childhood and she knew no different. He had that structured, polished thing going, and stability. Nothing to worry about with him. Definitely inside her comfort zone.

Sophie turned toward Zach, who still had his back to her. Those broad shoulders stretched his thin gray T-shirt to the max. Well-worn jeans hugged his backside, and work boots that had definitely seen better days spoke volumes about how hard the man worked. She watched as he flipped open the binder and flipped through page after page.

Everything in her life had been safe until she'd fallen for Zach Monroe. Then she'd been a foolish teen. Now she was a grown woman with more common sense.

So why did her stomach always flutter when this intriguing, infuriating man was around? She wanted it—no, *needed* it to flutter around Martin. She kept waiting for that moment to happen.

"My plans got canceled." She shoved her phone back into her purse without responding to the message. "Do you want help going through Chelsea's things? I don't mind, but I understand if you want to be alone."

Throwing her a glance over his shoulder, he shook his head. "I'll be fine."

Dismissed. Why would she be delusional enough to think he'd accept help from anybody, especially her? Did she seriously believe just because they'd shared a two-minute conversation about their past that he would be ready to play nice? Way too much angst lay between them for the gap to be bridged in such a short time.

She was about to retrieve her items from the bedroom and leave, but Zach's low, whispered, "You've got to be shitting me" had her moving to stand beside him.

What she saw in the binders had her just as stunned.

# Chapter Three

Damn it. He'd hoped Sophie was leaving. The spellbinding floral scent mocked him as she moved closer. So close, her bare arm brushed his and it took all of Zach's control not to step away. He couldn't let her know how she still got to him, and he damn well couldn't react to that slightest of touches.

After all this time, after every ugly thing in his life and having every reason shoved in his face as to why he shouldn't want this woman, he still did.

Yet in the midst of his Sophie-induced haze, the pictures and the words in Chelsea's handwriting stared back at him from the pages of the binder. Each plastic sleeve held details of exactly what Chelsea's vision was for the Sunset Lake property.

"A spa?" Sophie asked.

"Not just a spa." He flipped back to the first page, where Chelsea had written BELLE VOUS in bold letters. "A getaway resort for women. What the hell does that even say?"

Sophie laughed. "It's French for 'beautiful you.'"

"Of course she wouldn't just want to call it something in English," he muttered.

His sister had had a flare for all things over-the-top. Her dream had been to travel to Paris, but in all her escapades, she'd never made it there.

"So she wanted to open a resort." Sophie reached over, tugging the other binder from below his. "She laid out so many plans in these."

Everything from the rich hardwood flooring to the drapery tied back in the entryway of each service room, instead of doors. She'd even made notes about having little café chairs and tables along the patio that would overlook the lake, where the ladies could enjoy meals or just relax.

Zach glanced over at Sophie and the pages she searched. "She never mentioned this to you?" he asked.

Shaking her head, Sophie turned and met his gaze. "Not a word. I'm seriously just as shocked as you. Maybe she was afraid we'd laugh or talk her out of it."

Zach didn't miss the hint of hurt in Sophie's tone. More than likely she was upset that Chelsea had kept a secret. In reality, though, didn't they all have secrets? Some not as glamorous as others.

"I have no idea what to do with this now," he muttered as he closed his binder. He'd seen enough.

"I can't see you and your brothers getting into the resort and spa business." Sophie laughed. "Perhaps selling the property would be for the best."

Maybe in a logical way of thinking, selling the house would be best. Zach had never thought logically, though, and he didn't intend to start now.

"I'm still not selling." More than ready to get to the reason he came, Zach headed toward the bedroom.

He should've known Sophie would follow. Great.

"Have you even thought about it?" she asked, right on his heels. "Have you wondered what Chelsea would want you guys to do? You know the town would fix it up, make it beautiful and draw people in."

He didn't give a shit what the town wanted or what their vision was. He cared about Chelsea, and now that he knew her dream, he couldn't just laugh it off. Deep inside he knew that's why she'd kept these notes hidden. Fear of rejection. Rejection was something all four Monroe kids had in common. They'd experienced enough of it before they were rescued by Ed and Nancy Monroe.

Zach had never known the love of parents before he was adopted. Braxton kept to himself, but whatever demons he battled were pretty big as well. And Liam, well, he placed himself inside this bubble and refused to let anyone in, so his past had been riddled with rejection. He'd also not gone into details. That was one thing all boys had in common. They didn't want to get into the ugliness of their pasts. They'd fight those devils all alone to keep the outside world from seeing just how damaged they truly were.

But right now Zach wasn't going to focus on his past, or that of his brothers'. Yet again, that's not what Chelsea would have wanted. She'd want him to take a leap of faith, to be adventurous like she was.

So what now? Did he find someone who would want to take on such a business? Find a woman who would want to be the manager of a resort for women only? Did he do it himself? Chelsea would've gotten a kick out of her three brothers opening a spa.

The image nearly sent him into panic mode. He needed to thoroughly think about this. Somehow he had to make this work in order to honor his sister's memory.

"I'm not ignoring her dreams," he finally said. "Selling to the city will never be an option for me."

Granted, he was fixing up his own home, and that was taking up a chunk of his time and money. The old Victorian he'd been raised in from a teen was now his, and he'd been slowly renovating it to sell. He'd not mentioned that last part to his brothers yet. He'd certainly give either of them first dibs at the house, but Zach was ready for a change. And he was still up in the air as to whether or not that change would be just a different house or a different town altogether.

Now, though, this resort plan would have him reevaluating everything.

"The concept of a women's resort and spa isn't a bad idea," he went on, shocked at the thoughts flooding him. "Think about it. We're not far from Savannah. From a business standpoint this idea of hers could work, and there's nothing else like it that I know of. We're already a hot spot for tourists who filter over anyway. Why not add more appeal?"

Sophie stared, mouth open, eyes wide. "You're not seriously considering this."

Shrugging, Zach merely held her wide-eyed stare. He might not go through with this crazy plan, but he at least wanted to toy around with some of his thoughts and Chelsea's ideas.

The brief notes he'd seen had his mind spinning. Packages for groups of working women, mother-daughter specials, guest rooms in the mansion or renting one of the two cottages on the land. The ideas were really endless, and Chelsea had one hell of a start already outlined.

Damn it, he already had this business up and running in his head, like some damn kid daydreaming about what they want to be when they grow up. What the hell did he know about a spa? He had callouses, only shaved and cut his hair under duress about three times a year. From a business angle, though, he was pretty confident the spa would be a huge success.

Thinking about something and going after it were two totally different things. Case in point, the woman who stood before him. He'd attempted to go after her once, and that had turned into a living nightmare.

Sophie shook her head. "You're crazy. You want to discuss this with your brothers before you go any further? As far as Liam is concerned, the property can go to the city if Braxton is okay with it."

"If I want to move ahead, I'll buy their portion somehow. If this plan ends up falling through before takeoff, we'll all sit and discuss other options."

No matter how adamant Liam was, Zach knew deep in his heart he wasn't going to sell this property. He couldn't get rid of that last bond he had with his sister. Selling to the city would have her rolling over in her grave. She'd been so angry when Anna had broken off the engagement with Braxton, she'd actually confronted the woman. Thankfully, Zach had gotten there in time to break up the scuffle that was about to break out.

Sophie raked her hands through her golden hair and sighed, reminding him that she still stood way too close to him.

She pointed toward the bed. "That's the stuff I want to take. You okay with that?"

Zach glanced down at the photos, the clothes, the sketch of the Eiffel Tower. "Yeah."

He picked up the framed pencil drawing and studied the picture. Sophie didn't say a word.

"This is really good," he muttered before glancing up at her. "It looks similar to the pencil drawings in your office."

Sophie nodded. "I got them all at the same time and gave Chelsea that one."

Her eyes darted around. She was lying about something. Why? Or perhaps she was nervous being in the same room, a bedroom at that, with him. He didn't want to make her uncomfortable—or any more so than usual. Being alone together was a bad, bad idea.

When Sophie bent to scoop up the remainder of the items from the bed, Zach didn't step back. Torturing himself further wasn't a smart idea, but damn it, he couldn't force himself away from her. That floral scent of hers wrapped all around him, mocking him. Nothing good could come from allowing his mind to focus on how perfectly amazing this woman was. She belonged to someone else. A schmuck with a perfectly parted haircut and some sporty two-door car, but still.

As Sophie straightened, he passed over the framed artwork, but didn't move.

"What?" she asked, clutching the items to her chest.

Such a small gap between them now. So close he could see the black ring around her green eyes, see the slight smudge of makeup beneath one eye, as if maybe she'd shed a tear before he arrived. His perfectly polished Sophie was a bit imperfect, and damn if he didn't want to ruffle her up even more.

Wait. *His Sophie*? Only in his every waking fantasy.

"Do you need help out?" he asked, unable to come up with anything better.

She shook her head, sending a stray strand of golden hair gliding across her forehead. "I've got it. Are you sure you don't want help here?"

He wanted to reach out and smooth away the stray hair that had slid down across her cheek. He'd lost any right to touch her years ago. "I'm sure."

Sophie stared for another minute, then nodded. As

she turned to go, her limp seemed more pronounced than he'd seen before.

"Are you sure you're all right?" he asked. When she glanced over her shoulder with brows drawn down in confusion, he added, "From the fall."

"Nothing I can't handle."

Of course. Because she was tougher than he was. Zach couldn't handle seeing her like that, couldn't handle the fact that he could've killed her in that one, reckless moment.

"One more thing."

She sighed. "What?"

"Don't tell anyone about Chelsea's idea."

Her hesitation had him worried she wouldn't agree. Finally she nodded. "I'll wait to hear from you and your brothers regarding the city's offer."

Once she was gone and Zach was left in silence, he glanced around Chelsea's bedroom. Sinking to the bed, he rested his hands over his knees and dropped his head between his shoulders.

That was the most interaction he'd had one-on-one with Sophie in years. Even though she was gone, her scent lingered and Zach was finding it harder and harder to push her out of his mind. She'd been thrust back into his life in the past few days and he honestly wasn't sure he was strong enough to keep his distance.

Fortunately, he had enough to keep him occupied and he hoped his personal encounters with Sophie were coming to a close. Between clearing out Chelsea's apartment, renovating his own home, and now reeling from Chelsea's bombshell vision, Zach had enough on his plate. Thinking of things that would never be was a waste of time.

What he needed to focus on now was how to break this women-only resort news to Braxton and Liam.

Zach nearly laughed. He couldn't wait to see their faces when he told them they were going to have to start researching massages and facials.

Zach's ability to string a sentence together using every cuss word known to man, and some he'd invented himself, was rather impressive. What wasn't impressive was that he was a damn professional and he couldn't get the freshly cut ceramic tile to match up perfectly in the corners of his new shower. How the hell was he having issues? This was his livelihood, the one thing he devoted his existence to. The one thing he didn't screw up.

Renovating, making things new again or starting from scratch, kept him from going insane. Yet now he'd botched the tiles and would need to grab another sheet.

His personal issues were starting to seep into his professional life. Something he couldn't allow. He had no room for personal anything.

Zach was just about to take his hammer and smash the hell out of everything in that damn bathroom when his newly installed doorbell rang. At least that had turned out like he wanted.

Perhaps he wouldn't be having such a hard time right now if he wasn't so distracted by all the turmoil that seemed to keep growing. First the back taxes were looming over their heads, then the city wanted to buy the property that his sister adored and put her entire savings into, and now he'd discovered another layer to Chelsea's dream.

Wiping the sweat from his forehead, he headed down the curved, narrow steps to the front door. Darkness had settled in, and he realized he hadn't turned on any lights downstairs, other than the porch lights, which were on a timer. Obviously it was later than he thought.

Flicking the switch to the new antique chandelier that hung from the high ceiling in the foyer, Zach glanced through the glass panels on the sides of the door. He'd known before looking who'd be waiting on the other side. He resisted the urge to groan, but he wouldn't hide in his house and cower just because his new neighbor was overly friendly and very flirty. Okay, she was beyond flirty. The woman didn't know subtle.

Glancing down at his sweat-stained gray T-shirt, he was thankful he hadn't ripped it off earlier. No way would he ever want to greet this divorcée in skin and denim.

Flicking the lock on the door, Zach eased it open, just wide enough to stand in the opening, making it perfectly clear visitors weren't welcome.

"Ms. Barkley," he greeted without a smile.

Blond hair bleached within an inch of its life was piled high on top of her head. Blood-red lips pursed as her overly made-up eyes traveled down his body. Her visual lick did absolutely nothing to turn him on. In fact, always being under the microscope since this woman moved in last month was getting a bit creepy. Were there no other single men in this neighborhood? He knew for a fact that Mr. Mullins across the street was single, even if he was knocking on seventy.

"Call me Sherry," she reminded him, as she did every time. "I'm really sorry to bother you so late."

Yeah, she looked so upset about showing up at his door wearing a halter top that left several inches of cleavage all squished together and threatening to spill out. At this time of night did most women have on a fresh layer of bright red lipstick and perfectly teased hair?

"I have a leak in my roof right in my upstairs bedroom. Over my bed." She crossed her arms beneath her breasts, sending them to an even higher level. Some men might find her blatant approach sexy. He wasn't one of those men.

Zach tried not to sigh as he glanced around her at the perfectly clear spring evening, stars twinkling bright, full moon beaming down.

He brought his gaze back to her. "It's not raining."

She lifted a shoulder and smiled. "You never know when it will start. It is spring and all."

Cringing at her pathetic attempt to get him into her house, Zach gave her the only option available. "I can have a guy over there tomorrow."

"Oh, I was hoping you would fix it yourself. I'm not sure I trust anybody else."

Zach gritted his teeth and gripped the edge of his door. No way in hell was he setting foot in her bedroom. She'd probably chain him there and he'd never be heard from again.

"If I didn't trust my guys, they wouldn't be working for me." He had to remain professional, though she seriously tested his patience—and that was on a good day. "I'll have someone at your place by ten o'clock."

She opened her mouth as if she wanted to say something else, but Zach was already in a mood before her visit. Right now it was best he be left alone to his surly mood.

"I'm in the middle of something right now," he

told her, stepping back to close the door. "Nathan will be more than happy to help with your problem."

She nodded, but her pout remained. "Thank you, Zach. I knew I could count on you."

"No problem. Good night."

He closed the door, flicking the dead bolt back into a secure position. The thought of that woman sinking her sparkly red claws into him terrified him. There was a market for fake, processed, teased, perfumed, reconstructed bodies, but Zach wasn't in that check-out line.

He preferred the type of woman who was a bit more natural, a bit more discrete. A woman who was oblivious to her power, didn't exploit her assets.

Who knows, maybe Nathan went for that over-the-top type of woman. Either he'd be thrilled or pissed that Zach sent him. Either way, Zach was staying far away from that house and that woman if he could help it.

Cursing as he pounded back up the steps, Zach hated how his newly divorced neighbor was throwing herself at him, and he wasn't the least bit interested. Zach should want someone like Sherry. He was a man with breath in his lungs and he was turning down her not-so-subtle hint for a booty call.

Most men would call Zach a fool. Perhaps he was, but Miss Bleached and Baked wasn't doing it for him and there were certain things a man couldn't fake.

He stepped back into the bathroom, stared at the shower, and let out a sigh. The house was too quiet, and quiet led to thinking, which was not something he wanted to do.

If he started thinking, he'd start planning on things to do with Chelsea's mansion. That would turn into thinking about talking with his brothers. His brothers who still weren't on the same page as him and were contemplating Sophie's proposal. And once again his thoughts would circle back to Sophie.

So, yeah. He needed music, fast and loud, in order to finish this tile project and start planning his attack in regards to the Sunset Lake property.

There had to be a way to keep his sister's dream alive.

# Chapter Four

Later that evening, Sophie tied her robe around her waist, covering the evidence of the surgeries on her hip and abdomen. Hiding the physical marks was the easy part. How did she cover the emotional ones? The scars that cut so deep into her heart they left her crippled in so many ways.

And not that she thought of herself as crippled; her limp and inability to have children weren't what kept her emotionally scarred. It was the fact that each time she saw the marring on her skin, she thought of Zach, of how he continually punished himself by pushing people away. Maybe he'd come around now, with Chelsea gone. Maybe losing his sister would open his eyes to the fact that life was short.

Damp tendrils of hair clung to her neck from her jasmine bubble bath. Now that she was relaxed, all she wanted to do was crawl into bed with a good book and escape into someone else's life until she tumbled off into sleep. Many mornings she'd woken with a book still in her hand, or she'd find it had fallen to the floor.

She'd just stepped into the hallway to go through

the house to turn off lights when the doorbell rang. Glancing at the clock at the end of the hall, she was surprised anyone would be here this late. Padding down the hallway leading to the foyer, she took in the shape of the figure beyond the etched glass. A little surprised, she flicked the lock and pulled the door open.

"Martin, what are you doing here?"

Still dressed in a suit even though the spring evening was rather warm, he smiled and stepped over the threshold. Sophie eased back, allowing him room, and he shut the door behind him.

"I wanted to apologize for postponing our date again." He took her hands in his and brought them to his lips. "Forgive me?"

"It's not a big deal," she told him. Though she'd hated being put off at the last minute, she was at least used to it. She also refused to sit around and worry over a man. "I know you're busy. Besides, the free evening gave me a chance to go to Chelsea's apartment and get some things."

Martin's brown eyes studied her face. "What on earth did she have that you would want?"

Sophie didn't want to get into this. Martin had never kept his opinion of Chelsea and her free ways to himself. He'd thought Chelsea was a bad influence on Sophie, but Sophie ignored his misguided opinion. Chelsea died just after Sophie and Martin started dating, and Martin had offered a bit of comfort, but he just didn't understand the pain.

"There were some pictures and a few other things I'd gotten her through the years." Sophie turned and headed toward the living room. "Come on in and have a seat."

Her hip was so much better since soaking in a hot tub. Falling in front of Zach still left her feeling ridiculous, and she hated even more the amount of concern and anger she'd seen in his eyes when he'd looked down at her lying on the floor.

After leaving Chelsea's, Sophie had gone over and over in her mind about the revelation in those black binders. She had no clue what Zach would do with that information, but he'd asked her to keep it to herself, so she intended to do just that. Loyalties ran deep, even if their relationship had been severed.

"I can't stay long," he told her, as if there was ever a large chunk of time carved out for her. "I stopped by because I saw your porch lights still on, so I knew you were up."

Of course he wouldn't stay long. She totally understood he was a busy man. Still, just once she'd like to come first. They'd dated six months; maybe he was ready to move on. Maybe she was.

When he'd asked her out initially, she'd agreed to see him because, well, he was the exact type she'd been told over and over she should be looking for. Her parents had definite goals for her, but as time went on, Sophie realized her goals for herself were vastly different.

Dating Martin hadn't been bad, just boring. Boring meant comfortable, and Sophie found herself afraid to step from her comfort zone. So here they were, months later, and Sophie wasn't quite sure what step to take next.

She eased down on the sofa, but Martin simply leaned against the doorway. "Do you want to start seeing other people?" she found herself asking before she could filter the words.

Martin stood straight up, his eyes wide. "Why would

you ask such a thing? Of course I don't want to see other people."

Sophie crossed her legs, tugging the edge of the robe over her thighs when the thin material threatened to slide open. "We're both so busy, I just didn't know if it was the workloads that kept us apart or if you were trying to tell me something."

Martin crossed the room and sank onto the cushion next to her. Placing his hands on hers, he waited until she turned to face him before he spoke.

"You know we're perfect for each other, Sophie. Our lives and backgrounds are so similar. We have the same vision for the future." His thumbs stroked her knuckles. "This has just been a busy quarter, and we have another couple weeks of meetings. How about this Saturday we do something special? We'll go to that new restaurant we've been meaning to get to for a month now. Nothing will interfere. I promise."

The idea of him putting effort into their relationship warmed her. "Sounds good."

"Have you heard from the Monroes about the property? I figured you would've called me with an answer by now."

Sophie shook her head. While she knew where Zach stood, she wanted to wait until all the brothers had agreed on a decision. "They're getting back to me by Friday. They wanted to think about the offer."

Martin's jaw clenched. "I would've thought with your strong connection you would've convinced them this was the best decision."

"I gave them my opinion, but I can't make them take the deal." Irritated that he assumed she could wave her magic wand and get three very different men to agree on one major topic was ridiculous. "If they don't want to sell, there's nothing I can do. Or anybody else, for that matter. They're pretty strong-willed."

Instantly his face softened, and his hand came up to her cheek as he stroked her skin. "Sorry. Of course you can't. I just know how much we would love to get that historical property. It could be renovated and really bring in more tourists."

Laying a quick kiss on her lips, Martin came to his feet. "I need to get going. I'll wait to hear from you on Friday about the property and I'll call and get reservations for Saturday."

Sophie walked him to the door. "I can't wait."

Martin pulled her into his arms and kissed her good night before walking out the door. Even though she didn't get all tingly when they kissed, didn't crave or ache for his touch, Sophie was realistic. She read way too many romance novels. There was a reason they were labeled "fiction." People didn't actually yearn for someone, didn't have sensations shooting through them at just a touch.

No, what she and Martin had was easy. Isn't that how relationships were supposed to be?

So why did she keep going back to how Zach had looked at her earlier? When she'd fallen, when she was leaving? Both times he looked torn, almost scared. And she'd definitely felt something beneath that heavy-lidded gaze of his.

Shutting off all the lights, Sophie headed back to her bedroom. The fact that Zach Monroe could make her insides tingle just proved her point. The romances she read about and realistic expectations were at opposite ends of the spectrum.

\* \* \*

Zach popped the top off his Mountain Dew and made his way out to his deck. The sun had all but set and he'd lit a fire in the fire pit a while ago. Nothing like a fire on a late spring night to end a shitty day.

At stressful times like this he wished he still drank. That lesson had been learned—several times over, as a matter of fact. Between the raging alcoholic sperm donor that helped create him, the strung-out woman who brought him into this world, and the mess he made of his life at twenty-one, Zach had promised himself never again. Because he knew if he started right now, he might never stop. Drinking did help numb the pain, blocking the reality that always loomed in the near distance. Unfortunately, that haze had to wear off sometime, and those were the moments Zach never wanted to face again.

The last time reality had smacked him hard in the face and he'd come to, he'd seen Sophie and Liam unconscious and bleeding . . . because of him.

Glancing down at his scarred knuckles, Zach didn't need the visual reminder. Every single day of his life he replayed the accident he'd caused. He replayed the terror that had gripped him. He could still feel the glass shatter against his skin, slicing deep as he busted the back glass in the cab of the truck to climb out and go find help. No matter the penance he paid in jail, no matter the distance he kept from Sophie, nothing would erase that nightmare movie that played over and over in his mind.

Dropping his head back against the chair, Zach focused on the crackling fire and the embers that were starting to settle at the bottom of the pit. Always focusing on the past was no way to try to move forward. He found himself wanting desperately to push ahead.

With Chelsea's death and now her vision coming to the surface, he wanted to come out on top. Wanted to take back control of his life instead of having life control him.

Relaxing on his patio after a day's work always helped him unwind. Settling into the chair his father had made brought him some sort of peace each evening. He needed that peace, no matter how small. Actually, discovering Chelsea's ideas might be just what he needed to focus on, to move into that area where he could be proud of something he'd done.

Zach's cell vibrated in his pocket and he fished it out. Braxton's name lit up the screen. He wasn't in the mood for a chat, but he wasn't in the mood for much else either, so he might as well answer.

"Yeah."

"Wow, always so chipper," Braxton greeted. "You home?"

"Yeah."

Where else would he be on a Saturday night? He randomly dated. Very randomly.

"A man of few words. Thought I'd swing by," Braxton told him.

"I'm on the deck."

"Be there in five," Braxton told him.

He hung up, figuring his brother had come to some decision regarding the property. Braxton lived about ten minutes away, but he taught college in Savannah. With Braxton on spring break, he shouldn't have to go back until next week. Plenty of time to get this decision finalized.

A car door slammed and within seconds Braxton rounded the house and stepped up onto the deck. He didn't say a word as he passed right by Zach, slid open the patio door, then came back out with a can of diet

Coke. He settled in the other Adirondack chair and sighed, stretching his legs out and crossing his ankles.

"That bad, huh?" Zach asked.

"That frustrating," Braxton corrected before taking a hefty drink. "What's got you sitting out here in the dark alone?"

"Just thinking."

"You're always so elaborate with words."

Zach shrugged. "You're the one who uses all the words, Professor."

Braxton taught history and economics. He'd always been the brainy one, the intelligent one. He even sported that polished cut with hair gel or whatever the hell he put in his blond hair to keep it in place. But Braxton did don the occasional scruff, just enough to avoid looking like an old, boring college professor.

At least all of his tats were covered. Apparently employers didn't like the ink. Just another reason Zach enjoyed working for himself.

Zach finished off his drink and tossed the can into the trash at the edge of the deck. "I assume you're here about the property."

Braxton's can tapped against the wood armrest. "Yeah."

Silence settled around them until Zach glanced over at his brother. "Are you keeping your answer to yourself, or do you intend to share?"

"I'm not ready to sell."

Relief slithered through Zach and he released a breath he hadn't known he'd been holding. "And Liam?"

"He understands my decision, but he doesn't want the burden of the house."

Zach tapped his fingers against the edge of the

chair. Once he informed Braxton of Chelsea's wishes, he might not want the burden either.

"I went to Chelsea's apartment yesterday."

Braxton turned in his seat. "Why didn't you call me? I would've gone with you."

With a shrug, Zach went on. "I started boxing up some of her things. I need to have the apartment empty by the end of the month."

"Stubborn ass," Braxton muttered around the drink as he took another swig. "I'm on break. Why not ask for help?"

"She doesn't have that much." Zach crossed his ankles, lacing his fingers over his stomach. "I found something."

"What?"

"Chelsea kept binders with pictures, notes, and detailed plans regarding the Sunset Lake house."

Braxton set his can down beside the chair and raked a hand down his face. "I can tell by the look on your face you're already worried what my reaction will be. Go ahead, tell me. Chelsea had some crazy ideas, so I doubt anything could shock me at this point."

Zach wanted to laugh. "She wanted to open a women-only resort and spa."

"Seriously? She would've been great at something like that. I knew she had some good business sense in that sometimes flighty head of hers." Braxton's smile faltered, his eyes narrowed. "Wait. Don't tell me—"

Zach allowed a smile to stretch across his face. Smiling always felt so foreign to him, he'd not had many reasons to do so in his life. Seeing Braxton's stunned expression and a hint of pissed-off thrown in was certainly an occasion to release the grin.

"At least consider the economic angle of this," Zach stated, hoping to appeal to Braxton's business side.

"You know how this town already gets an overflow of tourists from Savannah. This women's resort would be a great idea. Women eat that shit up. Massages, getting their nails done, wine, and all that other stuff."

Braxton eased forward in his seat, resting his elbows on his knees and shoving his fingers through his hair. "Can I ask why you're so hell-bent on making this happen?"

Zach had asked himself that same question. The answer was simple really. "I want Chelsea to live on somehow. If making this work honors her memory in any way, I don't see how we can't go for it. Do you really want to ignore this?"

"You're right." Braxton sighed, dropping his hands to dangle between his knees. "Damn it, I hate when you're right."

Reaching over, Zach slapped his brother on the back. "That was easier than I thought."

"Don't gloat."

"I plan on heading to the house Sunday morning, if you'd like to go. We need to get an idea of what needs doing so we can get a building permit to fix it up. I'm sure the electrical and plumbing aren't even up to code."

"This is going to be a long project." Braxton laughed. Not an amused laugh, more of a "what the hell are we doing" laugh. "Let's keep this under wraps. The last thing we need is for word to get out that we're working on a resort for women."

"If it helps, Sophie thinks the business is a great idea too."

Braxton's shoulders stiffened, his eyes widened. "You talked to Sophie about this?"

*Damn it.* "She was at the apartment when I got there."

"Really? And you two actually had a conversation without anyone else as a buffer?"

Zach stared at the fire, refusing to rise to the bait dangling in front of his face. This conversation had been about the property. Nothing else.

"Grouchy Zach is back," Braxton muttered. "Looks like I hit a nerve. Will you stop closing up when someone brings up a topic you're not comfortable with?"

"I'm not discussing this."

Braxton sighed, reached down for his can, and took another drink. "I know you have feelings for—"

"Shut up."

No way was he discussing his damn feelings, and definitely not regarding Sophie. Shit. Had he been that transparent? He didn't need to get his emotions out in the open. They were just fine living deep inside him where no one could see.

"Zach, it's me." Braxton shifted in his seat to glance over. "I'm not judging, I'm not telling anyone. I'm just telling you this thing you've got eating you alive has got to be dealt with. You give off some strong vibes. I'm sure she's oblivious to them, but I know you better. And the guilt you—"

Zach jumped to his feet. "Shut the hell up. I'm not having a Dr. Phil moment with you. I don't need anyone inside my head rooting around and trying to diagnose my problems."

There were too many for one person to handle anyway.

Braxton stared up at him. Nothing but an occasional cricket and the crackle of the fire filled the night. Zach clenched his fists, more than ready to take out his frustrations on someone. Damn it, he hated violence.

Unfortunately, that thread of evil was in his genes.

Another reason the fairy-tale daydream of him and Sophie was utterly absurd.

"Sit down," Braxton said in that low, controlled tone. "I'm not fighting you, and you don't want to fight me. You know I'd kick your ass."

Zach couldn't help but smirk. "Bullshit," he said, falling back into his chair. "You'd mess up that pretty-boy hair of yours."

"Don't let the hair fool you. I could still kick your ass and my hair would still look better than your mountain-man appearance."

Tension eased from Zach's shoulders at the quick way they always fell back into bantering. He missed that with Liam—not that he'd ever admit that to his older brother. Zach didn't blame Liam one bit for hating him.

"Why don't you just tell Sophie how you feel?"

Groaning, Zach dropped his head against the back of the chair. "Stop beating the dead horse."

"That's not a reason."

"She's dating someone."

"Martin is boring. That won't last."

Zach swallowed, hating how he could get so swept up into thinking of Sophie that he actually fantasized about having something with her. "Even if it doesn't, we are polar opposites. Throw in the accident and we have absolutely nothing to build on."

"You never know until you try." Braxton sank back into his chair. "I can't believe I'm doling out relationship advice. Anna ripped my heart to shreds, but I'm not letting that stop me from being open to another relationship. Well, as soon as I feel like it."

Braxton's heart got stomped on, and he'd turned into a playboy, refusing to get too close to another woman. One sleepover per woman had been the max lately for his once calm, family-seeking brother.

Braxton had always stated he wanted a wife, children, and a life like the one he'd had growing up with the Monroes, but after what happened with his ex, who knew what Braxton wanted now. The man had officially closed himself off from letting women in. Zach, on the other hand, refused to ever allow a woman to get so close that he had to reveal his dark childhood. And no way in hell would he pass those genes down to any innocent child.

Keeping people at a distance was the best decision for everyone involved. Besides, getting close to someone would only open his heart to emotions he knew he wasn't strong enough to handle. He didn't want the inevitable hurt to seep in. First his biological parents had damaged him so deeply he honestly would probably never recover. Then his adopted parents passed away, and now Chelsea. Letting anyone else in would just be emotional, soul-crushing suicide.

Zach eased forward on the end of his chair. He grabbed the poker from the edge of the pit and prodded the wood, sending orange sparks flying.

"You know I never want a relationship, let alone something long-term. So, whatever Sophie does or doesn't do with her life is none of my business."

"Why don't you make it your business? Maybe she's unsure because of you. Did you ever think of that? Maybe she doesn't want long-term, or maybe she could be the one to change your mind on relationships."

Resting his elbows on his knees, Zach shook his head. "You're not making sense and your babbling is giving me a headache."

"Maybe I'm wrong," Braxton went on, obviously not caring about the headache. "Maybe she does pick up on your vibes. What if she reads through your gruff attitude and sees the truth?" Braxton paused, really letting the words sink in before he continued. "Can you blame her for not wanting to confront you about her feelings? You've not exactly been easy to be around."

Zach gritted his teeth, willing Braxton to shut the hell up. The last thing Zach wanted was to think about what Sophie might or might not feel toward him. The last thing he needed was false hope where she was concerned. Opening his heart to bleed out again wasn't an option or a risk he was willing to take.

"I can't," he muttered.

Braxton came to his feet, staring down until Zach glanced up. "You mean you won't," Braxton corrected. "Live your life miserably if you want. But one day you're going to wake up and wonder why the hell you didn't grow a set and just take a chance."

# Chapter Five

Braxton entered Sophie's office Friday afternoon. She'd been eagerly waiting all day. She'd had a closing that morning, but had told her assistant if any of the Monroe boys called to make sure to get ahold of her. For several reasons, Chelsea's property was taking top priority.

Sophie wasn't a bit surprised the middleman of the trio had been the one sent to deliver the message.

Braxton eased his tall, broad frame into the same seat he'd sat in last Friday. The dark jeans and pale blue button-up showcased his tanned skin, his broad shoulders, and masculine physique. Today he wore his glasses, which only made him look more studious. No doubt the young girls on the campus were halfway in love with him.

"So, what did you decide?" she asked, lacing her fingers together and resting them on her desk. "And please, tell me you all came to a mutual agreement without black eyes and busted knuckles."

His rich laughter filled the office. Of the three brothers, Braxton was the most free with his emotions. Liam and Zach, on the other hand . . . she wasn't even sure they had emotions other than anger and bitterness. Well, Liam only had anger toward Zach. Zach, on the other hand, seemed to be angry with the world.

"Sort of," Braxton replied, crossing one ankle over his knee.

A knot settled in her stomach. "Sort of? You either do or don't want to sell."

"We don't."

As Martin's girlfriend, she was a little upset at the decision. But, as Chelsea's best friend and someone close to the Monroe clan, Sophie was elated.

She wondered what Zach had decided to do regarding Chelsea's vision, but since he'd asked her not to say anything, she'd keep that to herself.

"So where does the 'sort of' come into play?" she asked.

Braxton eased back into his seat, crossing his arms over his chest as he drew out a sigh. "Zach and I are going to buy Liam out so the house will just be mine and Zach's."

Sophie nodded. "I'm not surprised. Now both your brothers got their way."

"As an added bonus, I didn't have to break up a fight," he told her with a sideways grin. "Liam is happy with working in an upscale, city restaurant and he doesn't want another burden."

"What are you and Zach going to do with the place?"

Braxton shook his head. "That's what I came to discuss with you. Zach told me about the binders."

Sophie couldn't help the smile that spread across her face. "And?"

"A resort? What the hell would we know about running a resort?"

Shrugging, Sophie came to her feet and rounded

her desk. "Who says you guys would have to run it? Fix it up the way Chelsea envisioned and then hire someone to run it." She sat on the edge of her desk directly in front of Braxton. "It is a women's resort. Would be a little silly to have you two brutes hanging around."

Braxton massaged the back of his neck and groaned. "I know Chelsea is somewhere laughing at us. Leave it to her to have some harebrained idea we're stuck with."

"You loved her and her harebrained ideas."

A sad smile stretched across his face. "Yes, I did. I wouldn't expect less of her than to leave us this surprise."

"So you two are going to fix it up?" she asked, hopeful.

"Yeah. We haven't gone into any specifics, but that's the goal in mind. I'll be heading back to Savannah on Monday. We're figuring I'll be more of the financial backer and Zach will be the manual labor portion. We're partners for now."

Sophie couldn't be happier to hear this plan. Although telling Martin wouldn't be fun, she still was so excited that Chelsea's brothers were moving ahead with their sister's vision.

"Zach and I are planning to meet at the house Sunday morning to look over the structure and get a list of basic improvements to be done, to take to the zoning commission for a building permit. You can join us if you'd like."

Sophie quirked a brow and smiled. "Did you run that by Zach before you invited me?"

Braxton eased forward, placing his hand on her knee. "You and I are friends, Soph. No matter what turmoil lives between you and Zach, that has never, and will never, affect you and me. Got it?"

Sophie nodded, knowing he was right. The issues she and Zach had were a world apart from her relationship with anyone else.

"So, you want to meet us there to walk through? I know you've seen it, since you sold it to Chelsea, but I'd like your opinion, now that you've seen her vision."

Sophie smiled, reached down and squeezed his hand. "I'd love to."

"Great. We're meeting at nine."

Coming to her feet just as he did, Sophie wrapped her arms around him. "Thank you for seeing this through for Chelsea."

Enveloping her in a brotherly hug, Braxton patted her back. "I'd do anything for my family." Easing back, he looked her in the eye. "I include you in that, too."

"I know," she told him with a smile. "See you Sunday."

Once he was gone, Sophie sank back against her desk. The notes and pictures, drawings and dreams Chelsea had poured into two thick binders were going to become a reality.

The fact that hardheaded, impenetrable Zach had really thought this through said so much about the man he kept hidden from the world. He might want to keep people far outside the perimeter of that wall he'd erected around himself, but Sophie knew, deep down, there was a man with feelings. Knowing that Zach had a passion for something gave Sophie hope.

Zach had once been reckless, but he'd been full of life and they'd been friends. She wanted that back. Wanted to be close with all three men, as she used to be before the car accident that left her scarred, handicapped, and infertile. Before Liam had been injured and had pushed Zach out of his life.

Before Zach had been arrested for aggravated vehicular assault and sent to prison for a year.

But how could they possibly find their way back after all this time?

Placing the ever-pressing thoughts on the back burner, Sophie turned and reached for her cell. Right now she needed to call the other man in her life and break the bad news to him.

Letting this relationship go on this long had been a mistake. Being comfortable with someone, dating someone because that's what was expected of you, was completely wrong.

And everything about Zach felt deliciously right.

"I have a surprise for you."

With her arm linked through Martin's, Sophie glanced up at him. "What is it?"

They exited the restaurant after a romantic meal complete with candlelight, a trickling waterfall in the distance, and the most amazing meal she'd ever had.

They walked arm in arm down the narrow street with old-fashioned lampposts giving off a soft glow. The gentle breeze slid her knee-length skirt around her thighs and set her hair dancing about her shoulders. Martin steered her toward the bench nestled between two oversized ceramic pots overflowing with greenery and a pop of color from spring flowers.

When Sophie sat, Martin moved in right beside her and kept hold of her hands. "First of all, I want you to know I'm not upset about the property. I realize I came off as gruff with you yesterday. I think I was just more surprised than anything."

Sophie hadn't taken offense. She'd known he wanted that piece on Sunset Lake for the town. Actually, she'd still been reeling from the excitement of

Braxton's news about the plans to move forward with a resort. Martin's tone hadn't even entered her mind. He'd been understandably frustrated.

She also hadn't said a word to him about Zach and Braxton's plans. What went on now with Chelsea's home was private and nobody's business until the Monroe boys were ready to disclose the information.

"I know how much you all wanted it." Sophie was well aware, but she didn't want to get into this with him. "Let's not discuss business. Okay?"

Martin chuckled. "You've read my mind. I have much more important things to talk about."

Sophie glanced down at their joined hands and his perfectly neat nails, not a callus in sight. The man exuded office mogul. Whereas Zach's hands were damaged, rough.

*Stop it.* Why did she have to keep circling back to Zach? She was on a date with the man she'd been seeing for a while. A man who embodied everything she was brought up to look for in a man and someone she was comfortable with.

Zach made her feel anything but comfortable. Yet, she couldn't let this go on much longer. Martin wasn't the one for her. Who wanted to just be comfortable the rest of their lives? Guilt gnawed at her because Martin deserved to know exactly how she felt.

"I know we have such crazy schedules, and it's taken its toll on you, on our relationship."

He shifted so she had to lift her head and look directly into his face. With dark chocolate eyes, light brown hair that would turn blonder in the summer, Martin was a very handsome man. Very polished, but his career demanded perfection.

"Our jobs have taken a toll on our social time,"

she agreed. "I know you're busy and my career can be insane at times too. It's out of our control."

"Which is why I've booked us a room at a bed-and-breakfast in two weeks. A three-day getaway is what we need. We'll leave work behind and worry about nothing."

Sophie's heart kicked up—and not in a good way. Go away with him for an entire weekend? They hadn't slept together yet. She was always hesitant to let anyone see her scars. She wasn't ashamed of her body, but there was still that level of intimacy that went beyond the act of having sex by exposing her most vulnerable part.

"I have to say I'm shocked." She turned her head, meeting his brown eyes. "I didn't know you were planning on taking me away anywhere."

Martin wrapped an arm around her shoulders, pulling her into his side. "It was a last-minute decision and I was fortunate enough to have connections to get us a reservation."

As they sat, letting the evening breeze wash over them, Sophie couldn't think of an answer.

If she said yes, that would imply they would share a room, share a bed, leading them into a territory she definitely didn't want with him. If she said no, he would think she wasn't taking them seriously. She couldn't flat out break things off because she was still so unsure, but she certainly wasn't ready to have a weekend away, either. Damn emotions. She was torn and didn't want to make a life-changing mistake.

Being an adult sucked sometimes. She'd taken for granted the days when the biggest decision she needed to make was whether or not to wear pink nail polish or be bold and do black to piss off her mother.

She shifted in her seat when her hip started to ache.

Of course every time her hip ached, she instantly thought of Zach. The fact that she thought of another man while being held by a man she was supposed to be in a relationship with was rather telling.

Just because she thought of Zach didn't mean anything. By default he was part of her life simply because of Chelsea. But any romantic involvement between them had ended before it fully started.

"I didn't mean to leave you speechless." Martin's breath tickled her cheek. "I wanted to surprise you and let you know how serious I'm taking our relationship. I'd like to take it to another level."

Another level. Code for sleeping together without the sleeping.

"You certainly surprised me." She laughed, shifting and settling deeper into his side. "I have to be honest. I'm not sure I'm ready for the next step."

Inwardly she cringed when he didn't say anything. She wasn't going to lie or pretend. She wouldn't do that with anyone, especially a man she'd been dating.

Martin kissed her head. "Think about the trip. I'd like to take you away. Whatever happens once we get there would be up to you. No pressure."

"All right," she told him, worried how this would play out in the end. "I'll have to see if I have the time."

He'd said no pressure, but Sophie had a sinking feeling once they arrived she'd feel nothing but pressure.

Maybe it was time to let go, to finally end things with him. Her parents were thrilled she was dating him. Thankfully, though, they were out of town traveling through Europe for the next month.

Sophie closed her eyes as she rested against Martin. His thumb stroked her shoulder, his other hand settled onto her thigh. The man had waited for her to move on to the next level, and Sophie had to admit most men wouldn't have been as understanding.

Martin knew about the accident—who in this town didn't? He'd never brought it up, but Sophie figured he had to know why she was so hesitant.

If Martin was getting this serious, was he thinking long-term? Because if he was, Sophie had some more things to consider. What would Martin do if he found out she couldn't have children? Would he see her as flawed? Would he want nothing to do with her?

Sophie wasn't going to borrow trouble. She had no intention of telling anyone about her infertility. Unless she planned on marrying a man, there was no reason to disclose the final piece of her painful past, especially when she knew this relationship was most likely coming to an end.

Cool air enveloped Sophie as she stepped into the old Sunset Lake mansion. Early morning sun pierced through each and every window, dust particles dancing in the vibrant light.

The grand foyer was stunning, even with the scarred, filthy wood floors. It was the huge stained-glass window on the landing of the curved staircase that stole the show as soon as anyone entered the home.

She honestly had no clue what the guys would be facing as far as getting the property up to safety codes in order to open a business, but the end result would be nothing short of breathtaking. She only wished Chelsea was around to see her dream come to life.

"What the hell are you doing here?"

Sophie jerked around at the grouchy tone. Zach, complete with scowl and messed hair, stared back at her.

She was done catering to his moodiness, so she pasted on a smile. "I wanted to see the place again."

"I invited her." Braxton came from one of the side rooms off the foyer. "If you're going to be nasty, go to another part of the house. Sophie has just as much right to be here as we do."

Zach's eyes narrowed as he stalked past her and ran his gaze over the ceiling, the window frames, and muttered something under his breath. He'd dismissed her, but that was fine. She wasn't leaving, and if he wanted to be a jerk, that was his problem. Yes, she wanted to be here for Zach, but she wanted to be part of this endeavor too, because a resort and spa would be brilliant.

"Ignore him," Braxton said with a smile. "He hasn't had coffee yet."

"Is that the excuse for the past decade?" she half joked, but Zach's stiffening shoulders weren't lost on her. She hadn't meant to poke the bear. Okay, maybe she had, but come on. How long could a person brood?

"Want me to walk with you, or are you exploring on your own?"

Sophie looked back at Braxton. "I can look on my own. I'll just text you if I need you."

"Works for me. I'm heading upstairs." He tapped his notebook against his thigh and headed toward the steps before turning back. "Zach—"

Zach turned. "I know. Play nice."

Braxton threw her a grin before he ascended the wide, curved steps. The grand staircase itself was sigh-worthy. The rich beauty of the entryway was stunning. Sophie had sold this house to her friend, so she'd been inside several times. Now she was looking at the home from a whole new angle. A business angle, and one that would surely take off if done right.

First, though, they had to make a list of needed renovations and take it to the housing office to get them approved. Once the guys had a building permit, they could get started. Sophie could hardly wait to see this home start to take shape and come to life.

Sophie turned in a slow circle, taking in the windows, the high ceiling. Only a few feet from her, Zach crouched down and ran his hand across the old hardwood floor. Not the original from the looks of it. Again, he muttered something and Sophie decided to take matters into her own hands. She was done letting him hide behind pain and guilt. She would be spending a good bit of time with them now, because Braxton was right. She had every right to be part of this journey.

"What are you thinking?" she asked, crossing her arms. "Sand them or replace them?"

Those blunt fingertips ran across the grain, leaving a trail in the dust. He didn't answer and Sophie wasn't budging. Tapping her foot, she smiled when his eyes darted to her legs. She'd thrown on an old pair of tennis shoes, running shorts, and a tank. Sophie knew the closed-up house would be stuffy and hot.

While she may have ugly surgical scars on her hip, she knew her legs were in great shape from the water aerobics classes she taught twice a week and the runs she forced herself to do. Even her doctor had suggested exercise to keep the muscles strong and firm. He did warn her not to overdo and to listen to her body, and right now her body was saying she wanted Zach to take notice.

"Chelsea liked the look of dark, rich wood floors," Sophie went on as if they were actually having a conversation and this wasn't one-sided. "I think that would look really nice in here."

Rising to his full height, towering over her, Zach's

intense, hard gaze pinned her in place. "I'll figure it out once I see the rest of the place. I'm not concerned with cosmetic decisions right now. I'm more concerned about getting approved for the permit. I'll worry about 'pretty' later."

Wayward dark strands curled over his forehead; inky lashes outlined beautiful dark eyes any woman could get lost in. When he crossed his arms, mimicking her stance, she caught sight of the freshly busted knuckles on his left hand.

"Did you get in a fight?" she asked, nodding to his hand.

He didn't even glance down. "Yeah, with the bathroom I'm renovating."

That snarky side of his irritated her. "That looks serious. You need antibiotic ointment on that," she scolded. "Probably could use stitches."

When she started to reach out, he stepped back. "I'm fully aware of how to tend to my own wounds."

"You may be aware, but you're doing a piss-poor job of following through." She refused to let his sharp words or actions hurt her. He was Zach, sometimes crabby, sometimes quiet . . . yet always intriguing. "When that gets infected because you've opted to be bullheaded and you can't work, I won't be responsible if an 'I told you so' slips out of my mouth."

His eyes darted to said mouth, and Sophie resisted the urge to lick her lips. No doubt Zach went for the vixen type, the woman who didn't care about relationships.

Why was she so worried about Zach's type? Over the years Chelsea had mentioned a few women here and there, but as far as Sophie knew, Zach hadn't had a serious relationship since he'd gotten out of prison.

The fact that he had served time always bothered

her. Not that she saw him as damaged or below her in any way. His incarceration had eaten away at her each day he was away. He'd made a mistake. Yes, people were hurt, but he'd never been in trouble before and she'd wanted the judge to take it easy on him.

Chelsea had hinted at a horrific childhood Zach had lived through, and Sophie hated how he'd been doing so well for himself until one night when they'd all made poor choices.

To see his brothers and Chelsea struggle with the backlash from the town, then their parents' fight to hold their heads high and still be proud of the man Zach was had been difficult. Eventually people's whispers died down. Other gossip had taken its place.

Sophie had been in surgery the day Zach's sentence came down, and she'd been unable to be by his side, to tell him how sorry she was. She'd tried to visit him in prison, but he never accepted her as a guest. After he'd served his year, she'd gone to him, but he wasn't the same man anymore. He'd closed in on himself, turning away any friendship or anything more they could've had.

And that had sliced her deeper than any surgery or doctor's findings ever could have. Not only had she lost any chance of a romantic involvement, she'd lost a friend.

He'd gone straight back to working with his father until Ed passed away from a massive heart attack. Only a year later Zach's mother succumbed to cancer.

As if all the events leading up to the death of the two people who'd saved him hadn't been enough, Zach had lost them when he was just getting back on his feet. Perhaps he'd never recovered. Maybe he never would.

Sophie had to try, though. Chelsea wanted better for her brother, and to be honest, Sophie wanted more of a life for him, too.

"I have a busy day." Zach flexed his wounded hand and let out a tired sigh. "Look around all you want, but don't get in the way."

Turning on his battered work boots, he walked away and disappeared down the wide hallway. Sophie gave him a mock salute, which he couldn't see, but the childish gesture made her feel better.

Zach was in all-work mode and irritated, so looking around on her own was perfectly fine. Besides, she wanted to explore the mansion from a female standpoint, from the view of how to decorate and make use of each room for the grand spa and resort her best friend had envisioned. Yes, all the beautifying would come later, but that wasn't going to stop her from daydreaming now.

Zach and Braxton could look around at the mechanical, reconstruction side of things. They could work the electrical angle and worry over the pipes and plumbing. Their father had owned a construction company for years, teaching each of the boys the trade. Only Zach had taken to the work and turned it into a lucrative career. He was the most sought-after contractor in the town and surrounding areas. Apparently people didn't care about the gruff exterior since he did such an impeccable job.

While Braxton knew quite a bit about construction too, Sophie figured he was walking through the house doing figures in his head and forming a budget. Braxton was book smart, business savvy, and extremely intelligent when it came to economics. With these two in charge, there was no way this resort wouldn't take off.

Sophie just wished Liam was on board. She wished all three brothers would've joined together and completed this project for Chelsea.

She went from room to room on the main floor. She'd only seen Chelsea's notes for a few minutes, but already her mind was spinning with ideas. By the time Sophie had used her phone to snap countless pictures of the entryway, formal dining room, kitchen, and the sitting area, she'd lost track of time.

She'd been there a little over an hour and hadn't seen either of the guys. She'd heard movement a few times, but had been caught up in the nostalgia of the place. She couldn't even imagine what had transpired between these walls. The fact that a family had lived here and had taken such a risk to house escaped slaves during the Civil War was amazing and beyond brave.

Which reminded her of the old tunnels in the basement. When she'd sold the house, she hadn't gone through the tunnels. She had had an inspection done, and the inspector found the passageways to the two other cottages on the land to be sound. Now she wanted to explore.

She turned the old brass knob, and the door opened with a slight groan. She peered down the dark, narrow steps, sliding her phone out of her pocket to use the bright screen as her flashlight. She held tight to the rail as the familiar twinge in her hip kicked in whenever she did steps. Not painful, just there and enough to be annoying.

At the bottom of the stairs, she turned and spotted Zach. His flashlight roamed over the concrete walls, the furnace and water heater, pipes running along the ceiling.

Her tennis shoes shuffled against the grit and grime on the concrete floor as she made her way across the dingy space.

"You should've stayed upstairs," he told her, not taking his eyes off the task. "The floor is uneven down here and you could fall."

"How did you know it was me?" she asked, gripping her phone.

A grunt was her only response.

Warmth spread through her at his worry. Minor as it may be, she would take it. Not that she wanted his pity by any means, but the fact that he showed some caring emotion seemed like a step in the right direction in finding out if the old Zach still existed or if he'd died the night of the crash.

Sophie headed toward the old steel door that led to the tunnels. There wasn't a doubt in her mind Chelsea had explored these spaces. Chelsea had lived for adventure of any type.

Sophie hadn't seen the tunnels mentioned in Chelsea's notes, but Sophie hadn't gone through all of the notes either. Had her late friend planned on doing something neat with these secret passages?

"What are you doing?"

Sophie turned, shielding her eyes with her hand when his light nearly blinded her. "Am I under examination? Put that down."

"Don't go in there," he warned in a firm tone.

She tugged on the old metal latch. The door creaked as it was freed from the rusty lock. "I just want to look for a second. Don't you?"

"I will. I want you to go back upstairs."

"Why?"

His light shifted down, drawing closer to her as his work boots scuffed against the floor. "Because it's dirty down here, it's cold and it's dark."

Sophie ignored him and propped the door open, moving on into the narrow tunnel using the light from her phone. She wanted to see how long the tunnel was. She knew it came out at one of the servants' quarters, but she didn't know if it branched off in two different directions or if it led to just one of the homes and another tunnel led from that home to the second.

The eerie feeling that swept over her at all the memories, heartache, and fear held in this constricted space had shivers racing through her. Sophie couldn't even imagine hiding just to save your life, protect your freedom, all because of the color of your skin.

"Would you get the hell out of there?" Zach yelled as he started in behind her.

Sophie turned. "What is the problem? I'm fine. The ground is level and flat in here. I'm not going to fall."

She started to turn back around, but Zach grabbed her arm. "Maybe I want to look down here alone."

She couldn't see his face all that well, but his warm breath tickled her cheek, his strong hand held on to her bare forearm.

"Too bad," she told him, tilting her chin. "I'm already down here and I'm just as much a part of this."

Zach cursed beneath his breath as his beam of light bounced off the narrow walls. "I don't want you to be, Sophie. Can't you see that? I don't want you here."

Hurt spread through her and she jerked her arm away from his grasp. Damn stubborn man. Who did he think he was, ordering her around?

She refused to let him see the extent of the damage

his words had just caused. She'd wanted to pull the emotions out of him. *Be careful what you wish for.*

"I'm already here," she fired back, her tone harsh from the tears that clogged her throat. "If you want away from me so bad, then why don't you get the hell out? Go back to whatever it is you were doing out there. I want to look."

Zach's flashlight clattered to the floor as he took hold of her shoulders and all but forced her up against the wall. Damp concrete cooled her back while Zach's heated body pressed against her, molding perfectly and sending arousal shooting through her body. The narrow area didn't leave much room to wiggle.

"Don't you get it?" he said through clenched teeth. "I'm trying to stay away from you and you're not helping."

She wished she could see his eyes, wished she could see his face, but with her phone at her side and his light on the floor angling toward the door, all she could do was make out his shape, hear his low, throaty voice, and feel that hard, thick body on hers.

Sophie closed her eyes for a moment, terrified of her feelings for this man who obviously loathed her.

"I know you see me and still feel guilty about the accident," she said softly. "I don't want to always be that reminder—"

His lips crushed hers and for a brief second, Sophie was stunned. She snapped back into reality and sank into his kiss as he kept a tight grip on her shoulders, holding her firmly against the wall. His body trapped her, his kiss assaulted her, and that bulge in his pants all but mocked her.

This was the moment she'd waited for, the moment she'd dreamed about for years, and Zach Monroe blew every single expectation out the window with his talented lips and hard, taut body.

His tongue swept into her mouth and Sophie responded with a groan as she arched against him.

She wanted more, wanted to feel him, wanted to wrap her arms around him. She wanted to be rid of these clothes.

Never before had she wanted a man with such intensity.

Zach tore his mouth from hers with a string of curses.

"Not the way I'd hoped you'd feel about kissing me," she muttered, her lips still tingling, her body still revved up and aching for more.

His hands fell from her shoulders. "I won't apologize."

"Well, that's a move in the right direction."

His boots shuffled against the concrete as he shifted back slightly. "This means nothing."

"Felt like something to me," she countered.

"Obvious reasons this was a bad idea aside, you're dating someone. Or did you forget?"

The sarcastic, harsh question didn't deter her from defending herself and firing right back. "You kissed me. You put your hands on me."

Not that she hadn't enjoyed every delicious second of it.

He started to turn, but she reached for his arm. This wasn't over. She wanted, deserved answers. And she wanted more of what just happened.

Tensing beneath her touch, Zach froze. "What, Sophie?"

"Why did you kiss me?"

Now he did turn to face her, and with the light in his hand she could make out the torn expression on his face. An expression that matched the fear and vulnerability she'd seen when she'd fallen in Chelsea's apartment.

"Why?" he repeated. "Because I've wanted to kiss you since I was sixteen. Because I couldn't keep wondering what you tasted like. I had to know." He blew out a sigh and lowered his voice. "Because I will never have anything more with you, and I selfishly needed that moment. Looks like I'm human after all."

She started to reach for him, but his hand shot up, gripped her wrist. "Don't."

"You tell me all of that and then expect me not to react?"

And men thought women were confusing?

"You're with Martin. Even if you weren't, I won't do relationships or anything long-term. There's nothing between us."

"I'd say there's years of tension between us that we need to wade through before we can decide anything," she told him as anger bubbled within her. How dare he minimize the impact of that kiss? "Hard to ignore a kiss like that."

"You don't understand," he whispered. "You can't possibly know what I have in me, what I've been through. All I could ever give is physical, and you're better than that."

Frustration overwhelmed her and she jerked her arm away. "You won't let anybody in, damn it. Don't you see that I want to be here for you? That I want more with you than this awkward tension and occasional encounters?"

In an instant, Zach's hands framed her face, the warmth of those rough palms only adding to her growing arousal. Between the desire and the anger, she was ready to rip her clothes off and throw down the ultimate challenge.

"I'll never let anyone in," he growled, holding her firmly in place. "Nobody deserves to be subjected to this darkness. Can't you see I just want to keep you away from that? That's what I've always wanted."

The brokenness pouring from him made Sophie wonder what the hell he'd endured that had him hiding behind such a fortress of defenses. She'd heard Chelsea speculate on what they believed Zach had gone through before coming to live with the Monroes, but really nobody had a clue.

"Tell me you don't want me and I'll give up right now."

Okay, she hadn't meant to let that out, but now that the words were hovering between them in the darkness, Sophie wasn't sorry.

Slowly, as if he didn't want to let go, Zach's hands fell away, leaving her colder now than ever.

His stare turned cold. "I don't want you."

No four words had ever, ever hurt so bad. All this time she'd been holding out hope that she would be the one to break through to him, to be the one he lost control with.

"You didn't kiss me like you don't want me," she threw back. "In fact, that kiss felt like a stepping-stone to something more."

Forget the bulge in his pants that had settled against her stomach . . . no need to state the obvious.

"That kiss wasn't the start of anything more. It was a kiss, it's over. I'm sure Martin kisses you."

*Not like that.*

"Zach?" Braxton called from the basement.

"In the tunnel," Zach called back over his shoulder,

then looked at her once more. "Everything that just happened here, forget it."

If she thought for a second that he truly didn't want her, she would totally back away. But no man would have kissed so passionately, touched so tenderly, and tried to protect her from a past she knew nothing about, if he didn't care for her.

So if he wanted to use hurtful words to push her away, fine. She'd use hurtful words to pull him in . . . one way or another.

"I think I'll let you finish this tour alone since you're so set on living that way."

She was apparently a glutton for more torture and anguish, because she went up on her toes and laid her lips against his for the briefest of seconds before stepping away.

"Good luck on forgetting that kiss."

# Chapter Six

Zach slammed the door on his fridge and cursed the very moment his control had snapped and he'd kissed the hell out of Sophie.

How was he to have known she would kiss him right back, matching his passion with one all her own? How was he to know she'd taste better than he'd ever imagined . . . and he'd done quite a bit of imagining over the years.

Damn it, he could still taste her. Now what was he supposed to do? She was dating an asshat who didn't deserve her, but at least that man could offer Sophie a future. He wanted her to be happy, didn't he? He wanted her to have a perfect life. Zach was about as far from perfect as a man could get.

He was an utter fool to even be thinking of the word "future" where Sophie was concerned. He'd had his chance, he'd blown it, and he would continue to pay his penance.

Even beyond the unexpected kiss and bold reaction from Sophie, today had been interesting on the house front as well, and they were just getting started. He and Braxton had discussed all the renovations the house would need to get it up to code and all the foundation-type work. Cosmetics would come later, but for now they needed to get all the basics out of the way.

This wouldn't be a quick project, and it wouldn't be a cheap process. Zach figured all the money he got from the sale of his home, provided Liam and Braxton were on board, would go toward fixing up Chelsea's house. He could always bunk with Braxton until he figured out something else—not what he wanted, but that might be the only option for a temporary fix.

Unfortunately, Zach would have to tell his brothers about needing to sell their childhood home. He didn't need all the space the old Victorian provided. The house should be filled with a family, with kids and dogs and laughter. He'd been tossing the idea around in his head for some time, but now that he needed the extra money, selling the home he'd lived in since he was twelve was the only option.

Even though the home was in his name only, out of respect he'd still tell his brothers and explain his reasons for selling. Zach had a feeling this conversation would only cause more conflict, but he wasn't going to just outright sell and then drop the bomb on them. Going that route would definitely drive more of a wedge between them.

The bad blood since the accident had never settled, and Zach didn't want to cause any more of a rift between Liam and himself. Just because they couldn't be in the same room without arguing, didn't mean Zach wanted to hurt him or be deceptive. He'd be up front about this house, about the prospect of using the funds for Chelsea's dream, and Liam could get on board or buy their childhood home outright.

Zach took a long drink of his pop, his mind circling back to Sophie. He couldn't help but wonder if he'd crossed a line he could never recover from. Kissing her had been a mistake, but he'd barely had control over his emotions for years, and he'd finally snapped. As if things between them weren't complicated enough, now they had this added problem.

The problem being himself. He'd pushed Sophie away, he'd done everything possible to keep her at a distance, including lying straight to her face when he told her he didn't want her.

What a load of bullshit. Didn't want her? The second his lips had touched hers, he'd barely been able to stop himself from taking exactly what his body had craved for years.

She'd kissed him with a fire he hadn't known she possessed. But she was seeing another man, and that made Zach even more of a jerk for messing around with her physically and emotionally.

The reality check put him back in the mind-set where he belonged. Yes, he'd wondered for years what kissing her would be like. Yes, he'd wondered if she would kiss him back with an ounce of the emotion he had for her.

Everything he'd fantasized about had been so minute in comparison to the real thing. Remembering Sophie pressed against him, her little sigh of pleasure, would have to be enough. He wouldn't be touching, let alone kissing her again. And that heated kiss was already more than he deserved.

Zach's cell rang, pulling him from his thoughts. Setting his half-empty can on the end table, Zach fished the phone from his pocket and checked the ID.

"Miss me already?" Zach greeted Braxton in lieu of hello.

"You want to explain why you and Sophie were in the tunnel and the second I get down there she takes off, looking like you killed her puppy?" Braxton demanded.

Zach straightened against his couch, instantly on the defensive. "She doesn't have a puppy."

Did she? Hell, he had no clue. He'd been trying to avoid her for the past decade, and he'd done a pretty good job of it until lately. She could have a damn rabbit living in her house and a goat in her backyard for all he knew.

"Don't dodge the question," Braxton ground out.

"We were talking." *And kissing*.

Braxton's laugh pushed through the line. "I'm not an idiot, Zach. Whatever you did to her, you need to fix."

Dropping his feet from the coffee table, Zach stood. "You don't know anything that's going on between Sophie and me, so don't try to play mediator now."

"Why not? I've had to play referee with you more than once. I understand the tension with you and Liam, and I've even let you two go at each other to work off that steam. But I will not stand back and watch you with Sophie. If you're serious, fine, but I don't want her hurt anymore. She's different, Zach."

Raking a hand over his jaw, his coarse whiskers rubbed his palm as he blew out a breath. "I know. Damn it, I know she's different. That's why I push her away all the time. If she looked upset it's because I was rude and told her to get away."

Silence filled the line and Zach held his breath, waiting for Braxton's reaction.

"You can't act on these feelings." Braxton's knowing

tone was low, worried. "I know the other night I told you to risk it, but Sophie was torn up when I saw her. How could you—"

"Drop it."

No way was he getting into this discussion with anyone, especially one of his brothers. Anything he felt for Sophie, past or present, would stay locked away. They both led different lives, both had goals that didn't involve each other.

"If you're strong enough to keep your emotions in check, then you need to fix whatever you did to her," Braxton went on. "I'm not going to pry, but if I see her visibly upset one more time, I'll kick your ass."

A piercing pain sliced through his heart. Hurting Sophie even more than he already had, was not an option. Yet another reason he wouldn't even attempt a relationship with the only woman he'd ever truly wanted.

"I'll fix it," Zach vowed. No matter the struggle, no matter the heartache he felt, he'd sacrifice anything for Sophie's happiness.


Leaving Martin a voice mail telling him she couldn't go out of town with him seemed rather cold, but she'd tried several times and never could get him to pick up. She couldn't put off telling him any longer, because he deserved to know and time was running out.

Not only could she not go out of town with him, she couldn't see him anymore, but that conversation was definitely something she needed to do face-to-face, and she'd just have to demand a few minutes of his time.

Sophie didn't need any more time to think about her relationship with Martin. Not after that kiss she and Zach had shared. No way could she continue seeing one man when her mind remained fixed on another.

She'd always wondered what kissing Zach would be like, but now she knew, and it wasn't something she could ignore. The memory of the instant fire that had spread through her at Zach's rough, demanding kiss had her body heating up all over again.

For some asinine reason she was completely drawn to the gruff, grouchy exterior of a man who kept pushing her away. She could easily blame her attraction on the teenage girl who found herself falling for the town bad boy against her parents' wishes. If that had just been an infatuation, those feelings would've dissipated long ago.

Instead, everything she felt for Zach kept getting stronger, more powerful each time she saw him. She was to the point she was going insane with conflictions. Did she risk telling him, only to have him shut her out even more?

Regardless of the outcome with her and Zach, Sophie wouldn't be with a man she didn't have strong feelings for, so she needed to tell Martin they should see other people.

Sophie curled her feet beneath her on the sofa and slid her pencil in a smooth, easy glide over the clean sheet of paper. Flynn curled next to her and purred softly, as if he hadn't a care in the world. Soothing jazzy music filled her living room. Most times her favorite selection was her go-to in order to relax. Unfortunately, tonight she was anything but relaxed. Even her favorite band wasn't taking the edge off.

Her cell vibrated on the wooden coffee table. When she glanced at the screen, she groaned and went back to her drawing. No way could she deal with her mother.

No doubt the woman was calling to discuss some little shop she'd just been in or to complain about Sophie's father. No matter what, Sophie simply wasn't in the mood.

Breaking things off with Martin would be easier than telling her mother that the relationship was over. Her parents loved Martin, or rather they loved his social standing in the community and how he would look in the family. Not that her family was loaded, but they liked to play the part. They had, or rather her parents had, enough money to take trips and be comfortable, but they flashed their lives just for show and to appear "important." Sophie never cared what others thought . . . well, except for Zach.

Sophie sketched a bit more, with no idea where she was going with the new artwork, but she just wasn't in the mood. That had never happened before. Drawing and listening to Sinatra or Dean Martin had started out as therapy when she'd been dealing with tough times after the accident. The hobby had quickly turned into a passion and a talent she hadn't known she possessed.

Placing the pad and pencil on her table, she retrieved her phone and ignored her mother's voice mail. She'd listen to it tomorrow. Right now, she didn't have the emotional strength.

She was tired, confused. Sleep wouldn't come easy tonight. She had water aerobics to teach in the morning before work, and no doubt she'd show up looking worn and haggard, which pretty much matched how she felt at the moment. There was no way she could focus on much, when all she could concentrate on was the feel of Zach's lips against hers, the firm, powerful way his body had pressed hers against the cool wall.

His rough hands had gripped her in a way that she knew she'd be reliving for days, if not months to come.

Flynn darted down the hall and beat her to the bedroom. She wasn't sure why that silly cat always thought there was a race, but apparently there was, and Sophie always came in last.

She reached into her antique drawer and pulled out her favorite chemise. She loved silky things against her skin while she slept. Anything soft and thin that made her feel sexy was always a good thing. Every woman should treat herself to something that made her feel beautiful, whether it was flannel or satin. Sophie wasn't counting on a man to make her feel sexy; she was independent enough to do that for herself.

The cell on her dresser vibrated again and Sophie rolled her eyes as she glanced over. Only this time it wasn't her mother.

Her heartbeat lurched and she stared at the name on her screen for several seconds. She even blinked, sure she'd glanced at the name wrong.

With a knot forming quickly in her stomach, Sophie hit the button and answered. "Zach."

"I need to talk to you."

No greeting. Just to the point—whatever that point might be.

"Is something wrong?" she asked, gripping the phone and forcing her tone to remain calm.

His muffled laugh leaned toward the sarcastic side. "That's one way of putting it."

Sophie padded to her bed, where Flynn had already stretched out on the yellow blanket folded across the bottom. She took a seat, crossing her arm over her abdomen.

"What do you need to talk to me about? Is it the

house?" *Keep it professional. No need to jump to conclusions.* Though if she thought he was sexy before, he was doubly so with that low, throaty voice sliding through the phone.

"No."

She swallowed, glancing down at her pink polished toenails against the glossy, dark hardwood floors. "Oh. Well, I'll be in the office tomorrow after ten if you want to swing by. We can talk then."

"Are you alone?" he asked.

Shock and arousal spread through her at his demanding question. "Um, yes."

Who else did he expect to be here right now? Did he really think after the way they'd kissed that she would have Martin here for a sleepover? Granted, Zach had no clue about her private life or that she'd not been intimate with anyone in years. She just couldn't, for way too many reasons—mainly the man on the other end of the line.

"I'm on my way."

Sophie came to her feet, worry settling in. "You sound odd, Zach. What's wrong? Is it Braxton or Liam?"

"They're fine. See you in a few minutes."

He hung up. Actually hung up, as if inviting himself over was normal, like they were friends. What had happened since she'd seen him this morning? He'd kissed her like she was his lifeline to salvation. Then he'd completely pushed her away, using hurtful words that still stung.

Sophie dropped the phone on her bed and grabbed her silky robe off the small hook on her closet door. She had no idea where Zach was when he called, so she hurried and tied the robe, making sure she was fully covered.

Padding barefoot down the hall, she'd just flicked the porch light on when Zach's broad, powerful frame mounted the steps. Her heartbeat kicked up as she freed the dead bolt and pulled the old oak door open.

The instant Zach lifted his head, that heavy-lidded gaze of his raked over her body, leaving her tingling in spots she didn't know could tingle from a mere glance.

Gripping the doorknob, she straightened her shoulders. "Come on in."

"I'll stay on the porch."

O-kay. She stepped outside, pulling the door closed behind her. Now in the pale glow of her porch lights, she shivered at the intimacy. Folding her arms over her chest, she forced herself to look him in the eye and not be intimidated by his masculinity, which threatened to make her knees buckle. Seeing him after what they'd shared in the tunnel was difficult. How could they ever go back to the awkward relationship that they'd grown accustomed to? Now they'd reached a new level of awkward, because just looking at him had her aching, had her staring at his mouth, wondering how those lips would feel on the rest of her body.

"Do you want to have a seat?" She gestured toward her porch swing.

"No."

Sophie let out a sigh. "For someone who wanted to talk so bad you showed up at my house, you're not saying much."

Those eyes continued to accost her. How could he just stand there as though this crackling tension wasn't the third party in this difficult meeting?

"I know I shouldn't be here. I'm sure Martin wouldn't appreciate it."

Sophie took a deep breath. "Martin isn't an issue anymore."

She shouldn't have said anything. It was hardly fair to say that to Zach when Martin didn't even know yet. But the words slipped out and she couldn't pull them back.

Zach blinked, obviously shocked. "Because we kissed?"

At least he wasn't avoiding the topic. "Partly," she answered honestly. "But I'm not discussing him, because he has nothing to do with why you came over. Does he?"

Zach shook his head, the muscle in his jaw clenched. "I came by to apologize for the kiss, for how I handled things."

Sophie could easily have let those words deflate her, but she was stronger than that. Something Zach would do well to remember. Because there was no way in hell a man who kissed like that was sorry that it happened. He hadn't acted sorry . . . he'd acted just as needy as she'd felt.

"Really? You're going to go that route?" She laughed, knowing that calling him out would irritate him. She was done coddling him and his self-pity. "Don't lie to me. You can't kiss me with so much passion and desire and be sorry for it at the same time."

Those chocolate-brown eyes narrowed. "Fine. I'm not sorry I kissed you. I am sorry for the way I treated you."

"Which time?" she countered. "After the kiss or all the years leading up to it?"

Crossing his arms over his wide chest, Zach shifted his feet and continued to glare. A portion of his tat peeked out beneath the hem of his gray T-shirt. Broad muscles stretched the thin material. Zach came by his spectacular frame the old-fashioned, hardworking way, with intense manual labor.

The man exuded sex appeal, but there was so much

more to him than physical strength and an impressive exterior. Layers of emotions, some dark and some caring, made up the intriguing man.

"I didn't mean to hurt your feelings earlier," he told her.

Sophie jerked back. She'd never heard him sound this sincere, this broken. What had that kiss done to him? Something wasn't right, and she wasn't quite sure how to approach it because the man was so closed off.

"My feelings weren't hurt."

"Now who's lying?" he asked, raising a dark brow.

"Fine," she conceded. She didn't want him hiding his feelings, so she wasn't going to hide hers. "You did hurt me. It wasn't the first time, and I doubt it will be the last."

Zach raked a hand over his messy hair, glanced down to his scuffed boots, then back up to meet her gaze. "Hurting you kills me," he whispered. "That's the last thing I'd ever want to do. But you're not the type of woman who gets involved with someone like me, Soph. You're sweet talking and dinners, I'm rough and one-night stands."

His raw words washed over her, sending shivers racing through her as she rubbed her hands up and down her arms. Perhaps that was exactly what they were, but who's to say those worlds couldn't collide into something glorious?

Sophie didn't know what to say. Being around Zach had always been a battle of wills, and seeing him so vulnerable wasn't something she'd had any experience with.

"That's the main reason I came," he went on. "I won't lie and pretend touching you didn't affect me. Judging from the way you kissed me back, I'd say you were just as affected. But that's where things have to stop."

She started to reach for him, but he stepped back. Just like in the tunnels. Sophie closed her eyes and nodded, not accepting defeat but giving him the space he so obviously needed. "Why are you so difficult?"

Lifting her lids to meet his dark-as-night eyes, Sophie didn't know what to make of his pained expression.

"This isn't me being difficult. This is me saving both of us from a road that would only lead to destruction."

"And you're so certain that anything we would have would be a disaster?"

"You don't get it." He shook his head, throwing his arms wide. "I'm doing this for you."

Sophie pulled her robe tighter and laughed. "Great, now you're going to fall back on the 'it's not you, it's me' excuse? I took you for someone who could man up and not rely on lame comments."

Zach took a menacing step forward. He stood within an inch of her, his warmth spreading through her just as surely as if he was touching her. Those eyes pinned her in place and she gripped the vee of her robe to keep from reaching up and touching that coarse, stubbled jaw so set with determination.

"For the first time in my life, I *am* manning up." That growl-like tone did nothing to kill the desire she had for him. "I'm not running, I'm not hiding. I'm here, opening myself to you because I can't stand you to be hurt. Working on the house together is fine; I actually welcome your input. But I can't be that man you may think you want. That man doesn't exist inside of me."

Now she did reach up, unable to help herself. She wanted him to feel comfort, to know that whatever internal demons he was battling didn't scare her.

More than anything, she wanted him to know he wasn't alone.

"I'm glad you're done hiding." Sophie stroked his jaw, not intimidated when he stilled beneath her touch. "But now you're lying to yourself. If you think we can work together on this project, spend a great deal of time together, and not be drawn even more strongly to each other, you're mistaken. We've dodged each other for nearly a decade, Zach. That kiss proved we have something."

He gripped her hand, slowly lowering it from his face. "We have a past and now we have a mutual goal. There is nothing more."

When he turned to go, Sophie couldn't help but get in one last word. "You say you came here to apologize and to tell me you're done running." When he froze, without turning around, she went on. "You're still running, Zach. Which proves you came here for one reason. To see me. Because you know just as I do that something beyond our control is happening between us."

Without another word, without waiting to see if he would even reply, Sophie went back in her house, locked the door, and flicked off the porch light.

Sinking back against the door, she willed her legs to hold her up. Her body trembled at the breakthrough that had just occurred.

Perhaps through all of this heartache, these years of suppressed emotions, there was a light at the end of this dark, lonely tunnel.

# Chapter Seven

Zach wanted nothing more than to pound the hell out of something. Unfortunately, he'd done all the demolition on his current home and was now in the rebuilding stage.

He'd driven around for nearly an hour after leaving Sophie's house. The way she'd called him out on his emotions, the way she'd stood there so strong and vibrant, had nearly brought him to his knees. How was he ever going to make it through the renovations at the Sunset Lake property if she kept battling him? Because Zach was truly afraid he couldn't stand up to the new, fierce side of Sophie.

As he put his key in the back door, something rustled in the bushes. His first thought was that Ms. Barkley would be standing there when he turned, but as he came back down the steps to see what was causing the rustle, Zach realized it wasn't his overly deliberate neighbor with her cleavage up to her chin.

Nestled beneath his honeycup shrub was a dog, a very large dog, lying on her side. Zach knew the dog was a female because of the intense way she was breathing and the protruding belly that no doubt held puppies ready to be born . . . in his yard.

Zach muttered a curse. Not that he didn't love dogs. He actually loved animals, but what did he know about a dog in labor, or puppies? The only dog he'd had growing up was one the Monroes found on the street and brought home one night because it had a broken leg. They'd nursed it back to health and kept the stray for another eight years. No puppies involved, and the dog was a male.

Zach crouched down, squinting to get a better view. His back porch light offered enough of a glow, but the thick shrubbery shaded the dog.

"Hey there," he said in a soft tone he barely recognized. "It's okay, girl."

Was it? Hell, he knew less about labor than he did about puppies. Did he call the vet? Call an animal shelter? Was she delivering the pups now? Good grief, why his yard? What if he did something wrong and the pups got hurt or the mom died or . . .

Okay, he needed to get a grip because he was of no use if he was going to freak out. Dogs had puppies all the time . . . just not in his damn yard.

From what he could see, the dog appeared to be a yellow Lab mix. She let out a whine, and Zach raked his hands through his hair. Damn it, what should he do?

He jerked his phone from his back pocket and quickly looked up "dogs in labor." The image section was not an area he needed to go right now. He'd be seeing it up close and personal soon enough. Scrolling through the articles, he found a promising, helpful site.

After reading and learning way more than he felt necessary, he went into action. As tired and frustrated with life as he was, he couldn't just go in and go to bed when there was a dog in need and innocent puppies about to be born.

Softly, Zach ran a hand over the dog's head, letting her know she wasn't alone, before heading inside to gather towels and a bowl of water. He was definitely out of his element here, but that dog had either him or nothing. What if the pups weren't born for another day? Was he going to sit up all night?

Yes, he would. Because no matter what a jerk he could be, he wasn't one to abandon anyone or anything when they were in need.

An image of Sophie lying in a hospital bed after the accident slammed into his mind. He'd not seen her because he'd been arrested, but he'd heard enough to know she'd been through hell . . . because of him. No, he wasn't going there. He'd been no use to her then. He sure as hell wasn't now, either.

Pushing Sophie and his emotions aside, Zach gathered all he needed and headed back outside. Dumping the towels on the ground, he pulled his phone back out and looked up the town vet.

Marcie had graduated with Sophie and Chelsea, but he'd never had a need to call her office before now. He waited for the answering machine to kick on and left a message, hoping they were checked often and she would call back soon.

Zach took a seat on the ground next to the bushes and kept searching through his phone for any information about what to do for this dog. As he looked closer, he realized she didn't have a collar on. He didn't recall seeing such a beautiful animal in the neighborhood before, either. Surely she belonged to someone. Maybe Marcie would be more help once she called back.

Every now and then the Lab would let out a whine

or a howl. Zach hated that. Couldn't she have lain down in someone else's yard? Like maybe Ms. Barkley's? No, that wouldn't have been good. Zach couldn't imagine his stiletto-wearing neighbor catering to the needs of an abandoned, pregnant dog.

It wasn't lost on him that he was riding to the rescue of a canine and her unborn pups when he couldn't even figure out how to save himself from this mess he'd gotten himself into with Sophie.

She was obviously on to him, and she wasn't going to let him get away with lying to himself or lying to her. He had no clue how to approach her when he saw her again. All he could do, all he *should* do, was focus on finishing the renovations, focus on this asinine idea of opening a damn women's resort, because all of that was more than enough to make his head spin without adding Sophie into the mix.

Zach swallowed as images of Chelsea flooded his mind. When he'd come to live with the Monroes, the last of the four stragglers they'd adopted, Chelsea had been so sweet even when he'd been anything but. She would talk to him, that bright smile across her face as if her entire world were unicorns and rainbows. He'd hated the smile at the time. Hated how she constantly threw in his face how his pity parties were robbing him of his happiness.

But each time she came into his room, often late at night because they'd been insomniac partners, she would curl up on that window seat and just talk. Half the time he never said a word, but every single thing she said penetrated his thick skull.

Oftentimes she'd fall asleep in that window and Zach would take the blanket from his bed and cover her up. He almost felt as if she were staying with him, watching over him like some real-life guardian angel.

Chelsea had recognized a broken soul, having been one herself. But she'd turned that brokenness into freedom and had lived her life the way she wanted, through happiness, giving her darkened past the mental middle finger.

At first Zach had no idea how someone who had been basically abandoned could be so happy, so full of life. He'd endured nightmares he'd never wish on his worst enemy, and all he'd wanted to do was pick a fight or be alone. Chelsea hadn't let him do either. She loved him instantly, and he soon came to find out she was impossible to ignore. She was impossible not to love.

When Zach felt the sting in his throat, he muttered a curse and raked a hand down his face. He was tired. That's all. He wasn't going to break down. What would be the point? Crying wouldn't bring her back, crying wouldn't get him out of this emotional roller coaster he was on, and crying wouldn't help this current situation. Because if the way this Lab was shifting, as if trying to get comfortable, and the way she kept tightening her stomach, Zach had a feeling he wouldn't need to speak to Marcie once she called. The delivery would be over at that point.

Water aerobics always relaxed Sophie. Unfortunately, like the pencil sketches, nothing was really helping lately.

She'd gone through the familiar motions in the class, chatted with her regulars, and caught up on the latest town gossip. Her mind was still on her late-night visitor and his stubborn pride.

As she steered her car toward her office, her cell

rang. She tapped on her steering wheel to answer her hands-free device.

"Hello?"

"Soph, I'm on my way to a meeting, but I wanted to return your call."

Pulling into her parking spot, Sophie sighed at Martin's clipped, rushed tone. "I apologize for the last-minute cancelation, but this isn't a good time for me to get away."

Silence greeted her on the other end.

"Martin?"

"Is this because of that Sunset Lake property and the Monroes?"

Gripping the wheel, Sophie stared straight ahead at the tall fountain in the middle of town. "I'm busy with several projects," she answered. "Surely you understand."

Once again he said nothing for a moment.

"We need to talk," she told him. "In person and not in a rushed setting."

There. She'd gotten that out. She seriously hated confrontation, but staying with Martin any longer just wasn't possible, and he deserved to know.

"I don't like the sound of that," he said, his tone low. "What's going on, Sophie?"

"I'd rather speak in person. I'm showing a house this afternoon, but I'll be home all evening if you'd like to stop by."

"I'll see what I can do."

Sophie said her good-byes, not wanting to draw out the tension-filled conversation another minute. If Martin were in tune with other people's feelings, he'd most likely pick up on the fact that they'd grown apart. Even before Zach's bold step into her life recently,

Sophie just wasn't feeling a connection with Martin like she'd had early in their relationship.

On a sigh, Sophie grabbed her messenger bag and headed into her office. She'd showered and changed at the gym after her class, so she was ready to go. With her assistant still out on vacation, Sophie was running the place single-handedly and was doing quite well, if she did say so herself.

After letting herself in, she punched in the security code and headed straight to her office. She had a few phone calls to make, then an open house that afternoon on a newly listed property. She fully expected to receive multiple offers, which would hopefully drive up the asking price.

Just as she booted up her computer, her cell rang again. Glancing over, she was actually relieved to see it was Liam. Relieved yet curious, because he rarely called her.

Sliding her finger across the screen, she answered. "Hey, Liam."

"Do you have a minute?"

Surprised at the intensity of his tone, Sophie eased back in her cushy desk chair. "Of course. Something wrong?"

"No. But I want this conversation to stay between us."

Now she was really intrigued. What could Liam have to discuss that was so private?

"I won't say a word to anyone."

Since the accident years ago, Sophie had always had a special bond with Liam. He'd been at the hospital with her and sat with her after her surgery. Even though he'd been patched up and hurting, he'd stayed by her side. Since that time, he'd call her, check on her and offer that silent support. She knew without a doubt that he would do anything for her, and the bond they shared over a tragedy could never be severed.

But Sophie had wanted to reach out to Zach after the accident. On that she and Liam disagreed. When Zach had been sent to prison for a year, he'd refused her visits. Once he got out, he'd been even angrier, more closed off than ever. More than once Liam held her as she'd fought back tears, and he never said a word. He understood her feelings, just as she understood his where Zach was concerned, but Liam never judged her.

And while Liam was very much closed off to the world, Sophie could always get him to open up to her.

"Are you okay?" she asked.

"I'm fine. I want to know more about this project my brothers are taking on."

Sophie smiled. *So, the brother adamant on keeping his distance is now interested.* She truly hoped he'd get on board. Chelsea would've loved knowing her disgruntled siblings were working on a project in her memory . . . and a women-only resort and spa, no less. Chelsea was no doubt smiling down from heaven.

"Actually I want to know what's going on with the property now. With the payments on the back taxes coming due, can you tell me what the next step is?"

This was an area Sophie didn't want to get in the middle of. She didn't want to play both sides, or all three, technically, with the Monroe brothers. Everything she was doing now was for Chelsea.

"When Braxton was home he and Zach did a walk-through of the property. They made several notes on what needed updating to get the place up to code. I'm not sure what the final numbers are. Zach was going to do some figuring before they looked at costs for the cosmetic work."

Even thinking about the day of the walk-through, the turning point with Zach in the tunnel, got her flustered. She hoped her voice remained strong and steady because every single time she thought about that moment when he'd kissed her so passionately, she seriously felt like a puddle of emotions.

"Why didn't you ask Braxton about all of this?"

"I didn't want a speech on why I should be contributing," Liam answered. "I'm still not sold on this project and it could be a huge failure. The only reason I'd want in is because of Chelsea."

Sophie swallowed the lump of remorse at the thought of how much they all missed the feisty, free-spirited friend and sister. There was a way to make her legacy live on, and Sophie desperately wanted all the guys on board.

"We're all doing it for Chelsea." Sophie eased forward in her chair, pulling up her list of e-mails. "Do you honestly think Zach and Braxton had their hearts set on a resort and spa?"

Liam laughed. "Honestly, with those two, knowing it's for women only, I think that's their draw."

Sophie didn't like the stab of jealousy that speared through her at the mention of Zach's interest in other women. She knew he didn't date much, knew he kept to himself. But he was a man, and there wasn't a woman around that could deny his sex appeal. Between the beard, the broad, muscular frame, and his brooding attitude, he screamed alpha, and Sophie knew she was completely out of her element to even think they were on the same level.

Still, that didn't stop a girl from desiring everything she shouldn't.

"Are you telling me you want in on the project?" she asked, circling back to the real reason he called.

Liam blew out a sigh. "I honestly don't know. I don't want to put you in the middle, but I just needed to know what was going on."

"You could move back," she told him softly. "You could still work there, but live here with us."

"I'm only thirty minutes away. Savannah isn't that far."

Far enough when there was already a world of emotions wedged between the members of his family.

"So what do you want me to do?" she asked, glancing at her e-mails. None that couldn't wait until after the open house. "Do you want me to keep you updated, or do you want me to try to talk you into jumping on board?"

Liam's gentle laugh filled the line. "I have no idea. I guess I just don't want to be out of the loop. I've already lost Chelsea. I don't want to feel like my entire family is slipping away."

Sophie's heart broke for Liam. He'd distanced himself from Zach after the accident, but Sophie knew Liam would never have left to begin with if he and Zach had been able to get out their anger and resentment toward each other. But once Zach had gone to prison, Liam hadn't tried to visit. Each brother had let the hurt fester, and now here they were, ten years later, and all of that pain was just bubbling below the surface.

One day, they were going to blow.

"Maybe if you could keep me updated. Just let me know the costs and where the guys stand? I'm not giving input," he informed her. "I don't want to weigh in on this, but if I decide to jump on board later, and that's a big if, I don't want to be going in blind."

Sophie smiled. Liam wouldn't be able to stay away. He'd want to be part of this, he'd want this as an outlet to feel closer to Chelsea, but he had to figure that out on his own. Every man wanted his ideas to be his own, so Sophie would let him draw his own conclusions.

Perhaps this would be the thread that sewed this broken family back together.

"I promise to keep you updated," she assured him.

Perhaps some persuasion would accompany her updates when she checked in.

Sophie and Liam said their good-byes, and as much as Sophie tried to concentrate on digging into work, she couldn't get her mind off of the Sunset Lake property. Chelsea had had a vision, one that meant so much to her that she'd taken time to plan this out, to hold it close to her heart and not share it with those closest to her.

Chelsea had purchased the property she'd loved since she was a little girl. She'd always joked that she'd own it one day, but Sophie always played it off as a little girl's dream . . . She knew all too well how those dreams could be crushed in an instant.

Refusing to allow that one life-altering night to ruin her day or the current dream she was fulfilling for a friend, Sophie opted to focus on what needed to be done to help Zach and Braxton with the property now. She might not be able to do much grunt work, but she would definitely be with them through 100 percent of this journey.

Sophie glanced at the time on her cell and calculated how long it would take her to run a last-minute errand before the open house in a couple of hours. She liked to arrive early at the homes to make sure the staging was properly set up before potential buyers strolled through.

Chewing on her bottom lip, she shut her computer off, grabbed her bag, and headed out the door. She wasn't going to hide behind the awkward tension between her and Zach. This project was a huge undertaking and they were all in this for the long haul.

As she drove toward his house, she wondered just how well she'd be received, showing up so unexpectedly.

# Chapter Eight

The bright afternoon sun kept Sophie's spirits high during her drive to Zach's house. A beautiful day usually helped to draw more people out to an open house, plus Sophie needed that extra boost of sunshine from Mother Nature. Anything to keep her mood high as she tried to tamp down the nerves.

Why was she so nervous? Was she afraid of facing Zach's grumpy attitude? That wouldn't be new. Was she worried he'd look at her with that angst-filled desire? Also not new. He might not even be home, and she'd been getting worked up for nothing.

Sophie's confidence level and her mood plummeted as she pulled into his drive and spotted a very leggy, busty blonde in killer heels strutting back across the lawn to the house next door.

The blonde threw a look over her shoulder, a smile on the woman's blood-red lips, toward Sophie.

Sophie couldn't put her feelings into words, because if she sat there and analyzed them too much, she'd be hurt. She had no claim on Zach. They'd shared a kiss. No, two kisses. But that was all. He'd made it clear there could be nothing else.

Yet there was clearly something else going on, whether he wanted to fess up to it or not.

That didn't mean he didn't have a thing going on with his neighbor, who Sophie seriously doubted just came to borrow sugar.

Killing her engine, Sophie shook her head and stepped from the car. After smoothing her green pencil skirt and tucking her hair behind her ears, she straightened her shoulders and made her way to his front door. She refused to feel inferior to a woman she didn't even know.

So what if Sophie didn't have silicone to fill out her shirt? So what if there was no way in hell she could ever wear heels like that with her limp? And so what if red lipstick made her look washed out and she always chose a sheer gloss? She was proud of who she was. That didn't mean she had to like someone so blatant sniffing around Zach.

Sighing, Sophie raised her fist and pounded on his door. She didn't care if he wasn't decent. It was the middle of the afternoon and his booty call schedule wasn't keeping Sophie from working on her ideas for Chelsea's home.

The door jerked open. Zach's eyes darted to her, then behind her, then back to her.

"Not who you were expecting?" she asked, quirking a brow.

She had no idea how she expected him to answer the door, but shirtless with a pair of running shorts low on his hips hadn't crossed her mind. When she'd thought of him not being decent, she hadn't thought far enough ahead to an actual scenario . . . not that any image in her mind could compare to the real, beautiful vision.

That tattoo she'd seen peeking from his shirt scrolled

up and over his taut shoulder. Ink over muscle . . . She'd never thought about it before, but this was a new level of sexy.

"Get in here," he growled as he turned from the door.

"You look like you've had a rough night."

The lady leaving the scene of the crime might have played a part in that, if Zach's messed-up hair was any indication. Sophie hated the thought of another woman raking her nails over Zach, but she was also realistic and knew he wasn't a monk.

By the time she stepped in and closed the door behind her, Zach grunted in response and disappeared down the hall. Sophie followed, assuming that's what her gracious host had intended.

As soon as she rounded the corner to his laundry area, she stopped short.

"Not one word," he grumbled. "We've been up all night and I'm not in the mood for a snarky comment."

Big, bearded, burly Zach cradled a puppy in one bulky, muscular arm and tried to wedge the tip of a bottle between the pup's little lips.

Sophie didn't know if she wanted to laugh at the image, sigh over the sweetness, or stand back and keep taking in the view. Yet again, the man continued to surprise her, and in the end laughter won out. Maybe he hadn't been burning up the sheets at all. Yes, this made her happy. No, she didn't care if that was childish.

Zach muttered a curse when the bottle didn't ease in. He murmured something sweet to the squirmy puppy. She'd never seen such a caring side of him. Nor had she seen him bottle-feeding anything at all before. Laughter bubbled up.

His eyes cut her way. "Stop laughing. You'll scare them."

"I'm sorry," she said, holding her hand over her mouth as she glanced down at a tired mommy lying on a very cushy pile of blankets while roughly six puppies nestled against her belly. "It's not you I'm laughing at. Well, it is, but not for the reasons you're thinking."

Zach shifted his broad frame, muscles flexed all over the place. "I'm not in the mood for games."

Sophie shrugged and leaned against the dryer. "On a good day you're not in the mood, so lack of sleep doesn't really change you much, does it? I laughed because I thought I'd just witnessed your booty call doing the walk of shame, but I find you in here nursing puppies."

"My booty call?" Zach finally got the bottle into the puppy's mouth and the ball of fur stopped moving around. Apparently he was just a hungry little guy. "I'd never sleep with my neighbor, and I sure as hell wouldn't label it as a booty call."

"What would you call an afternoon romp, then?" she asked, unable to help herself.

With a sigh, Zach pinned her with his heavy-lidded gaze. "Did you have a reason behind your visit? Because I'm sure you didn't come here to discuss my bedroom partners or what label I place on it."

No, no she hadn't, and she'd gotten so far off track it took her a minute to figure out what she had come here for.

"I'm sorry I dropped in on you last minute and that you were up all night with your mama dog."

"She's not mine." He held the puppy up, stroked its golden fur, and gently placed it back down with the rest of the litter. "I found her in my bushes last night after I came back from your place. I'm looking for a home for her and the pups, but the pups can't leave the mom for six weeks. There's got to be someone who will take them all. I sure as hell can't."

Yet he had. Sophie didn't think her heart could swell any more for this man at this exact moment. "Looks like you're the daddy for the time being."

He cursed, raked a hand through his mop of messy hair, and propped his hands on his hips. "Then the vet couldn't get here in time for the delivery because she had an emergency, but a tech helped me over the phone with my questions. The puppies came, that little guy was too small, so I called back and was told to bottle feed it for a few days. I ran out this morning to get everything I needed and here I am. Now that you have the entire story, do you want to tell me what you need?"

Stepping toward him, Sophie smiled and tipped her head back. "You're a remarkable man."

Zach lowered his brows. "That's what you needed to tell me?"

Still smiling, Sophie gently squatted down and ran her hand over the head of the beautiful Lab. Completely ignoring the slight twinge in her hip, she stroked the soft, golden fur and wondered how many times Zach had done something like this without a soul knowing. Because that would be his way. He'd play hero to anyone and anything and expect zero recognition. In fact, he most likely hated that she'd witnessed him being so selfless.

"I wanted to see those binders of Chelsea's, if you don't mind," she said, throwing a glance over her shoulder. "I figured while you were working on the main renovations, I could be getting things in place and seeing what I can do to save money regarding the decorating and finishing touches. I know we're a long way off, but I have some connections, and with home sales, I'm always finding cheap buys of furniture and odds and ends."

"They're in the living room. You can have them."

Sophie gave the now sleeping dog one last stroke before she went to stand. That twinge earlier turned into a full-fledged shooting pain, and Sophie hissed as she froze before she could even stand.

In an instant, Zach was at her side, his arms wrapping around her. "Don't move. Just lean against me."

She had no choice. It was either lean on him or fall on her butt. She'd really like to save this outfit and her pride.

"Sorry," she muttered, hating once again how her humiliation liked to rear its ugly head around him. "I just moved wrong, that's all."

"If I help, can you stand?" he asked, his breath tickling the side of her face.

Sophie nodded and gritted her teeth as he slowly eased her up, taking her weight back onto his body as his arms remained locked around her.

They fit. As if clicking into place perfectly without even trying, they fit together like nothing she'd ever experienced. That hard, broad chest against her back had her practically melting into him. She'd never felt this level of desire with another man, certainly not the man she'd been in a relationship with for the past several months. She hated to compare the two, because they were polar opposites on the man-scope, but how could she not?

"Do you need me to carry you to the couch?"

Sophie closed her eyes. "No. Just give me a second."

The pain in her hip had definitely lessened. The second she requested was purely selfish, purely for her own enjoyment. Sophie hated playing games, but she just wanted one more moment with his arms wrapped around her. One more moment not worrying about why Zach kept pushing her away. For right now, he was everything she needed, but saying so would cause him to close off even more and she needed him open, she needed him to be as raw and exposed as she was.

"Soph."

That tone did amazing things to her body, her heart. Still, this wasn't what she'd come here for, and she wouldn't be throwing herself at him each time they came together. He wanted to distance himself from feelings he was obviously fighting, and she refused to be that woman who kept trying to gain his attention.

Which meant no more melting into his arms. She'd have to stand on her own two feet, no matter the pain in her hip. Damn it, that shooting pain came at the most inopportune times.

"I'm okay," she assured him, easing away from the comfort of his embrace. "Hardly a twinge now."

Pasting on a smile, she smoothed her hands down her simple silk blouse and pencil skirt before she turned to face him. Those dark brows were drawn in again as his eyes assessed her. This was the precise reason she refused to lean on him, to use her slight handicap as a crutch to gain more attention. She'd never be that girl.

"The binders?" she reminded him, hoping to pull him from the guilt he most likely flooded himself with. "I have an open house soon, and I need to get there early."

Zach hesitated, then nodded. When he turned and

left the room, Sophie exhaled a breath and applauded her performance and her self-control. It would've been so easy to use Zach's remorse to gain his undivided attention, but she wanted him to look at her and not see the night of the accident, not see the mistake he made or the year he spent in prison. She wanted him to look at her and see a woman. Not his sister's best friend, not anything other than a woman who was attracted to a stubborn, hardheaded man.

Glancing down at all the sleeping puppies again, Sophie crossed to the sink in the corner to wash her hands. While she loved animals, she didn't necessarily want to go to the open house smelling like a dog. Although a cute puppy sleeping on the living room rug would make for a picturesque setting and tug on some family's heartstrings.

She'd love to take a pup for herself, but she wondered how Flynn would accept a newcomer . . . probably not very well at all, considering he'd had the run of the house for years now.

By the time Sophie made it into the living room, Zach had stacked the thick black binders on the coffee table.

"Just keep them," he told her, crossing his arms over his still bare chest. "If I need them I'll let you know, but it's going to be a while before I can focus on her designs and plans."

Sophie crossed to gather the binders. "Thank you for not pushing me away on this project. Helping with this really makes me feel close to Chelsea. I'm just not ready to part with you guys just yet."

She laughed as she reached for the binders, but Zach placed a hand on her forearm. Her eyes darted to his scarred hand moments before he snatched it away.

"What do you mean, part with us?" he asked, standing way too close for her emotional comfort.

She straightened and faced him. "I just meant that with Chelsea gone, you guys still have each other, and it's not like any of the Monroe boys are going to call me up to go shoe shopping or to go watch the latest chick flick."

"Braxton might. He's a sucker for those damn movies."

Sophie smiled. "You know what I mean."

On a sigh, Zach nodded. "Listen, I know there's been tension between us. Just because Chelsea is gone, doesn't mean we're all not still friends."

Sophie stared at those dark eyes, so intense and mesmerizing. The sprinkling of chest hair, the tattoo, and the random scar were spellbinding as well. But she had to concentrate on what he said . . . and then use his words against him.

"Are we friends, Zach? Because that's not the vibe I've been getting from you."

He continued to hold her still with just his gaze as he raked a palm over his beard. The bristling sound against his hand had her trembling. She knew what that coarse hair felt like against her skin, her lips, and she craved more.

"We're friends, Sophie," he muttered. "I've let you in about as much as I've let anyone."

He'd let her in? In what? His house? Certainly not his life. Could one person be that closed off from the world? Other than Liam and Braxton, Zach really didn't have people deeply rooted in his life. His business didn't count. No doubt he even kept his employees at arm's length.

"Wow, you really aren't a people person, are you?"

Shaking her head, she reached for the binders, because this conversation was going nowhere fast and she had somewhere to be. Getting into a verbal sparring match each time she saw him was only going to make this process more difficult.

Clutching the binders, she turned and smacked into Zach's chest. "Excuse me."

He didn't move. He didn't speak. He didn't touch her. The man simply stared down at her as if he was trying to figure out the next move in this delicate game of chess.

"What?" she whispered, afraid he'd say something that made her more confused . . . afraid he'd say nothing and let her walk away. "You can't keep doing this to me."

His hands came up to cover hers. "What am I doing?"

"I need a truce. You want to be friends, fine. But you can't look at me like that, you can't push me away with your words and draw me back in with a look. I deserve better than to be yanked around."

Zach's hands tightened on hers briefly before dropping away. "You're right. You do deserve better."

When he stepped back, Sophie cursed herself. "You're taking my words wrong."

Zach walked to the front door, his eyes on the death grip he had on the knob. "No, I'm taking them exactly how I should. You do deserve better, Soph. Better than anything I could give, friendship or otherwise. Sometimes I need to be reminded of that."

Forgetting the binders, the open house, the outside world entirely, Sophie dumped the binders onto the couch and crossed to Zach. Grabbing his broad shoulders, she forced him to turn and face her. No way was she leaving him here to beat up on himself.

But before she could utter a word, he'd taken back control of the situation and himself. Framing her face with his rough palms, he backed her against the door and came nose to nose with her.

"You can't touch me," he murmured against her lips. "I barely hold it together when I'm with you. Can't you see that? I don't know how else to warn you."

"You'd never hurt me."

His thumb stroked her bottom lip. "I already have."

Anger bubbled through her. "Get past it, Zach. You've done your penance."

His forehead came to rest on hers. "I pay it every time I see you, think of you."

"Why do you do this to yourself?" Her heart literally ached for him. "Why can't you just take what you want? What we want?"

The all-consuming ache for him to close that miniscule gap and kiss her was killing her. She could practically taste him, yet he still held himself back.

"Because selfish needs stole everything ten years ago."

When he pushed away, Sophie took a moment to process his words as she stared at his back. "If that's how you truly feel, then you should've stayed in prison. It's no different than the steel walls you've put around yourself, only this time you're the guard. You refused to see me for a full year."

Her voice broke on that last word and she cursed herself.

"I won't beg you to start living again," she told him as she went back to retrieve the binders. "If you want to live like this forever, then go ahead. But don't look for me to be an enabler, because I think you're being selfish. Do you see me sitting around feeling sorry for myself because I have issues from that night? You have no idea what I lost. No idea. I had plans, Zach, and they were instantly taken from me. But I don't focus on all of that or place blame. I've learned to live with the life I have, the cards I've been dealt, because otherwise I'd never make it."

She stormed back to the door and jerked it open as tears threatened to spill. "So don't worry about your emotional battle over me. I assure you I won't come around again without Braxton or Liam as a buffer."

She slammed his door, feeling like a fool and hating herself for being so open and harsh with him. But damn it, the man was infuriating and she wanted to shake him. Then she wanted to kiss him.

And that was the crux of her problem. No matter how frustrating and hardheaded he was, no matter this guilt he kept wrapping himself in, Sophie still wanted to be the one to uncover all of those layers and help Zach heal.

Since when had she become a masochist?

# Chapter Nine

Later that day, he'd left the binders on her porch and run away like a child afraid of getting caught. So what if her words had been dead-on? So what if she had him pegged in ways he hadn't even considered?

Sophie was his light. Whether he would ever admit the truth aloud or not, she was the light pulling him back into the world he'd so desperately wanted to escape. Concentrating on work, focusing on the grief and self-imprisonment had been his go-to since getting out.

Not long after he'd been released, his parents had passed, leaving him even more angry and bitter with the world. Yet Chelsea and Sophie continued on. Both women were important to his life, both women found ways to move past their individual hurt and continue to thrive.

Thrive. Zach sat on the floor in his utility room and fed the runt of the litter from a bottle as he had that afternoon. He honestly didn't know if there was ever a time in his life when he'd actually thrived.

As a child he'd been in a less-than-stellar environment, thrust into ugly, horrendous situations no child should ever endure. Once he came to the Monroes, the damage had been done, but they'd loved him anyway.

Then he'd gone and gotten all cocky when he'd finally confessed to himself that he had a thing for Sophie. He'd shown off at that party, and when Liam had argued Zach wasn't in any shape to drive, he'd wagered a bet that he was.

A damn bet. A bet that changed so much in so many lives, all because Zach's ego had taken center stage to common sense.

His cell vibrated in his pocket, but he ignored it. There wasn't anybody he wanted to talk to, and he highly doubted this would be work-related on a Saturday night.

Focusing on the pups, Zach wondered who would want to adopt these little fur balls. Marcie had said they wouldn't be ready to go for several weeks. How the hell did Zach keep a houseful of dogs when he was trying to finalize his own renovating so he could put the place up for sale?

And he was definitely selling. No question about it. He'd done some of the initial number crunching, and there was no way he could move forward with the Sunset Lake property if he didn't sell this house first. He needed that chunk of money, plus a loan from the bank to fully dig into all of the updating that mansion needed.

Zach smiled. Despite this mess and the uncertainty that awaited him, he couldn't help but smile at Chelsea and her larger-than-life dream. She might have been spontaneous, but she never did anything halfway.

After Zach finished feeding the runt, he refilled the water bowls, let the mom outside to do her business, and put fresh newspaper down for the puppies . . . not that they were making use of it other than to shred it to pieces. But perhaps they'd get the hang of using it for their bodily deposits as opposed to leaving little surprises on the freshly tiled floor.

Zach's stomach growled and he realized he hadn't eaten since his early lunch. He'd been preoccupied with the dogs, his overly blatant neighbor, and then Sophie.

The dogs he would have to deal with until he could find them good homes. The neighbor . . . hadn't he pawned her off onto his trusted employee, Nathan?

And Sophie. Zach sighed. There was no easy answer when it came to her. Even thinking her name flooded him with a multitude of emotions.

Yes, he used the accident as a wedge to keep his distance, especially from her. Even if he could get beyond the fact that he'd altered her life, he couldn't give in to his selfish desires and tell her how he truly felt. The ugliness that lived in his past was a part of him. He came from parents who were full of evil, and no way would he ever risk passing that on to a child. And he had no doubt Sophie would want children. She'd be the perfect mother.

Zach rested his palms on the island in his kitchen and dropped his head. What the hell? How did his thoughts instantly go to Sophie and children? Yes, he'd wanted her for years and had briefly lost his mind and wanted to see if they could be more than friends, but with the accident, the prison, and life standing in his way, Zach had circled back around to the realization that she needed someone who wouldn't taint her life.

One day Sophie would meet a man who was worthy

of her, they'd marry and start a family. And when that time came, Zach would have to leave Haven, because seeing Sophie with another man would absolutely kill him.

Seeing her around with Martin was bad enough, but Zach knew Sophie wasn't in love with him. She wouldn't have kissed Zach with so much passion if she loved another man.

"What the hell?"

Zach jerked around at Braxton's cursing and the slam of the side door in the utility room.

"Don't bother them. They're down for the night," Zach called back. The last thing he wanted was for those puppies to be disturbed again, because last night had nearly done him in. They'd yipped and made noises all night. But he couldn't be angry, because they were too damn cute. Even when they yawned in his face, that sweet puppy breath got to him.

Zach turned, leaning back against the island as Braxton climbed over the gate in the doorway to the utility room. Braxton stood on the kitchen side, still staring back into the room and shaking his head.

"What the hell?" he repeated, jerking around to focus on Zach. "You starting a kennel or something?"

"What are you doing here?"

"I tried calling, but you didn't answer." Braxton moved to the refrigerator and opened it to examine the contents.

So that had been the missed call.

"Looking for something?"

Braxton straightened with a pizza box in hand. "Yeah. You need to go to the store."

Zach sighed. He might as well get this uncomfortable talk over with and move on, because Braxton was definitely going to be the easiest one to share the news with and now was as good a time as any.

"I'm selling the house."

Braxton dropped the box on the island and stared at Zach. "What?"

"This house," Zach clarified. "Not the Sunset Lake one."

"Regardless, why?" Braxton flipped the lid on the box and surveyed the few remaining pieces. "Are you asking or just telling me? I assume you haven't told Liam or he would've called me."

Zach pulled the pizza box away. "Forget this. We'll order a new one. There's not enough here for both of us."

Braxton crossed his arms over his chest. "Then order it, so we can talk about this ridiculous idea of selling the house."

"It's not ridiculous," Zach muttered, pulling out his phone.

He hated the look on his brother's face, hated having this entire conversation, but Braxton would see this was the only option at this point.

Zach placed the order and made his way into the living room. He assumed Braxton would follow. After they ate, maybe they could finish that final bathroom project so the place could be put on the market. Not that Braxton was big on manual labor; he'd probably hate to get dirt on his expensive teacher pants, but Zach could always use an assistant.

Zach sank into his oversized leather chair as his brother stepped into the room and leaned against the door frame. "You want to tell me about the dogs or why you're suddenly selling our childhood home?"

Resting his hands on the thick arms of the chair, Zach shrugged. "Pizza will be here in forty-five minutes.

I can cover both topics pretty fast. The dog was a stray in my bushes. I couldn't leave her, and the vet couldn't get here to help, so I brought her in last night and she delivered puppies. I'm looking for homes for them."

Zach refused to shift in his chair under his brother's intense stare. The decision was made, for reasons beyond his control, and regardless of emotions or memories or anything else that might factor into Braxton and Liam's point of view, Zach wasn't giving in.

"As far as the house, I need the money to help with Chelsea's project." When Braxton continued to stare, Zach shrugged. "That brings us up to date, and we still have forty-four minutes left if you have anything to add."

Pushing off the door frame, Braxton moved farther into the room. "Yeah. I have a hell of a lot to say. First, good for you with the dogs. I guess you do have a heart when it counts."

Standing by the fireplace Zach had just finished re-facing, Braxton toyed with picture frames that had been their mother's. Zach had put them in a box when he'd added the new stone, but as soon as he was done he'd gotten them back out. His mother's treasures couldn't be kept in a box, even if one of the photos was of Zach in his cap and gown at graduation, looking like he was fake smiling for the camera . . . which he was.

"Second," Braxton went on as he turned to fully focus on Zach, "did you already discuss this potential sale with Sophie?"

Zach jerked. "Sophie? Why would I ask her?" As if he needed another reason to contact her.

"If you put it up for sale, I assume you wouldn't use anybody else."

Well, damn it. He hadn't thought of that. He hadn't gotten quite that far in his plans. Basically he knew he would need the funds from this house to pay for the other, and he had to get the bathroom completed in order to sell it.

Blowing out a breath, Zach laced his hands over his abdomen. "Yeah, I'll use Sophie. I wouldn't trust anyone else with this."

"So you haven't called her." Braxton rested his hands on his hips, his eyes moving around the room as if to take it in for the first time. "Did the taxes get paid?"

Zach nodded. "I took our money down to the courthouse and paid them yesterday morning. Another reason I'm eager to get this sold so I can have the funds for Chelsea's house. My savings account is nearly dry."

"There's no other way?" Braxton asked. "What if Liam was one hundred percent on board with the project? He hoards nearly all of his money."

Shaking his head, Zach replied, "I still don't see that we could do it the way it needs to be done. Though having him participate financially would be a definite plus."

"When are you going to tell him about selling?"

Zach eyed his brother.

"Oh hell, no." Braxton shook his head and laughed. "I'm not telling him. I'm not always going to be the buffer, and you're not a child."

"Then I'll call him. I'm not waiting on him to breeze back into town, because I never know when that will be."

Zach eased forward in his chair, a slight weight taken off his shoulders. One brother down, one to go.

"You took that better than I thought," Zach stated.

Finally taking a seat on the couch, Braxton picked up the remote and clicked the television on. "I wasn't delusional. I never thought you'd live here forever. Hell, you lasted longer in Haven than I ever thought you would."

"What's that supposed to mean?"

Flipping through the channels, Braxton propped his feet up on the coffee table. "I'm just saying you never acted like you wanted to be here. Then when Dad gave the business to you, I figured you'd work long enough to save money and go."

Zach hated how dead-on Braxton was with the original plan. Zach had been a restless teen, a reckless teen, but he'd stuck around because of his parents, because of this family they'd brought together.

Even when Zach had gotten out of prison, he'd been dead set on getting the hell out of Haven, but he was good at construction, and his father's impeccable reputation had helped Zach land job after job, and now he was in demand.

"Where will you live?" Braxton asked, turning his attention from the television.

Yeah, that was the tricky part. There was going to be some maneuvering, and the timing on certain things had to be perfect.

"I figure I'm going to have to stay at Sunset Lake."

Braxton busted out laughing, then sobered when he realized Zach wasn't smiling. "Stay at the house that doesn't even have electric right now?"

Zach didn't want to tell his brother he'd slept in worse places. He'd *lived* in worse places.

"I can throw down a sleeping bag. I'll be fine, and we'll all save money. Besides, who says this house will sell fast?"

"I just think you need to fully think this through," Braxton told him. "You need to have a backup plan. I assume that will be my place. You might as well just stay with me anyway, instead of practically camping."

Zach wanted to laugh now. Backup plans weren't part of his life. He had one plan and he fully executed it.

"I'm going to stay in the house if this one sells fast," he repeated. "There's no reason I can't. Right now I can at least work on one bathroom and get it done fairly soon. I already had the water turned back on, but I may need to redo some of the pipes to the kitchen."

Braxton opened his mouth just as the doorbell rang.

"Go ahead and pay for that, would ya?" Zach asked as he settled deeper into his seat and laced his hands behind his head. "I'm practically a poor, homeless man."

Braxton flipped him the bird. Zach laughed until the puppies started yipping again.

Muttering a curse, Zach closed his eyes. "No, no, no. I should've thought of the doorbell."

Braxton went to open the door. "Go care for your babies, honey. I'll make dinner."


Nerves rolled through Sophie's stomach, but prolonging the inevitable would only make her anxiety skyrocket. She needed to get this over with.

Martin was on his way over. Nothing like squeezing in a breakup between a late business meeting and bedtime.

Sophie yawned as she stood by her floor-to-ceiling

window and held her glass of Riesling. Not that she needed a cup of courage. She loved good wine, and if loosening her fear of confrontation was a by-product, then she wouldn't turn it down.

Car lights cut through the darkness and slowly turned into her drive. Taking a sip, Sophie went to unlock her front door. She wasn't nervous about breaking things off. There was no love, nothing that indicated she wanted a future with a man who put work above her. Besides, there were no sparks. Kissing him was just . . . a kiss.

Kissing Zach was an experience. An experience she didn't have time to focus on right now.

Before Martin could knock, Sophie had gone to the foyer and opened the door just as he mounted the steps. Gripping the edge of the door in one hand and her wineglass in the other, Sophie offered a smile.

"Thanks for coming by," she told him, feeling rather silly trying for small talk.

"Is everything okay? You sounded different earlier." Martin stood just inside the threshold, but shifted as Sophie started to close the door. "I couldn't get here any earlier, but I've been worried about you all evening."

Which meant he'd actually thought about her during a business meeting. That would be a first.

"Why don't you come in and sit down," she suggested.

Before she could walk away, Martin stepped to the side, blocking her path. "Just tell me what's wrong."

Holding on to her glass with both hands now, Sophie tipped her chin up and looked into Martin's worried eyes. She wanted to feel a connection, a spark . . . something to show her that these last six months had led them somewhere, but the longer she stared, the more she realized she'd been with Martin for the wrong reasons. She'd been with him for security and comfort. At first she'd been attracted to him, and they'd been on friendly terms. He'd asked her out and she'd been excited, but the longer they were together, the less he made her a priority.

Not that she was a needy female, but she would like to come before every other thing in a man's life.

"Martin, I think we need a break."

There. She said it. Sophie held her breath as she waited on his reaction. She didn't need to wait long.

"I was waiting for this," he said, shaking his head with a soft chuckle that held no humor whatsoever. "I knew once you started getting cozy with Zach over this project—"

"No." Sophie held up her hand. "Zach has nothing to do with this."

Seriously, he didn't. She'd been having doubts about Martin and her for a while, but kissing Zach just confirmed that she had no feelings for Martin anymore.

"I just need to concentrate on some other things in my life now, and to be honest, I don't feel like you're putting a lot into this relationship."

She wanted to cringe as those last words left her lips, but she wasn't sorry she said them. He deserved to know the truth about how she felt.

"So you're blaming me?" he asked, propping his hands on his hips. "I'm the one who rescheduled everything so I could take you out of town. You're the one who canceled after you spent some time with those Monroe brothers. You never will break away from them, will you? You'd think after that accident . . ."

Martin trailed off, muttering a curse beneath his breath. "You know what? Fine. If you want to move on with a guy who doesn't deserve your loyalty, then you two deserve each other."

Sophie didn't have time to say much else as Martin stormed out of her house, leaving her front door wide open. Warm evening air filled the foyer. Sounds from the neighbors filtered in. A car door slamming, kids screaming and playing, laughter. Life around her continued to go on as she stood there wondering how this breakup had turned on her, leaving her feeling guilty and like a terrible person.

On a sigh, Sophie closed the door and locked it. After setting her alarm for the night, she took her glass to the kitchen and finished off the wine, placing her glass in the sink. She wasn't quite ready for bed, though it was getting late. No way could she sleep now, not when Martin's parting shot still resounded in her head.

Sophie truly didn't want to think that her breaking things off with Martin had anything to do with Zach, but she was lying to herself. The breakup with Martin would've inevitably come, but since Zach had been part of her life more recently, the split just came a bit sooner.

And mixed in with the guilt also came relief. She didn't want to keep stringing Martin along, not when her heart wasn't in their relationship. Anything between them had fizzled out long before Zach's lips touched hers.

Still, she should've known, the moment she realized she'd never sleep with Martin, that he needed to be out of her life. She'd only been with two men in her life. Partly because of her scars from the accident, partly because she just didn't feel a connection to many people. Intimacy wasn't something she took lightly, but if she couldn't be with someone that way, then she didn't need to waste time dating him.

Sophie turned off the lights in the house and headed to her bedroom. She wanted to look through those binders Zach had left on her porch. She'd come home earlier and there they were on her porch swing. No note, nothing but the binders. Stupid jerk couldn't even leave a note.

What would he say if he did write something? *Sorry I'm a jerk. I've been this way since you've known me. Here are the binders.*

But seriously, what did she expect? Zach was a man of few words when they were face-to-face. Did she honestly figure he'd pen something on a Post-it note?

The fact that Zach took up so much of her head space was ridiculous. If he wanted to ignore the obvious attraction between them, then Martin was right that Zach didn't deserve her.

After changing into her silky tank and matching tap pants, she sat down on the cushioned, floral seat at the corner desk. Since sleep wouldn't be coming for a while, she wanted to look through Chelsea's ideas and really get a good feel for the overall theme, then dissect each room in her head to figure out the best plan of attack.

The more she flipped through and studied pictures and small notes written in Chelsea's elegant hand, the more excited Sophie became. So excited, she pulled out her sketchbook and started outlining the foyer and sketching in a chandelier, cushioned bench seating, and a large circular table with a vast floral arrangement adorning the center.

These sketches were going to keep her sane. She'd used her pencil art to concentrate on healing after the accident. Now she would use it to keep her mind on the project, and not on the man in charge.

# Chapter Ten

Already a hell of a day and it wasn't even lunchtime.

Zach pulled his work truck into a parking spot right in front of Knobs & Knockers. He could've had Macy bring him the supplies when she closed for the day, but he needed to speak with her anyway, and he needed a break from that damn pipe in the main floor bathroom of the Sunset Lake house before he threw a stick of dynamite in there and called it a day.

But if he wanted to sell his home and stay at the mansion while fixing it up, he preferred the bathroom renovated . . . or at least in working order.

First, though, he had to talk to Liam. And wouldn't that be a fun time on top of all the other bundles of excitement he'd already experienced?

Yanking on the door to the hardware store, Zach stepped inside as the bell chimed over his head.

Wearing her signature plaid shirt and dark hair in a ponytail, Macy greeted him with a smile.

"Hey, Zach." Her smile quickly died on her face. "Oh no. Whatever the project is, you don't look happy. It's the Sunset Lake property, isn't it?"

Sighing, Zach leaned onto the scarred wood counter. "I've just started. I swear it's trying to kill me, and Chelsea is somewhere laughing her ass off at my expense."

Macy reached across the counter to pat his arm. "You know everything you're doing would make her happy, and that's all that matters."

Zach grunted, though he knew Chelsea would love that her brothers were moving ahead with her dream. Well, two of the three. And that was all that was keeping him partway sane.

Rubbing his eyes with his forefinger and thumb, Zach shook his head. "I need some PVC pipe cut."

Macy straightened, tipping her head to the side. "You look exhausted. What else is wrong?"

Zach couldn't prevent the sarcastic burst of laughter that slipped out. "I have puppies. They yip all night. I think they're in cahoots with Chelsea's spirit."

Macy stared at him, her lips quivering. "Dogs?"

"If you laugh, I will bring the mom and her little fur balls and drop them off to you. Then we'll see who's laughing."

She didn't hold back another second. Macy laughed so hard she ended up with tears running down her face. She waved a hand toward him.

"I'm sorry, Zach," she said between fits of laughter. "I'm just trying to imagine you taking care of a litter of puppies."

When the door chimed again, Zach glanced at the robust man with silver hair and dark eyes that matched Macy's.

"Maybe your dad will cut that pipe for me instead of laughing," Zach muttered.

"I'll cut your pipe," Macy told him as she wiped

beneath her eyes. "Come on back and tell me what you need."

Phil Hayward came around the counter and eyed his daughter. "Hassling the customers again?"

"Oh, it's just Zach." Macy smiled up at her father. "He doesn't count."

Zach wasn't offended in the least by her words or that he'd been the fodder for her laughter. Macy was one of the few people he was comfortable around. She was easy to talk to and joke with and he knew she felt the same or she wouldn't go out of her way to agitate him.

"If you're done mocking me, I'll meet you in the back."

Macy gestured for him to go ahead. "After you, dog whisperer."

Zach headed to the pipe area and searched through the sizes until he found the piece he'd need cut. When Macy came in beside him, he pointed to the pipe.

"I need a three-foot piece," he told her. "And even though you nearly doubled over with laughter, I'm sorry I haven't gotten back with you about those house plans."

Macy pulled the piece from the others stacked along the wall. "No worries. I know you're busy."

"I'm not too busy for friends. Would you want to come over to the house Friday night and we can discuss this more in depth?"

Holding on to the pipe, Macy nodded, her ponytail shifting over her shoulder. "Sounds good. I'll close up at six and head on out. Is this the only piece you need?"

Once he finished giving her his entire order, because

he really didn't want to have to make another trip, he waited for Macy to get it all together.

His cell vibrated in his pocket. Pulling it out, he cringed when he saw the number. Martin's office. Fantastic.

Zach slid his finger across the screen and held the phone to his ear. "Zach Monroe."

"Zach, this is Martin."

Shoving a hand in his pocket, Zach leaned against the door frame leading into the room where Macy had gone. He waited for Martin to continue.

"I'm calling about your building permit."

Words no contractor ever wanted to hear, let alone from the man who annoyed said contractor just because he breathed. From the tone of Martin's voice, Zach was already pissed.

"What about it?" Zach asked.

"The plans you submitted were not approved."

Did he sound smug? Zach gripped his cell and gritted his teeth. "And why not?"

"The plans for the kitchen were not satisfactory in regards to the exhaust and how the electrical would be run."

Zach cupped the back of his neck and dropped his head. There wasn't a doubt in Zach's mind that Martin was taking great delight in this moment. That suit-wearing jerk had never made it a secret he didn't like the Monroes. Not that Zach cared, but there was no way he would let this small-town politician ruin Chelsea's dream.

"What exactly is the problem?" Zach wanted details, not just a smug asshole telling him he couldn't do something. Although there was no doubt in Zach's mind there was nothing wrong with the plans, other than his name had been on them.

Martin went into some nonsense about the exhaust needing to be on the other exterior wall to free up the second exterior wall for the double ovens and stove. Because the house was so old, they felt it best to be routed differently.

Focusing on the bright yellow sale sign hanging above a display of lightbulbs, Zach replied, "Fine. I'll draw up new plans and have them for you by the end of the week. Is there anything else?"

Because once he drew up new plans, Zach didn't want Martin coming back and saying there was a problem with the bathroom or the steps or some other issue. Zach could see Martin being a pain in the ass during this entire project.

"Nothing regarding the house," Martin told him. "But there is something I want to say."

Macy came back through with the pipe. "I'll put it up at the counter," she whispered as she passed through.

Zach nodded, then focused back on the sign. Whatever Martin was about to say was only going to make Zach even pissier. "And what's that?" he asked, eager to end the call.

"You may think you have some hold on Sophie, but I know you're just stringing her along."

Zach jerked at the bold statement from the prick. "What?"

"Don't act like you don't know she broke things off with me," Martin retorted. "I'm sure you were just waiting for this to happen. She's always been infatuated with your family, and I see how you look at her."

Sophie broke things off with Martin? Good for her. Martin was an ass. And how had anyone seen how

Zach looked at Sophie? He tried his hardest *not* to look at her.

This breakup was not good news for Zach. There went one of his best excuses for keeping his distance from her. She deserved better than Martin, but definitely better than anything Zach could offer.

"Whatever you and Sophie have going on is none of my business," Zach told him, purposely sounding bored, as if he couldn't care less. "If that's all you have about the house, then we're finished. But I will tell you this: If you're jerking me around on this project because of your personal life, I suggest you rethink your strategy."

"Are you threatening me?"

Zach laughed. "If I threaten you, you won't have to ask."

He disconnected the call before he really did something that would cause problems down the road. Zach would love nothing more than to punch Martin in his smug face, but Braxton and Sophie would not approve. Added to that, Zach's business had an impeccable reputation, started by his father. No way would Zach tarnish it, not when his father was the main person to help Zach turn his life around and give him chance after chance at redemption.

Zach couldn't help but smile. Sophie had finally ended things with Martin. Smart girl, but what did this mean? He shouldn't care what she did with her spare time, her personal life, but damn it, he did. He couldn't push her away and still want to know what was going on in her life. He had no right to anything from her. Yet the fact she was free and single now, especially after they'd kissed and she'd admitted her attraction, would only complicate things further.

Shoving his phone back in his pocket, Zach headed to pay for his supplies. He had a bathroom to tackle and new frustrations to get out. Between the new plans he had to draw up and the bomb about Sophie being single, Zach was ready to do some demolition.

Sophie rubbed her head. "Yes, Mom. I'm doing fine."

She loved her mother, she truly did, but the woman hovered. No, hovered wasn't even the correct term. The woman controlled . . . or tried to, anyway.

"Martin and I just needed a break, and it's really for the best," she repeated for what seemed like the fifth time in as many minutes.

"Why on earth would you end things with him?" her mother asked yet again, her tone even more shrill than the last four times. "He was perfect for you."

No, he was perfect for her mother and the ideal family her mother wanted Sophie to have. Her mother was still in denial about Sophie's infertility, but that topic wasn't one she was getting into today. Of course, even if Sophie wanted to discuss it, her mother always blew it off as something a specialist could fix. Yet another area they argued about. Hard to fix what wasn't there.

"When are you and Daddy coming back?" Sophie asked.

"Changing the subject won't make it go away," her mother stated.

"Martin and I are over, and I'd rather discuss your fabulous trip."

Her parents were constantly taking trips, whether it be to an exotic country or an ocean cruise, they were always on the go. Sophie often wondered how she could be so different from her mother, because being home was all that mattered to Sophie. She had no desire to travel the globe.

"Oh, darling, I just had the best massage and facial."

Sophie eased back in her office chair as her mother went on about the masseur and his magical hands. Sophie knew all she had to do was turn the topic back to her mother and Martin would be all but forgotten. Her mother was a bit of a narcissist, but at times like this the selfish manner came in handy.

Sophie printed out the forms for the property she'd just done an open house on. The first offer had come in and she needed all parties to sign the agreement before further steps could be taken.

"But, darling, I really must get off of here," her mother told her. "Your father has scheduled a lunch for us at my favorite place, before we board the ship."

Sophie said her good-byes and realized her mother never did tell her when they'd be home. The cruise was due to end in a week, but that didn't mean anything. Her parents were known for moving from one adventure to another without coming up for air.

Her cell chimed once again, this time lighting up Braxton's name.

She slid her finger across the screen. "Hey, Braxton."

"Got a minute?"

Pulling the papers from the printer, Sophie placed them in a folder. "Sure. What's up?"

"Can you meet Zach and me at the new house? Apparently there was an issue with getting the building permit because of the kitchen layout and the electrical work with the exhaust."

"Seriously?" Sophie eased back in her chair and shifted to relieve the pressure from her hip. "What could be the problem? Has he ever run into issues before?"

Zach might be grouchy, moody, and flat-out frustrating, but he was the epitome of professional when it came to his job. When his father had passed the business down to Zach, Zach had been so surprised at the amount of faith his father had invested in him, he'd thrown himself into the job. Sophie knew he took pride in the business his father had built up and he wouldn't do anything to tarnish his dad's reputation.

So the fact that the building permit had been declined was absurd and hard to believe. The timing was too perfect to be a coincidence.

Dread slid through her. Surely Martin wasn't taking this breakup out on Zach and Braxton.

"Never, that I know of," Braxton replied.

"Who told you guys of the problem?" she asked.

"Zach just said he received a call from the city office."

Sophie had no doubt who'd placed that call, but she wasn't going to start stirring the pot, because if Zach and Martin talked, there was already trouble brewing.

"When do you want to meet?" she asked.

"Zach is working there now. I'm free whenever, so just tell me your schedule."

She glanced over her planner, though she tried to keep it memorized. "I can be there in a couple hours. I just have to get some papers signed and run a few errands. Does that work?"

"Sure. See you there."

As eager as she was to get the new listing under contract, Sophie was more eager to get Chelsea's project under way and find out exactly who had called Zach, though she suspected she knew the answer to that one.

After making a few calls and setting up two showings for other properties, Sophie gathered her folders and slid them into her messenger bag. By the time she got out of the office, she realized she was running late.

The early summer sun had her squinting as she stepped out onto the sidewalk and walked the half block toward her car. The streets in town were becoming busier during the day now that school was out. More kids were playing in the park, splashing in the fountain, and riding bikes along the designated paths. Families were setting up picturesque picnics on checkered blankets, and Sophie couldn't help but feel that familiar tug on her heart at the sight.

With the park being across the street from her office, she often got a view of all the activities. She didn't feel self-pity for her circumstances. Pity wouldn't give her the ability to have children. But that didn't stop her from feeling that clench to her heart each time she saw a happy family.

She was human. She hurt. She'd like nothing more than to be immune to the sight of children running to their mom's or dad's open arms. Adoption was an option, sure, but she'd really like to be married before diving into that process.

And at this rate, she wasn't walking down the aisle anytime soon.

She also wasn't focusing on Zach. Nope. She refused to do so. She refused to relive over and over how amazing he felt against her, how he kept trying in some Zach-style way to protect her from himself. The man was noble to a fault, and damn if that didn't make him even more appealing each time he pushed her away.

As she slid behind the wheel of her SUV, she glanced at her watch. She'd be meeting him in just under an hour. Hard not to think of the man when she was constantly seeing him or . . . damn it. She couldn't *not* think of him. She tried, somewhat, but he just kept popping into the forefront of her mind.

He wasn't only stubborn in real life, he was quite infuriating in her thoughts as well.

Sophie focused on her potential sale as she went to meet the parties for signatures. Once she was finished, she drove toward the edge of town and up the small incline toward the property. Sophie absolutely loved this setting. The sprawling two-story Civil War–era home certainly had seen better days, but that was all cosmetic. With all the rich history and beauty, something with all this charm couldn't just be built. The old mossy oak trees had stood for decades, providing that perfect Southern backdrop for such a magnificent home.

Smiling as she approached the two-story mansion, Sophie could almost see the place as it had once been in its grandest of forms. She could picture horses and buggies coming up this slope, women in full skirts greeting their men as they came home from the war.

She glanced toward the two small cottages in the distance near the pond. If this place could talk, Sophie knew the stories would be epic.

Braxton's shiny truck sat next to Zach's beat-up work truck. A slight difference in the vehicles, much like the differences in the men themselves. One always seemed to be polished and put together. The other was rough around the edges but definitely reliable.

Leaving her bags in the passenger seat, Sophie slid her cell into the pocket of her skirt. The sun had really warmed things up today, so she left her cardigan in the car. Making her way up toward the front door, she made a mental note to figure out something grand for this entryway. The landscaping and path leading to the main entrance should really make a statement . . . something other than "this place has been neglected for decades."

The old handle wiggled beneath her hand as she pushed the door open. The creaky hinges gave off a haunted-house vibe, but Sophie knew that was just another item in the long line of things that needed replacing. Though she hoped Zach found a door that was similar to the one currently hanging. She really wanted to capture the essence of the original house with some modern-day touches.

"Zach? Braxton?" she called, her voice echoing in the open empty foyer.

"Kitchen," Braxton yelled back.

Sophie smoothed her hair back over her shoulders as she made her way toward the back of the house. The musty smell was almost overpowering, and she only prayed they didn't find mold, or at least a very minimal amount. Mold in older homes was a financial suck and extremely dangerous. The last thing they needed was too many unexpected problems, though renovating was never as simple as anyone planned and unfortunate expenses always happened.

As she stepped into the wide entryway leading to the kitchen, she spotted Braxton with his hands on his hips, standing over Zach, who was on his hands and knees beneath the old, rusty sink.

Zach muttered a curse from inside the cabinet and Braxton threw her a look. "He's getting crankier. You've been warned."

"You mean it can get worse?" she joked.

Pushing out from beneath the cabinet, Zach came to his feet and wiped a hand down his face, no doubt ridding himself of the cobwebs he encountered. She recalled how much he hated spiders. Even as a rough and tough teen, he'd get one glimpse of a spider and start trembling and stomping on the thing until it was beyond dead.

Best not call him on his fear right now if he was in a mood. Then again, when was he not in a mood?

Still, he looked fantastic with dirt smudges across his face, his ratty T-shirt pulled taut across his broad chest and those holey jeans that fit his lean hips like the proverbial glove.

Whatever his mood was, it wouldn't ruin the scenery. He was still the sexiest man she'd ever laid eyes on, and she hadn't forgotten the image of him bottle feeding a puppy. Could the man be any more adorable?

Sophie bit the inside of her lips to keep from laughing. If she called him adorable she'd see a whole new side of grouchy.

"It's doable to rework the entire kitchen," he stated, resting his hands on his narrow hips. "Damn it, I shouldn't have to. I've been over this and over it, and I know there was nothing wrong with the original plans."

Sophie crossed her arms to ward off the chill of the old home, now wishing she'd grabbed her cardigan from the car.

"Martin did this, didn't he?" she asked.

Zach's dark eyes landed on her, sending a whole host of new shivers racing through her. "It doesn't matter."

"It does if this has anything to do with me."

Braxton stared back and forth between them before letting out a sigh. "Martin called, didn't he?"

Zach ignored the question as he walked around the perimeter of the spacious room. He studied the exterior walls, muttering under his breath, and the fact that he wouldn't address the question told her all she needed to know.

"I'll talk to Martin." And let him know exactly how his misuse of power could get him into trouble, because acting like a toddler not getting his way, he was just asking to be called out. "Don't draw up any more plans for now."

Zach jerked around. "Like hell you will. This has nothing to do with you, Sophie. Leave it."

"Then tell me Martin didn't call you." His eyes continued to hold hers, but she wasn't backing down. "He's abusing his authority and we all know it."

"I'm not afraid of him," Zach stated with a laugh. "He can't hold off on this forever."

"So it was him who called you."

Zach's eyes narrowed. "Drop it."

"Can you two cool it so we can get this figured out?" Braxton asked. "Arguing won't fix this, and we need to get the building permit so Zach can get started and move in."

"Damn it, Braxton!"

Sophie glanced from brother to brother. "What's going on? What does he mean, you're moving in?"

"Nothing," Zach muttered, shooting death glares at Braxton. "Let's figure out the best layout."

"No, I want to know what he meant," Sophie insisted. "Why are you moving in here? You have a house."

"I'm not getting into this." Zach crossed to his notepad on the counter and started jotting something down. "I think the industrial stove we discussed will still work fine on this wall near the back door. There should be no problem running the exhaust out here. What do you guys think about keeping the fridge over here, too? For a cook, it would make sense and save steps."

"You should ask Liam his opinion," Braxton said.

"Yeah, well, he had his chance to help and chose not to." Zach moved his gaze from the wall in question to his notes, as he scrawled down something else. "And the other exterior wall could have more cabinetry and a long counter for prep. I want to keep the sink in the new island."

"Excuse me?" Sophie chimed in. "I'm not done with the topic of Martin or the fact you think you're moving in here. Can you guys please clue me in?"

Zach dropped his pencil and rubbed the back of his neck as he stared up at the ceiling. "I'm putting my house on the market. Martin will always be a pain in my ass, but nothing I can't handle." He brought his eyes back down to her. "There. Can we move on now?"

Crossing the room to stand directly in front of the stubborn man, Sophie crossed her arms. "No, we can't move on. I want to know why you're selling your house."

And why hadn't he called her to list it?

What was going on here? There was no way Liam knew this was going on, and this was one situation she wasn't going to clue him in on. It wasn't her place to tell.

"I don't have time for this. I'm figuring up the new plans, refiguring the cost for extra wiring, and the last thing I want to talk about is my house."

Zach's voice was dangerously low, but Sophie was done tiptoeing around him and his moodiness.

She turned to Braxton. "What do you think about the sale?"

Braxton shrugged. "It's not my house, but I agree with Zach's reasoning and I'd do the same if I were in his shoes."

"And Liam? What does he think?"

Braxton threw a glance over Sophie's shoulder. "We haven't told him yet."

Sophie closed her eyes and sighed. There was so much hurt in the family, she didn't even know where to begin trying to help them patch all the pieces back together.

"Don't you think he should be in on that decision?" she asked, turning back to Zach, who kept his back to her as he studied his notes.

"He's coming in sometime this weekend," Zach replied without facing her. "I'll tell him then."

Before she could reply, Zach turned and brought that dark, intense focus directly down on her. "This is none of your concern."

Why did he continue to say things to hurt her? Why did he act like she had no personal connection to this family? And more importantly, why was she standing there beating her head against a brick wall?

With a slight nod, Sophie backed up a step. "You're right. None of this is my concern. I don't know what I was thinking. Just because I was part of your family for years, I practically spent my teens in that house and loved your parents like my own, I couldn't possibly care about you guys or that house."

She turned to leave when Zach called her name.

Sophie merely held up a hand and kept walking. She was done. Officially done with Zach Monroe and the way he treated her . . . treated everyone, for that matter. He'd not even mentioned anything to Liam, and regardless of the bad blood that flowed between them, Liam deserved to know what was going on.

Still, she wasn't the one to drop that bomb and she was washing her hands of this. If they needed help during the cosmetic phase, Sophie would step in, but only to honor Chelsea. Other than that, they were on their own.

Anger and hurt fought for top place in her heart, and she didn't know which one was crippling her more. As she reached her car, Sophie rested her hands on the top of the door and cursed herself for the blurry vision and the sting of tears. Zach Monroe wasn't worth it.

Okay, he was, but she deserved better. All this time he'd tried telling her that, but now she knew. He pushed and pushed her away, and now she understood why.

Why did she have to love a man who was so wrong for her? And why, even after all that just happened, did she still ache for his affection?

# Chapter Eleven

There was a level of hell that certain people belonged in for purposely hurting others. Zach was going to be first in that line after the way he'd treated Sophie earlier.

Damn it. He kept telling himself he wouldn't hurt her and he'd done nothing but. Over and over he'd said things, done things that only expanded that wedge of pain between them. He was best alone, because when he hurt, when he was scared, he lashed out, and every damn time, Sophie had been in the crosshairs.

Now here he stood on her porch, beneath the glow of the antique-style light above her door, ready to grovel if need be. He'd never groveled in his life.

Tapping his scarred knuckles on her door, Zach took a step back and waited. As much as he hated being there, he hated knowing he'd hurt her even more.

And speaking of hurt, his face still throbbed where Braxton had silently voiced his opinion on how Zach handled the situation earlier.

Sophie had been right, though. She'd grown up

with Chelsea, loved his family like her own, and often sought refuge when she wanted to get out of the stuffy environment her parents provided. Sophie was part of his life, past and present, whether he wanted to admit it or not. Whether he wanted to face his true feelings for her or continue to hide them, she didn't deserve the ugliness he kept using as a defense mechanism.

The dead bolt clicked just before the door swung open. Sophie's eyes widened, then narrowed as she stared back at him. Pulling her silk robe tighter around her curvy body, she clutched the top of the vee. That damn robe . . . the same one his hands had itched to peel off her body the other night.

"What happened to your face?"

"Braxton."

Sophie nodded as her cat slid against her leg and stared up at him. "Good."

Leave it to her to not sugarcoat her feelings . . . exactly opposite of him, who hid behind his at every opportunity.

"Can I come in?" he asked, shoving his hands in his pockets, feeling like a complete moron.

"Why should I let you? So you can hurt me again?"

Zach swallowed. He'd known he'd hurt her, damn it, but he hadn't been able to stop his words. Hearing her say it so boldly, though, did something to him that nearly crushed his soul. He'd die before he hurt her again.

"I want to apologize."

She said nothing as Zach waited. Waited for her to slam the door in his face, which he deserved. Waited for her to step aside and let him in. Waited for her to verbally attack him and tell him what a jerk he'd been to her for years.

Without a word, Sophie turned and walked away, leaving the door wide open. The cat darted off down the hall, disappearing into what Zach assumed was a bedroom.

He figured the fact that she'd not slammed the door in his face was his cue to come on inside. He crossed the threshold and closed the door behind him, trying like hell not to inhale the familiar floral aroma that seemed to hover everywhere Sophie was.

When he stepped into the living room, Sophie was shuffling papers together on the coffee table. One slid to the floor and he crossed to pick it up for her, but froze when he saw the drawing.

A pencil sketch. Similar to the ones in Chelsea's old apartment. Similar to the framed prints in Sophie's office.

No, not similar. Exactly the same.

Zach stared another moment before looking back up at her. She held the other sheets against her chest as she stared down at the sketch he held.

"You drew all of these?" he asked, amazed that she had such talent and he'd never known about it.

"Give me the paper, Zach."

"Why aren't you selling these?" His eyes roamed over the perfectly placed shadowing, the strong lines of the house.

He stared at a sketch of the Sunset Lake house and was utterly baffled at her ability to capture every single detail. She'd not portrayed the house as it stood now, but a vision of what it would be, what it probably once was.

"I was just doodling. No big deal."

She reached for the paper and he let her have it. He'd already ingrained the image into his head and there was no way she was blowing this off as a random drawing or a hobby to pass the time.

Sophie took the stack of papers and laid them on top of an antique secretary in the corner of the room. When she turned back around, the opening in her robe had inched farther down, giving him a glimpse of something equally silky and lacy beneath.

He deserved this penance. She was all polished and perfection, smooth and classy. Zach was everything on the opposite end of the spectrum—rough, hard, and dirty.

"I shouldn't have said what I did earlier," he started, knowing full well she wasn't going to say a word and the floor was all his. She wouldn't make this easy, but she hadn't kicked him out, so the fact that he was still there was more than he deserved.

"I can't take it back and I can't make it right, other than saying I'm sorry. When I hurt, I lash out, and you're the last person I want to be on the receiving end."

Her shoulders relaxed as she crossed her arms and remained silent. Zach swallowed, wondering how much he should reveal, how far into his soul he needed to go in order to receive her forgiveness.

"I'm not using my pain as an excuse," he continued. "There's no excuse for what I did. I know you love my house, I know you have memories there just like I do, and I know you care about my family, even though I've been an ass to you. But I can't focus on what's best for everyone and still carry out Chelsea's wishes, because at the end of the day, that's what I'm focusing on."

Sophie nodded. "I know you are, Zach, but after all we've been through, after everything in our past, whatever is happening between us now only makes this new pain harder to deal with."

He didn't want to address what was going on with them now. And he sure as hell didn't want to keep getting sidetracked by that creamy exposed skin.

"Nothing is happening now," Zach stated, wondering if the words came out as strong as he'd intended. "You know why it can't."

Sophie tipped her chin in defiance. "I know what I feel. I also know I'm done with trying to get you to open up to how you feel, to face that all of these emotions haven't gone away in years. Years, Zach. But if you haven't owned up to your feelings by now, you never will."

She started across the room with a slight limp, her eyes never meeting his as she walked by. "You've apologized, now you can go and feel better about yourself."

Zach remained still. He didn't feel better about himself. He didn't feel good at all, because even though he'd apologized, Sophie was still hurt. Years of his actions, or non-actions, had damaged her.

"Why do you feel anything for me?" he whispered as he stared at her back. "After all I've done, why?"

When they were teens he figured she'd developed a crush on him because he was Chelsea's brother, but Sophie hadn't looked at Braxton or Liam in such a manner. Then he'd wondered if she wanted someone opposite of her posh upbringing and stiff lifestyle. Being seen with the town bad boy would surely stick it to her snotty parents.

But the more he'd been around her, the more he'd seen she was with him because she liked him. He'd never questioned it until now. Perhaps he'd been too afraid of her answer.

With her back straight, she replied softly, "I'm not talking about this."

Zach closed the space between them and stepped up behind her, not touching her, though he'd give anything to have that right.

"I need to know." He inhaled her sweet, floral scent, closed his eyes for a brief second and savored the moment. "Help me understand what you see, Sophie."

She whirled around, her eyes blazing. "You know what I see? I see a broken man who won't let anyone in. I see a man who has so many people who care for him, but he continues to push them away. I see a man who took in stray puppies because deep in his heart he cares, though he doesn't want to admit it."

Zach listened to her, watched her lips move, and each time she moved her hands to emphasize the words, that robe slipped open a little more.

"I see a man who looks at me with desire and holds himself back," she murmured. "A man who deserves to be happy, but won't afford himself the chance."

Reaching out, Zach slid his rough fingertips over the silky edge of her robe and slowly pulled it back up over her exposed shoulder. When the material was back in place, Zach couldn't remove his hand. He kept telling himself to, but the message wasn't fully computing.

Sophie trembled beneath his touch, her eyes locked onto his. "Go, Zach. I can't take any more of this back-and-forth. Please—"

He cut her off with a kiss.

Zach wrapped an arm around her waist, pulling her lush body in against his. Cupping her cheek with his other hand, he had no control over his actions. She'd begged him to go, not because she really wanted him to but because there was so much angst between them.

And kissing the hell out of her wouldn't solve anything, but it sure felt perfect right at this moment.

Sophie sighed and leaned further into him. Her delicate hands slid up his shoulders and around his neck. Her fingers slid through the hair on the nape of his neck and sent tingles down his spine. Tingles. He'd never experienced tingles with any other woman in his life.

Slowly easing her back against the wall, he placed a hand on either side of her head as he held her body up with his own. She fit against him perfectly . . . as if he needed any further confirmation of how amazing they'd be together.

But that didn't make it right.

Zach lifted his mouth, resting his forehead against hers.

"Don't say you're sorry," she muttered. "Don't regret this."

"I don't regret kissing you, Sophie. I regret knowing this can't go anywhere."

Sliding her hands around, she framed his face and lifted his head to look him straight in the eyes. "I'm not asking you for anything, Zach. All I want is for you to be honest with yourself, with me."

"You don't want my honesty," he groaned.

"Maybe it's you who doesn't want to own up to the truth."

How could this one woman reach inside his heart and squeeze it? How was it that anyone could have pegged him so perfectly?

Damn it, his hands were shaking.

"I want you," he confessed. "More than anything I've ever wanted in my life. But there's so much about my past, so much darkness that I can't subject you to. And beyond sex, I have nothing to offer."

"In case you haven't noticed, I'm not shying away from sex. And as for your past, I'm not afraid," she told him with a soft smile. "You think I don't know you had a rough childhood? I may not know the details, but nothing you tell me would change how I feel."

There were only a handful of people who knew the truth: the social workers and his parents. Chelsea had known some of what he'd been through because they'd shared stories on occasion.

But having that ugly truth enter Sophie's life, having her look at him with pity—or worse, disgust— would kill him.

Sliding his thumbs along her jawline, he watched as her lids lowered and her lips parted. Unable to help himself, he covered her mouth with his again.

He'd never taken such time with kissing a woman before, but he wanted to know Sophie's touch, taste. He wanted to know every bit of her, but he still couldn't let himself get beyond that last hurdle.

Because nobody had ever mattered as much as Sophie. There were other women, too many women, but they weren't Sophie. She'd always been special, always been on a higher level. And the fact that she made him face his feelings scared the hell out of him.

Pulling away, he stared down at her. Flushed from his kisses, robe falling off her shoulder again to tempt him with all that exposed skin, and her eyes filled with passion, Sophie was the most tempting woman he'd ever known, and she wasn't even trying.

"I'm going to go," he told her, using every bit of

his willpower not to take what she was offering. "I'm not leaving because I don't want you, I'm leaving because I do. I'm giving us both time to figure this out."

Giving her time to change her mind and come to her senses.

"Ten years hasn't been enough?" she asked with a smile. "Don't make this more complicated than it needs to be."

"For the first time in my life, I'm thinking something through." Reaching out, Zach slid a finger over her forehead and pushed her hair away from her face. "Trust me, next time we're alone, if you still want this, you better be ready. It's all I have to give, and you need to be fully aware nothing could happen beyond the bedroom."

"You better keep that promise, Zach, because I've been ready for you for years."

Sophie's bold statement had him fighting to walk out her door and do the right thing. Now that she was fully aware that he was on board, she needed to think about this. Hell, he needed to process it fully himself.

Was he really going to get involved with Sophie? Did she really believe that this was not complicated? How could it *not* be complicated? Their twisted past had so many curves and highs and lows, he never knew what life was going to throw at them next.

But he knew one thing: He deserved a damn medal for walking out of her house knowing full well she was aching for him as much as he was for her.


"Are you sure you have time for this?"

Macy sat at the island in Zach's kitchen with a worried look on her face.

"I'm positive," he assured her as he pulled out the takeout she'd brought. "If you feed me each time we get together to discuss your house plans, the process may even go faster."

Laughing, Macy pulled out her phone. "Well, I have several pictures, and I'm afraid they're all different designs, so you may change your mind."

The puppies in the next room were yipping louder than usual. Most likely they smelled the takeout.

"Your friends in there want attention," Macy stated.

"They're fine. They just like to make noise and they never seem to care what time it is. Feel free to take them when you leave."

Macy laughed. "Poor baby. Are they keeping you up?"

He glared back. "Shut up or I'll drop them all off at your place."

"Speaking of my house, the pictures I have for you to look at are all over the place in regards to design."

"I'm sure they have some features in common." He pulled out two plates and started filling them with rice and chicken. "Most people won't see that, but if they're all your style, then there's usually a common thread."

He handed Macy a glass of tea and her plate before settling next to her on the other bar stool.

"You gonna tell me about that shiner?" she asked as she scooped up a healthy forkful of rice.

"My brother."

Her brow quirked. "Liam? You tell him about the house?"

Shaking his head, Zach cut into his chicken. "Braxton took out some frustration. I deserved it, so I let it slide."

Macy laughed. "So you haven't told Liam? You may have a matching eye after you do."

"Let's look at your pictures while we eat," he suggested, turning the topic away from his slight differences with his brothers. "After we're done we can get into more details."

"I'll let you change the subject, but only because I'm anxious to discuss my house."

She pulled up her images and as Zach studied them, he realized quickly how her tastes matched his own. He was going to enjoy this project, especially because Macy had a good amount of sense when it came to what was possible. Too many clients asked for the impossible and occasionally got angry when they realized he wasn't a magician.

"You're wanting a two-story," he muttered as he scrolled through her images. "You like stone, but there are several variations in color and sizing here."

Macy took a drink and pointed to the current picture on the screen. "That's the stone I'm not in love with. I want the type with more of a variation of colors. I have that picture because I like the style of that entryway and the narrow window above the door."

Nodding, Zach kept flipping through her images, studying each one with a skilled eye. As they ate and discussed the photos, he was able to get a better idea of what she wanted and was pretty confident he could narrow it down to a couple different designs that should please her.

"If you're finished, just leave the plates," he told her. "I'll clean up later."

"I'll at least put them in the sink." Macy gathered the two plates and took them across the kitchen. "I'm not one hundred percent sold on the two-story. The main thing I know I want is a large garage with an apartment on the back for Dad."

Zach paused. "Is your dad okay with that?"

Macy turned, leaning back against the counter. "We've had a few heated debates over the matter, but he sees my reasoning. We're really all each other has, and he still wants to keep his independence. I've stayed at home with him long enough. We both need our space, but we also still want to be close."

Macy was a noble, loyal woman. She'd gone to college on a softball scholarship, but ended up coming home when her mother had a stroke and passed away. Macy always said she'd go back, but she'd started helping her dad in the store and now she was co-owner of the popular business.

Zach admired her for putting her family first, for giving up her dreams without hesitation or complaint.

"We'll make sure it's something nice for him," Zach replied. "I'll grab my sketch pad and let the dogs out. Go on into the living room."

"I'll let the dogs out," she told him. "You go get what you need."

Zach hesitated. "Do you know what you're saying? Those little ones are evil."

Macy laughed. "I can handle puppies. Why don't you take a break from potty training and let me deal with this."

Zach shrugged as he headed from the room. "You asked for it," he muttered.

As he went to get his sketch pad from the office, someone banged on the front door. Zach froze. If Ms. Barkley stood on the other side of that door, he was going to have to tell her once and for all that he wasn't interested.

As he made his way to the foyer, he tried to figure out if he'd ever given her the impression that he wanted more than a neighborly "hi" in passing. Apparently she didn't care or she was just really determined to get him into her bedroom . . . or anywhere else he'd be willing to go with her.

Flicking the lock, he jerked open the door.

"Liam." Zach gripped the door, shocked to see his brother there. "What are you doing here?"

Liam pushed through and entered the house. "I talked to Sophie earlier. She asked if I'd spoken with you. Then I called to talk to Braxton and he asked if I'd talked to you."

Zach closed the door and folded his arms over his chest. Nothing like being thrust into revealing the secret. But the truth coming out was inevitable.

"You might as well come on in." Zach gestured toward the living room.

"Is that Macy's Jeep out there?" Liam asked.

Holding on to the smallest of the puppies, Macy stepped in behind Liam. "Yes, it is."

Liam turned, then stared back and forth between Zach and Macy. "Am I interrupting?" he asked, his eyes narrowed.

Interesting. Zach hadn't known Liam to show much emotion, but apparently he didn't like the idea of his brother entertaining the hometown hardware store owner.

"I'm working on something for Macy."

Zach left it at that because whatever he or Macy did was none of Liam's concern. If Macy wanted Liam to know anything, she could fill him in.

Liam stared at Macy holding the wiggly puppy for

a moment before he turned toward the door. "I'll come back."

"No." Macy took a step forward. "Talk with Zach. I can go play with these cute little guys."

Macy held the puppy up to her face, and she was awarded with a lick on her chin. The yipping started again from the laundry room.

"Are you running a damn kennel?" Liam asked.

"I need to put some food down for the mom." Zach started from the room before turning back. "Neither one of you leave."

"I'm not staying," Liam argued.

Zach sighed. "You drove all this way when you could've called."

"Well, I thought something major was happening and you needed to talk to me. Heaven forbid you actually call me and tell me what the hell is going on. I have to get veiled hints dropped from second parties."

Macy backed up a step. "I'm going to go put this little guy back. I'll take care of feeding the mom and keeping the dogs occupied. You guys talk. Zach, don't worry about the plans tonight. We can do it another night. I'm in no hurry."

She disappeared before he could tell her to stick around because he was sure once Liam realized what Zach needed to say, Liam would leave in a snit.

"Tell me what the hell is going on." Liam propped his hands on his hips. "I took my one night off this week to drive here."

"You could've called."

"From the way Sophie and Braxton seemed worried that I hadn't spoken with you, I figured this was more than a phone call. And you've obviously gotten into a fight—I'm assuming with Braxton."

Zach raked a hand down his beard and shook his head. "Our fight has nothing to do with why I need to talk to you."

Liam said nothing. He didn't blink. He merely stood still in that angry pose, glaring across the space between them.

"I'm selling this house."

The muscle in Liam's jaw clenched as he crossed his arms over his chest. The scar running down the side of his face seemed redder, as if his anger had spawned the shade.

"I wouldn't have put it up for sale without telling you, but I just officially decided."

"What the hell are you thinking?" Liam asked in a low growl. "How could you sell this house? Where are you going to go? Did you even think that maybe Braxton or I would want this, before you decided to get rid of it? Just because this is in your name doesn't mean we aren't invested in it."

Liam spun around, muttering obscenities that would have had their mother scolding them no matter their ages, and then he turned back. "This is just like you, to be so damn selfish," he continued. "You do whatever you want and to hell with the rest of us."

Anger slid through Zach, but he'd expected nothing less from Liam.

"Maybe before spouting off you should consider the reasons." Zach marched through to the living room, knowing Liam would follow. "Braxton and I can only afford to spend so much on Chelsea's property. That property tax took a good chunk of my savings, and those renovations are going to be expensive. There's no way around it."

Zach stopped at the mantel where the photos were, his eyes zeroing in on his late sister. "I'm not going to let finances get in my way of fulfilling this dream of Chelsea's, because if she were alive she'd do anything possible to get this done. She'd sacrifice everything, and I plan on doing the same."

Spinning back around, Zach faced his brother, who stood leaning in the doorway. "You can be angry all you want, but shut the hell up when it comes to me and my reasoning. You had a chance to be in on this and you opted out."

"I didn't know you'd be making rash decisions without discussing them with your family first."

Zach hadn't had to discuss his decisions with anyone. He sure as hell never had to discuss things with his brothers, because they had little to nothing in common other than being taken in by amazing parents who were complete saints.

"I'm telling you now."

Liam laughed. "I came to you. When were you going to tell me you were selling our childhood home?"

"I would've told you before Sophie put it on the market."

"I'm honored."

Macy stepped up behind Liam. "The dogs are all taken care of. I'm just going to go, and we can talk later."

"No." Liam held his hand up and glanced down at her. "You can stay and finish your date. I'm leaving."

*Well, hell.*

"I'm not on a date," Macy told him. "I want Zach to build me a house."

Liam dropped his hand. "Regardless, I'm interrupting and I've heard what I came to hear."

"You're just leaving?" Macy asked. "You can stay."

Was that hope in her tone? Did Macy have an interest in Liam?

Zach continued to watch the two before him, wondering if this was new or something that had been in front of his face for years. Liam was trying his damnedest not to look Macy dead in the eye. Granted, he rarely looked someone dead in the eye because he usually tilted his head just far enough to keep the scarred side of his face turned away.

But Macy was ringing her hands, looking up at Liam with wide eyes. She wasn't being coy or playful, she was simply showing a side Zach hadn't seen before. A side that showcased a woman interested in a man.

"I have no reason to stay, especially since the house won't be in my family any longer." Liam glanced at Zach. "There's nothing for me here."

Zach watched as Liam stormed out of the house. There was nothing he could do about Liam's anger. Actually, Zach had expected more of an altercation.

But when he looked at Macy, she almost seemed deflated or disappointed. Did she and Liam have something going on that no one was aware of?

Surely not. This town was too small for word of a relationship not to get out, and Macy would've said something. The way she was still staring at the door, though, told Zach that she was definitely hung up on Liam.

As much as Zach hated to admit it, he feared Macy's longing after Liam would only lead to heartache down the road. But he sure as hell wasn't one to offer advice in the romance category.

Because the one woman he wanted was tempting him like he'd never been tempted before, and he knew the second he caved and gave in to her, he'd be facing a whole host of heartache himself.

# Chapter Twelve

Zach swept up the mess in the main floor bathroom. Finally, the building permit had come through and it had only set him back five days.

In that time he'd stayed busy working on various odd jobs and had started new projects where he'd placed Nathan in charge of the crew. This Sunset Lake property was going to take the majority of his time. He intended to focus on this project until it was complete. At that point he truly had no clue what to do, no idea how to run a spa/resort for women.

Yeah, definitely an area where he'd need Sophie's expertise.

The only interaction he'd had with Sophie was via text, setting up a time to meet in her office to officially put his house on the market. That appointment was later today, and he was torn up just thinking about it. Between being alone with her again and putting the only haven he'd ever known on the market . . . he just hoped he made it through the meeting.

Had he seriously admitted to her that he was ready to try something? What had he been thinking? What if he couldn't? There were so many issues he had, so much darkness inside him, he seriously was afraid of taking another step with Sophie. But how would he know if he never tried? He'd avoided her and this sexual tension for a decade. That hadn't worked out so well, now had it?

On another note, Zach had not heard from Liam at all. Braxton was pretty quiet lately too, but he'd most likely been spending time with a woman. Braxton tended to seek comfort from strangers, but that was his cross to bear. None of Zach's business.

Whatever issues Braxton carried around, he never shared them. That told Zach that the past Braxton kept to himself had deeply damaged his brother. Would anyone ever be able to penetrate Braxton's outer shell? Zach had thought Anna might, but then she'd cheated on Braxton and he'd closed up even more after the breakup.

All three brothers and Chelsea had carried different pasts into the Monroe home. Braxton had been the most secretive. Zach knew that when Braxton was about ten, his parents were killed, but he didn't know how and Braxton never offered the information.

When Zach came to live with the Monroes, Braxton was quiet, always wanting peace in the house. Zach and Liam had rubbed each other the wrong way from day one, and that never sat well with Braxton. He'd always tried to intervene and keep everyone calm.

Whatever happened in Braxton's past had made him determined to see those around him happy and calm. Whatever he'd experienced was rooted so deep, Zach wondered what the young Braxton had gone through.

They all had their problems and they were all dealing with life in different ways . . . or not dealing with it at all, as was the case with Zach. He'd much prefer to ignore his aching for Sophie. He'd give anything to block out the pain of losing Chelsea. And he sure as hell hoped he had the ability to complete this resort and do it justice the way Chelsea would've wanted, and have it be a success. Wasn't that the biggest risk in all of this?

Swiping his arm across his sweaty forehead, Zach dumped the dustpan full of debris and mess into the heavy-duty black trash bag. He needed to have Macy place a bulk order for more—which reminded him, he still needed to get with her.

The last two nights, thanks to the yipping pups, he'd lost even more sleep and had used the time to jot down the main concepts for what he felt Macy would be looking for in a new home. Once he ran those by her, he could start doing a mock-up on the rough sketch.

Stifling a yawn, Zach had no idea how to get sleep. There was no way he could put the dogs outside. He'd not been much of an animal person, simply because the opportunity hadn't presented itself, but he never liked seeing dogs tied up outside. He never quite understood why people owned a pet they were just going to hook on a chain and toss food to a few times a day.

So outside was out. But how did he sleep, and how the hell did he train them to sleep or at least keep quiet at night? It was like those little things never shut up. If one was asleep, the others were playing and barking. One of them was always awake. No wonder the poor mom just lay around. The poor dog probably just wanted to be ready for a moment's peace if the opportunity ever came.

Tying up the sack, Zach hauled it into the kitchen and set it by the back door with the other sack he'd filled only an hour ago.

Something scooted against the floor upstairs.

Zach froze, listening for the sound again. After a moment of utter silence, and questioning if he'd actually heard anything at all, he shrugged. Old houses always made odd sounds.

He cracked his knuckles as he moved down the hall, the familiar puckered skin on the backs of his hands always a reminder of his carelessness.

When his cell vibrated in his pocket, he pulled it out and eyed the screen before answering.

"What's up, Nathan?"

"I know you're working and I hate to interrupt, but your neighbor called again."

Zach withheld a groan as he stopped in the hallway and cringed as he tipped his head back and eyed the ceiling. "And what's wrong with her house this time? I swear on my life, before that house sold it was solid. I helped build the damn thing myself just seven years ago."

Nathan chuckled. "It seems the faucet in her master tub is leaking."

*Bullshit.* "Did you go check it out?"

"I offered, but she asked if we could both come over," Nathan said slowly. "That woman is bold. I told her we were busy and I'd have to call her back. What the hell, man?"

Zach gripped his phone and headed back toward the bathroom. "Call her back. Let her know that we're too busy to spare both of us. Keep it professional, because that woman reads into everything. If she needs the pipes looked at, tell her she should call a plumber. I hate to turn away business, but we both know that's not why she's calling."

Zach had worked too hard to maintain the company's reputation for high standards, which his father had established in the community and surrounding areas. No way in hell was he going to let it get tarnished because of some divorcée with an itch to scratch.

Yeah, he was a guy and appreciated an attractive woman. But what he didn't appreciate was a blatant woman, a woman who had no class, and a woman who felt it was okay to disrupt his working hours. He had actual clients, and she was getting to the point of pissing him off.

"I'll let her know," Nathan stated. "I'm over at the Butchers' place now. We're nearly done shingling the garage and we'll start on the house tomorrow."

"Great. You're too busy to check out a leaking faucet."

Laughing, Nathan replied, "Got it. Let me know if you need any help out there."

Zach glanced around the nearly gutted bathroom. "I've got it covered. Thanks, man."

Sliding the phone back into his pocket, Zach started looking around the room. He had the layout of the plans in his head, and he also knew a portion of one of the walls had to go. Glancing at his watch, he saw it was late afternoon and he'd yet to have lunch. Where the hell was Braxton? He'd promised to be there and so far he was a no-show.

Zach sent off a quick text, telling his brother to stop by somewhere and bring some lunch and get his ass in gear so they could get this wall out. Time was not on their side, because Zach wanted to get this place done, get it open, and start seeing a return.

Yes, he knew all of that would take time, years most

likely, which was all the more reason he didn't want to wait any longer than he had to.

Braxton replied he was already on his way, he'd stop to get Zach's food and to "chill the hell out."

Might as well get the tools ready, because once lunch was devoured, the wall was coming down. The bathroom needed to be expanded, and the wall he'd wanted to remove wasn't a load-bearing wall, which would make the new design absolutely perfect.

Zach knew he'd have to sink every spare dime into this place, but it would be worth it in the end. He wished Chelsea were here to see it, to guide him and Braxton through the process, but all he could do was honor her wishes per her notes and binders.

And Sophie. Sophie was the thread that would tie this all up in a nice, neat package, because she knew design, she knew Chelsea's tastes in such things, and Sophie was the only woman in on this entire renovation.

Zach would swear Chelsea was looking down on him, laughing her ass off. He would get this done, it would be spectacular, and women from all over would come to enjoy a getaway and just relax. The draw from Savannah would get them started, and he hoped like hell word of mouth spread like wildfire.

Now all he had to do was finish fixing up this massive home, the two small cottages, learn about facials and cucumber sandwiches or some other ridiculous things women ate to stay thin, and watch the money roll in.

Sounded about as easy as keeping his feelings about Sophie to himself.

Zach was nothing if not determined. On the upside, the landscaping wasn't terrible. Being in the South, the tall, mossy trees stood strong and provided shade all over the property, including near the pond in the backyard. Mostly they'd need new shrubbery and flowers around the porches, but Zach knew an amazing landscaper he often recommended to other people. But that was the last thing they'd need to worry about.

After pulling in the necessary tools and another box of trash bags, Zach's cell vibrated again. If that was Braxton saying he'd be late, Zach was going to kill him.

Glancing at his phone, he was shocked to see Liam's name. The message simply said: Count me in.

Okay. Not what he was expecting. Zach shot off a quick reply: In on what?

He stared down at his phone, eager for the response, knowing most likely his brother meant the resort, but he didn't want to assume and he wanted to make his brother just say it.

The girly resort.

Zach smiled. He hadn't expected Liam to jump in, especially after the blowup at Zach's house several days ago.

The front door opened and closed as Zach messaged Liam back: Then you better take time off from that fancy restaurant and bring your tool belt, city boy.

For all the frustration they caused each other, for all the ways they simply didn't click, Zach actually felt good about this. He wanted Liam to be part of the project. Chelsea would've wanted all of her brothers to be in on this, and Zach admitted to himself he couldn't wait to get started with both of his siblings.

No doubt they'd argue, most likely fight and swing fists, but in the end they were coming together for their late sister because they loved her. It was as simple and as complicated as that.

Braxton appeared in the doorway, holding up a large brown bag. "Hurry up and eat. We have a lot to do."

Zach grabbed the bag from his hands. "Shut the hell up. You've been MIA for days."

A shadow fell over Braxton's face. "Had some things to work through."

Of all the boys, Braxton was the last one to show emotions. He had his shit together . . . or he put up an outstanding front.

"You okay?"

Nodding, Braxton pulled in a deep breath. "Just unfinished drama I had to put to rest."

Zach wasn't going to pry; he had enough secrets and drama in his own life. Besides, that was one area the brothers all silently agreed on. If one of them wanted to talk, they would. They weren't going to sit around and try to force one another's feelings out in the open.

"Then let's eat." Zach inched around his brother and headed toward the kitchen. "Afterward you can swing the sledgehammer to knock that wall out. I'm looking forward to you getting some calluses on your pretty hands."

Behind him Braxton snorted. "These pretty hands gave you a black eye the other day, if you recall."

Setting the sack on top of the old chipped countertop, Zach shrugged. "I deserved it. Besides, I'm sure I'll repay the favor one day."

After pulling out the cartons of burgers and fries, and the bottles of soda, Zach leaned against the counter and started digging in. Braxton took his stuff to the tiny island that would soon become scrap.

"When I was at the house earlier I fed the pups, let

them out, and had quite an interesting conversation with your new neighbor."

Of course he did. No doubt Ms. Obvious was hitting on Braxton as well.

"She's pretty bold," Zach replied around a fry. "Don't encourage her."

Laughing, Braxton nodded. "I got that. She was looking for you, though. I'm not sure she wanted to talk to me."

Shocked and a bit disturbed, Zach swallowed. "Don't feed her any information about me, either. That woman cannot take a hint."

"She's smokin' hot."

Zach didn't reply. He wasn't drawn to the voluptuous blondes who painted on red lips and poured themselves into their clothes. And he sure as hell wasn't attracted to someone who just assumed she could get anyone into bed.

He refused to stand there and think about the type of woman he was drawn to, because there was only one.

There would always be only one.

"I have an appointment with Sophie later to put the house on the market."

Braxton froze, his bottle halfway to his lips. "You're going through with this, then?"

"I see no other way." Zach focused on choosing the perfect fry instead of the questioning glare of his brother. "It'll be the best decision in the long run."

"Liam didn't take the news too well."

That sick feeling in his stomach grew. "No, he didn't. But he's in on this project."

"What?" Braxton set his bottle on the counter and

straightened. "You mean he wants to be part of this? The resort?"

Nodding, Zach turned to fully focus on Braxton. "He sent me a text just as you got here. He hasn't mentioned the sale of the house to me, but he said he was in on this. That will help financially too. Slowly things are clicking into place."

As they should, because Zach couldn't handle his world falling apart too much more.

"I'm busy later, but if you want to reschedule with Sophie I could go with you."

"No. I want to get it on the market."

"What about the dogs? You find homes for the puppies?"

Zach finished his lunch and wadded up the papers. "Not yet. I'm focused on trying to figure out how to get some damn sleep."

He'd figure something out with the animals. They were just too damn cute to be angry with. Still, he couldn't keep them.

"Let's get started on tackling that wall," Zach stated. "I've got an appointment in three hours, and I'd rather not show up smelling like I've worked my ass off all day."

"Heading home to get fancied up for Sophie first?" Braxton teased.

Zach flipped him the finger and headed from the room. No way was he responding to that, because he would have to admit the statement was too damn close to the truth.

When the door chimed in her office, Sophie's stomach flipped. She was technically closed, but had told Zach to go ahead and meet her at six.

Besides being a ball of nerves at the prospect of being with him after their heated encounter in her living room, she knew it was emotionally difficult for him to list his home. She was having a rough time as well, but she knew without a doubt that the Monroe boys were not taking this move lightly.

Liam had called her the other day and was angry and upset, but in the end he admitted Zach probably had the best plan. Not that the stubborn Liam would tell his grouchy brother such things, but Sophie knew. She also knew these boys loved each other more than they might ever admit.

Zach filled the space in her doorway, standing in the spot as if he were afraid to step inside. She knew his nerves were most likely all over the place as well. The man was so hardheaded but he cracked when he realized when he was at fault.

Sophie came to her feet and offered what she hoped was a reassuring smile. "You don't have to do this," she told him. "We can figure out another way."

Zach's dark eyes held hers a moment before he shook his head. "No. Let's get it over with."

He crossed the office and sank down into the chair opposite her desk. He'd recently showered, if his damp hair was any indication. That wasn't sweat, because the man smelled positively sinful and absolutely yummy. His black short-sleeved shirt stretched across muscles that had been gifted to him after years of hard labor, and those kissable lips surrounded by sexy beard mocked her.

*Keep it in control, Sophie. The man is having a personal crisis at the moment.*

Taking a seat, Sophie rolled her chair up to the edge of her desk and picked up her favorite pen. "What I want to know first is the recent renovations you've done. I know the basics of bathrooms and bedrooms, so I've got that down already. Tell me everything that's been updated."

Zach listed the rooms he'd remodeled over the years as well as the roof he'd replaced two years ago. He'd added a brick patio complete with pergola, and new landscaping in the last year as well. The more improvements he listed, the more Sophie knew they would get for this house. Added to that, knowing that a man who owned a construction company lived in the house would make buyers more apt to stay as close to the asking price as possible. With Zach's reputation, people in the area knew he did good work.

"Your house is twenty-two hundred square feet, right?" she asked, scribbling down the last of her notes.

"Twenty-four."

"What year was the house built?" she asked.

When he didn't answer, she glanced up. Zach's focus was on the far wall, where her pencil sketches of various buildings around the town were hanging.

"Zach?"

"Your talent is wasted," he murmured, still looking across the room. "Your talent is hanging on walls where people won't see it."

Sophie gripped her pen. "I didn't do those sketches to gain recognition. I did them because it's relaxing, almost therapeutic for me."

Okay, not almost therapeutic, they *were* therapeutic.

When his heavy-lidded gaze landed back on her, Sophie willed herself not to fidget in her seat. Those eyes could make a woman go weak in the knees, though, and she knew full well what that mouth could do.

"When did you take up drawing?"

So he wanted to get personal? Was this Zach extending that proverbial olive branch?

"After the accident."

The silence in the room enveloped them and she knew he'd been instantly thrust back to that night, because he glanced down at his scarred hands. Those beautiful hands that had broken glass in the truck to get her and Liam out.

Those hands that had slid along her skin only days ago, leaving her aching for so much more.

Before she could say anything more, though she wasn't sure what she could say, Zach jerked and pulled his phone from his pocket. When he glanced at the screen, he closed his eyes and sighed.

"Everything okay?" she asked.

"Nothing I can't handle."

He laid the phone on her desk without answering it and eventually the vibration stopped.

Sophie glanced between the cell and Zach, who had settled back into the seat as if moments ago he hadn't been silently dealing with his own personal hell.

The phone started vibrating once again.

"Ignore it," he told her. "It's my neighbor."

Sophie remembered the very voluptuous woman she'd spotted the other day. "Apparently it's an emergency."

Zach shook his head. "No, it's not. She's starting to become a nuisance."

Zach was one of the sexiest men Sophie had ever known. He had that mysteriousness about him, he had the body carved from perfection. It was no wonder women were literally begging him for attention. But Sophie wouldn't beg and she certainly was no match for someone so flawless and beautiful as Zach's very obvious neighbor.

When the cell vibrated again, Sophie reached across the desk. "Hello?"

"Um . . . I'm looking for Zach Monroe."

Sophie smiled across the desk to a stunned Zach. Never in her life did Sophie recall a time when his eyes had been so wide with utter surprise as they were now.

"He's busy at the moment," Sophie replied. "Can I take a message?"

"And you are?"

Sophie couldn't help herself. "The woman he's with right now. Are you a client?"

There was no response from the neighbor as Zach eased forward in his seat. Sophie sent him a wink, suddenly feeling a bit saucy. This wasn't her. She was quiet and reserved and didn't get in the midst of other people's issues.

But there was something about Zach that made her want to stake her claim. Not that she had a claim over him, but she sure as hell did over this woman.

"I can take a message," Sophie stated when the silence stretched too long.

"No. No message."

With a wide smile, Sophie disconnected the call and handed it back across the desk. "She didn't have anything to say."

Speechless, Zach kept staring at her. Sophie didn't know whether to applaud her performance or cringe at her boldness. On one hand, the neighbor was beyond beautiful, but on the other, Zach had made it perfectly clear he wasn't interested.

"Did I go too far?" Sophie asked, biting her bottom lip.

"Not at all," he told her, taking the phone and just

barely grazing his fingertips along the back of hers. "I'm just . . . I have no words."

Sophie shrugged. "I didn't think before acting. I'm sorry I grabbed your phone and just . . . well, implied things that aren't true."

Zach shoved the phone back into his pocket. "Don't worry about it. Maybe she'll stop harassing me. I tried to steer her toward one of my employees, but that didn't last long."

He wasn't addressing the fact that she'd pretty much told someone that she and Zach were together . . . as in, *together*. In this small town, if his neighbor started talking, everyone would know. Granted, Sophie hadn't identified herself.

This is why she preferred a game plan. She was the one to always think things through, looking at the scenario from all angles so she could choose the best option. And she truly wished she knew what was going on between Zach and her.

"You're overthinking this," Zach chimed in, interrupting her wayward thoughts. "Forget the phone call."

He obviously wasn't too concerned as he relaxed in the chair, fingers laced over his flat abs, so why was she?

"Okay." Sophie blew out a breath and glanced back down to her notes. "We've got the basics down. I'll have an appraiser go through the house and get back to me. Then you and I can discuss the price. I'm sure you'll want to talk with Braxton and Liam about that as well."

Sophie came to her feet, wincing when that familiar pain gave her pause. Zach instantly stood, reaching across the desk.

"No, it passed." She stepped around the desk to face him. "See? Nothing to worry about."

His eyes roamed over her, affecting her body just as if he'd actually touched her. Those beautiful lips thinned as his eyes narrowed in on hers.

"I'll call the appraiser tomorrow," she told him, purposely trying to keep tension from settling between them. "I'll let you know what he says."

Zach took a step forward, minimizing the space between them and effectively towering over her. "Are you always going to ignore the pain? Are you expecting me to ignore it every time I see you hurting?"

"I don't ignore it," she replied, tipping her chin up to meet his gaze. "I'm used to it and it will pass. It's really nothing more than a twinge most times. Besides, you're pretty good at ignoring things. You've pushed aside your feelings for years, so just add this to the list."

"I've not pushed them aside." He leaned in, still not touching her, but his warm breath tickled her face. "I live with them every single day."

"Well, you should be commended for your self-control. After what happened at my house the other day, I would've thought . . ."

Sophie shook her head and pursed her lips. After a moment of staring at each other in some sort of modern-day standoff, Sophie sighed. "Go home, Zach. Go to the Sunset Lake property or wherever. We're done here. The ball is in your court, so whatever happens next is up to you."

Just as she turned, he reached for her shoulder. He didn't grip her or demand she stop, but that subtle touch halted her movements just the same.

"Soph." His soft tone washed over her. She closed

her eyes, absorbing his words. "The last thing I want you to think is that I'm rejecting you."

"What am I supposed to think, then?" she whispered, her heart hurting for the years of angst that remained between them.

His hand dropped. "It's difficult to take something so precious from you."

Sophie whirled on him. "I'm not a virgin, Zach."

"Damn it." He slid a hand along his jaw and smoothed his beard down. "I'm not saying that. I'm saying I know you wouldn't take intimacy so lightly and there's no way I would ever take that from you. You deserve more than . . ."

Sophie nodded. "You can't even say it. It's fine. Just go."

After a moment's hesitation, he nodded and headed toward the doorway. Just as he started to leave, he slapped his hand on the frame and muttered a curse.

"Is it always going to be this push-pull between us?" he asked, throwing a glance over his shoulder. "Because I don't want you hurt. You have to know that everything I'm doing, I'm doing to protect you. I won't hurt you again, Sophie. It would kill me. I know you said this doesn't have to be anything more than what we desire, but that's not fair to you. I won't be that man to you."

She said nothing. What could she say? She'd never heard such vulnerability in his tone before, let alone heard him utter such heartfelt words.

She didn't get to respond. Zach was gone and the front door chimed as he exited the office building. Easing back, she sat on the edge of her desk and stared at the doorway where he'd just been.

In the span of thirty minutes, so much had happened.

Zach had opened up more than ever before, revealing that he truly did want her. Between the house going on the market, the untimely call from his neighbor, and Zach's comments on her sketches, Sophie really didn't know how to process all of this.

She did know one thing, though. She was done making this situation between her and Zach so complicated. It didn't have to be that way. *They* didn't have to be that way.

Now he could either listen to her or he could truly be alone, because he had one more shot.

# Chapter Thirteen

If he were a drinker, tonight would be one of those nights Zach could get lost in the bottle.

But the bottle was what got him into this damn mess to begin with.

Zach fed the baby puppy, noticing the little guy was finally bulking up. He needed to take them into the vet's office for an official checkup and to get shots scheduled. That would be time away from work, but these fur balls had no one else, and he couldn't just abandon them. He knew what that felt like all too well.

Great. Now not only was he angry with himself over Sophie, he was equating himself to a stray dog. He was definitely sleep-deprived.

He had no desire to do anything but crawl into bed. Wow, it wasn't even eight o'clock yet. Wasn't he just a party animal?

Zach squatted down and played with the pups. One nipped at his wrist with those sharp baby teeth, another tugged on the shoelaces of his boots, while another tripped over the other boot and squatted to pee.

"Seriously? I just let you guys out and you piss on my boot?"

He stood up and glanced at the mom in the corner. She looked back at him as if to say *I can't control them.*

After Zach cleaned up the mess, washed his hands, and put out fresh water for the urinaters, he climbed over the child gate and figured he'd try to find something for dinner.

Nothing appealed to him, so he opted to make a list of materials he'd need Macy to order for him for the immediate bathroom remodel. He needed to run by her store anyway and apologize for his asshole brother interrupting the other night, and tell her he had some new ideas for her house.

Just as he'd settled onto his couch with pen and paper, someone knocked on his door. And not just a knock, but a pounding, like it was urgent.

Oh no. No, no, no. If this was Ms. Barkley again, he was seriously going to have to just be rude. There was no other way he knew to manage her.

Gearing up for a confrontation, and practicing a speech in his head, Zach flicked the lock and jerked the door open . . . and his guest wasn't his annoying neighbor.

Sophie stood on his porch, her eyes wide, her hand over her chest. "I wasn't expecting such a rough greeting."

"I wasn't expecting an FBI knock." Zach's shoulders relaxed as he gripped the door. "What are you doing here, Sophie?"

Seeing her over and over was both a blessing and a curse. It hurt to look at her, but he'd die if he had to go without seeing her.

"I-I'm not sure now." On a soft exhale, she closed her eyes. "I was fine until you opened this door."

Confused, Zach opened the door wider, reached out

to take her hand, and eased her inside before closing the door behind her.

"You were fine before I opened the door," he repeated. "So tell me why you came and why you look terrified now."

Those bright eyes came up to meet his as she shoved her hair away from her face. "I talked myself into coming here and seducing you, and I wasn't taking no for an answer. I wasn't going to beg, but you admitted that you want me. This doesn't have to be any more than what it is."

Her words registered quickly and Zach had to take a second and really think, because they were teetering on the point of no return.

"And what is it?" he asked, surprised his voice was strong.

Passion stared back at him. If he thought the tension between them was high before this, right now the air crackled with it.

"This attraction hasn't gone away," she told him. "In ten years, even with ignoring each other, whatever this is between us has only gotten stronger. I know you're scared, you don't have to say it. You don't think I'm terrified? Coming here like this, risking rejection has me so nervous I can hardly stand it. But I'm willing to take that chance because I want this. I want you."

Rejection? The second he'd opened his door and pulled her in he knew he couldn't turn her away. He'd pushed and pushed and there was no strength left in him.

She'd come to him. His sweet, unwavering Sophie had put aside her fears and landed on his doorstep. He knew she came here to put everything on his playing field. He knew she presented herself to him because she had feelings for him, and damn, if that didn't humble him.

Sliding his hands over her face, his rough palms against her smooth cheeks, his fingers fisted into her hair as he tilted her head back.

"Be sure, Sophie." He stared into her eyes, so set with determination and desire. "Be sure of what you're asking for and know this is all I have."

Could he actually do this? Could he selfishly take what she was offering and go into this so casually? He'd had casual sex before, but Sophie was different, special.

"It's simple." She reached up, held onto his wrists. "You either want me or you don't. I'm not looking for a ring on my finger or a declaration of love."

"What if you want more later?" he asked, needing to clear all the bases to avoid hurting her again.

A corner of her unpainted mouth kicked up. "What if *you* want more?"

Damn. Maybe that's what he'd been afraid of this entire time. Because he did want more, but there was no way he'd take it.

Right now, this was all they could have. And he was going to relish every single moment.

Zach backed her up against the narrow wall between the door and the window. "Don't say I didn't warn you."

Capturing her mouth like a man starved for a taste of perfection, Zach aligned his body with hers. Sophie's hands slid up his arms to grip his shoulders as she opened for him.

Nothing else existed in his world. Sophie in his arms, in his home, was all he needed. How could every single thing in life be absolutely perfect when she was with him? How did all the anxiety and worry just fade to nothing with this vibrant woman in his arms?

As much as his body ached for her, as much as he needed her, Zach knew this was a night he didn't want to forget, and he sure as hell wasn't going to rush. Sophie deserved more. They deserved more.

When he pulled his mouth away, she let out a moan in protest. Without a word, he lifted her into his arms, a move he'd never made before because there seriously wasn't a romantic bone in his body. But holding Sophie like this seemed . . . right. That word seemed to keep popping up in his mind. He couldn't think of that now. He refused to let anything else take up space in his mind other than Sophie and the fact that he was carrying her to his bedroom.

As he started up the steps, she laid her head on his shoulder. "You don't have to carry me."

Zach froze on the second step. Yes. He did. "I know you can walk, but I know you also hurt more at the end of the day. Let me do this."

Lifting her hand to his jaw, she stroked her fingertips along his coarse beard. "Do whatever you want."

Zach closed his eyes and willed his self-control not to snap. Did she have a clue what her soft tone, her trusting words did to him? Did she have any idea how sexy it was that she'd humbled herself and put her fears aside, coming to him with her eyes wide-open?

With his heart pounding a bruising rhythm in his chest, Zach continued up the steps toward his master bedroom. Had he even picked up the dirty clothes lying around? Not that anything could be done about it now, and he honestly didn't care about his underwear on the floor, but . . .

Damn it. He was overthinking again. He had the woman of his dreams in his arms and his thoughts had drifted to laundry? He needed to get a grip before he totally screwed this up.

Sophie's fingertips continued to stroke his beard. Just that slight tingling sensation shot waves of pleasure through him. He wanted those delicate hands on his body. He wanted them there now.

"You're trembling," she muttered.

He hadn't even realized.

"It's me, Zach." Her gentle hand went to the side of his neck. "Don't hold back, don't treat me like I'll break. I'm here for you, your needs. Because fulfilling those will fulfill mine."

How did she have all the right words, all the comforting words, when he had a jumbled mess in his head? He couldn't even form a coherent thought because he was so damn scared right now. This had to be perfect for her. How could he not treat her like she'd break? Hadn't he nearly broken her before? He was a shattered man and she still wanted him.

Zach entered his room and winced at the disaster. "I, uh, wasn't expecting company."

Gently he put her on her feet and she laughed. "I grew up around you guys," she said, taking in the unmade bed and random clothes in piles. "I'm used to a little chaos."

Sophie was in his bedroom. He couldn't wrap his mind around it.

"This is it," he told her. "Your last chance to back out."

Smile wide, she shook her head. "You think I came this far, waited all this time for you, just to leave?"

Zach slid his hands around her waist, his pinkies sliding under the waistband of her skirt to encounter smooth, warm skin. "I'm barely hanging on here, Soph," he muttered as he rested his forehead against hers. "I want to do this right, but I'm about to snap."

Sophie shoved her hands beneath his shirt and started yanking it up. "I've been wanting you to snap for years. Don't make me wait any longer."

With her bold declaration, he helped her to jerk the shirt over his head and throw it onto a pile of other discarded clothes. When her hands went to the button on his jeans, he stopped her.

"I'll do this part."

The last thing he needed was for her to touch him there right now. He wasn't joking when he told her he was hanging on by a thread.

Sophie slid out of her cardigan, sending it silently to the floor. When she reached for the hem of her silk tank, Zach gripped the material.

"I'll do that too." No way was he going to miss an opportunity to undress Sophie.

He removed her hands from her tank and glided the flimsy material up and over her head. Zach swallowed at the sight of her standing there in a pale pink bra and her skirt. She was everything his fantasies were made of, and so much more that he didn't know he'd been missing.

"Stop thinking here, Zach." She smiled and stepped out of her flats. "The way you keep stopping is making me nervous."

Control snapped as he wrapped his arms around her and pulled her flush against his chest. She arched her back, and Zach kissed a path down the column of her throat. Her hands fisted in his hair as she threw her head back. With a skilled move, Zach flicked her bra open and quickly removed it without taking his lips off her heated, silky skin.

This was the moment he'd been craving. Her chest against his with no barriers. Zach's hands roamed all over her, and in the process he found the tiny side zipper on her skirt and got rid of that problem fast. By the time he got her fully undressed, he was beyond the point of no return.

Sophie did her own exploring over his bare chest, and her touch was anything but gentle. This woman knew what she wanted, which just bumped her up another notch on the scale of sexy . . . as if she needed a boost.

Zach made quick work of his jeans, shucking those and his boxer briefs to the floor. Stepping out of them, he hoisted Sophie up, her legs instinctively wrapping around his waist, her arms around his neck.

"Tell me if I hurt you."

Sophie kissed him. "You'd never hurt me."

Now wasn't the time to start that debate. He followed her down onto the bed, resting his hands on either side of her head.

He couldn't get enough. He couldn't touch her, taste her, or explore her enough to satisfy this craving he'd had for so long. He wanted to take everything in all at once, but savor each second at the same time.

He rained kisses over her shoulders, her breasts, down her abdomen . . . where he encountered scarring.

He'd not noticed moments ago when he'd fully undressed her because he'd been kissing her. But now, up close, he couldn't ignore the sight before him.

"Don't," she told him, coming up on her elbows. "They're in the past and we aren't. We're right here, right now, so don't go back there."

Swallowing, Zach forced himself to remain in the present. He had to do this, for Sophie. Later, when he was alone, he could torture himself with what he'd done to her. His careless, ego-inflated actions had left her physically and emotionally scarred.

"I know they're ugly," she went on. "I hope that—"

Zach placed a finger over her lips. "They're not ugly. Nothing about you is ugly."

It was damn hard not to relive that night right now, but he wouldn't bring that nightmare into the bed with them. Zach traced the surgical scars across the skin below her belly button, then moved to the puckered scar along her hip. After he'd fully committed them to memory, he kissed each one.

Too many emotions pulled him in different directions. He could easily be overtaken by any of them, but he refused to allow hurt and guilt to steal this moment. Sophie was naked and trembling beneath him—nothing else mattered.

Crawling back up her body, Zach settled between her legs and captured her mouth. His hand trailed down her side, her body trembling beneath his touch. He loved the feel of her beneath him, loved knowing his sheets would smell like her long after she was gone.

When he reached for the bedside drawer, she gripped his shoulders. "No."

Zach froze. "No?"

"If you're clean, I know I am," she told him, her gaze darting away as if this was uncomfortable for her to discuss. "I've only been with two guys and that was years ago. I've had physicals since then. There's no risk of me getting pregnant, either."

So she was on birth control, yet hadn't been intimate with anyone? That she hadn't slept with Martin shouldn't have thrilled Zach as much as it did, but he couldn't help it. He was human and he was a jealous bastard.

"Unless you're not sure," she added as she brought those wide eyes back to focus on him.

Making love to the woman he'd wanted for years with nothing in between? He'd be a fool to turn this away.

"Look at me," he demanded a moment before he joined them.

Words didn't even describe this euphoric state. Everything he'd ever fantasized about was absolutely nothing in comparison.

Kissing Sophie, having her moving in unison with him, was everything he'd ever wanted and everything he didn't deserve to have.

"Stay with me," she murmured against his lips. "Just us, Zach."

Pressing his lips to that tender spot below her ear, Zach concentrated on Sophie. His Sophie. His everything. Her fingertips dug into his shoulders as her back arched. Her body sliding beneath his, on his bed, was every single fantasy come to life.

Sophie's soft pants and moans nearly undid him, but he held her, made love to her, and focused on her needs.

He didn't know who was comforting who here. He had no idea if she was rescuing him from the ugliness that consumed him from within, or if he was giving her something she'd wanted from him for so long . . .

There was just too much to think about, and all he wanted was to get lost in her touch, her soft cries, her body wrapped all around him.

Just as Sophie's body tightened and she cried out, Zach followed her over the edge. He trembled against her, forced himself to keep his eyes locked onto hers, and staring back at him was one emotion he feared would enter this scenario . . . love.

But more than being afraid of her loving him, Zach was terrified she saw the same thing staring back at her.

Flowers. He was surrounded by a field of flowers.

Zach shifted beneath his sheets, pulling in a deep breath of that familiar scent. Sophie. He wasn't surrounded by flowers, he was surrounded by all woman.

The bed shifted and her hair tickled his bare shoulder. Just the slightest touch had him smiling. But he didn't open his eyes. He didn't want to be removed from this moment, didn't want to face the reality that their night was over.

Zach eased closer, reaching out and encountering . . . more hair?

His eyes flew open and Sophie wasn't in his bed. A sleeping, furry Lab was.

Seriously? What the hell was the mama dog doing in his bed? Where was Sophie?

He glanced around, not seeing any of her clothes, but his eyes landed on the dog bed and the puppies. Sleeping puppies.

Confusion hit him hard as he rubbed a hand down his face and glanced at the clock on his nightstand. No wonder he'd slept so well. Between the sex and the lack of barking, he'd caught up on some much needed sleep, but where was Sophie and why were all of these dogs in his bedroom?

Having Sophie in his bed had been beyond amazing, but he'd never expected to wake to canines.

Had she left? She'd obviously put the dogs in here because that dog bed didn't climb the stairs. Why had she done that? There was no way he was going to start letting these dogs sleep in his room. They could stay in the laundry room where they . . .

Zach eyed the pups, all curled and intertwined with each other, sound asleep. Okay, so maybe they didn't like the utility room. There had to be another option. He wasn't a dog person.

Yet here he was waking up to eight dogs after he'd spent the night with an amazing woman. Here he was keeping these puppies until they were ready to be adopted out. He'd brought them in when he could've left them out.

Okay, fine. He was a dog person. Who knew animals could reach into your heart so quickly and fill areas you never knew were empty?

Glancing back to the Lab in his bed, Zach laughed. Yeah, seriously not how he envisioned waking up today.

Zach showered and threw on clothes to head over to the Sunset Lake property. When he came back into his room, the pups were awake and the mom was sitting beside them as if to try to keep some type of control. She glanced at him and just stared.

"Hey, I'm new to this too," he told her, then shook his head. "And now I'm having a conversation with you like it's perfectly normal."

Definitely a dog person.

After letting them out, feeding them, and giving them fresh water, he put them back in the utility room and arranged the gate back in place. The room was big enough for the pups to play in and he'd made it a point to stop back home every couple hours or so to let them out to run a bit.

Another reason he needed to find a home for them

as soon as they were old enough to be adopted. He was losing time on projects by rushing home for bathroom breaks.

As Zach climbed into his truck, he knew his biggest issue wasn't the dogs. Was he ready to face what had happened last night? Was he prepared to see Sophie and pretend everything was as before? Because as much as she'd said she wasn't getting any more involved than physical intimacy, he doubted she felt the same this morning.

Sophie was loyal, she was loving, and she was completely open with her heart. There was no way she could go into this so casually. Hell, he wasn't so sure he could. Not with Sophie. Not with the only woman who'd ever truly mattered.

By the time he made it to the Sunset Lake house, he was even more confused and anxious than ever. On one hand he'd been relieved she'd called him on his feelings and had come to his house. But she'd left him in his bed and not said a word. Why? Was she afraid of what he'd say? Was she regretting her actions?

Zach gripped the steering wheel as he stared up at the house. He prayed she didn't regret what they shared, because even as unsure as he was this morning, he knew one thing for certain. He didn't regret what had happened in his bed. She was absolutely everything he'd ever wanted, and for a brief time, she was his.

Zach's cell vibrated on the seat beside him. Liam's name lit up the screen.

"Yeah," Zach answered.

"I'm heading into town in a couple of days. The restaurant is closing all next week for renovations before the summer crowd hits. Figure out what you need me to do and I'll help. None of that spa shit, though."

Zach couldn't help but smile. That actually felt good, especially when talking to Liam.

"And here Braxton and I wanted you researching chemical peels."

"Chemical what?" Liam sighed, muttered a curse. "Do you have some cabinets to bust out or flooring I can haul away? That's more my speed."

"You sure you don't want to work on the cucumber sandwiches?" Zach teased.

"Kiss my ass. You're only hurting yourself if you don't put me to use while I have the free time. Just wanted to give you a heads-up."

Zach appreciated the gesture. He knew it took a lot for Liam to call him and offer, but Liam had a stake in this as well now. Not to mention they both loved and missed Chelsea. Everything they did came down to her and what she would've wanted them to do . . . as a team.

"Do you want to stay at the house?" Zach asked before he could think better of it. Maybe that was pushing the comfort zone for both of them. "You don't have to, I was just offering."

Silence filled the line. Zach continued to stare at the second-story windows when he thought he saw a shadow pass in front of a window. But as soon as he thought it, there was nothing there. Must be the early morning sun hitting just right.

"I'll probably stay at Braxton's," Liam replied.

Zach didn't expect him to say any different, but he'd had a bit of hope in those few seconds of silence. Maybe hoping for closure or even attempting to bridge this gap was too much to expect. Years of anger and holding grudges weren't going to go away so easily . . . if ever.

"I've got to get back to work," Liam told him. "See you in a couple days."

Zach clutched the phone long after Liam hung up. Maybe one day his brother would forgive him for ruining his life. Maybe one day Liam would find happiness and not feel the need to hide behind his fear.

But who was Zach to offer advice to anyone on how to recover? He was still a jumbled mess. A year in prison hadn't done anything but give him time to think about how angry he was at himself, how things could've been so much worse and he could've killed two of the people he loved.

They'd all survived, and each day they pushed forward in their own ways. Not surprisingly, though, Sophie had emerged as the strongest. She seemed to be the only one of the three with her head on straight, able to come to terms with the past.

Which circled him back around to last night. Was she truly only looking for more? Did she not want anything else?

Part of him wished that to be the case, but the other part of him hated knowing he may never be with Sophie again. He'd thought for sure once he let her in, he'd be able to move on. He'd been lying to himself, because now that he and Sophie had been as physically intimate as they could be, he wanted more. And damn, if that didn't just confuse him even more.

# Chapter Fourteen

"Yes, Martin, I understand."

Sophie sat in her car, head back against the headrest, and gritted her teeth. She hadn't looked forward to calling Martin, but she'd had no choice. Her assistant was back from an extended vacation and apparently there was an offer on a city building that Sophie had been trying to sell. The buyer had questions that Sophie needed answers to—answers her ex could provide.

"I'm just asking if the building were to be purchased and turned into apartments, would the buyer be responsible for all the safety codes, or would the city help, since the building is an historical one?"

"Who's the buyer?" he asked.

Rolling her eyes, Sophie brought her hand to her forehead to try to rub away the tension headache. She'd not slept well after her night with Zach.

Her night with Zach. As if a life-altering experience could be summed up in such a simple way. As if having your entire world flipped upside down by the man you were completely in love with could be simplified and contained into just one night . . . not possible. And now more than ever she knew she loved him, and damn, if that didn't complicate her whole "this doesn't have to be more" speech.

Even though she'd run home and showered, Sophie could still smell him on her skin. Her body still tingled where he'd touched, and he'd touched her everywhere.

"Sophie," Martin growled. "Are you still there?"

*Unfortunately.* "It doesn't matter who the buyer is, Martin. They have made a generous offer and personally I think turning the building into apartments will be a smart move for the city. I also think you all should help if the coding needs a major overhaul."

"Not if it's a slum lord buying them."

*Oh, for pity's sake.* Sophie grabbed her purse and stepped from her car. Her hip was a bit more tender than usual today, but she'd take the extra pain considering the amazing night she'd had.

"I assure you, it's not a slum lord." She stepped into her office, waving at Tasha, who greeted Sophie with a smile. "I need your answer by the end of the day."

Without waiting on him to ask another ridiculous question, Sophie disconnected the call and sank onto the cushioned bench with scrolled arms that sat against the wall opposite Tasha's desk.

"I'm sorry." Her assistant wrinkled her nose. "I didn't know you two had broken up or I would've just called and gotten the information myself. I just assumed you'd get it faster than me."

Waving a hand, Sophie propped her purse on the bench beside her. "It's okay. A lot happened while you were away."

How could things be summed up so easily? Lately her life had been anything but easy. Frustrating, thrilling, worrisome . . . so many emotions to really nail it down to one.

"Well, I'll try to stay on top of things now that I'm back."

Sophie smiled. "You're all tan. I assume the weather was nice?"

"I didn't want to leave." Tasha eased forward on her desk and clasped her hands. "But I don't want to talk about my family vacation. You look exhausted but happy, and you're not with Martin. What's up?"

Exhausted? Yes. Happy? Deliriously so.

The dogs had started barking just as Zach had drifted off to sleep. Sophie wanted him to rest; the man deserved it. So she brought the dogs up to his room, hoping they'd be happy if they were with their "master." That plan had worked, but left no room for her in the bed.

Okay, that was an excuse. She was terrified of sliding back between those sheets and nestling in next to Zach's hard, lean body. She had to distance herself emotionally. Being with Zach was more than she'd ever hoped for, but she'd promised him only physical, and she was going to keep her promise.

"You're looking pretty content," Tasha said with a tilt of her head and a smile. Her pretty blue eyes crinkled at the corners. "You've met someone new?"

Tasha knew everything about Sophie's life, from the overbearing, controlling parents to the accident that left her scarred. Though she didn't know about the infertility caused by the accident, and Sophie wasn't going to let her in on her relationship with Zach, either. Zach was her secret, tucked safely away in that special place in her heart.

"I've just had my eyes opened," Sophie explained. "Martin wasn't for me, and now that I'm single again, I'm just really enjoying myself."

Thoroughly enjoying herself.

"I think there's more," Tasha said with a knowing grin. "But since I'm swamped this morning, I'll let you off the hook. You have a message from a doctor who's moving into the area and he's looking for a two-story home with charm. His wife is pregnant, so they want a yard. I left all the specifics in a note on your desk and I told him you'd be getting back to him today."

Sophie nodded, grabbing her bag and coming to her feet. "I'll see what all we have available to show him."

"I looked through our current listings." Tasha turned her attention back to her computer screen and started scrolling through. "Really, all I see is the old Marsh house on Campbell Avenue, but it needs a lot of work. I didn't get the impression the doctor wanted a fixer-upper."

Sophie knew of a place that wasn't in need of any renovations. She'd spent the most amazing night of her life there.

"I'll see what I can come up with," Sophie replied. "I'll be in my office."

Closing herself off from the world was best right now. Sophie wasn't sure she could handle dealing with people just yet. She was still trying to process how her entire life had changed after last night. She'd known there was a risk going to Zach. There was a risk in being rejected, there was a risk in getting intimate. No matter what she'd decided to do, her life would've changed.

And it had. Mercy, had her life ever changed. Now she knew for a fact just how perfect they were together, just how vulnerable he was and how much they needed each other. Still, he'd throw that past of his up again as a barrier if she let him . . . she didn't intend to allow him that out. He could face what was happening while they were in that bed together, and there was no way he could deny how fierce and even more intense their relationship had become.

Sophie hung her purse on the hook beside her door and crossed the room to the window overlooking a small pond. The town had installed a fountain in the middle of it a few years ago, complete with a few ducks swimming around, and added picnic tables around the perimeter for the local businesses. She didn't get much time to enjoy the area, but she loved the view and would often find it calming.

Not so much right now. She wasn't calm. If she were being honest with herself, she was confused. Her wants were pulling her in all directions. No, her wants were all pointing in the same direction. It was her wants versus her common sense that were currently at odds.

A little row of yellow ducks followed their mommy in the pond. Sophie smiled at the picturesque sight. Working today was going to be quite challenging when her mind was still on the last twelve hours of her life and the man who occupied her every thought.

She'd not even left him a note. She'd been so worried about him sleeping, and getting out without waking him, she'd forgotten. Was he angry when he woke? Was he relieved he didn't have to face her?

Sophie wrapped her arms around her waist. Did he have regrets? Please, please, please, she prayed he didn't. As much as she wanted more—she wanted everything, actually—she couldn't regret the most perfect night of her life and she truly hoped he felt the same.

She'd known Zach would be a tender lover, but she hadn't realized just how emotionally broken he was. He'd done everything for her, cared for her and pleasured her. He'd had a controlling, dominating, sexy way about him, but at the same time she'd sensed his inner battle.

Turning her attention to her desk, Sophie decided she was useless today. After all that had happened, she needed to talk to Zach. She needed to keep the upper hand over her emotions and clear the air. The last thing they needed was a new level of awkwardness to settle between them. They had a long journey ahead with Chelsea's project, and they couldn't afford to be overrun by their past, or sex.

The door to the main office chimed, but Sophie knew Tasha would handle anyone who came in. On a sigh, she tried to wrap her mind around what she needed to do. Talking with Zach was first and foremost.

The door to her office opened and shut. Before Sophie turned, she knew who stood behind her and it wasn't Tasha. The air in her office seemed to thicken, hum even. Sophie's quickened heartbeat told her all she needed to know.

"You left without saying good-bye."

Nerves had no place here. What was there to be nervous about at this point? Zach had literally seen her at her best, her worst, and now intimately. She had nothing left to hide.

Turning, she forced herself to remain calm. But seeing Zach after knowing just how quickly he could turn her entire world into something of a fantasy . . .

"You not only left," he said, stalking his way across the room, his gaze locked onto hers. "You left me with a bundle of fur in my bed."

Sophie couldn't help but smile at the image of Zach waking up to a dog in his bed. Sensing he wasn't too angry, she didn't try to hide her laughter.

"I'm sorry." She kept her arms crossed in a piddly attempt to control her giggles. "I was trying to help. You'd just fallen asleep and I heard the dogs, so I tried to think of something to calm them."

He kept inching closer. As the gap between them grew shorter and shorter, Sophie's words started coming out faster and faster.

"I remember when I was a little girl and we had a dog, I would sneak her to my room and she'd sleep better." Now she had to look up at him, he stood so, so close. "My mom would scold me in the mornings, but it was worth it."

Zach slid a hand along her cheek.

"I thought maybe if they were close to you . . ." His other hand settled on the other side of her face. "Wh-what are you doing?"

"What I would've done had you been in my bed when I woke up." His lips hovered over hers, barely caressing her. "Just because we agreed on nothing more, doesn't mean I won't take advantage of touching you, kissing you when I want."

He consumed her as he leaned into her, holding her face just at the right angle to deliver the most impressive morning kiss she'd ever received. That hard body leaning against hers, backing her up a step until her back hit the window.

Zach lifted his head, his heavy-lidded eyes zeroing in on her mouth. "Don't leave my bed again."

Sophie gripped the windowsill. "I'm not going to be in your bed again. We agreed we wouldn't look beyond last night, so that was another reason I left. I was saving us both the awkward morning after."

He brushed his lips over hers once more. "Does this feel awkward?"

A tremble rippled through her. "No," she whispered.

"Do you want to stay away from my bed?"

She was in over her head here. "I-I should."

Gripping her face, Zach tilted her head up so she looked him directly in the eyes. "You won't."

She could hardly think for the way he was plastered so beautifully and perfectly against her. She shouldn't sleep with him again. Once was enough to ruin her, because she was positive she could never, ever have sex with another man. How could she? She'd waited years to be with Zach, and he didn't disappoint. He fulfilled every fantasy and then some. She'd become emotionally attached when she promised herself she wouldn't.

Sophie pulled from his grasp and stepped away. Holding a hand to her tingling lips, she paced. How had this spiraled so far out of her control? Last night when she'd stood on his porch, she'd felt so confident and full of power. But the second he opened that door looking all angry and rumpled, she'd started losing the fight. The tight grip she'd had on control started sliding away.

And now here she stood in her office, wanting nothing more than to take him up on his offer, but knowing if she did, she'd inevitably have heartache and even more hurt in the end.

"I can't be with you again." She kept her back to him. If she had to turn and face him, she didn't know if she could be strong enough. "I promised you that I wouldn't want more, that we just needed to keep this simple. If I'm with you again, I won't be able to keep that promise."

She had to stick with honesty here. Zach knew how she felt, he had to understand. She couldn't afford for him not to, because if he opted to fight her on this . . . she'd lose.

"So what do you want?" he asked from behind her. "Are we back to friends? Were we friends before last night? I'm not asking for a label, but I want to know my boundaries. I said no relationships, but I can't ignore the sex."

After taking a deep breath, Sophie turned and smoothed her hands down her bright red pencil skirt. "We're working on Chelsea's house. I'm going to try to sell your house. We aren't having sex. Well, not anymore."

A corner of Zach's mouth tipped up beneath his beard. He nodded as he crossed his arms over a most impressive broad chest. A chest she could still feel against her own.

No. She wasn't allowed to still be feeling him. She wanted absolutely everything, but if she didn't let him go now, she worried one of them would get hurt . . . quite possibly both of them. He was adamant he wasn't looking for more.

"I think that simplifies things," he told her. "So, does that mean no kissing either? Because I have to tell you, you're one hell of a kisser."

"Definitely no kissing."

Kissing Zach was a stepping-stone to sex. Some men kissed with their mouths; Zach poured his entire body into a kiss.

"I'll respect whatever you want," he stated with a brief nod. "That doesn't mean I have to like it."

Yeah, well, she didn't like her own rules, but they

were necessary boundaries. She had to keep both of them safe.

"I may have someone who is interested in your house."

Zach's brows lifted. "We go from sex to you selling my house? You haven't had it appraised yet."

"No," she agreed as she moved to her desk to lift the note Tasha had left. "There's a doctor moving to the area and his specifications match closely to your house. But I haven't called him because I wanted to talk to you. I want to make sure you are one hundred percent on board with this."

His chest expanded as he pulled in a deep breath, blowing it out slowly. "I don't really have a choice. This is moving faster than I thought."

Those dark eyes darted around the room as he rubbed his palm over his beard. She could practically see the wheels turning, but she didn't want him stressing over this.

"Nothing is done, Zach. He hasn't seen the place and a price hasn't even been mentioned. Don't start worrying just yet."

"I could store my things at the resort house," he murmured, "until I find somewhere else. No storage fee that way."

"You can store some stuff at my place too," she offered. "Or Braxton's. I'm sure he wouldn't mind."

Zach brought his gaze back to her. She hated that look of regret that passed through his eyes. Without a doubt, Sophie knew he didn't want to sell and was only doing so for Chelsea. What would Chelsea have wanted? Would she be on board with Zach selling their home to pay for a dream?

"Just think about all of this." Against her better judgment, she reached out and placed a hand on his tense forearm. "Nobody will think anything of it if you opt not to sell. We can find another way to get funding. I have some ideas."

One dark, thick brow quirked. "You're thinking of going to the historical society, aren't you?"

Sophie removed her hand. The last thing she needed to be doing was touching him. Wanting him was already an issue; she didn't need to make things worse. Besides, Zach was under pressure, and the last thing he needed was added stress from personal issues.

"There are grants that we could apply for. They take time, but I can start on the research tonight and we can see what's available."

Ideas started spinning around in her head. Too many ideas, ideas that could take up the bulk of her work time, but she couldn't let Zach or his brothers go through this alone. Chelsea would want Sophie to continue helping, and family came first. Always.

"I can still have your house appraised," she added. "We can get the ball rolling in two areas so we have a plan B. I won't put your house on the market or advertise it until you give me the official go-ahead."

"How much do you know about grant funding?" he asked.

Sophie went to her computer, booted it up, and took a seat. "I researched it before, but not for a small business and not for a home that had so much historical value."

Her fingers flew across the keys, hesitating when his hand rested on the back of her chair. His other hand came to rest on her desk beside the keyboard. Great, now he was looming over her. How could she concentrate? He smelled so, so good. If she turned just so, she could probably . . .

*No. Focus, Sophie. Focus.*

She found a few sites that would help them in their search. As she was filling out information for one of them, her cell rang. Both she and Zach glanced at the screen. Her mother.

Sophie waved a hand. "I'll get it later."

"She wouldn't like you helping us."

Turning slightly, Sophie looked him in the eye. "I slept with you last night. I'm pretty sure my looking up grants is the least of her worries."

She couldn't help but smile when Zach's jaw nearly dropped.

"Besides," she went on, focusing back on her computer. "What I'm doing is none of her business."

Suddenly, her chair spun around and she was hauled up against Zach's hard chest, his hands gripping her arms in that powerful, controlled manner he had.

"I like this Sophie," he told her, his eyes blazing into hers. "I like the confident, take-charge woman. Maybe I can convince her to come by my house again later."

He knew all the right words. As if she hadn't had feelings for him for years, the man knew exactly what to say to cause the most impact on her girly emotions that were all over the place.

"Zach," she protested, though her body leaned into his further. "You know this would go nowhere. You've said it yourself. I would want more, you wouldn't, and one or both of us would end up hurt."

Zach rested his forehead against hers. "If I could give myself to anyone, Soph, it would be you."

Those raw words said on a strangled breath had her nearly choking on those emotions she'd tried so hard to keep hidden. Just as her eyes closed to shield the unshed tears, her phone rang again.

Placing a kiss on her forehead, he murmured, "I'm heading to the house. You take that call."

He walked out of her office, leaving her alone with her jumbled thoughts and her ringing phone. How could he drop a bomb like that and walk away?

Sophie sank back down into her chair, ignored her phone, and cradled her face in her hands. Whatever haunted Zach's past was interfering with the progress she'd made with him. Would he open up to her? Would he let her in? Sophie didn't think he was distancing himself because of the accident; if that were the case, he wouldn't have taken her to his bed.

Something had damaged Zach so deep, he was afraid to take risks, afraid to let himself go and believe in the possibility of . . . love? Yes, love.

Sophie patted her damp cheeks and reached for her phone. That was two calls she'd missed from her mother. She'd have to call her back or the woman would have the entire police department on the hunt.

But first Sophie needed to get control of herself, because Zach was right. Her mother wouldn't like Sophie getting this chummy with the Monroe boys now that Chelsea was gone. Her mother had tolerated, barely, Chelsea's free-spirited behavior, but the polished woman loathed the Monroe men because they were a rowdy bunch.

Granted, they'd had their days, but they were upstanding citizens now. Of course her mother still saw them as hellions and teens, but Sophie knew the truth. She knew those men were more loyal than anyone she'd ever known. They were damaged on the inside and didn't get too close to people, and they might bicker and occasionally throw a punch at each other, but they loved each other deeper than any set of siblings she'd ever seen, blood-related or not.

Now Sophie had to figure out how to save Zach's home, get money for Chelsea's dream, spend an exorbitant amount of time with him to get this project off the ground, and try to keep her heart out of the mix.

She dropped her head back against the seat on a groan. How could she keep her heart out of the mix when he'd stolen it ten years ago?

# Chapter Fifteen

"What's happening in that room?" Zach asked, sure he'd heard wrong.

Braxton removed his glasses and pointed to the laptop screen. "The room for the hot-rock massage."

Zach stared at the screen. Some woman who appeared to be nude, save for the white towel across her backside, had large, black stones going down the length of her spine. What the hell had he gotten into?

"How do you know about this?" Zach asked. "No, wait. I don't want to know what you do in your off time."

Braxton flipped him the finger and shut his laptop. "I've been researching different spas and resorts. There are certain things that are a must-have for this to work right. Women eat this shit up."

Zach had to start thinking like that or this business would tank. But how the hell did he think about hot stones on bare skin? How was that relaxing? People paid for the most ridiculous things.

As a young boy, he'd feared if his next meal would come, or if his mom would be alert enough to even care he was still alive. Dirty, smelly apartments, random men filtering in and out, always on the move from one filthy place to another was Zach's childhood. He hadn't kept toys because he never knew when they'd have to gather their meager belongings and go somewhere else. Secretly he'd wished she'd just go off on her own and leave him. He figured he couldn't be any worse off on his own than with a mother who paid him no mind except when she needed him to do something for her, like steal a loaf of bread. She claimed nobody would look twice at a kid and think he was stealing. He'd actually gotten pretty good at swiping groceries. While other kids were playing baseball and going to the movies, he was trying to figure out how to stuff a jar of peanut butter in his jacket.

Now he was renovating a mansion to open a women-only resort and spa. Talk about making a complete one-eighty.

"I'm not that far in my thoughts, yet." Zach came to his feet and headed back to the bathroom they were working on. "I've ordered the tile for all of the bathrooms and it should be here by tomorrow. I'm doing heated floors in all of them as well."

"Don't go overboard until we have more funding," Braxton warned, following him down the wide hallway. "When is the house going up for sale?"

Zach stopped at the bathroom doorway. He'd not mentioned anything to Braxton or Liam about Sophie's plan. When he thought of her idea, his mind instantly went to her office yesterday morning, when he'd exposed too much of his heart. Why had he told her something so intimate? He never wanted her to know how much he wanted her. He couldn't afford for anyone to have such leverage over him.

"Actually, Sophie is trying to get us some grants."

Braxton's brows lifted. "I hadn't thought of that,"

he muttered, shaking his head. "I guess with losing Chelsea, trying to get the taxes paid, and figuring out what the hell we were doing, the obvious just slipped my mind."

"I think we've all had our minds on other things lately."

Braxton smirked. "Like a certain real estate agent?"

Zach moved into the bathroom and ran his hand over the drywall mud where he'd finished the edge of the partial wall he'd taken out. To this day, too many walls made him antsy. The confining spaces, the enclosed areas once made his anxiety run high. He wasn't near as bad now, but he still preferred the open spaces.

"Your silence only makes you look guilty," Braxton commented.

"I've been found guilty before."

Braxton muttered a curse. "You know that's not how I meant that."

Zach shrugged. "I'm not offended. But I'm not discussing Sophie."

Braxton laughed. "You don't have to. She's standing right here."

Jerking around, Zach spotted Sophie, her face tinted pink as if she'd heard a bit of the innocent conversation. They'd said nothing wrong or demeaning about her, not that he ever would, but that she was a topic at all would only make this harder on her. And even though he couldn't give her what she wanted, he didn't want her embarrassed.

Damn it. Why couldn't they just enjoy each other, as both friends and lovers, and not worry about the rest?

Because Sophie was the type of woman who would want a house with a devoted husband without a criminal record, and a yard full of screaming, happy kids.

She would want church on Sunday, family vacations to the beach, and hot chocolate by the Christmas tree.

Zach swallowed as he met her beautiful, bright eyes. One day she would fall in love, and Zach would have no right to stand in the way of her happiness. Isn't that why he kept his distance? Well, other than last night.

"Am I interrupting?" she asked, looking at the two brothers.

"Not at all." Braxton smiled and wrapped an arm around her shoulders. "I hear you're looking into some grants?"

"Actually, that's why I'm here." She pulled up her phone and started scrolling through, her eyes squinting slightly at the screen. "There's a good chance we can get all we need from this one outlet."

Zach moved closer, wanting to see more, because if he could get what they needed to renovate this house, then he could keep his own. Could life be that simple? Could things be going his way?

A dull *thud* sounded from overhead.

"What was that?" Braxton asked, glancing toward the high ceiling.

Zach shook his head. "Not sure. I've heard a few things when I'm alone working. I figure it's the old house settling. I'll go up and check. Who knows, maybe another stray followed me."

Sophie laughed as he walked away. He loved hearing her laugh, loved seeing her smile. To know he caused either of those made his heart swell with an emotion he couldn't label because if he did, he'd have to admit that Sophie meant everything to him. Absolutely everything.

As he climbed the steps, he heard the murmured chatter of Braxton and Sophie, but he tried to focus on any sounds from above. The random noises were so few and far between, he'd assumed they were all due to the old house. But you never knew what you'd find in an abandoned house.

The second floor was actually in better shape than the first floor. Whoever had lived here last, and that was decades ago, hadn't bothered doing anything up here. Other than the thick layer of dust, grime, and the outdated decor, the second story wasn't terrible. Ugly, but workable.

Zach glanced into all of the six oversized bedrooms, the bathrooms, and even the large linen closet. Not a stray animal or a rodent to be found. Spiderwebs the size of a Volvo, but nothing that would cause a sound. Damn, he hated spiders, though.

When he went back down, Sophie and Braxton's heads were tipped in toward each other. They were talking in low tones and Zach hated the surge of jealousy that spread through him. Why was he jealous of Braxton? Sophie had never shown any interest in his brother that way.

But Braxton was that silent ladies' man. He was quiet, had that whole professor thing going for him, and women found brains sexy . . . didn't they? Braxton had a master's degree, he was an overachiever, and he probably polished his silverware for fun and put it all back in nice, neat order when he was finished.

Braxton was the type of man Sophie would end up with. Someone with a classy, honest job that required dress pants and a shirt with a collar. She would find a man who didn't come home from work with new holes in his already tattered jeans. She'd have a smile on her face and greet him at the door with a kiss.

Zach's hands fisted at his sides as he stepped off the last step and crossed the spacious room.

"You look pissed," Braxton stated. "What did you find?"

Reining himself back in, Zach shook his head and forced himself to relax. "Not a thing unless the spiders weaving those webs are bigger than we think." He shuddered at the thought.

Sophie slid her phone back into the pocket of her skirt. This one wasn't fitted like her others. This skirt stuck out from her body just enough to make her legs look even more appealing. Not that they weren't appealing in any state of dress . . . or undress.

"I was telling Braxton that I stayed up last night and filled out all the forms to apply for this grant."

The night before she'd been up most of the night too.

"You can't work yourself to death," Zach told her. "Tell Braxton what needs to be done. He's a nerd, he'd love to fill out forms."

Braxton's punch to his stomach caught Zach off guard, but he retaliated by turning slightly and sending an elbow straight into Braxton's abs.

"When you boys are finished, I have more to say."

Sophie's bored tone made him smile. Damn, she was even cuter when she didn't put up with his nonsense. She'd been around his family enough to know they oftentimes threw fists, elbows, whatever, and discussed after the fact.

"Just because I teach history and econ doesn't mean I'm a nerd," Braxton said, rubbing his stomach. "The ladies happen to find my intellectual side sexy."

Zach snorted. "Yeah, they're totally into you when you recite Chapter four of the ancient history textbook."

"Can we focus?" Sophie asked, her voice rising to

get their attention. "Some of us have another job to get to."

Zach cleared his throat. "Sorry, Soph. What were you saying?"

She stifled a yawn. "A rough estimate is thirty days, but I'm hoping to hear something sooner. All the paperwork is done and sent. Everything was electronic, so once I started I kind of just went with it. I really think we have a good shot at this because we meet all the criteria. Small town, new business that will generate income and boost our local economy, plus the house is over one hundred years old, so they want it preserved."

"So does this mean you're not selling?" Braxton asked Zach.

Sophie smiled. "It means he most likely won't have to. As much as I was looking forward to that commission, I'm keeping my fingers crossed that he doesn't sell."

Braxton picked Sophie up and spun her around. "This is awesome."

"Put her down."

*Damn it.* Zach hadn't meant to go all territorial, but he didn't want any other man's arms around his Sophie.

His Sophie. She wasn't his. She'd been his for a night and he'd let her in, knowing that he wouldn't give her what she deserved. He was a selfish prick, but he wouldn't have changed that night for anything.

"Looks like my brother is staking his claim," Braxton pretended to whisper to Sophie as he eased her back onto her feet with a loud kiss to her lips. He threw Zach a lopsided grin.

Sophie winced, but Braxton kept his arm around her as he jerked his attention back to her face. "You good?"

Hesitating a second too long, Zach stepped forward

and wrapped an arm around her waist. "Go sand that wall," he told Braxton. "I'll be back."

Braxton raised a brow as if to silently say *Told you so,* but Zach didn't care. He knew Sophie was exhausted and her hip was obviously giving her fits.

"I can walk," she informed him. "I just needed a second because I stepped wrong. That's all."

*That's all.* She had to deal with intermittent pain, and he couldn't ignore it or pretend everything was okay.

Once they reached the front door, he turned to face her, gripping her waist with both hands. He loved the feel of her beneath his touch. She might not come to his bed again, but that wouldn't stop him from touching her. He'd already passed over that friendship threshold, and he intended to take full advantage.

"Go home." Zach tipped his head down to look her in the eyes. "Get some rest."

A faint smile spread across her face. "I have work. I have a showing in an hour and a closing at the end of the day at the bank. I'm too busy, but your concern touches me. Sometimes I wonder how much you care."

He cared. More than he should.

Kissing her softly on her forehead, Zach stepped back, physically and emotionally. There was no other option.

"After you're off work, go home and rest. Don't worry about this place and don't worry about the grants. Everything will work out, but you working yourself to death won't help any of us."

A hint of a smile flitted around the corner of her lips. "You need me. Admit it."

If only she knew how much. He couldn't even fully wrap his mind around the extent to which he needed her.

"Liam's due here in a day or so," he told her. "So

we'll have all hands on deck for a while. You better rest up while you can."

When he turned to walk away, she called his name. He froze, glancing over his shoulder. The sight of her radiant smile had his breath catching in his throat, a bad tightening around his chest. Damn it. What was he going to do with all these feelings he had zero control over? He had no clue where to put them all, because dumping them on anyone was impossible.

"Thank you for doing this," she told him. "Chelsea would love seeing her brothers coming together and working as a team. I know a women's resort isn't your ideal project and the renovations are just the beginning, but . . . thanks."

He tried not to think too much beyond the renovations, because if he started focusing on chemical peels and hot stone whatevers, he'd run away and never look back.

Zach nodded and headed back toward the bathroom. He needed to make sure Sophie took care of herself, because she would put everything ahead of her own needs. She would do all she could for Chelsea's dream to come true; that's what made Sophie so special. She didn't care that her parents had frowned upon the Monroe kids, she didn't care that she had a prosperous business to keep running, and she didn't care that she would be working closely with a man she'd fallen in love with.

Zach stopped in the hallway and placed his hand on the wall. He needed support. She'd never come out and said she loved him, but he'd seen it in her eyes when they'd been in his bed. The woman couldn't mask her emotions. Now he just needed to figure out how to keep from hurting her . . . again.

But more so, he needed to figure out how to stop from falling in love with her.


Surprisingly, her hip wasn't killing her tonight. After the day she'd had, she'd managed to get through the showing, another unscheduled showing, and a closing, all without the accustomed annoyance.

Still, she was nearly crawling from sheer exhaustion by the time she pulled into her drive. When she spotted the familiar truck parked in her spot, her heart did a little flip. What was he doing here? She couldn't ignore the flutter of nerves in her belly . . . nerves she'd never experienced with any other man. Not that there had been many, but these nerves had Zach's name all over them. They always had.

She pulled in behind him and grabbed her bag. By the time she let herself in the back door, she was smiling. Somehow he'd let himself in, but she wasn't questioning or complaining because her house smelled amazing.

"I have no clue what you're making, but I've never been so happy to have a trespasser."

Turning from the stove, Zach held a wooden spoon in one hand and had some type of red sauce in his beard. Sophie laughed, hung her bag on the post by the back door, and crossed the tiled floor.

"Sampling the goods?" she asked, reaching up to swipe her finger over the coarse hair.

"What?" he asked, then spotted her finger. "Oh yeah. It's ready. Perfect timing."

She licked her finger and oh, mercy. The man could cook too? Did he have to be so imperfectly perfect? Couldn't his flaws be annoying? Instead, all his faults were either adorable, like the sauce in the beard, or heart-wrenching, like the prison he continued to keep himself in regarding his past.

Either way, the closer she got to him, the sexier he became.

"Hope you like spaghetti." He flicked a burner off and started looking through her cabinets. "It's really all I know really well."

Sophie reached beneath her center island and pulled out two plates, setting them on top of the granite. "As long as I don't have to make it, you could've made me a bologna sandwich."

Grabbing the plates, he started scooping up healthy portions. "Now you tell me."

Normally she had wine with pasta, or wine with anything really, but she wasn't about to pull out alcohol with Zach there. Not that he had a drinking problem. As far as she knew he hadn't touched the stuff since that night, or that's what Chelsea had once told her. But she wasn't going to be disrespectful.

"I made some tea yesterday," she told him, glancing through her fridge. "Does that work for you?"

"Fine."

By the time they sat on the bar stools at her island eating area, her exhaustion from the day had practically faded. With Zach in her kitchen, looking more at home than he should and playing the domestic king beautifully, she'd suddenly gotten her second wind.

"Your cat darted off as soon as I came in."

"He's not overly friendly. He'll come out when he wants me to feed him."

"I picked your lock." He forked up a hearty bite. "You need new locks, by the way. I got in way too easy."

"Haven isn't known for its high crime rate." She

spread her napkin out over her lap and picked up her fork and knife. "And if someone wants in to cook me dinner, I'm not going to make it more difficult."

She took a small bite, nearly groaning at the amazing flavor of the sauce. When Zach didn't have a snarky comeback, she glanced his way.

"What?" she asked after she'd swallowed.

Using his fork, he pointed to her lap and spoke around a mouthful of food. "Your manners are a bit different than mine."

She realized exactly what he meant. "Yeah, well, if you'd been reprimanded for having your elbows on the table or not properly using your utensils, you'd be brainwashed too."

Zach slid her napkin from her lap and tossed it on the counter. Then he reached over and took the knife from her grasp and set it aside as well.

"There. Now you can eat comfortably."

Sophie stared at him as he dug back into his dinner. "What if I get something on my skirt?"

"Take it off."

"And sit here in my underwear?"

He grunted as he chewed. Yeah, a bit different than dinners she was used to with other people. Even when she ate in front of her television, she still had her lap protected and her fork and knife. Years of being ingrained with the importance of table manners wasn't something she really thought about, she just ate the way she was taught.

"You're not eating," Zach stated, dropping his fork to his plate. "You don't like it, or are you not sure what to do now that I took away your manners?"

Intrigued, Sophie tipped her head. "Does that bother you? My manners?"

"No, but you're in your own home. Relax."

He went on to finish his plate and get a second helping. Sophie got through her meal without dropping a hunk of sauce onto her skirt. Now, had she been wearing white, she would've been wearing the sauce for sure.

She started to stack the plates, but Zach covered her hand with his. "Go and sit down. I'll do the dishes."

"You cook, you clean, you build houses." Sophie smiled. "What can't you do?"

He laughed. "I can't swim."

Sophie laughed, then realized he wasn't joking. "Seriously?"

Zach shook his head and gathered the dishes. "I probably could if my life depended on it, but before I came to live with the Monroes, I never went to a pool, so I just never had a desire by the time I came to live here."

"I'll teach you," she promised him. "And you won't even have to come to one of my classes, either."

"I'd best stay out of the pool."

Zach never talked about his time before the Monroes. Ever. At least not with her, and Chelsea had been pretty tight-lipped about it as well, so Sophie had never pushed. She couldn't help but wonder what made him so talkative tonight, or what had made him push his way into her home and make dinner. Not that she was upset about either, just curious.

She watched him move about her kitchen, cleaning and stacking dishes in the sink. No man had ever made her dinner, let alone in her own kitchen.

"You're still in here." Without turning around, he

ran a sink full of sudsy water. "Go into the living room and relax."

"What if I'm relaxed right here watching you?"

Throwing a slight grin over his shoulder, he shrugged. "You have a warped way of relaxing."

Not if her version included a sexy man doing domestic chores. She was relaxed and aroused . . . a lethal combo with Zach in the house.

"How are the pups?" she asked.

"Well, they like my room." He rinsed a pan and stacked it in the drying rack in the sink. "I talked to the vet earlier. She said she may have found a home for two of them when it's time, but I need the other five adopted out as well as the mom."

"Why don't you keep her?" Sophie suggested.

Zach drained the water, grabbed a towel, and wiped his hands before turning to face her. "And what would I do with a dog?"

Sophie shrugged. "Same thing you've been doing. Love her."

"Do I look like a dog person?"

Biting the inside of her cheek, Sophie still couldn't suppress the smile. "You looked like a dog person when you were cuddled up with her."

"Funny." He crossed to the island and leaned on his forearms. "Why don't you take a puppy?"

"Me?" She'd not really thought about it. "I wouldn't know what to do with it when I was at work."

"Take it with you," he suggested. "You've got that park across the street. You could take it on walks when you had a break. You know you want one."

That little one had cuddled against her neck when she'd carried it to his bedroom. Even his little puppy breath was adorable. But Flynn would not be happy. Granted, Flynn didn't socialize much with Sophie, so most likely her grouchy cat would ignore a dog too. For a while she could keep them separated while she was gone, just until they grew more accustomed to each other.

"You're considering it," Zach said with a smile. "Boy or girl? I've got both."

Sophie groaned and came to her feet. "You should've been a salesman. Give me a girl. I don't want a boy hiking all over my furniture."

Zach laughed. "And you think a female will hold her piss?"

"I don't know," she cried, throwing her arms up. "Just give me any of them. They're all adorable."

Zach sighed and glanced around the room. "I'm going to head home and let them out. I'll be sure to save you one when the time comes to find homes."

"You're leaving?" she asked, lifting her brows. "Why don't you stay for a bit?"

His heated gaze nearly sizzled her from across the center island. The man was that fast, that powerful . . . that potent. He could stop her with a look and have arousal shooting through her entire body.

"You afraid I can't keep my hands to myself?" she joked. "I promise to be on my best behavior."

"Yeah, well, I can't promise because my best behavior would still have you stripped in no time."

The veiled promises made her shiver.

"Seriously." She rested her palms on the granite top and leaned forward. "Just stay. I like talking with you, Zach. This has been good. We can even discuss the Sunset Lake property if that would be better. Just . . . don't go."

He held her gaze and said nothing. Finally he nodded. "We're discussing the property only."

Sophie wanted to jump off the stool and skip into the living room, but she felt that might be a bit overkill. Still, she felt as if she'd achieved some grand victory. This was such progress . . . Granted, they'd slept together, but they were making headway beyond physical. She wanted more though, and if all she could get was friendship and an evening of working on this project, she'd absolutely take it.

She led him to the living room and took a seat on her favorite oversized floral chair. The pattern was muted, but it was still an accent chair she'd fallen in love with at an estate sale. She couldn't wait to start finding rare gems for Chelsea's place. Her late friend wouldn't have wanted everything to come from a cookie-cutter store.

Zach sank onto the sofa and propped his feet on the coffee table, boots and all. Sophie smiled. Her mother would've absolutely died at the sight, but Sophie didn't care a bit. A home should be a place people were comfortable, and Sophie wanted Zach to feel comfortable here. She wanted him to come back, to let himself in, and think of her as a friend. If that's all she could get, she wasn't going to turn it away.

"So what's the overall plan," she asked, curling her feet up in the chair beside her. Smoothing her skirt down her thighs, she didn't miss where Zach's eyes had gone. "Do you have a goal in mind when you want to be finished, or are you thinking that far ahead yet?"

Zach sighed and tipped his head back. "I know when I'd like to be done, but I'm not sure it will happen. I'd love to be ready to go with the business by fall so we can work on Christmas specials or gift certificates."

Sophie smiled, rested her elbow on the arm of the chair, and propped her chin on her fist. "Sounds like a true businessman already working. But I agree. If you can get some buzz going and you're up and running before Christmas, think of all the gift certificates or the New Year's bookings you'll have."

"We have a lot of work, and there's always unforeseen circumstances as well as shipments that don't come in on time." Zach glanced down at his boots and lifted them from the table. "Sorry. Wasn't thinking."

"You're fine. Put them up there. It's a table, Zach. It's not white sheets at Buckingham Palace."

"Talk to me about your vision for the decorating, and beyond, into the actual rooms of the resort." He shifted, bringing his arm up and stretching it along the back cushions, his boots remaining on the floor. "I just want to make sure we're still all on board with everything."

She'd decorated that place over and over in her mind. She'd go from her tastes to Chelsea's. Sophie had to keep reminding herself she had to do what her friend would've wanted. And Chelsea loved all things vintage or Paris-related. Both themes could blend beautifully together and be done in a tasteful way that would appeal to women of all ages.

"I think the main floor should be kept as a community-type area," she told him. "You have the kitchen, the main bathroom, the foyer, and a beautiful sitting room. Then there's the room that appeared to have been a library. Why not keep that as such?

Women love to read. We can keep the latest copies of popular books in there."

When Zach didn't respond she took that as a sign that he didn't hate the idea.

"The glass room that overlooks the pond, I think we need to make that the eating area. It's close to the kitchen and the view is breathtaking."

Zach nodded. "I agree. Braxton had already planned that in his notes that he passed to me."

"What are your thoughts on the two cottages?" she asked. "Are we planning on renting those for a higher price? Have those as the gold star of weekend getaways?"

"That's what I assumed we would do. Chelsea's notes were pretty specific when it came to those houses." Zach laughed. "She was so laid-back about everything in her life, but when it came to this property, she knew what she wanted and kept detailed descriptions, didn't she?"

Sophie ran her fingertip over the tonal pattern of her chair. "That proves to us how important this place was to her. We really need to stick as close to her wishes as possible."

"I plan on it."

"I've been researching various spas and resorts in my downtime."

Zach eyed her, quirking a brow. "And when is that? Because as far as I've seen, you have no downtime."

Leveling her gaze, she replied, "Are you the pot or the kettle?"

Shrugging, Zach glanced around the room. She knew what he was looking at. The pencil sketches. She had them all over her home. She couldn't count the number of drawings she'd done over the last ten years. Some she framed, some she gave away to random people and friends, some she had in a folder in her dresser drawer.

"I want these in the house," he told her, his eyes coming back to land on her. "No matter what else, I want you to do some sketches for the house. Maybe one in each bedroom, and definitely the entryway. Maybe a grouping or whatever you want."

She swallowed. Did he realize she'd used the sketches to recover from the accident as a form of mental therapy? If he was aware, Sophie knew he wouldn't be asking her, but she didn't mind one bit. She loved drawing and Chelsea had loved the simple designs too.

"I'd best get started now," she joked. "Anything else?"

"Sorry," he said with a slight cringe. "I don't know how long one takes you."

Sophie swung her feet down, shifted to the other side of the chair, and pulled her feet back up. "Depends on my mood, how much I need the relaxation, and if I already know what the subject will be."

"I'll leave everything up to you when it comes to the sketches," he assured her.

"Well, I was thinking for the bedrooms, maybe they should each be a theme. You know, one could be Paris, one could be London. Whatever. Chelsea was so prone to take off and travel, but she never got to the places she truly wanted to see. Why don't we do each room as one she'd had on her bucket list?"

When he remained silent, she wasn't sure if he was processing the information or afraid to reject her ideas for fear of hurting her feelings.

"If you'd rather—"

She stopped midsentence when he jerked and

reached for the cell in his pocket. Staring at the screen, his brows drew together before he answered.

"Hello?"

His eyes widened as he jumped to his feet. "I'm on my way."

Clearly alarmed, Zach shoved his phone back into his pocket. Sophie came to her feet. "What is it?"

Without looking back, he raced from the room. "The Sunset Lake property is on fire."

# Chapter Sixteen

Sophie darted after Zach. She didn't ask, she just hopped up in the passenger side of his truck and buckled up as he tore out of her driveway.

"Who called you?"

He punched his hazard lights as he accelerated through town. "Braxton. The fire department was on the way."

A ball of dread filled her stomach. Could fate be this cruel to pull Chelsea's dream right out from under them? After they'd all finally come together, they had a plan and a real purpose to work as a team, could it all be gone?

Beyond that, this home was a piece of history for the town. The grand estate had always stood tall on the small hill, overlooking Haven for over a century.

As they drew closer, Sophie couldn't help but let her mind flood with possible scenarios they'd face once they arrived. Would the entire home be engulfed? Would it be minor and they could rebuild with just a slight setback? How would this affect the grant funding? Was it arson?

Oh no. She seriously prayed it wasn't arson, because

heaven help the one who set the fire if the Monroe boys discovered them.

As Zach pulled into the long drive, Sophie sat up straighter in her seat and clicked her seat belt off. Relieved that flames weren't shooting out of each window, she struggled to see exactly where the fire was. Two fire trucks sat in the drive; hoses were pulled and disappeared into the front and side doors.

Zach had barely put the truck in park and killed the engine before she was out and running up the walk. Well, running as fast as she could until the twinge in her hip kicked in.

Strong arms encircled her, lifting her off the ground and back against a familiar, firm chest.

"Slow down. There's nothing we can do until we see how bad the damage is."

Sophie nodded, gripping his arms. "I'm okay. You can put me down."

He eased her down but kept an arm around her waist. "We'll go in together, but you're coming back out to sit in the truck if you pull a stunt like that again or if I even think you're hurting."

The way he cared, putting her needs ahead of his fear for this house, was all too telling. But she'd have to pick apart all of that later because right now she was terrified of what they'd find inside.

Just as they hit the porch, Braxton stepped from the house. A streak of black covered his gray T-shirt and his hair stood on end.

"It's under control," he told them with a long exhale. "I came by earlier to sand some more in the bathroom. I was only here a few minutes when I smelled smoke. The kitchen where you ran new wiring along that outer wall was on fire. I grabbed that small extin-guisher we keep here and got most of it before I called the fire department and then you. But there's some damage."

Sophie stepped from Zach's grasp and turned to look at him. He rubbed his forehead, closed his eyes, and muttered a curse. "I was just here," he stated, clearly frustrated. "There was nothing wrong when I left and I can run wire in my sleep."

Braxton shrugged. "That's where I found the flames. The fire department is in there now, looking for the point of origin or anything suspicious."

"How much damage was done?" Sophie asked, shifting her weight to her good side.

"I don't think much." Braxton brushed his hands down his shirt, ran his hands through his hair, and sighed. "It's going to put us back, but I don't think for very long."

"Did someone call Liam?" she asked.

Braxton nodded. "He's on his way."

"There's no way that wiring was faulty," Zach muttered, almost as if he were talking to himself. "I've never had a problem."

An SUV roared up the drive. Liam had arrived, coming in as fast and frantic as Zach had.

Sophie placed her hand on Zach's arm. "I'll go talk to him."

As she started to step away, Zach reached for her. "You okay?"

"I'm fine. You and Braxton go inside."

She didn't hang around to see the concern staring back at her. No doubt Liam would be angry and confused at this unfortunate turn of events, and if she could play buffer, then she certainly would, because the last thing any of the boys needed was to get into an argument over how the fire started.

She met Liam at the end of the walk. His eyes searched beyond her.

"Braxton and Zach are inside," she told him, stepping so he wouldn't pass. "Calm down and look at me."

With his focus centered on her, Sophie reached for his hand. "We don't believe there's much damage and the fire was contained to the kitchen. Nobody was hurt, so that's what's important."

"How did it start?"

Sophie swallowed, leading him up the walk. "They think the wiring in the kitchen."

"The old wiring?"

"No. The new."

Liam cursed as he came to an abrupt stop and pulled his hand back. "How the hell can new wiring go up in flames?"

"Don't go there," she warned. "Accidents happen and placing blame now will get us nowhere. The kitchen was getting an overhaul anyway, and fighting now will only set us back."

The muscle in Liam's jaw clenched. He was angry and looking for an out, and Sophie wasn't about to let him storm inside and zero in on his target. If he wanted to yell at someone, he could use her . . . not that he would, but she was going to stay in his face until he cooled down.

"Zach is inside with the firemen and he'll get it figured out," she went on. "You know he's never had anything like this happen before."

The muscle in Liam's clean-shaven jaw clenched. "That doesn't mean this isn't his fault."

Sophie placed a hand on Liam's firm chest. "Listen to me and calm down. He's as upset as you are, but check your rage before you walk inside. Got it? I won't have you going in there and starting a fight."

Liam's dark brow lifted. "You're pretty territorial with Zach. I don't want to know why."

"Good, because it's none of your business."

Sophie pivoted on her heel and started back up the walk.

"He's going to hurt you."

The low, bold warning had her freezing. With her back still to Liam, she replied, "It's a chance I'm willing to take."

Because she was. Zach might not want more, he might not be ready for more, but that didn't mean she wouldn't keep trying to chip away at his defensive walls. And having anyone, including his own brother, cause more harm, would not happen while she was around.

The firemen had gone. Braxton had given Sophie a ride back home when Zach insisted she go rest because it was so late. And now Liam was practically looming over Zach's shoulder.

"Back the hell up." Zach couldn't focus on the wiring with his brother waiting to call him on a mess-up. "I'm going to be a while. You might as well go home too."

Liam took a step back, a small step. "I'm not leaving. This is my project too, and I want to know what the hell happened."

Zach honestly had no clue. The fire department said faulty wiring, but Zach knew that wasn't the case.

As he looked over the blackened wires, he was starting to grow concerned. Some of this was not his work. Who else would mess with the new electrical?

Braxton didn't know how to do this, and Liam sure as

hell wouldn't attempt it. Which placed the speculation straight onto Zach, but . . .

He blew out a breath, raked his hands over his beard, and turned. "I have no clue what happened. I didn't wire this like that. There are rookie mistakes here."

The average person might not see what Zach saw, especially with some of the wires black, but there were wires running in areas he hadn't even touched yet.

Zach didn't add that they were lucky the entire house didn't go up in flames. Luckily Braxton was here when it happened. Zach didn't even want to think of any other outcome, because this old house would've gone up fast and unforgiving. There would've been chimney and foundation left had no one been around to catch it in time.

"Maybe you're too busy burning the candles at both ends." Liam crossed his arms over his chest, narrowing his eyes. "Why don't you try focusing on the house instead of sniffing around Sophie."

Zach shifted his stance, turning fully to Liam. "What?" he asked, sure he'd heard wrong.

"Leave Sophie alone," he warned. "You've done enough to her and the last thing she needs—"

Zach's fist connected with Liam's jaw. Before Liam could recover, Zach had hold of his brother's shirt and was backing him across the room until they collided with the wall.

"Don't you ever talk about Sophie to me," Zach growled. "Our relationship is none of your business."

Liam punched Zach in the stomach, forcing Zach to release his hold and double over as the wave of nausea consumed him. Damn it. He was too old for this.

"I don't want to see her hurt again," Liam shouted. "I won't sit back and watch you use her for a time and then push her away when you're finished. You weren't a friend to her when she needed you most, so don't act like you're anything more now."

Trying to pull in some much needed air, Zach held on to his stomach as he straightened. "What are you talking about?"

"You turning her away when you were in prison," Liam spat out. "For some asinine reason she went to see you. Often. You always declined her visit."

Because he hadn't wanted to see her. He was humiliated, and there was no way in hell Sophie was going to see him behind glass . . . not when he was there partly for the damage he'd caused her.

"I had reasons." Finally he was getting air and breathing without too much pain. Definitely too old to be getting into a fistfight. "None of that matters now. Sophie and I have an understanding."

Liam's mocking laugh really grated on Zach's nerves. "Do you?" his brother asked, propping his hands on his hips. "Because she defended you earlier. When I arrived she was quite determined to keep me away from you until I calmed down. She's special, Zach. Even you can't be that much of an asshole to think you can just mess around with her."

No way was Zach getting into this with Liam. Partly because it was none of his business, but mostly because Liam was right. Zach had no right to think he deserved any part of Sophie's beautiful world shining into his. But he wanted . . .

What? What did he want? A commitment? A chance at forever with her? Marriage and babies and sharing bills?

When anger rolled into guilt meshed with reality, he had no choice but to look at the grand scheme of things. He'd slept with Sophie. He wanted to sleep with her again, but there had been a bond that had formed when they'd been intimate. And if he slept with her again, he knew that bond would only bind them even tighter. There would be no way to sever it later without completely breaking her heart. Or his.

Zach turned and stared across the room at the frayed wires, the blackened wall, and the mess he'd have to clean up. It was late, he was beyond tired, and he wanted to be alone.

"I'm going to clean up, then head out," he said without turning back to his brother. "I'll meet you and Braxton here in the morning and we'll regroup."

"Fine." Footsteps pounded over the floor, then stopped. "Don't think I'll let this go," Liam warned. "Sophie is my friend and I would look out for her no matter what. If you're honest with yourself, you'll know this is wrong from every angle."

Continuing to stare at the wall, Zach clenched his fists. The front door opened and closed with a slam. Alone with his thoughts was a dangerous place to be. Alone with his thoughts after Liam pounded common sense into him could prove to be crippling.

Zach had never begged for anything in his life. When he was a kid and his father brought home women and his mother was too strung out to care, Zach didn't say a word. When his biological parents would be gone for days, Zach searched for food. When he came to live with the Monroes he'd struck the parent lottery and definitely never asked for anything, because he'd just been given more than he'd ever hoped for.

But at thirty-two years old, he wanted Sophie. He wanted her with a need that had become all consuming.

Having her meant exposing her to the past he'd fought to keep behind him. Having her meant opening himself up to someone and risking loss all over again.

And having her meant she would have to choose between her parents and him, because there was no way her family would sit by and watch her grow closer to someone like Zach. Accident aside, they'd never liked him. When he'd wrecked and Sophie had been injured, he'd been warned to stay away from her or face their lawyers.

At the time Zach hadn't wanted any more trouble for his parents, so he'd avoided Sophie, in prison and when he got out. He would only see her when Chelsea brought her around, but even then Zach would do everything in his power to avoid her.

It had been the most difficult decade of his life.

But now he was an adult, and he wasn't afraid of her parents, but he was afraid of putting her in a tight spot . . . something else she didn't deserve.

So now he faced trying to figure out how to get through each day working closely with Sophie, because he had just come to the conclusion that he could never be with her again.

But just like when he was a kid and had come to live with the Monroes, he had something more than he'd ever thought possible for his life. Being with Sophie was absolutely beyond any expectation he'd had. He just had to hold on to those memories, let them replay over and over in his mind as he—

A *thump* came from the basement. A *thump* that couldn't be ignored, and there was no way in hell that was the house settling. He kept a knife in his truck and contemplated going out to get it for about two seconds, but decided to grab the hammer from the kitchen island instead. There were enough tools here he could use for a weapon . . . unless whoever was downstairs had a gun.

Zach eased the basement door open, paused, and listened. Nothing. One step at a time, he listened for further proof of an intruder. Had this person started the fire? What on earth were they still here for? It wasn't uncommon for someone to break into abandoned homes, but in Haven that was something he'd only experienced once in all his years of working construction. Still, this could be some random stranger just passing through.

By the time Zach got to the bottom of the steps, he gave his eyes a moment to adjust to the darkness, but he needn't have bothered by the time his focus landed on the far corner behind him. A boy stood at the electrical box, flashlight in hand, muttering something under his breath.

*What the hell?*

"Turn around," Zach stated loudly.

The boy jumped, dropping the flashlight until it rolled across the floor, coming to a stop halfway between them. Zach kept his eyes on the boy as he slowly moved to get the light. Once in hand, he held it right on the stranger's face. His bruised, swollen face. But the bruises weren't fresh, so whatever he'd endured had been a while ago.

"What are you doing in my house?" Zach demanded.

The boy, wide-eyed, tipped his chin up a notch. So, he was afraid but he wasn't about to give in. Zach ran the light over his clothes, torn T-shirt and holey jeans. Could be a normal outfit for some kids these days, but Zach seriously doubted this boy was a typical teen. From the look of him he might be sixteen.

"Either tell me what you're doing in my house, or

you can tell the cops when I call them. I imagine they'll have you tell the story to children's services too."

Those wide eyes were instantly filled with fear, and Zach cursed himself. Maybe he should stick with dogs. Clearly people weren't his strong suit.

"I'm leavin'," the boy muttered and headed for the steps, forgetting his lost flashlight.

Zach ran, cutting him off at the base of the stairs. "You're not going anywhere until I know who you are and why you're here."

"This place was empty," the boy murmured.

Warning bells sounded all through Zach's head. "It was. Now it's not. Who are you hiding from?"

The boy shrugged. "Doesn't matter."

An inkling of familiarity slid through Zach. Suddenly this boy mattered, because Zach wondered if he was looking at a version of himself years ago.

"What's your name?" When the boy said nothing, Zach sighed. "I'm Zach. Now you go."

"Brock," he mumbled.

"Where do you live?" Zach was pressing his luck in the questioning, but there was no way this boy was leaving without Zach learning more. Those bruises came from somewhere, and Zach had a sinking feeling. "Or are you trying to live here?"

Brock's haunted eyes came back up. "Listen, man, get out of my way. I'll leave and you can forget about this."

Some people might let this guy go and forget he was here, but Zach wasn't about to just turn a lost boy loose. Zach had been a lost boy once too . . . still was, if he was honest with himself.

"I'm not going to hurt you." Zach should've led with that, because right now those words were the most important ones. "I just have some questions."

"Did you call the cops before you came down here?" the boy retorted.

"No. And I won't as long as you answer my questions honestly."

Zach truly had no intention of calling the cops about the kid. Now, if he discovered who'd used their fists on his face, he might reconsider.

"How old are you?"

The boy took a step back. "Old enough to defend myself."

Zach muttered a curse. Brock was definitely a younger version of Zach, chip on his shoulder and all. And the fear in his tone was all too telling.

"Sixteen?" Zach guessed.

"Yeah," he mumbled.

"You've been staying here a few days, haven't you?" Putting all the thumps and creaks together, Zach had to assume this boy had been hiding for some time. "How have we not seen you?"

"I'm pretty good at hiding."

Zach nodded toward his face. "Not too good. Who did that to you?"

"Car accident."

Rolling his eyes, Zach snorted. "I'm not stupid, so don't treat me like I am. You get in a fight with a friend?"

Brock kicked his worn sneaker against the cracked concrete floor. When he remained silent, Zach's heart literally ached for the boy. Damn it, he didn't want to have this conversation. He didn't want to be in this situation. Brock didn't want to be in this situation either.

If the Monroes hadn't stepped in, Zach wouldn't be where he was today, so there was no way in hell he could turn his back on this kid.

"Do you have parents who are wondering where you are?"

Brock merely snorted and shook his head. Okay, so clearly this boy was keeping his cards close to his chest, which was fine. Easier on Zach that way, but that wouldn't prevent him from caring. Damn it, he instantly cared. Caring is what caused hurt to seep in. Caring for people is what made you vulnerable.

"You're not hiding out here anymore." Zach turned, heading toward the steps. "Follow me."

Hitting the second step, Zach glanced over his shoulder to the boy, who remained still.

"That wasn't a question." Brock met his stare and Zach stared back into the depths of hurt and vulnerability. "I'm not going to hurt you. I plan on feeding you and letting you rest somewhere besides an old, dirty house."

Brock's eyes widened. "I'm not going anywhere with you. I don't know you. Listen, man, just don't call the cops and I'll leave."

"You're leaving," Zach confirmed before turning to mount the steps. "With me."

Zach was surprised when he heard footfalls behind him on the steps. He figured he'd have to do more coercing. The boy was coming, but Zach hadn't earned any type of trust, which was fine. That didn't mean he was going to ignore Brock, and he sure as hell wanted to uncover what Brock knew about the fire . . . and who had put those marks all over his face.

When they reached the first floor, Zach headed toward the kitchen. "I need to lock the back door, then we're heading to my house."

"Dude, I'm not—"

"Listen." Zach held up his hand. "You can take your

chances that I'm not lying to you and come with me, or we can let the cops deal with you. Those are your options."

Zach didn't like scaring the boy, but there was no way he was just letting him go wander out to who knew where. Zach cringed at the thought of what could happen to Brock if he was truly out on his own.

Brock stormed around Zach and jerked the front door open. "Fine. But you touch me once and you'll regret it."

Those words told Zach more than he wanted to know, and everything he'd feared. There was no way in hell Brock was going anywhere for now, except to Zach's home, where he could rest without worry and have a warm meal. After that . . .

Zach sighed. After that he didn't know what, but he'd make damn sure this young boy was safe from whatever he was hiding from.

# Chapter Seventeen

After leading the dogs out to go to the bathroom, Zach had another pressing matter to deal with.

Easing the spare bedroom door open, he checked on Brock, pleased to see the young boy making use of the antique queen mission-style bed that had once belonged to Chelsea. It was nearly seven o'clock in the morning, and Brock was completely out of it—on top of the covers with his ratty tennis shoes still on.

Zach gently closed the door and headed down the hall. At least Brock had fallen asleep, even if he couldn't fully relax and trust his surroundings. No child should have to worry about where they were sleeping or if they were safe. Zach had been awake most of the night, making sure Brock didn't try to run again. Worry kept Zach fully aware of how delicate this situation was.

Today Zach was getting some answers. First, he needed to know if anyone was missing Brock. No dancing around the topic. Zach wasn't going to get in trouble with the law for having Brock stay here. On the other hand, Zach also wasn't turning Brock out into the world until he knew exactly where he was going and if he'd be safe.

Time for some breakfast. Zach wasn't the greatest at cooking. Okay, fine, he was flat-out awful other than the spaghetti he'd made for Sophie.

Sophie. Should he call her? Was this a day she taught water aerobics or not? He honestly should learn more about her life.

Intimacy aside, he wanted her to be a friend if nothing else, and as a friend, she needed to know he cared.

He led the dogs into the utility room, refilled their water bowls, and fed them before heading to the kitchen. Pulling his phone from the charger, he sent Sophie a quick text.

Busy this morning?

While he waited for a reply, he scrounged around in his cabinets to see what he could come up with. The bread seemed to be all white, nothing questionable growing on it. Now if his milk wasn't chewy and he had eggs that didn't smell, maybe French toast would be an option.

His cell vibrated on the counter.

Just got out of the shower and getting ready for work. Why?

Did she have to add the bit about the shower? Was she trying to torment him? Knowing the new, sassier Sophie . . . yes.

I'll give you 50 bucks if you swing by my place asap.

Okay, bribing was taking it a bit far, but he was desperate. He really didn't want to give Brock a piece of toast and a glass of water. The boy deserved more. Last night he'd insisted he wasn't hungry, and Zach wasn't fighting with him any more than he had to. Brock had come to his house, so Zach needed to take that victory.

He kept his eyes on the screen of his phone and smiled when she replied.

**Be right there.**

Relief slid through him. Sophie didn't even ask why he needed her, and she was heading over. Maybe he should warn her or at least give her a heads-up.

**If you have eggs and milk or any other breakfast item, bring it.**

One of the pups scratched at the gate Zach had put in place. "No," he told the pup, glancing across the kitchen into the utility room. "You stay in there for now. You've been out and you have food. I need to work on breakfast for someone else."

Damn it. He was having a full-on conversation with the dog. One-sided talks were not normal.

The dog yipped as if talking back.

"Nope. I'm not giving in. You need to listen."

Zach rolled his eyes and pushed off the island. He was losing his mind. For a man who thrived on being alone, he now had eight dogs, and a teenage boy he'd known all of twelve hours, staying in his home.

Jerking open his fridge, he surveyed the meager contents. Seriously, he was due at the store about five years ago. Problem with buying food was you had to prepare it, so that was a waste of money. It was much easier for a single person to grab something on the way home.

When the dog continued to scratch and bark, Zach moved the gate. "Fine. But don't think you're always getting your way," he scolded as the pup strutted by. "You're only getting out because I don't want you waking our guest."

"Do you normally talk to the dogs like people?"

Zach spun around to see Brock in the doorway, his hair stuck up on one side . . . apparently the only side he'd slept on.

"Not always," Zach replied, propping the gate against the wall. "Only when I've lost my mind."

A corner of Brock's mouth tipped up, but he quickly killed the look with a scowl. "I'm going to head out now. Thanks for letting me crash."

Zach crossed his arms over his chest. "Sit down. Reinforcement is coming to help with breakfast."

Brock glanced around the kitchen, probably contemplating whether he should stay or go. Zach waited. He didn't want Brock to feel like he was a prisoner. This was a fine line they were both treading, because Zach didn't trust this boy. Yes, he felt a tug of familiarity and there was no denying the sympathy he felt toward Brock, but Zach knew he had to stay a step ahead of this kid.

Finally Brock crossed the room, reached down to pat one of the pups, and let it nip on his hand before he pulled out a stool at the center island. Zach stared back at the questioning eyes. Before Sophie arrived, he wanted to get some answers.

"What's your last name?" Zach asked, bracing his palms on the other side of the island. When Brock merely stared, Zach sighed. "I'm going to get the answers. I know you don't trust me, but you slept here all night with no problem."

"Taylor." Brock shifted in his seat, his eyes darting down to the dog, pouncing around the floor. "My last name is Taylor."

Great. A start, as long as he was telling the truth.

"And who do you normally live with when you're not hiding in Civil War–era basements?"

Brock let out a soft laugh, and Zach couldn't help but smile himself at the brief action from such a sad-looking kid.

"My mother."

Zach snapped his fingers at the pups when two more came from the utility room and were fighting a bit too rough. They jerked around and darted across the room. Great. Now they'd want to play. He should've let them continue to bite each other.

They nipped at his toes, and Zach reached down to scoop them up, one in each arm. "Is your mother worried because you're not home?"

One pup took a bite at Zach's ear. "Damn it," he grumbled before placing that bloodsucker back on the tile. Little bundles of fur were still too damn cute for him to get angry with, but those little teeth were sharp.

"If she notices I'm gone, then she's probably relieved."

Zach swallowed the lump of hurt. He'd definitely been that kid. Too many kids knew this type of pain and emptiness. It was all too easy for others to look away, because oftentimes the truth was ugly and uncomfortable. And the truth was, Brock was alone, scared, and desperately in need of love and the proper affection.

"What do you know about the fire at the other house?" Zach held the boy's gaze, refusing to back down. Arson was a serious offense and he needed to know just how deep this kid was into illegal activity. He hoped Brock was innocent; he hoped he was just trying to get away and start a better life.

"I didn't mean to," he muttered beneath his breath

as his eyes shifted to the patterned granite beneath his fisted hands. "I was trying to help you."

Confused, Zach drew his brows in. "Help how?"

"I took electrical classes at my vocational school." He traced a finger over the dark pattern as he spoke. "I really liked learning about it, and I was at the top of my class this semester, but I have another year and I'm not sure I'll go back."

So much to take in from that statement. Zach started to reply when his doorbell rang. Brock jumped up from the stool, eyes wide, his feet braced.

"Relax," Zach said, putting the wiggling pup down to scamper to the front door with the others. "It's a friend of mine. You're safe here."

Brock didn't look any more relaxed, but he gave a brief nod.

Zach danced around pouncing pups as he made his way to the door. As soon as he flicked the lock and turned the knob, Sophie was pushing through.

"Okay, what's the emergency and why am I giving up my turkey bacon?"

Zach smiled as she whizzed by him and stopped short. Just as he closed the door he glanced over his shoulder and spotted Brock in the wide opening between the foyer and kitchen. The dogs were nipping at Brock's worn shoes and biting on the hem of his jeans.

"Come on," he said, clapping his hands at the puppies. "Don't bite his pants."

"You called a woman to cook you breakfast?" Brock asked, glancing back and forth between Zach and Sophie.

"No." Zach took the sacks from Sophie. "I called Sophie because she's a friend, and if you want real food, you'll be glad she's here. Otherwise I can pour you a glass of chewy milk."

Brock's eyes raked over Sophie. Zach held his ground between them, unsure how the boy would react.

"I can go," Brock stated. "This—I'm . . ."

Sophie took a step forward. "How about we have breakfast before you dart off? Okay?" Her quiet tone managed to do something Zach hadn't been able to do, and that was put a brief flash of trust through Brock's eyes. The boy nodded and bent to play with the puppies, but not before Zach spotted moisture gathering in those big brown eyes.

"Go ahead and play with the dogs." Zach headed toward the kitchen. Meeting Sophie's questioning gaze, he jerked his head in a silent motion for her to follow him. "We'll yell when breakfast is ready."

"What is going on?" Sophie whispered as soon as they hit the kitchen. "Who is that?"

Zach purposely rattled the sacks to mask his voice. "He's been hiding in the Sunset Lake property. I found him in the basement last night. His name is Brock."

"Did you see his face?" Sophie asked, her voice shaking as if she were on the verge of tears. "He's been beaten, Zach."

Zach swallowed as he surveyed the contents she'd brought. Bless her, she'd thought of everything.

"Move over and let me cook." She shoved him aside and started pulling everything out of the sack and placing it on the counter by the stove. "You explain."

For a moment he was stunned at how perfect she looked standing at his stove, the same stove his mother used to use. There hadn't been another woman in this kitchen, other than Chelsea, since. Something warmed him, but he didn't have time to dig into all the reasons why having Sophie here just made his day brighter and more manageable.

Holding a roll of sausage in one hand, Sophie snapped her fingers in front of his face. "Zach. Talk."

"I don't know much," he told her, leaning in so he could talk low. The puppies in the other room, barking at Brock, helped. "He's obviously running from something or someone. I gather he's been abused at home and his mother is at the heart of all of this."

Soon the sausage was frying, filling his kitchen with an amazing aroma he'd missed. Real food, not takeout.

"He claims he was trying to help with some of the electrical work and didn't mean to start the fire."

Sophie's head whipped around. "He set the fire?"

"I don't think it was on purpose. He's alone, from what I can tell, and he's afraid to go home."

A sad smile spread across Sophie's face. "Reminds me of someone," she murmured.

He knew she'd see the similarity too. "I couldn't let him stay there and I wasn't about to kick him out or call the cops."

Reaching up, Sophie framed his face with her hands. Such a simple gesture, yet he felt the impact throughout his entire body. She had a hold on him, and he had to figure out whether he was willing to risk holding her back or letting her go.

"You're giving him a chance," she said, her eyes misting. "What can I do to help?"

Zach took her hand and kissed her palm. "Don't let that sausage burn."

With a laugh, she turned back around and grabbed a large spatula from the crock next to the stove. "Why don't you go talk to him? I've got things covered in here. I don't have to be at the office until ten, so we're good."

"Thank you." Without thinking, Zach reached out and smoothed her hair behind her ear so he could fully see her profile. "You didn't hesitate to come when I asked, and you didn't ask questions."

Smiling and working on breakfast, Sophie shrugged. "You never ask for anything, so I knew it was pretty important. Either that, or you just really missed me."

Snaking a hand around her waist, Zach shifted their bodies until her side fully connected with his chest, his hips. "I can't count the number of times I've missed you over the years, sweet Soph."

She concentrated on the meat sizzling, but he didn't miss the tremble that rippled through her. He slid his hand up her back, cupping the nape of her neck.

"You look good in here," he whispered into her ear. "And I've missed you in my bed."

Zach left her with those parting words as he tore himself away. If he stayed longer he'd make a fool of himself and start proclaiming things he wanted, things he was wondering if he could ever have. How insane was that? Who was he to get a happily ever after?

Fortunately he had enough to occupy his thoughts and his time, between the resort renovations, the grants, the dogs, and now Brock. How had his life changed so much in the last few months? He'd gone from being a recluse, minding his own business and doing his job, avoiding Sophie and her boyfriend as much as possible, to sleeping with Sophie, somehow starting a new bond with his brothers, and building a women's resort and spa.

Zach raked a hand over his coarse jaw. He didn't even recognize himself anymore.

Just as he stepped into the living room and spotted

Brock on the floor playing with puppies and looking like a normal kid, the doorbell rang. Zach hated that instant look of fear in Brock's eyes.

"I didn't call the cops, if that's what you're jumpy about." Zach crossed the space to the door. "I promised you'd be safe here, and you are."

After breakfast, though, there would be some definite answers and some decisions to be made.

The second Zach jerked the door open, he regretted not looking out the glass side panels to see who the unexpected visitor was.

"Oh, you're home." Ms. Barkley stood on the other side with her hair all fluffed and sprayed as if blond teased-to-shit hair was a turn-on. Her blood-red lips tipped into a grin. "I was hoping I'd catch you before you went to work."

Zach gripped the knob and shifted so she couldn't see into the house. She didn't take the hint and stepped up onto the threshold to peek over his shoulder.

"Oh, um, hello."

Shifting back so he didn't get pushed over by her cleverly exposed cleavage or knocked out by her dousing of musky perfume, Zach glanced over his shoulder to Brock.

"What brings you over this early?" he asked, turning his attention back to his blatant neighbor.

"What? Oh, well, I have a project I'd like priced." She kept her gaze on Brock, most likely trying to figure out where the young boy fit in. "If you have time, I'd like to talk to you."

Hadn't they done this before? Couldn't she set her sights on someone else—someone who actually showed interest?

"Right now I'm busy, but I can call later or send Nathan over. He's the best worker I have."

Her eyes darted over his shoulder. Zach knew who stood behind him. He resisted the urge to smile, especially after how Sophie had talked to his neighbor on the phone. This should be interesting.

"Breakfast is ready," Sophie said, a smile in her tone. Zach couldn't have planned her timing better. "Are we having an extra guest?"

Zach shook his head. "No. Just us, babe." Turning back to his neighbor, who stood with her glossy lips parted in surprise, Zach said, "I'll be sure to get in touch later and we can discuss details."

As the neighbor stuttered incoherently, Zach ushered her right out the front door. As soon as he turned, he caught Sophie's eye. The second she busted into laughter, he couldn't hold back. Damn, that felt good to laugh, to share the experience with Sophie—even if it stemmed from something petty.

Seeing Sophie smiling, knowing they were having the same thoughts, only added to that special bond they shared. Another lock clicked into place . . . another layer added to their intimate, growing relationship.

"Did I miss something?" Brock asked, coming to his feet and glancing between Zach and Sophie.

"Just my neighbor, who likes to make her daily trips over for random questions. If she doesn't stop by, she calls twice." Zach pointed toward the hallway. "There's a half bath in there. Go wash your hands and then come in and eat."

Once Brock left, Zach followed Sophie into the kitchen. "I have a feeling she may not care so much about that deck anymore. Unless she had another phantom project she wanted done."

"She thinks you're cheating on her," Sophie joked,

still smiling. "She may call Braxton and have him console her."

Zach wouldn't put it past his brother to do just that, but whatever Braxton was dealing with and however he chose to battle his demons was none of Zach's concern. And he sure as hell didn't want to know about his neighbor and Braxton.

Sophie searched through two cabinets before she found his plates. She pulled two down and started dishing out some type of omelet with sausage. It smelled delicious.

"Where's your plate?" he asked when she placed two on the island. "You're joining us."

Smoothing a hand down her silk top that she'd tucked perfectly into her green skirt, she shook her head. "I think it's best if the two of you talk, and I have a feeling he's not going to be too chatty with an audience."

Brock stepped into the room and headed straight to the island. "I'm not too talkative with just one person, either. You can stay and eat." He sat down and shoveled a forkful of food into his mouth and spoke around it. "I'm heading out after. Don't let me interrupt whatever it is you guys do."

As much as Zach would love the alone time with Sophie, he didn't like the implication Brock was making. Had he been pushed aside before so whoever he lived with could be alone?

"Sit, Soph," Zach ordered. He crossed the kitchen and pulled out another plate. "You made it, you're eating."

Without arguing, she took a seat next to Brock's. Zach placed a plate in front of her, then poured three glasses of milk. Thankfully Sophie's was still in good standing with the calendar.

Breakfast was quiet, and a bit awkward. The dogs were nipping at Zach's pants and Brock's pants. A strange teen sat in Zach's kitchen eating like a starving boy, and Sophie, sweet as you please, quietly stood up and started to make more food for Brock before she'd even finished her own plate.

Questions circled Zach's head and he couldn't get into the personal ones just yet. He needed the basics, and he needed them now.

"Where do you live?" Zach asked, looking across the island at Brock.

Shoving his empty plate aside, Zach waited for the boy to shrug or make an excuse not to answer.

"Bellville."

An hour away. Sophie kept her back to them as she prepared more food. Her silent support meant everything, and Zach knew she would be taking all of this in and making her own opinion. They would no doubt discuss it later when they were alone.

"And you live with your mother?"

Brock nodded, draining his milk glass. "And whatever boyfriend she has at the time. She's had the same one for a little over a month, though. I'm afraid he's staying."

Sophie's shoulders stiffened. Zach placed his palms on the counter. "They don't know you left, so what are your plans?"

Now Brock did shrug, the signature move for most teens who don't want to answer or even discuss the current topic. Too damn bad.

"You don't want to go home and you don't want me calling CPS. My hands are tied," Zach told him honestly. "I want to help, but I need to know exactly what's going on and why you left. If you want help, you need to help me."

Brock glanced over his shoulder just as Sophie carefully stepped beside him with the hot skillet. She scooped the food onto his plate.

"I'm heading out," she stated, placing the pan back on the stove. "I'll be at the office if you need me." She eyed Zach. "For anything."

He nodded. "Thank you."

The dogs tried to follow her as she headed toward the front door. Zach whistled to get them back into the kitchen. His home had turned into a refuge for strays. The irony was not lost on him. His parents would love to see this, would love the fact that Zach hadn't turned anyone or anything away. They'd instilled in him that need to help others. Their love, loyalty, and dedication had made him the man he was today.

Zach took the empty bar stool next to Brock. "Okay. Start talking, and I want the entire truth so I can figure out how to help you. You lie to me and we're done."

Brock remained so still, Zach didn't know if he was going to say anything or not. Finally Brock nodded and sighed. "All right. I'll tell you everything."

# Chapter Eighteen

After meeting with the new doctor in town and his wife about their needs for a new home, and double-checking the building permit at the courthouse, Sophie was exhausted. Still, the day was a success since she'd managed to get in and out of the courthouse without running into Martin. Now she just had to drop a FOR SALE sign off in a new client's yard and she could head home.

Well, she could head home, but she planned on stopping at Sunset Lake to check in on Zach. She'd not heard from him all day, and she was desperately worried about Brock . . . and Zach. There was no way the man could be untouched by having a near mirror-image of the boy he'd once been thrust into his face.

But Zach would do the right thing.

She also had some good news to share and she wanted to do so in person.

Sophie maneuvered her car through downtown, taking in the busy sidewalks with laughing kids, smiling families, couples holding hands. Summer was just getting started and with Savannah only twenty minutes away, the town would be even busier as tourists trickled in.

She loved tourists. Loved seeing her beautiful town thrive even when the economy wasn't the greatest. This community took care to make the area look lovely, the garden club always keeping fat pots over-flowing with flowers at the base of each lamppost lining Main Street. Volunteer groups from local high schools kept litter picked up for extra credit— yay to those smart teachers—and the city council was adamant about storefronts being freshly painted. Haven was most definitely a picturesque town, which would only help the new resort attract clientele.

Pulling into the long, curved drive, she spotted Zach's old truck at the top of the incline. As she rounded the curve, she saw Liam's SUV as well. Blowing out a breath, she pulled in behind the vehicles. With no Braxton, did this mean Brock was playing referee? Was Brock even here? Well, if nothing else came from this project, maybe Zach and Liam would learn to actually talk and get along. Sophie didn't care if that was all wishful thinking; she'd keep wishing until the day came when those two burned the guilt-and-anger bridge.

The late afternoon sun was hotter than she'd an-ticipated and the silk blouse she wore was starting to cling to her in some very unpleasant areas. Nothing like sweat rings to polish off that professional look she prided herself on. She had her gym bag in the trunk, but it mostly had a spare bathing suit and a pair of shorts. Not the look she should put forth here either. She was going to have to start keeping a change of clothes with her since she planned on being here after work most days.

Digging in her purse for a clip, she twisted her hair

and quickly piled it on top of her head. The air on her neck helped. Maybe she wouldn't have a heat stroke.

Her car door opened and Sophie screamed.

With an arm on the roof of the car, Zach leaned in. His lopsided grin, sweaty shirt, and rugged looks were nearly enough to have her overheating again.

He laughed. "Easy there."

With a hand to her heart, Sophie smiled. "I don't care that you scared me if you'll laugh like that again."

When he extended his hand, she let him assist her from the car. He didn't back up. With two strong arms caging her against the open door, Zach leaned into her.

"We're both sweaty . . . you more than me."

He ran his nose along the length of her jaw and traveled up to her ear. "I like being sweaty with you."

Whatever had gotten into this new affectionate Zach, she wanted more of it. But right now she couldn't think beyond the fact he was turning her inside out up against her car in the middle of the day.

"Wh-what are you doing out here?"

His hands settled on her shoulders, squeezing. "Maybe I was waiting on a beautiful woman to drive up."

Her body trembled, ached. "What are we doing?" she muttered, then gasped when his lips slid over her throat. Her head fell back and all she could do was stand here and let him touch her so perfectly, yet so tenderly.

"I'm ignoring warning flags and tasting you." His mouth eased back up, hovering a breath away from hers. "Unless you'd rather I stop?"

"No. No stopping."

She felt the smile against her lips seconds before he captured them. Sophie opened, welcoming that familiar thrill she'd come to know only from Zach. She slid her hands around his waist and wished they were somewhere other than the driveway of an old historic house with people inside.

Before she could melt into a puddle, Zach pulled back. "I'm glad you're here."

"Yeah?"

He nodded, releasing her. "I know I shouldn't touch you or kiss you because I have no idea where this is going, but resisting has become near impossible."

"I never said I wanted you to resist, Zach." She had to make that clear. "I didn't want you to be torn. You know what I want. You. That's all. Nothing more complicated than that."

His eyes nearly blazed right into her. "Everything about you, about us, is complicated."

He'd admitted there was an "us." She wasn't going to state the obvious. This was a step in the right direction. A long time coming, but she'd take this victory.

"Is Brock here?"

The warmth in Zach vanished and his face hardened. "He's inside with Liam. Those two have clicked."

"And you're upset about this?"

"What? No." He shook his head and raked a hand over his messy hair. Taking a few steps around the drive, he stared out toward the pond. "Brock filled me in on everything earlier. I'm just torn right now. I'm going to have to call someone because he needs out of that environment." Clasping his hands behind his head, he looked down to his worn boots. "Damn it, he won't trust me if I do that, but this has to be done the legal way."

The battle Zach was fighting was going to be difficult, there was no way around it.

"I'm afraid to ask what he told you." Sophie pushed off her car and pulled at the damp silk clinging to her back. "What I want to know is what your plans are where he's concerned."

Zach's dark eyes cut to her. "I've known him less than twenty-four hours and already I want to help him. I have no clue how. He needs to live with someone who cares, but I know the system doesn't always work, and if he gets placed somewhere . . ."

Shaking his head, Zach muttered a curse. "He'll take off again and who knows what will happen to him."

Sophie's heart melted. Zach may have tried to push people away, he may have hated the world and been punished for one tragic mistake, yet here he was taking in stray dogs, nursing pups until they could be adopted, and now he was trying to save a young, broken boy, all while restoring an old mansion because his late sister had a dream.

If she hadn't fallen in love with him years ago, she was 100 percent head over heels now.

"Why are you smiling?" he asked, his brows drawn in.

"You know why." Sophie closed the space between them and kissed the side of his face. His prickly beard tickled her lips. "I'll do whatever I can to help you."

"Braxton has a fancy lawyer friend. I've got a call out to him. This has to be handled the right way."

The right way. Sophie didn't know what his exact intentions were, she wasn't sure Zach fully knew, but he was going to do something, and that was more than Brock had been offered so far.

"I have some good news," she told him. "Let's go inside since Liam is here too."

Zach tipped his head. "Tell me now."

"You'll have to be patient." Sophie started down the sidewalk. She'd taken maybe three steps when she was lifted off the ground and flung over Zach's shoulder. "Why am I looking at your butt?"

Zach laughed. "Because you were limping and I'm carrying you inside."

"Your concern is sweet, but the execution could use some work."

"You dumped the polished man, Soph. Now you have me." Zach carried her to the porch and gripped her thigh. "You know you love this."

He knew her so well. Better than anyone, actually. Which made him perfect for her. Now if she could just get him to realize how they were imperfectly perfect together.

As soon as they were inside, he set her down. "No steps today. We're working in the bathroom and kitchen anyway."

Sophie nodded. Arguing with the stubborn man was useless. Besides, she liked knowing he cared so much. Not that she ever intended to use her limp as a means of gaining attention; she'd never want to be that pitiful and desperate. But knowing he zeroed in on how she was feeling without her saying a word proved how much he'd settled himself into her life. She hadn't even noticed she was limping more than usual.

"Hey, Sophie." Liam strutted through the foyer. With a ball cap on backward, his dark hair curling around the edges and a stained white tee, you'd never guess he was a prominent chef at a popular Savannah hot spot. "We've got sandpaper with your name on it."

Laughing, Sophie glanced over his shoulder at Brock, who hung back. "Hi, Brock. How are you?"

The boy shrugged, but gave her a passing glance. Her heart literally ached for the kid. No doubt he was terrified of his future, and to be honest, so was she. But Zach wouldn't give up on this kid and neither would she.

Focusing back on Liam, Sophie could barely hold back the happy news another second. "I've heard back on the grant." She turned to make sure Zach was behind her still. "We've been approved!" she squealed.

"Already?" Zach asked. "That was fast."

Nodding in agreement, Sophie said, "It's been a week. They said up to thirty days, but this was much faster than I figured. If you're changing any renovations on the original list, I just need to let them know."

"I can't foresee any changes," Zach told her. "Wow, I didn't expect to hear back so soon. You are awesome, Sophie."

Beaming with pride, she was so excited she'd spent sleepless nights working on this for them, for Chelsea. She screamed when Zach picked her up and spun her around, placing a loud smacking kiss on her lips. The second he put her down, Liam wrapped his arms around her and spun her in the other direction.

"Keep your lips off her," Zach growled just as Liam's mouth pressed to hers in a brotherly manner. "I'll kick your ass."

Liam laughed, easing Sophie back down but keeping an arm around her waist. "I'd like to see that. I believe Braxton gave you a black eye the other day and I punched you in the gut. Don't make me remind you who's stronger here."

"You're full of it," Zach retorted with a snort. "I deserved it the other day, but you lay your lips on her again and—"

The back door slammed and Sophie jerked her attention in the direction of the hall leading to the kitchen.

"Shit," Zach muttered, taking off in a run. "Brock."

Why did Brock leave? One second they'd been joking and . . .

Sophie closed her eyes as realization dawned on her. The poor boy didn't know the difference between playing and real life.

"I'm going after him too."

Sophie watched as Liam took off after Zach. No way would they let Brock escape thinking the worst . . . thinking they'd ever turn their fists on him. How sad that a teenage boy didn't recognize the brotherly banter and joking manner. Sophie had been so thrilled with the news, with Liam and Zach laughing and joking with each other, she hadn't even stopped to think.

She wrapped her arms around her waist and headed back out the front door. Maybe he ran around front. Regardless of where he went, Sophie was confident Zach would find him and set him straight in the most loving of ways.

After frantically searching for nearly thirty minutes, Zach finally found Brock behind one of the two old cottages on the property. Brock sat on the ground just outside the back door and didn't even look up when Zach took a seat beside him.

Zach shot off a quick text to Liam that he'd located the boy.

"You take off like that again and I'm going to think you don't like our company."

A pebble poked Zach in his rear end, so he shifted, stretching his legs out before him and crossing his ankles. The sun was getting lower, sending radiant orange rays spreading out along the horizon, making a stunning reflection in the pond.

"Liam and I have a history," Zach started, staring at the pond and wondering about building a new dock, because focusing on work was so, so much easier than digging into his past. Unfortunately, this boy needed help, and Zach was going to have to put himself on the line. "Liam, Braxton—who you haven't met—and I were all adopted. We had a sister, Chelsea."

From the corner of his eye, Zach saw Brock stiffen. "Had?" he asked.

Zach nodded, plucking a clover from the ground beside him. He brought a knee up and rested his elbow on it, twirling the clover between his thumb and finger. He couldn't sit still, not when he was about to open his heart to a virtual stranger.

"She passed away several months ago," Zach told him, hating how he had to speak of his vibrant sister in the past tense. "She was in a skiing accident."

"And you liked her?" Brock asked, as if family love was foreign. The question and the manner it was delivered broke Zach's heart.

"I loved her more than anything. She was literally the glue that held us together."

Zach heard footsteps seconds before Liam came into view. Catching his eye, Zach nodded. Liam quietly moved around to sit on the other side of Brock.

Having Liam here only made this that much harder. But maybe he needed to be here; maybe this was perfect timing.

"Liam and I have always rubbed each other the wrong way," Zach went on, tossing the clover aside. "From day one he irritated me and I purposely irritated him. Braxton battled his own issues but kept trying to make peace between us. Chelsea loved us all and always tried to pretend we were one big, happy family. We were, but Liam and I definitely made things harder."

When Liam didn't chime in, Zach continued. "We were always hitting on each other. I'd get mad, throw a punch. He'd get mad, throw a punch. On rare occasions Braxton would join in, but only when he was really angry."

"Yeah, I get that you guys punch a lot," Brock mocked. "That's what I was getting away from."

Zach appreciated his honesty, but he was missing the point entirely.

"Even though Liam and I have our issues, I can speak for us both when I say we love each other." Zach had to swallow. He'd not said those words aloud . . . ever. But he did love his brothers and should've said the words well before now. "We're family and we're always there for each other. Why the hell else do you think three dudes are working on opening a resort for women only? It sure as hell isn't because we love to read up on massages and facials. We're doing this to honor our sister. In the end, we've got a bond that nothing can break. And when we fight, we aren't trying to show our power and anger. It's just how we are."

Zach glanced over Brock's head at Liam. His brother met his eyes, held them, and nodded in agreement. Something coursed through Zach . . . love, relief. He hadn't been lying. He truly loved his brother, and having Brock here only helped Zach face the truth he'd known for years.

"I've hurt Liam in more ways than I can count." Zach prayed like hell he wasn't going to have to dig into the accident portion of his past—or worse, start sobbing like some pathetic guy who couldn't control his emotions. "But I hope he knows I'd do anything for him."

"Do you get what he's saying?" Liam asked Brock. "We'd never hurt you. Ever. We might throw a punch at each other, yes, but we love each other. We piss each other off, but that's just how we show our love. It's warped, but you have to know you're safe here. We'd never let anyone lay a hand on you."

Zach's chest ached. He replayed all the things Brock had told him earlier and Zach wanted nothing more than to go throat punch a few people. What kind of monsters laid their hands on children out of anger? There was a special pocket of hell for those people.

Brock glanced at Liam. "Did you get that scar from your parents?" he asked as if a parent harming a child was a normal conversation. Completely heartbreaking.

Liam reached up and ran a fingertip over the red line down the side of his face. "Car accident when I was twenty-three."

Zach stared, waiting for more of an explanation, shocked when Liam left it at that. A bit of relief filled him, followed quickly by even more love. Even now, after everything, Liam was protecting Zach from retelling that story until he was ready.

"I don't know who to believe," Brock muttered, jerking on the blades of grass by his side. Pluck, toss, pluck, toss. "I hate my life."

"I admit, you were dealt a rough hand," Zach agreed. "I'm here to tell you that I'm going to do everything in my power to make sure you never have to go back again."

Brock grunted. "Foster care is a joke, man. I did that once and they put me right back with my ol' lady once she got out of jail."

"You're not going back to her," Zach promised, praying like hell he could keep it. "Foster care, I hope, isn't an option."

"Where would I stay?" Brock asked, searching Zach's eyes. "With you? What do you know about raising a kid?"

Liam quirked a brow, silently agreeing with Brock's concern.

Zach shrugged. "About as much as you know about living with an adult who cares for you, but I'm damn well going to try my best and not let anyone hurt you again. Besides, I could use help with work."

"There are child labor laws."

Zach laughed. "You're of age to work, and I think once we hone your electrician skills, you'll come in handy."

For the first time since Zach first spotted Brock in the basement, Zach saw hope. No matter what, he planned to deliver on his promise to keep Brock safe. He hadn't intended to keep the boy, but he'd damn well settled in with the idea the second he said it.

# Chapter Nineteen

Sophie sanded in the bathroom around the vanity. The new layout was going to be gorgeous, especially if Zach opted for the paint color Chelsea had in her notes.

But paint, renovations, and Chelsea's binders were the last thing on her mind. Zach, Liam, and Brock had been gone well over an hour. The sun was starting to set and she was getting worried. She knew they'd found Brock, Liam had texted her, but she was still worried. That poor boy. What all had he endured? He was tough, though. He'd get through this, and with help from the stubborn, hardheaded Monroe boys, Brock had no choice but to head in the right direction.

"As much as I love watching you work, I think you should go home and rest."

Sophie glanced over her shoulder. Zach stood in the doorway with a smirk on his face. "I'm not tired," she told him, laying the sandpaper down and turning to face him fully. She swiped her hands together, ridding herself of the drywall dust. "How's Brock?"

"Right now? He's okay. Overall?" Zach sighed and shook his head. "He'll be okay. I'll make sure of it."

"Why do you want me to go?" she asked.

"I don't want you to go. But Braxton is on his way and—"

"Ah, I see. Some testosterone-filled evening of working, burping, and farting? The male bonding ritual?"

Zach grinned. "Something like that."

Knowing they needed some time to get Brock used to them and hopefully earn more trust, Sophie nodded. "If you need anything at all, call me. Promise?"

"We'll be fine."

She knew he'd never call, but that was fine. Zach didn't need a sitter and he didn't need her hovering. Besides, she had work to do.

Once she said bye to the other guys, she headed home. A couple new listings had come through and she was hoping one of them would suit the doctor who was moving to town, because she was not about to show Zach's house. He was keeping it.

Sophie found herself smiling hours later as she sat in her favorite floral chair, Flynn purring beside her as she sketched some of the rooms in the Sunset Lake house. These sketches were visions of what she thought the rooms once looked like in their grandest of times. Most likely the first-floor parlor had housed ladies with skirts swishing about as they had afternoon tea while the gentlemen in the study drank whiskey and discussed ways to end the war and solve the world's problems.

She couldn't wait to do the various exterior images with the old mossy oak trees, the porch stretching across the house. The entire property was absolutely breathtaking, and once word got out about the resort, women would come from all over the country for a relaxing getaway, whether alone or for a girls' retreat. Sophie might even check in herself.

Her pencil slid easily over the paper as she shifted her bare feet beneath her, careful not to disrupt her sleeping feline. She added curtains to the floor-to-ceiling windows in the parlor. Sophie just knew they would've been made of thick velvet, probably in dark green or sapphire. A rich shade held back by gold tassels.

Once her parlor and study images were done, Sophie's hand was cramping. She wanted to draw that grand staircase, but that would require a good amount of time and dedication. Yawning, she set her tablet on the coffee table, laid her pencil on top, and had just put her feet on the floor when her doorbell rang. The chime pulled Flynn from his sleep. He stretched back, then arched up on his paws before prancing from the room, as if he didn't have time for visitors.

Sophie had lost track of time, but when she glanced at the antique clock on her small corner desk, she saw it was nearing ten. She wasn't a bit surprised she'd been at it for nearly four hours.

At first glance through her etched-glass door, Sophie knew the shape of those shoulders. A thrill shot through her that he'd want to see her at the end of his day. She hated setting her hopes so deep into him, into whatever this was between them, but she couldn't help herself. She'd been denied for so long.

With a flick of the dead bolt, she tugged open the heavy oak door. The porch light lit up one side of his face and the dark of night shadowed the other. That image right there summed up her Zach in the proverbial nutshell.

Wait . . . *her Zach*? Yes, he was hers. Always had been, if she was honest with herself.

His eyes raked over her body and Sophie resisted the urge to wrap her arms around herself. She'd shucked her bra when she'd changed, and now she wore a black tank and old gray cotton shorts. Had she known she'd have company . . . nah, she still would've chosen comfort.

"Your light was on," he stated.

Smiling, she reached out and tugged him inside before closing the door and sending the dead bolt back into place. "You can always stop, even if the light is off."

Zach took a step closer, narrowing the gap between them. "I have no reason to stop. I just found myself driving here and . . ."

Sophie reached out for his hands and squeezed. "Stop there. That's good enough. I don't care if it's because you were afraid to go home to your crazy neighbor or you were afraid of facing the worries with Brock, or even that you weren't wanting to share your bed with an eighty-pound dog. I don't care. You're here. That's all that matters."

With a smile stretching across his face, Zach stared down at her. The gesture had his dark eyes crinkling in the corners. She wished he'd smile more. The man was absolutely breathtaking when he did.

"Can it be that easy?" he asked. "Can this between us be that simple?"

"It already is that simple. You just have to accept it." She stepped in closer, lifting their clasped hands and holding them between their chests. "You ready to admit this isn't casual anymore?"

"I'm ready to admit I don't want to spend this night without you." He rested his forehead against hers. "I'm ready to admit these past few weeks have been the best I've had in a long time and I'm ready to admit . . ."

Zach closed his eyes and Sophie waited.

"I'm ready to admit I want more with you than just sex."

Her heart swelled at his quiet statement. This was all she'd waited for, all she'd prayed for and dreamed of.

"Why now?" She asked because she had to know.

Zach eased his hands out and framed her face. Easing back just enough to look her in the eyes, Zach stroked her cheeks with his thumbs.

"Because you matter. We matter." He kissed her lips softly. "This matters."

She'd waited on him to say those words, to come to that realization on his own.

Sliding her hands up his hard chest and over his shoulders, Sophie smiled. "Where's Brock?"

Zach settled his hands around her waist, started walking her backward. "Liam is staying at my house. Those two are bonding."

She fully allowed him to take the lead and steer her down the hallway toward her bedroom. "And they're going to take care of the dogs?"

A beautiful, toe-curling smile spread across Zach's face. "Everyone is taken care of and all I'm worrying about tonight is you. And all you're going to worry about is doing nothing but focusing on my touch."

Definitely something she could handle.

When she reached to turn on her light, Zach's hand covered hers. "Leave it. Go open your blinds. I want you wearing nothing but moonlight and me."

Sophie shivered once more. Every now and then Zach's romantic streak made an appearance, and when it did, she could hardly control herself. She wanted him—now.

Flynn rubbed against her leg as she made her way slowly across the hardwood floor. Her eyes had adjusted to the darkness and she knew the floor was spotless.

She figured Flynn was already out the bedroom door, not interested in having people disrupt his nap.

Once the blinds were open, the full moon cast a glow into the room. Thankfully her bedroom faced the back of the house and a yard full of flowers and large live oak trees, decades old, covered in Spanish moss. Total privacy.

"I've missed you." Zach's footsteps slowly moved across the room. "Missed touching you, kissing you. Making love to you."

Sophie closed her eyes, her breath caught in her throat as Zach's hands settled on her shoulders. She eased back against his chest.

"Stay the night," she whispered. "I want to wake up with you."

Kissing her forehead, then turning her in his arms, he murmured, "I have no intention of leaving."

Zach's rough hands slid beneath the hem of her tank. He spanned her waist and jerked her even closer. Sophie smoothed her hands up and over his shoulders, threading her fingers through the hair at the nape of his neck.

"I know we said this was not going to get complicated." Zach laughed as his thumbs stroked her bare skin. "But I'm beyond complicated when it comes to you, Soph. I'm falling here."

She never thought he'd be so open, never thought the bedroom was where he'd choose to loosen up.

"I love you," she told him. "I don't know where your feelings are for me, but you need to know how strong mine are for you."

Zach kissed her, softly, gently, and absolutely perfectly, as if she was the most precious thing in the entire world and he just wanted to savor her. When he eased back,

Sophie swiped her tongue over her bottom lip, wanting to taste more.

"I know how you feel," he told her, whipping her tank up and over her head. "I see it when you look at me, I can feel it when you touch me."

Sophie gripped the bottom of his T-shirt and pulled it off, flinging it to the side. "I want you to know it, in everything I do. I never want you to doubt where you stand with me. Even if you can't love me back, I won't hide my feelings from you."

Those rough, strong hands roamed down her sides, dipping in at her waist and rounding over her hips. "I never want you to hide anything from me, Sophie. Never."

Zach dropped to his knees. Slowly he eased her shorts and panties down. Bracing her hands on his shoulders, Sophie stepped out of her clothes and stared down at the top of Zach's head. One hand gripped her hips as he stared at her abdomen. A lone fingertip traced her scars, causing her stomach to quiver, her nerves to kick into high gear.

Before she could utter a word, Zach leaned forward and kissed her imperfection. Then he moved to her hip, where she'd had a pin put in. He did the same, tracing the scar with his fingertip and following that up with a kiss.

His eyes roamed up her body, settling on her face. "I love you too. Maybe I always have and could never let myself admit it."

Sophie's breath caught in her throat, her heart clenched. "Zach—"

In an instant he was on his feet, framing her face between his large, callused hands. "You deserve to be loved, deserve to know passion and have every desire come true."

"I only want you. That's every desire."

Wrapping his arms around her, Zach pulled her flush against his body and captured her lips once again. She'd never expected him to declare his love. Oh, she'd hoped, she'd dreamed, but she'd also been realistic.

Sophie eased back, gripping his biceps. "One of us is very overdressed."

Zach quickly removed everything, leaving him standing in the glow shining through the open blinds. Placing his hands on her hips, Zach backed her toward the bed. As soon as she sat on the edge, he followed her down, pressing her back against the thick covers. His weight was absolutely perfect on her. He settled perfectly between her legs as his lips slid along her neck, nipping his way toward her breasts.

Sophie arched her back, threaded her fingers through his hair, and let him do whatever he wanted. His beard tickled her bare skin in the most delicious way possible.

His hands roamed all over her, heating her with each pass. Without words he loved her, he cherished her, and he made her feel like she was absolutely the only one in his life. Finally. Finally their time had come, and Sophie wasn't going to let anything come between them. Zach was hers, she was his. Nothing else mattered.


"We can stay here all day, right?"

If Zach had his way, he'd never leave. Unfortunately, life wasn't stopping just because he and Sophie were lounging in bed because they'd been up most of the night, unable to keep their hands off each other.

"Sorry," he told her as he smoothed her hair off her

shoulder and down her back. "Eventually I'm going to have to get home and start this ball rolling with Brock."

Sophie settled deeper against his side, her leg flung over his. "I guess you, Liam, and Brock had a long talk yesterday?"

Zach curled his fingers around her bare shoulder and stroked his thumb along her smooth skin. "We did."

"Are you going to elaborate or keep it to yourself?"

He hadn't planned on discussing their time together. Not that he was keeping it from Sophie, he just hadn't thought about it.

"I told Brock as much as I could, as much as I felt he could handle and not be terrified." Zach hadn't disclosed the full truth behind his own childhood. "He is fully aware of the dynamics that make up the Monroe family, and he knows Liam and I have had our share of issues."

Zach's other hand rested on his abdomen. Sophie reached out, lacing her fingers with his in silent support.

"I explained to Brock that no matter what happens here, we would never let anyone hurt him and we would never lay a hand on him," Zach went on. "I told him we may throw a punch, that's how we are, but we still love each other."

Sophie tipped her head, resting her chin on his chest, and stared into his eyes. "You told Brock you love your brothers? And Liam was sitting there?"

Zach nodded, shifting on his side so he could face her fully. "Yeah. It was time he knew. Even if he never forgives me for that night, even if he hates me forever, I needed him to know. I didn't realize it until I was talking to Brock about Chelsea and our family. I do love my brothers, even if I want to punch them on occasion."

The second Sophie's eyes filled, Zach cursed. "Don't cry. There's nothing to cry about."

A smile spread across her face as a tear slid down her cheek. "After all this time, you and Liam may have a chance at a relationship not centered around bitterness and guilt. I'm so glad you guys talked, so happy Brock was there to witness this, even though he has no idea what a milestone he witnessed."

It wasn't news that Sophie had forgiven him long ago. She'd never blamed him, never acted as if he'd ruined her life or held a grudge for that night. Proof she was a better person than he was, because if the tables were turned, he honestly didn't know if he could do the same.

"Were you ever angry with me?" he asked before he could stop himself. "I know you never took your anger out on me. Maybe because I avoided you for so long after the accident, but did you ever hate me?"

Blinking the tears away, Sophie shook her head. "Never."

"How could you not?" he whispered.

Propping herself up on her elbow, her head resting on her fisted hand, she reached out and traced the back of his scarred knuckles. "Because of this. You never intentionally hurt us, and when I woke up after my surgeries at the hospital, I was told you busted out the glass to go get help. You saved my life. You saved Liam's life."

Zach swallowed the lump of guilt. He was moving on, airing out the past, and guilt had no place . . . not if he wanted a future with this beautiful, forgiving woman at his side.

"Had I not been showing off, had I let Liam drive like he'd asked, I wouldn't have had to worry about saving your lives."

Zach had replayed that night so many damn times over the last decade. Liam had been perfectly sober, but Zach had a new truck and wasn't about to let Liam drive it. Hell no, not when Sophie had been smiling at him all night, and Zach figured once they dropped Liam off there might be more than just flirting.

But that never happened.

"I'm sorry I turned you away when you came to see me," he went on. If they were going to pull everything out into the open, he needed to dredge up every single aspect. "I was humiliated. I didn't want you to see me there, and I had no clue how you'd react once you saw me. Had I looked at you and seen hate, I don't think I could've gotten through that year. I knew in my heart I'd never have a chance with you, but I just couldn't handle knowing you hated me."

Sophie slid her hands over his shoulders, easing him back down onto the pillow. Her entire body covered his as she rested her elbows on either side of his head and looked him straight in the eye.

"I have never hated you. Ever. I've loved you since the moment we met. I loved how you treated Chelsea like she was precious, and then you were a hard-ass with your brothers. I loved how you made me feel, like you were interested in me but weren't quite sure how to approach me. You were everything from tough to vulnerable, and I loved every single layer."

Sophie slid her lips over his, straddling his hips before sitting up. "I don't want to talk about the past. I want to live right here, right now with you in my bed and know that we have a future."

Before he could respond, her doorbell rang. Sophie

jerked as if she'd been caught doing . . . what? This was her own house and if she wanted to spend her morning making love, then she had every right.

"Expecting company?" Zach asked, quirking a brow.

"No."

Sophie contemplated ignoring the uninvited guest, but the bell chimed again.

"Seriously," she muttered, climbing out of bed. She jerked her robe off the hook on the back of her door and threw it on, knotting it in a hurry. "I'll be back. Don't move."

Zach laced his hands behind his head and smiled. With the sheet draped around his waist, his ink and his muscular chest on display, Sophie had a hard time turning to leave.

Flynn was stretching in the hall as the doorbell chimed for a third time. Who in the world needed to see her at nine o'clock on a Saturday morning? Clearly someone who had no manners.

The second she flicked her lock and eased her door open, her heart stopped.

"I was beginning to think you weren't home."

Sophie had to step aside as her mother and father charged right through her door. But when her mother gasped, Sophie glanced down the hall and spotted Zach wearing nothing but a sheet wrapped around his waist.

Wasn't this going to be fun?

# Chapter Twenty

"Mom, Dad, if you want to sit in the living room I'll be right back." Because excusing yourself to go get underwear on and have your lover put on clothes was perfectly normal. "Give me five minutes."

"Sophie Ann," her mother gasped. "Tell me this isn't what I think it is."

Sophie couldn't help but laugh as her mother's wide eyes darted to Zach. Her father crossed his arms, his jaw clenched and his nostrils flared. Yeah, they were angry, but this was her house, her life, and if she wanted to sleep with Zach then that was really none of their business.

She wished she'd ignored the persistent doorbell now.

"If you think Zach spent the night, then you're right." Sophie turned toward Zach, who still clutched the twisted sheet at his side. Just as she started toward him, she threw a glance back at her mother. "I don't need, nor do I want your opinion."

Sophie's mom gripped her arm before she could move away. "After all this time, are you still this careless? This hung up on a man who ruined your life?"

Sophie glanced to Zach, but he'd closed himself off again. She couldn't read his stony expression, and after all that had happened with them in the last few weeks, she prayed to God this was not going to be a setback.

Pulling her arm free, Sophie rounded on her mother as she pulled her robe tighter over her chest. "What I'm doing with my life now is not your concern. I know you love me, but Zach and I have something and—"

"No." Her mother cut her off with a shake of her head, holding both hands up. "No, Sophie. Do you forget what you went through because of this man's recklessness? The surgeries, the therapy?"

"That's enough," Sophie stated.

"Or maybe you forgot that a family was stolen from you, since you can't have children."

Dread consumed her. Heat washed over her as she froze in place. Of all the things her mother could've said, Sophie never expected her to play the infertile card. But the woman was desperate to crush everything that Sophie wanted with Zach.

Risking a glance at Zach confirmed her mother's jab had hit home. He barely looked at her before turning and disappearing into her room.

Anger flooded through Sophie as she whirled on her mother. "Get out. Your damage has been done."

"Honey, your mother—"

"Don't defend her, Dad. Both of you just go."

Sophie pushed past her mother and jerked the door open. Crossing her arms, she stared down the hall, knowing full well that Zach was now getting dressed and had most likely fully detached himself from any emotions he'd been feeling only moments ago in her bed. She wanted to go back thirty minutes, she wanted to be snuggled up against Zach's warm body, talking about the Sunset Lake house, Brock, or anything else that pertained to the happy life they were just getting started with.

Sophie didn't even spare her parents a look as they passed through the door. She couldn't focus on anything other than getting back to Zach, talking to him to see what he was thinking, if he would even open up to her. For so long he'd felt so guilty for causing her limp. How would he react to discovering her infertility, a result of the emergency surgery after the accident?

Once on the porch, Sophie's mother started to say something, but Sophie cut her off.

"We're done for now," Sophie said before closing the door and flicking the lock back into place.

It was no secret her parents didn't like Zach, but Sophie hadn't expected them to find out about this newfound relationship this way. She'd been unprepared, and now she had some damage to clean up. In all honesty, she would've told them in her own time, in her own way. But their surprise visit ruined everything . . . literally.

Heart beating fast, Sophie stepped into the bedroom just as Zach was tugging his shirt down his abs. He searched the room until he found his socks and boots. Sophie crossed her arms and leaned against the door frame. He knew she stood there, she could tell by his tense shoulders and his jerky movements, yet he never made eye contact.

Fear flooded her, but they'd come too far for her to let him back away now. He loved her, and she was holding on to those precious words. Zach wouldn't have told her his feelings if he hadn't truly meant them, and she could tell by the way he'd loved her all night, the way he'd treated her so delicately, as if she were everything to him.

"Don't let my parents ruin this."

Zach paused in tying up his work boot. "They didn't ruin it. They opened my eyes to reality."

Sophie gripped the material on her arms, but didn't move into the room. Zach needed space, she could give him that, but she was blocking his only exit. They were going to talk and he wasn't about to run just because things were uncomfortable now. Okay, that was a major understatement, but how did she put into words how their relationship had just taken another drastic turn?

"This didn't change anything," she said, needing him to know she meant every word. "I'm the same person you spent the night with. I'm the same woman you claim to love."

Pushing off her bed, Zach propped his hands on his narrow hips and finally met her gaze. Everything he'd been feeling last night was gone, she could see it in the pity staring back at her. The guilt-ridden Zach had returned, and in the span of only minutes, their relationship had taken a major nosedive.

"I don't want pity." She tipped her chin and squared her shoulders. "Don't look at me like that."

"Why didn't you tell me you couldn't have children?"

Sun flooded through the slats of her blinds. She'd never be able to look at them again without hearing Zach tell her to open them so he could see her naked in the moonlight. He'd filled her bedroom, her home, her heart, and now she had to fight to keep him there.

"I would've," she admitted, realizing at some point she wouldn't have been able to keep it from him any longer, not with the way their relationship was going. "I never said anything before because nobody knew other than my doctors and my parents. Chelsea didn't even know. I couldn't risk her telling you."

Zach raked a hand over his beard. "Damn it," he muttered, then started to pace her room. He reminded Sophie of a caged animal. There was so much rage, so much anger in him, and he no doubt directed all his negative feelings toward himself. Right now he was doing the blame game again, reliving that night. Still, no matter how many times he went over what happened, it wouldn't change her feelings.

He stopped just beside her window, his back to her as he looked out onto her yard. "So you had more than a pin put in your hip from the accident."

Sophie didn't respond. Zach wasn't asking, he was working through the demons that had reared their ugly heads.

He slammed the side of his fist against the wall. Sophie couldn't handle the separation another second. As she crossed the room, Flynn darted in and scurried beneath her bed. Sophie would love nothing more than to hide, but ignoring feelings and shutting everyone out was the crux of the problem here.

"Don't, Sophie." Zach didn't turn, but he stopped her with his low, hurt tone. "Don't come closer, don't touch me."

She continued to move toward him until she was right behind him. Wrapping her arms around his waist, she laid her cheek against his taut back.

"I won't let you push me away."

He didn't reach down to touch her joined hands, but he didn't step away either. A minor victory in her fight.

"I'm not pushing you away," he corrected. "I'm facing facts. We can't be together. You know that."

Sophie squeezed him tighter for a moment before

dropping her arms. She wanted him more than her next breath, but she refused to be a clinging woman or someone who used guilt to keep a man.

"I don't know any such thing," she countered as she took a step back. "At least look at me if you're going to end things. If everything we did last night doesn't matter to you, then look me in the eyes when you tell me you're leaving."

He might be hurting, but she was getting a good dose of mad going right now. How dare he let her go because he was afraid, because he was feeling guilt, or whatever the hell excuse he was going to use.

Slowly, Zach turned. She almost felt bad for the tired look on his face, but she refused to let him go down this path again.

"Everything we did matters, Soph." He started to reach a hand out, but shoved both into his pockets. "I'm not saying this meant nothing. What we did meant everything and I do love you. But knowing I literally stole everything from you, your goals for the future, your family, I can't be here."

Sophie listened to his words, his excuses, and something hit her she hadn't thought of before. "Do you not want to be with me because I can't have children? I guess I hadn't thought you would want your own—"

Zach reached for her, gripping her arms. "No. Never once even think that. I would never bring a child into this world. Not with my genes."

Sophie waited for him to elaborate. He'd mentioned his past a few times over the years, but now she wanted to know more.

"Your life with the Monroes changed the man you are," she told him. "Whatever was passed to you biologically shouldn't have you this afraid."

Zach snorted. "I'm not afraid. I'm not running from anything and I'm not having this discussion."

He started to step around her, but Sophie moved to block him. "What did they do to you?" She laid her hand over his heart. "What was so bad that you won't talk about it, that you won't even let me in?"

Zach closed his eyes, sighed, and turned away from her. "My father had women. It was like a revolving door at our apartment. When my mother was home, she was too strung out to care or she had her own share of men."

Sophie didn't know if she was more shocked at the story itself or that he was finally telling her what happened.

"My dad finally disappeared one day. I assume he went off with one of his women." Zach raked his hand over the back of his neck and turned to face her. "For the next two years my mom would come and go, mentally and physically. We moved around all over. Her drug habit had us getting kicked out of every place we stayed. Sometimes we'd sleep in the car, sometimes she'd prostitute herself out for a place to stay."

Sophie swallowed, but kept her eyes locked on his. Reliving this part of his life wasn't easy, and she couldn't even fathom what his life had been like before the Monroes rescued him.

"More than once my mom offered me up. She didn't try until I was a teen, and by then I could fight. I was never . . ." Zach glanced away as if he couldn't look at her. "I wasn't sexually assaulted, but there were times I worried I wouldn't be able to fight everyone. Luckily I was old enough and fast enough to run away. I'd be gone a few hours, sometimes a whole day before I went back. I didn't know where else to go except the last place my mom was. By then they'd forgotten about me because they were high again."

Just the thought of a young boy worried about such evil things hurt Sophie's heart. "How did you finally get away?"

"A cop drove by our car one day. I was sleeping in the backseat. Mom had parked illegally and that's what drew his attention. I'd been in the car for two days without her. I told the officer I hadn't seen her and he took me. I went into the system and hit the parent lottery. You know the rest."

The way he summed everything up like he was relaying the plot of a bad movie proved just how detached he was from that life, from that young boy. He'd left that nightmare behind and he'd overcome all the ugly filth he'd endured.

"You're not your parents, Zach." Sophie wrapped her arms around herself and tipped her head back as she stepped closer. "We both have things to overcome. You can let your past define you or you can choose to take control of your life. If you're so hell-bent on finding reasons to push me away, then go. Walk out that door, because you know what? Even with everything you just told me, and I believe you really condensed it, I still love you. Nothing has changed on my end. You're still Zach, the man I've loved for years despite all the reasons I shouldn't."

Zach's phone vibrated on the nightstand by her bed. Neither glanced that way, but she knew he was pulling away from this situation.

"Being with you was more than I thought I'd ever have." His eyes held hers, but he didn't reach for her like she'd hoped. "For a short time I let myself believe I could have a life with you, that loving you would be enough. But seeing you with your parents . . . I won't be the one to come between you guys and I can't love you in all the ways that you deserve. I would damn well try, but . . ."

The phone vibrated again and this time he went for it. When he answered, she could tell it was Liam on the other end. Sophie turned from the room and walked out. She couldn't be in there. Couldn't see him in her bedroom knowing he'd never be back.

She headed to her living room and stared out the wide front window. The sun was so bright and beautiful, totally opposite of all the hurt and darkness that had settled deep into her heart.

Zach's heavy footsteps hit the hardwood, growing louder as he approached. From the corner of her eye, she saw him in the foyer, standing in the doorway to the living room. Silence settled between them. A new level of fear weighed heavy in her heart.

"I know you think you need to go," she said without turning. "But know this. I gave you ten years. I waited for you to come around for so long that I'm exhausted. If you walk out that door, if you leave with the knowledge that we love each other and this ending is all on you, then don't come back. You won't be welcome in my life again, Zach."

Her voice cracked. The words gutted her in ways losing her ability to have children never had, but she had to be honest. She couldn't do this again . . . not when she'd come so close to having everything she'd ever wanted.

"I know." His soft tone filled with angst sliced through her heart. "I'll always love you, Soph. But there's only so much I can give, and in the end, it wouldn't be enough."

Sophie whirled around. "You're a coward."

He stood still for only a moment before nodding and turning away. The front door opened and closed, leaving her broken and destroyed.

"How long will he be pissed?"

Zach spun around and slammed his wire cutters on the island. "I'm not pissed."

Brock jerked as Liam settled a hand on the boy's shoulder.

"Damn it." Zach rested his palms on the old counter and dropped his head between his shoulders. "I'm frustrated, okay. That's all. It'll pass."

Yeah, and he was going straight to hell for lying. He was pissed, beyond pissed, actually. He was a raging ball of pain, fury, and rage all rolled into one, and he only had himself to blame for getting caught up in some damn fairy tale, thinking he and Sophie could actually have something normal. They weren't normal people.

"This have anything to do with Sophie?" Liam asked.

Didn't everything? Years ago he'd started weaving his life around her and now he was so damn caught up, he had no clue how the hell to break free. He'd walked out of her house yesterday—the hardest thing he'd ever done in his life. She'd issued the ultimatum, and he'd had no choice but to call her on it and leave.

He'd been in a mood since, except for when Braxton's lawyer called to say a judge would hear an emergency case for Brock on Monday. But he couldn't sit home today. He couldn't be at his house and not see Sophie in the kitchen, Sophie petting the puppies, Sophie in his bed.

"This wiring is done." Zach pushed off the island

and turned toward the wall in question. "We can start on these walls today if you guys are up for it."

"You're avoiding the subject," Liam stated. "What the hell happened with Sophie? She hasn't been by at all yesterday or today."

The dead-last thing he wanted to talk about was this situation with Sophie. Liam and Braxton would give him hell . . . a place he deserved. Zach turned back to his brother, knowing he couldn't keep this truth hidden.

"I doubt she'll be coming by, at least for a while." If at all. Maybe when Zach wasn't there, but that would be very infrequently.

Brock's wide eyes darted between Zach and Liam. "Don't start fighting."

Liam shook his head. "We won't. But I want to know what you did."

"We're not seeing each other anymore." Damn, that killed him to say, but it would get easier as time went on . . . wouldn't it? "I'm not sure she'll want to be here with me."

Liam muttered a curse and smacked his hand against the countertop. "Are you for real? What the hell happened? That woman has been in love with you for years, and now you're not seeing each other? I want to kick your ass, but I can already see you're miserable."

Well, that was something. "Drop it, Liam. I don't want to talk about it."

Zach's cell vibrated in his pocket. At one time he would have jumped to answer, hoping it was Sophie. Now he only answered hoping it was work-related, because he wanted to completely submerge himself in projects and not think of anything else.

Pulling his phone from his pocket, he saw Macy's name and relaxed.

"Hey, Macy," he answered, ignoring Liam's narrowed gaze. Whatever was going on there was none of his concern. Zach had his own issues. "What's up?"

"Is this a bad time?"

Was there ever a good time anymore? "No, this is fine. Did you get a chance to see the ideas I e-mailed you?"

"I did. I actually wanted to discuss when you could get started. I know you're busy at Sunset Lake, but if we could just discuss a realistic date."

Zach stepped from the kitchen, away from Brock and Liam to head into the foyer. "Honestly, this project will take several months, but I can start sooner. It may just be slow moving at first, if that works for you."

"Oh, Zach, really?" Macy's tone hit that excited-woman octave. At least he could make someone happy. "I don't want to pressure you. I know we're friends, so I'm fine waiting, but if you can start sooner, that would be amazing."

"I'll start working on the final designs before we stake off the land."

"Just tell me what I need to do and I'll do it." He could hear the smile in her voice. "Thank you so much, Zach. You're the best."

That was rather debatable. "I'll be in touch."

When he disconnected and turned, Liam was glaring at him. "Get the hell out of my private conversations. I'm building her a damn house. Chill."

"Whatever you have going on or not going on with Sophie, fix it." Liam turned to glance over his shoulder before lowering his tone. "I promised that kid we wouldn't throw punches and I intend to keep that promise, but Sophie is special. You need to apologize for whatever you did. She's our friend, she was Chelsea's friend, and she's going to be a major part of this project if you haven't scared her away."

Zach shoved his phone in his pocket and crossed his arms. "For now, it's best if I don't talk to Sophie. You're more than welcome to call her, or Braxton can, but she won't talk to me."

Liam raised his brows. "Are you sure about that?"

"When I left, she told me I was never getting back into her life again." Zach's throat tightened, and his chest felt as if it was being squeezed by a vise. "I'm pretty sure she won't talk to me if I call her."

Liam raked both hands over his face, one fingertip lingering a second longer over his scar. "You've hurt her. How did you hurt her this bad that she won't even talk to you?"

"Reality hit me and I broke things off. I can't be with her, Liam. I just . . . damn it, she can't have children because of the accident."

He hadn't meant to blurt that out, but now that the words hovered between them, he couldn't take them back. It wasn't his place to share Sophie's private information.

"Are you serious?" Liam asked. "And you won't be with her because she can't have kids? What the hell, man?"

Shoes scuffed against the hardwood as Brock slowly came into the open area. Zach wasn't holding back; he had nothing else to hide at this point. He'd lost all that mattered and he had to remember what it was like living without her.

"That's not the reason I'm not with her," Zach clarified. "Discovering the truth, knowing all this time she's had to change the focus of her life because of me, kills me. I can't give her anything, Liam. I can't be the man she needs or deserves."

"That's ridiculous." Liam threw his arms out and laughed. "So, what . . . you're deciding now what's best for her? Did you even ask what she wants?"

Zach moved over to the staircase and sank onto the bottom step. He didn't have the energy to fight with Liam, with Sophie . . . with himself.

"Can I talk to him for a minute?"

Zach glanced at Brock, who was staring at Liam, waiting for permission. Liam let out a sigh and nodded. "Sure. I have to head back to Savannah tonight, so I'm going to go get some work done in the kitchen. Braxton texted me a minute ago, and he'll be here soon."

Once Liam was gone, Brock came over and sat next to Zach. The old worn jeans and sneakers Zach first found him in were still a staple in his wardrobe, even though Braxton had rushed out and bought him a pair of jeans and a new pair of shoes. At least Brock did have on a different T-shirt, compliments of Braxton's shopping trip.

"I barely know any of you, but I can't help but form an opinion." Brock rested his elbows on his knees and stared down at the scarred wood floor. "This accident that you caused, it left Liam and Sophie dealing with their own shit."

"Watch your mouth." Yeah, this kid was like looking into Zach's own past. "Yes, though."

"And Liam loves you. He seems to have forgiven you," Brock went on. "I figure Sophie loves you or she wouldn't have gone to all the trouble with breakfast the other day. Plus she looked at you like you really mattered."

Yes, she did. He'd seen that look and now he'd have

to keep that memory locked away, only pulling it out when he was truly desperate.

"I want that," Brock stated. He glanced over at Zach. The bruises were faded now, but the yellowish tinge was still evident. "I want to find a woman one day who will look at me like I matter. Regardless of the sh—stuff I've been through, I hope I find someone who will still love me no matter what. And I don't mean in that weird I-need-a-mommy way. I mean a woman I want to spend my life with."

Zach hadn't heard Brock speak this much since they met. Granted, that had only been a few days ago, but still. The sincerity in the boy's tone, the hope that filled his eyes when he spoke of his future, warmed something in Zach.

"You want a family?" Zach asked.

Brock nodded, turning his focus to the threadbare knees on his jeans, where he started picking at a thread. "I know it sounds crazy since I'm so young, but I want a wife and kids. I just want normal. I've never had it and that's all I want."

"I hope you'll want an education and a job," Zach stated, nudging Brock with his shoulder. "Let's try to keep an order to your goals."

Brock smiled and nodded. "Yeah, I hear you. I'm just . . . I'm confused as to why you let Sophie go. I mean, you love her, right?"

Zach couldn't speak for the lump in his throat so he nodded.

"Then why do you think you can't give her what she needs? I figure if she loves you, then that's all she needs. Right? I know your childhood wasn't much different than mine, but I'm not giving up on finding happiness. I don't think you should either."

Zach listened to each word of advice given by a kid half his age and wondered how the hell this boy who'd come into his life only days ago could put Zach's entire messed-up, warped life into perspective so easily.

"I don't want you giving up." Zach blew out a breath and came to his feet. "As for me, it's too late."

Brock pushed up and cracked his knuckles. "It's only too late if you're quitting. I thought you'd be one of the guys who fought for what he wanted."

Before Zach could reply, Brock walked away. How the hell did that kid add another layer of guilt? Zach wasn't giving up, he was moving on and setting Sophie free. She was going to be much happier in the long run.

And not fight for what he wanted? He was rebuilding a house for a damn resort and had had to fight to get this ball rolling, hadn't he? Granted, this was Chelsea's dream, but still, Zach wasn't about to give up on this house and he sure as hell wasn't going to give up on Brock. That boy was looking for someone to let him down, and Zach refused to be that person.

The back door opened and slammed. Braxton's angry voice sounded through the hall leading to the foyer. Zach heard the name Sophie and knew he was in for it.

Just as Zach headed for the kitchen, he heard Liam call out, "We promised Brock no punching."

Braxton gripped a folder in his hand as he came down the hall. He closed the gap between them and smacked the folder against Zach's chest. "These are from Sophie. They're some images you'd asked her to do. She said she'd try to get the others, but she's not sure when she can do them. You want to know why she's not sure?"

Not really, because Zach didn't want to relive this

entire nightmare with Braxton right now. Apparently he'd been to Sophie's house and it took all of Zach's self-control not to ask how she was doing . . . which would've been an absolutely stupid question.

"She's thinking of moving." Braxton shoved Zach back a step. "And as she's rambling on about relocating and how she'd start her business over in another city, she's trying her hardest not to cry, though her eyes are swollen and red, which leads me to believe you're an asshole and you hurt her yet again."

Moving? What the hell? Where had that come from? She loved it here in Haven and she had a reputable real estate agency. How could she think of leaving?

Life continued to smack him in the face. Every time he thought he was doing the right thing for those he loved, the plan absolutely blew up in his face, leaving him even more scarred than before.

Zach gripped the folder and opened it slowly: flawless drawings by Sophie, images of her late best friend's dream. Even through all of this, Sophie wasn't giving up on Chelsea, not giving up on this project, even though she'd let him go.

He glanced through each one and wondered how much time each picture had taken her, what she'd been thinking as she drew. She'd told him she had started drawing when she was recovering from the accident. Had she drawn any of these after he left yesterday morning?

How narcissistic did that make him, wondering if she'd drawn to get over him? Sophie would move on, she'd be fine eventually, and Zach would be . . . in the same hell he'd been in before he'd had her. No, actually he'd be in a deeper level because now that he'd been with her, tasted her, touched her, he knew exactly how amazing they were together and he'd have to live with those memories for the rest of his life.

"If we didn't have to be in court tomorrow for Brock, I'd kick your ass."

Zach glanced from the sketches up to his angry brother. "Liam already promised Brock no more punching."

"I'd find another way to hurt you," Braxton vowed, crossing his arms over his chest.

Even with his professor glasses on, Braxton was still a badass who rarely showed his anger. Apparently he saved it for Zach.

"We have work to do here," Zach stated, closing the folder. "If you want to bitch at me, do it while putting up new Sheetrock in the kitchen."

Braxton narrowed his dark eyes. "Are you seriously going to stay here and work, knowing Sophie is home crying? Are you that heartless?"

Zach shoved his brother aside. "I'm not heartless. I can't be with her. Drop it."

Zach headed into the kitchen. Liam was taking a drink, Brock was trying not to look at anyone, and Zach focused on the wall that needed new Sheetrock. Holes for three outlets and one light switch would need to be cut.

"You're such an asshole." Braxton pushed Zach from behind. "You left Sophie when things got complicated because you're afraid."

Zach whirled around, slapped the folder onto the island, and clenched his fists.

"Easy there," Liam demanded. "No fighting."

"Since when are you the mediator?" Zach called over his shoulder. "You guys don't get it. You have no idea—"

"I know her parents came by and you freaked out,"

Braxton interrupted. "Sophie told me everything, which only makes you more of a prick."

Zach sighed. "You know what? You all can work. I'm taking a break."

"Better cool down if you're going to see Sophie," Liam stated.

Zach flipped him a finger before storming out the back door. Damn his family for being so . . . concerned. He didn't want concern, he wanted . . .

At this point Zach didn't know what he wanted. If anything was possible in the do-over category, he'd take the night of the accident. Hindsight always proved what a selfish idiot he'd been.

He got in his truck and headed home to let the dogs out, feed them, play with them. Spending a few minutes around something that actually enjoyed his company was what he needed, because he was trying like hell not to go to Sophie's house and beg her not to shut him completely out. But that wasn't fair to either of them. She needed to move on, though the idea killed him, but in the long run she'd be okay and she'd find love with a man who would . . .

Zach slammed his palm on the steering wheel. He didn't even want to think in those terms. Brock's words kept playing over in his mind. Could it be that easy to take Sophie's love? Could she truly love him as much as she said she did? He'd taken everything from her, yet she claimed none of it mattered now.

Could she be that forgiving? She'd forgiven him when he'd clearly never forgiven himself. But he'd walked out on her yesterday. Walked out when she likely needed him most.

Yeah, he had decisions to make and a comfort zone to step out of. He could live his life, *his* life, and take control, or he could watch the woman he loved move on without him.

The choice was clear. She may have told him never to come back into her life, but that wasn't going to stop him from staking his claim. Sophie had fought for them long enough. Now it was his turn.

# Chapter Twenty-One

Sophie gave her assistant several errands to run, then told her to take the rest of the day off. Basically, Sophie just wanted to close herself in her office, turn the CLOSED sign around, and hide. She could still answer e-mails and phone calls, but right now she wasn't in the mood for much of anything.

Nearly a week had passed since she'd seen Zach. Six days, to be exact. She'd told him not to come back into her life, but she thought he might at least try something . . . anything.

Sophie pulled up her e-mails, but her focus drifted to the pencil drawing on the far wall in her office: the row of connected buildings, her office tucked right in the midst of them all. She'd done this drawing the day she'd bought the building for her office . . . nearly four years after the accident.

What started out as therapy had definitely become a passion, but she was having the hardest time trying to come up with more sketches for the Sunset Lake house. Each time she sat down to draw, she thought of Zach, of the diligent way he was pushing forward with this project. Even after all he'd done, and not done, she admired him for honoring Chelsea's memory.

She would fulfill her promise in spite of Zach and his stubborn ways. She would finish the sketches, she would get them to one of his brothers, and she would promote the hell out of this new business when the time came. And she'd do it all because no matter the end result, Sophie loved Zach's family.

The main door chimed and Sophie sat straight up. Time to put on the professional smile . . . she should've just turned the CLOSED sign around like she'd wanted to.

Before she could get to her feet, her office door opened.

"I was hoping I'd find you here."

A sliver of disappointment settled in as Sophie stared across the room at her mother. She'd not seen her parents since the bomb that had been dropped on Zach.

"Can I come in?"

Sophie gestured to the chair opposite her desk. Easing back, she waited for her mom to have a seat. Hopefully this would be a peaceful visit because Sophie wasn't in the mood, nor did she have the energy to get into it with her mother.

"You've not returned my calls," her mother stated, crossing her legs like the proper lady she was. "I know you're angry, but I never thought you'd shut me out."

"I never thought you'd purposely try to ruin my life." Sophie sighed and shook her head. She didn't want to become that bitter person who blamed everyone else for their own actions. Sophie was the one who'd chosen not to reveal the truth about her infertility. "That was harsh. I'm sorry, but you have to know what you did is hard to forgive."

"What I know is that I wanted to surprise my daughter, and when I came into the house and saw a man who nearly killed her standing there half naked, my motherly instincts went on high alert." She leaned forward in her seat just enough to rest her arm on the desk and meet Sophie's gaze. "What were you thinking, Sophie? I'm truly trying to understand this. I know you're an adult, but that doesn't stop me from worrying."

In her mother's own way, she loved Sophie. That much was apparent, but there was a point where the woman had to let go of control and relax.

"I'm assuming you're not getting back together with Martin?"

Sophie shook her head. "I don't love him."

Her mother stared for a moment before nodding and easing back into her seat. "And you love Zach."

Tears threatened to prick her eyes, but Sophie willed them away. She thought she'd dried up at this point and she'd promised herself she wouldn't break down again.

"Honey, he's only going to hurt you."

Sophie laughed. "Yeah, well, I think we've hurt each other. That doesn't stop how I feel."

"So what are you going to do now?"

Shrugging, Sophie tipped her head back against the chair and prayed for divine intervention. There had to be an answer, there had to be some way to make this pain less crippling and actually move on without feeling like she was moving through wet concrete.

"I'll get through this and so will Zach," she answered honestly. She wasn't mentioning her thoughts on moving. Her mother didn't need to know that little nugget of information. "I'm—"

The door to the main office chimed once again. Sophie's mom came to her feet. "I won't keep you," she said, smoothing her hands down her crisp khaki pants. "Would it be okay if your father and I stop by later?"

Sophie pushed away from her desk and stood, crossing to the doorway. "How about I call when I get off work and we can go out to dinner or something?"

"I'd like that."

Sophie's office door flung open, causing her to jump back. "Oh, I'm sorry. I thought you were alone."

"Brock?" Sophie took in the sight of the boy. Fresh new T-shirt, jeans that fit, without the threads unraveling, and shiny new shoes. This was the work of the Monroes. "What are you doing here? Is everything all right?"

His eyes darted over Sophie's shoulder, then back. "Uh . . . yeah. I just . . ."

"Oh, sorry. Brock, this is my mother, Catherine Allen." Sophie gestured behind her. "Mom, this is Brock. He's been working with Zach."

Her mother smiled. "Pleasure to meet you. I'll just let you two talk."

"Nice to meet you, ma'am."

Once Sophie's mom stepped out, Brock held up a folder Sophie hadn't noticed he'd been holding. "These are for you."

Confused, she took the folder and opened it. She flipped through the familiar images, then looked back to Brock.

"What are these for?" she asked, closing the folder. "I gave them to Braxton last Sunday."

"Yeah, he gave them to Zach, but Zach said he doesn't want them unless you deliver them."

Sophie narrowed her eyes. "He said that, did he?" What kind of game was he playing? Did he honestly think she could face him right now? Did he truly want her to?

Sophie crossed her office, laid the folder on her desk, and turned back to Brock. She crossed her arms and leaned against her desk as she eyed the boy, who still stood by the door.

"What's really going on?" she asked. "Why are you here and why did Zach really send those back?"

"I just told you. He said he'd take them, but only from you."

Sophie continued to study him. The bruises had faded, revealing an adorable young man who might just have a promising future. She knew the guys were taking him to court this Monday, and Liam had called to tell her the judge had agreed to let Zach have emergency custody, provided Social Services found nothing in their home inspection and investigation.

"Are you staying with Zach now?" she asked.

Brock nodded. "We've been working on the house. You should come see it."

"I'm not sure I'm ready for that." Sophie still wanted to know what part Brock was playing in all of this. Zach wasn't one to play games. "Who brought you here?"

"Zach."

Sophie straightened. "Is he waiting in the car?" Was he afraid to come in? What on earth was going on?

"No, he ran to Knobs and Knockers. He said he'd be back out front in ten minutes."

"Am I supposed to deliver this folder then?"

Brock shrugged. "He didn't tell me that."

Sophie couldn't help but laugh . . . she was either going to laugh or cry, because she was so confused right now she didn't even know what to feel.

"You can wait in the lobby for Zach, and when he

gets here, you tell him he'll get his sketches when I'm ready to give them back."

Brock's eyes widened. "He won't like that. I think he was hoping for today."

"Was he now?" And why was that? Did he have something planned? She knew for a fact they weren't near ready to hang the sketches, and she still had more to work on. "He'll have to get over it."

"How long are you guys going to fight?" Brock asked, shoving his hands in his pockets. He glanced down at his new shoes. "Sorry. That's not my business. It's just, you look like you've been crying, Braxton is mad at Zach, and Zach hates the world right now. Liam went back to Savannah, but he was pissed at Zach when he left, too."

"I haven't cried for a few hours, actually. I just didn't bother with much makeup today. As for the rest of it, sounds pretty normal for the Monroe boys."

"Are you really planning on moving?" he asked. He stared at her as if he were afraid of the answer.

Sophie tipped her head and weighed her answer, editing it in her own mind. "It's been a thought. But I've not decided anything. Why? Who told you I was?"

"Braxton mentioned it to Zach the other day and then they were trying hard not to hit each other."

Sophie was impressed they'd had any self-control. They really cared about Brock, to keep their fists to themselves.

Brock turned to head out the door. "I'll go wait on Zach and I'll give him your message."

Sophie crossed the room. "I'm glad you stopped by, even if you were playing the middleman. You look great."

A smile tipped Brock's lips. "Thanks. It's been a

good week, all things considered. And Zach might even let me keep one of the puppies."

"Just one?" Sophie quirked a brow.

Brock laughed. "I'm still working on the others. He talks to them like babies. He's pretty ridiculous. I don't think when the time comes he'll be able to get rid of them."

Sophie knew he wouldn't. She'd seen how he cared for the dogs, even if he pretended to still be a badass. He bottle fed one, had kept vigil during the night of the birth like some nervous father, and he was talking to them like children. The man had seriously grown attached to those pups.

"I better go wait on him," Brock stated. "You promise you'll bring those back. Right?"

"Promise," she said with a smile. She didn't have to say when.

Once Brock was gone, she waited another twenty minutes before she went to turn her sign to CLOSED. She was done with this day. She sank back into her office chair and flipped the folder open once more.

Flipping through each sketch, she froze when she found an extra paper at the end. Another drawing. It was terrible, but she couldn't take her eyes off of it.

It was a drawing of Zach's house with a man and a woman in the front yard. Stick people, actually, but one of them had on a triangle "dress" and there was another boy off to the side.

At the bottom, in Zach's scratchy handwriting, it said: WHAT FAMILY LOOKS LIKE TO ME.

Did he mean . . . no. He couldn't mean this would be them and Brock. He'd said he'd never marry, he'd never have a family, and Brock wasn't "his" technically.

Sophie stared at the image until the lines blurred

and a teardrop landed on the paper, smearing the F in family.

That man was so infuriating and confusing all at the same time. Now she had to go to him and see what he wanted, what he meant behind this drawing, because she truly had no idea.

She'd told him he wasn't welcome in her life anymore if he walked out, and at the time she meant it. But now, yeah, she didn't think she could turn him away if he wanted back in.

That didn't mean she had to make it easy for him, though.

Zach finished putting the last bit of grout over the new tile in the main bathroom. He'd wanted to be alone, so when Braxton had finished up with his classes for the day, he'd come by and taken Brock to dinner.

Honestly, Zach didn't know what was worse, being alone with his thoughts or being with his brother, who was still pissed.

When he'd picked Brock up from Sophie's office earlier, Brock seemed both amused and confused. He was smiling, but then said Sophie would bring the sketches when she wanted.

Had she not looked through them? Did she even get what his pathetic attempt at art had meant? He deserved to suffer for how he'd treated her, how he'd walked away again, but was she going to give him anything to go on?

He'd obeyed her wishes and kept his distance. Using Brock as a middleman hadn't been his first choice, but Zach was desperate and he wasn't about to just let the love of his life go without a fight.

Sophie was too kind, too sweet to totally ignore him. But she had told him he wasn't welcome back into her life if he left. Would she hold on to those words? Would she protect her heart even more now?

Pushing up off the hard floor, Zach stretched and twisted until his back popped. Just as he reached down to get his tray of grout, a spider the equivalent of his size-thirteen work boots scurried by. Damn pests nearly gave him a heart attack every time.

He stomped on the bug with more force than necessary, but he really wasn't taking any chances. Anything with eight legs that could move that fast could not be trusted.

The front door opened and closed before Zach could grab the empty tray or take off his knee pads. He moved down the wide hallway toward the foyer and froze.

Sophie stood in the middle of a dirty, dusty construction zone wearing a spotless yellow dress with little brown sandals. Her hair was down and straight, not a curl in sight, and her face was completely devoid of makeup. She looked as tired as he felt, but she was the most gorgeous sight he'd seen since he left her place last weekend.

His eyes darted down to the folder in her hand. There was no doubt now as to whether or not she'd seen his picture.

"Here are the sketches." Sophie extended the envelope but moved no closer.

Slowly, Zach crossed the open space and took the folder.

"I don't know why we had to pass this back and forth," she went on, crossing her arms over her chest. "Braxton already delivered it once."

She didn't know why? Zach flipped the folder open and leafed through the pages. His sketch wasn't there.

"Was this all there was when you got it?" he asked, dumbfounded.

"Of course," she replied. "Those are the drawings I put in there. Should there be something else?"

"I had . . ." Zach flipped through them once more. Maybe it had fallen out.

"What?" she asked, taking a step closer. "What are you looking for?"

Focusing back on Sophie, he saw the shimmer in her eyes as she tried in vain to blink tears away. "With all of your images of this home in the past, I put my image of my future, our future."

"Ours," she repeated. "And you think we have a future together? Because I'm positive you were the one who never wanted to marry. Never wanted a relationship, and you walked out on me."

Zach gripped the edge of the folder. "I am guilty of all of those things. I've never denied that I'm no good for you, Sophie, and I deserve every bit of penance you give me."

Damn it, now his own eyes were burning. This moment meant too much. He couldn't let her slip out of his life again. Nothing else mattered but her forgiveness.

"You saw the drawing."

Sophie nodded. "Yes."

"Tell me you understood my sad excuse for a love note."

Sophie swiped at her damp cheeks. As much as he wanted to reach for her, the ball was in her court. She was in complete control, because when he'd tried to be in control of things, his life had gone all to hell.

"Explain it to me."

Zach ran a dirty hand over his equally dirty, sweaty beard. "You're not going to make this easy, are you?"

"When you work for what you want, you appreciate it more."

Zach dropped the folder with a *smack* onto the wood floor before he reached for Sophie. He couldn't stand the separation another second. Framing her face between his palms, he used the pads of his thumbs to swipe away fresh tear tracks.

"I've never appreciated or loved anyone more than you," he vowed. "I've just got a terrible way of showing it."

"Yes, you do." She closed her eyes and rested her forehead against his. "I don't know what you want, Zach. I only know I can't keep doing this. I can't—"

He cut her off with his mouth. He'd missed that sweet taste, those soft sighs when she gave herself to him. Zach wrapped his arms around her waist, pulling her flush against him. By the time he eased his mouth away, Sophie was gripping his shoulders as if she wasn't sure if she wanted to hold him or not.

"Relax," he murmured against her lips. "I've got you, I've got us. I don't care if you have to think about this or if you need to wait and build your trust back up. I'll fight for this until you're in my life permanently. I won't lose you, Sophie. I'll never walk away from you again and damn it, I'm going to marry you."

Sophie gasped. "What?"

He nipped her lips once more before pulling away and running his hands up and down her back. "One day, if you'll have me, I want to marry you. I know you deserve better than anything I could ever offer, but I'll love you more than anybody else could ever think of."

He hadn't even realized he'd shed a tear until Sophie's delicate fingertips slid across his cheek. "I know you don't want kids, and I can't actually give them to you, but could we adopt?"

Zach laughed. "Does this mean you'll marry me one day?"

Sophie looped her arms around his neck, and her wide smile only made more tears slip down her face. "I'll marry you any day you want. You're mine forever, Zach Monroe."

Those words coming from her lips were more than he ever dared to hope for. "I'll adopt and raise a family with you in my old house," he told her. "For now we have Brock, and I'm hoping to get custody of him. He's legally living with me now. If his mother shows up, then a hearing will be necessary. I will definitely fight that, but she's nowhere to be found and I doubt she's even concerned he's gone."

Sophie threaded her fingers through his hair and kissed him. "He's so lucky to have you, and so am I."

"What do you say we head home?" he suggested as he held on to her hips. "We can tell Brock the good news. He was worried."

Sophie stepped out of his arms and reached for the hem of her dress. "Why don't we stay here and make our own memories?"

The dress slid up and over her head as she toed off her sandals. Sophie stood in the foyer wearing nothing but a smile and a matching pale pink bra and panty set.

"I'm sweaty," he protested.

Sophie laughed as she closed the space between them. "That's just the way I like you."

When she jerked his shirt off and started on his belt, Zach wasn't about to protest. "I love you, Sophie Allen. I'm going to marry you as soon as possible."

With a wicked grin, she unfastened his jeans. "I'm a

little busy at the moment. I'm about to make love to my fiancé."

Zach moved her hands away and lifted her into his arms, laughing when she squealed. As he carried her to the sitting room to a sheet-covered sofa, Zach knew this was just the start of the family he'd always said he didn't want.

Thankfully, Sophie had managed to break through his stubborn, hardheaded ways.

Please turn the page for an exciting sneak peek of
Jules Bennett's next Monroe Brothers romance,

**CAUGHT UP IN YOU,**

coming in December 2016
wherever print and eBooks are sold!

*Just try it*, she said. *It will be fun*, she said.

And that manipulative conversation with Sophie, his soon-to-be sister-in-law, is why Braxton now found himself wearing nothing but his boxer briefs and a towel, waiting for a massage.

A massage. He might as well turn in his man card now and go ahead and sign up for a facial and a pedicure while he was here.

Braxton Monroe and his brothers were gearing up to open a women-only resort and spa, in honor of their late sister, Chelsea. The business had been her dream, so how could they ignore something she'd been so passionate about?

With the resort set to open the first of the year, and the open house just a week before Christmas, they needed to hire a masseuse. In the beginning, they weren't sure if they wanted one on hand the first day the resort was open, but finally decided they wanted to do this up right and do it up big, just like Chelsea would've wanted.

Sophie had just sold a house to a new lady in town, and after some apparent girl bonding, Sophie wanted the guys to check out this applicant for the masseuse position.

And because the woman was new to the small town of Haven, Georgia, and not currently employed, Braxton was now in this stranger's home. He'd been half naked in a strange woman's house before, but usually under much different circumstances. Braxton hoped like hell Sophie hadn't lied when she'd said she'd checked out the woman's credentials.

Thankfully, Sophie had driven him over here to help with the awkwardness of the situation. Though he'd questioned her in the car when she started acting weird. She never gave him a straight answer when he asked about the naughty grin on her face, and he was almost afraid to see how this was going to play out. Okay, he wasn't almost afraid, he was flat-out terrified.

He also had no clue why he couldn't meet the potential employee before she came in and rubbed her hands all over him. But Sophie had insisted he was to undress and wait in the room, because he needed to have the full "client experience." Yet again, how the hell had he ended up with his ass up and his head in a doughnut-shaped hole?

Braxton groaned as he realized how foolish he looked lying there. For all he knew, this was a prank orchestrated by his brothers. No doubt Zach and Liam were back at the resort laughing their asses off at his expense. There would be payback.

The door behind him clicked and footsteps shuffled across the glossy wood floor. Braxton didn't lift his head, didn't want to see whoever had just walked in. He'd had more than enough of pampered rich girls to last him a lifetime. He'd seen the designer bag by the front door, Prada if his ex had taught him anything.

The last thing he wanted was to deal with another label-snob.

Bitterness was a pill he'd been trying to swallow for months . . . It still wasn't going down.

Braxton wanted to get this humiliation over with so he could go back home to his punching bag, drink a beer, fondle his remote, and try to regain some of his masculinity. First, he had to get this damn warped interview process over with.

The pocket door to the room slid open, then shut with a soft *whoosh*. Braxton attempted to mentally prepare himself for the next hour of the unknown.

"Good morning, Mr. Monroe." The soft, almost angelic voice washed over him, hitting him straight in the gut with a punch of lust. That was definitely something he hadn't prepared for. "My name is Cora. Have you ever had a massage before?"

Braxton grunted out a laugh. "First, call me Braxton. Formalities aren't necessary when you're going to have your hands on me. Second, no, I haven't, but I lost a game of rock, paper, scissors with my brothers, and my so-called friend drove me so I wouldn't be able to back out."

Her soft laugh seemed to caress his bare skin. "I assure you, by the time I'm done, you'll be glad you lost that game."

Between that laugh and her sultry tone, he was getting more turned on than he should. Seriously? That was new to him. For the past several months he'd been a bit . . . social with the ladies. Normally it was a flirty smile, a heavy-lidded lingering gaze, or a blatant touch that set him in motion.

Did Cora have a sultry smile or bedroom eyes? Tall, short? Did she have curves, or more of an athletic build?

Did she dress classy to match that Prada bag, or was she more laid-back?

He gritted his teeth. He was here for a job interview, not to visualize the body that belonged to that sexy voice. He shouldn't care, because the last thing he needed was to be tied in knots over a woman . . . any woman. Physicality was his best friend lately, and he was just fine with that.

Braxton closed his eyes, listening to the soft movements, the subtle clangs of containers being opened, closed. He had no clue what to expect, but when something small and warm rested against the top of his spine, he stiffened.

"What's that?" he asked.

"Hot stones. I'll be placing them down your spine. Would you like me to explain each step as I go so you're more comfortable, or do you prefer quiet? Each client is different, but since this is basically an interview, I feel I should tell you everything so you understand what it is that I can offer."

What she can offer? With a voice like that . . . Braxton bit the inside of his cheek. He couldn't start hitting on a potential employee. Yes, he'd gotten a bit more outgoing since his engagement debacle, but there was a time and a place. This was neither, nor.

Cora carefully rested the stones down his spine, which he had to admit was rather nice. Damn it. He refused to like this. He was here under duress. Why was he already thinking of her on a first-name basis? Oh yeah, because she was about to rub him.

"While I'm working I can tell you about myself."

Yeah, something he should've thought of. This was his chance to interview her for the position, and they desperately needed someone to fill the role. Sophie absolutely swore this woman was the one for the job, but she'd insisted one of the brothers interview her to make sure. Focusing while getting a rubdown was a bit difficult, in his defense. Damn it, that felt too good. Should he be enjoying himself this much?

"I've been a licensed masseuse for two years." Her calm, relaxing voice cut off his thoughts. "Not very long, but I went to college first and I have my degree in accounting."

Okay, so that told him two things: She had her head on straight for getting a degree, which the nerdy professor in him admired. And she was still young, almost a decade younger than him, which was just another reason he needed to keep his lustful thoughts out of his head. Just because her voice was silky smooth didn't mean he had to react to it or start to fantasize about what she looked like.

While the rocks stayed in position, Cora's hands started gliding in short, smooth strokes from the middle of his back down to his side. Braxton had to catch himself from groaning. No, he wasn't here to enjoy the process, he was here to see if she would work out in their spa. In his defense, though, he could see how women would eat up this type of pampering. And that's precisely what they needed for this women-only resort and spa he and his brothers were going to open.

Belle Vous was a vision of their late sister, Chelsea, and the Monroe boys were fighting like hell to make sure this resort was unlike anything around. They didn't want to just open their doors and hope for the best. They wanted, just like their beautiful sister had, to make the business thrive. They wanted this to be a place women came to relax from work, from family, from life in general. Chelsea had wanted that because their adoptive mother had put her life on hold to ensure they all had an amazing life. The woman had never asked for anything for herself; everything was for her family. Chelsea's dream was to cater to those women who were constantly giving.

"Why aren't you working as an accountant?" he asked, impressed he could form a coherent sentence while she worked her magic. Oh man, those hands of hers were talented. And he had no idea why there were rocks down his back, but this was absolutely amazing.

Fine. He was enjoying every second of this, but that didn't mean he had to admit it to anyone.

Her hands stilled for only a split second before she replied, "Personal reasons. Being a masseuse gives me more freedom. I love helping people relax. In a world where everything is rushed and hectic, I think people need to take more time for themselves. To work at a resort as unique as this one would be perfect."

Something about her passion, her need for freedom, reminded Braxton of Chelsea. His late sister would already love Cora for this position in the spa. And Braxton had to admit, he could get used to this treatment . . . still without anyone knowing, of course.

"I'm going to use some oil now," she told him, still in that soft, made-for-the-bedroom voice. No, damn it. She wasn't made for a bedroom, at least not his. "Do you prefer a scent or unscented? I keep both for allergy reasons, and for men who prefer not to smell like flowers or fruit. Everyone is different and I like to please each client."

Oh man. She was killing him. Killing. Him.

His mind drifted to areas it shouldn't. He didn't need to think about being pleased in any other way than by finding the perfect employee.

Braxton laughed at his wayward thoughts and how quickly he'd strayed off course. "Unscented is fine. Do you have many male clients?"

"I did where I was working," she replied easily. "I had quite a variety, actually. CEOs, blue-collar workers. Granted, most of them were private about their guilty pleasure, but that's fine. I understand the need for them to feel masculine. I've learned how to keep secrets, and every client has them."

Her hands slathered together seconds before the warm, oily glide took over. He had to swallow back the groan that threatened to slip out. Mercy, he hadn't expected to really enjoy this. Braxton didn't know if all massages were this sensual or if he'd hit the masseuse jackpot, but this woman and her clever hands could rub him all day.

Best. Interview. Ever. Maybe he needed to hold more interviews for possible masseuses. Or not. That was one thing he'd never live down, if either of his brothers thought he actually liked this.

"Why the move to Haven?" he asked. "I was told you lived in Atlanta."

Her hands traveled to the other side of his back. The oil slid easily between her palms and his skin, making him think of other, very unprofessional thoughts.

"My family is in Atlanta, but I've never wanted to stay there. I'm not a big-city girl. Too rushed, too chaotic for me." She finished his back, then moved to shift the towel over his backside as she placed more oil on the tops of his thighs. "I love Savannah, always have. Several summers ago I came to Haven with a friend and instantly fell in love with the small-town charm."

Was she trying to get away from the city or her family? Or both? There was a story there, but right now Braxton was having a hard enough time controlling his urges. With her digging into the backs of his thighs . . . he couldn't delve into her personal issues.

"Can you tell me more about the resort?" she asked, moving down the table to work on his lower legs. "Sophie told me enough to have me interested in what three guys would want with a women's resort."

Braxton chuckled, lifting his hands to settle on either side of his face on the cushy doughnut pillow. "We're either really smart or we're about to make total fools of ourselves."

"Personally, I think the idea is brilliant. Working moms, young, single women looking for a getaway, sisters, moms and daughters. You'll have a whole host of women flocking to this resort."

He didn't know why her approval pleased him. Cora with the sultry voice and the talented hands had clearly taken control of his mind and every single thought. Who knew a masseuse held so much power?

"Our sister, Chelsea, bought this house a few years back. She always loved to travel and take off on a whim. The one place she always wanted to see was Paris." He focused on the story, not on the fact she was now on his thigh again, up near very personal territory. "She had a vision for this place that none of us knew about until she passed away almost a year ago."

Cora's hands froze. "I'm so sorry. I had no idea you'd lost someone that close."

Braxton still couldn't believe it himself. Not a day went by that he didn't want to send Chelsea a text, but just as quickly as that thought would hit, the pain of the emptiness would replace it. That ache, it hadn't lessened one bit. The pain was just as fierce, just as crippling; he'd just grown accustomed to living with a hole in his life. He didn't like this new chapter without her, but he would go on living and honor her memory. The alternative of letting his grief consume him wasn't an option. Chelsea was a strong woman, and he'd be damned if he'd let her down.

"We're getting along." The simple reply for emotions that were anything but. "We're doing this for her, to keep her alive the only way we know how."

Cora smoothed the towel back in place. She brushed against the side of his leg as she moved toward his feet. "You must be a strong family to support each other like this."

There was a wistfulness to her tone, almost a longing. None of his concern. Sexy women were one thing, baggage and anything personal was a whole other level he ran fast and far from. Being jilted by a so-called love could make a man a bit jaded . . . or at least wake him up to how careless people were with other's hearts.

"We have our typical moments where we don't agree, but we know we can always depend on each other."

"Sounds perfect," she murmured.

Oh yeah. There was a story. A story he had no reason to care about. Even if she came to work for his family, getting personally involved on any level would be a mistake.

"Chelsea left behind several binders with notes and pictures, detailing exactly what she wanted out of this new property she'd purchased." He still couldn't believe the whirlwind of activity over the past year. "She wanted to name it Belle Vous, which means 'beautiful you' in French."

"She must have been an amazing woman," Cora replied. "This idea, it's all so perfect."

"That's what we're holding on to," he said honestly. "We want every woman who hears about the resort to have that same reaction. We figure at first there will be all kinds of interest, but we don't want that newness to wear off."

"Tell me more about my position," she went on as she gripped the arch of his foot with her fingertips. "Will there be appointments, like at a spa, or would you prefer someone there all day to be ready for spur-of-the-moment clients?"

Sticking to the reason he was there, Braxton replied, "We will have set hours for the spa, but you will be doing your own appointments. We want the spa workers to feel like they have control over their schedules while still meeting the needs of the clients."

"Smart."

Braxton smiled. He'd be sure to tell his brother Liam that, since Liam wanted all spa employees to be there all day and all evening. Braxton and Zach had finally talked some sense into him. They'd burn out their workers in the first few months working them to death like that. Growing could come later. Right now they needed a good, solid base to keep things running smoothly while they focused on catering to the guests.

By the time his massage was over, Braxton didn't know if he could move. Would it be unprofessional to lie there and take a nap, now that he was all relaxed?

"I'll let you get dressed," she told him. "Just tell me when you're done and I can come back in so we can talk more. I just have a few more questions, and I assume you have more for me."

He should, but with his loose muscles all he could think of was *When can you start?*

The door opened and closed. Braxton sat up, twisting his neck from side to side. Damn, he felt pretty good. After working on that house, getting everything fixed and repaired, he'd had his fair share of aches and pains. He wasn't twenty anymore, and his body was reminding him with each crack and cramp. Not to mention he was used to working at a college and not a construction site.

He quickly dressed because now he wanted to see the woman behind the magic. Would her tone match her appearance? For all he knew, someone's elderly grandmother had just felt him up and he'd liked it.

Wouldn't be the first time he'd found himself in the company of an older woman. Unfortunately, Zach's overeager neighbor had been a one-night mistake he still couldn't dodge.

But Cora wasn't a grandmother, of that he was sure. She'd sounded young, and she'd given him a hint as to her age when she'd discussed her education. Regardless of how instantly attracted he was, that was only because of her voice, her talented hands. What man wouldn't be instantly turned on? He was human.

He needed to get into professional mode fast, because he refused to be taken off guard again by this woman.

Fastening his watch, Braxton glanced at the closed door. He'd been in here for all of an hour, and he'd never felt this calm. She truly was a miracle worker, and perfect for the spa. As usual, Sophie was right.

Braxton turned the knob, easing the door open, but stopped short at the sight of Cora standing in the hallway talking with Sophie.

Swallowing his shock, Braxton stared at the beautiful woman who'd just rubbed his body to complete relaxation: the long, rich auburn hair tumbling down her back, the petite build, the way she tipped her head toward him but didn't meet his gaze.

Sophie smiled. "I'll let you two talk. I'll just wait in the living room."

Braxton noted the large yellow Lab sitting obediently next to Cora. He hadn't seen the dog when he'd first arrived, which was strange. Didn't all dogs bark and run like mad toward the door when a visitor arrived? Zach's dogs certainly did . . . all eight of them. Well, the seven puppies did. The poor mom tended to remain still, as if she didn't even have the energy to greet a new guest.

"Would you like to go in and sit, or stay in the hallway?" Cora asked, a wide smile spreading across her face, her gaze still locked over his shoulder.

Braxton returned her infectious smile. "We can go back in here. I only have a few more questions."

"Great."

Braxton watched as she reached out her hand. He thought she was reaching for him but realized she was feeling her way. She also hadn't looked him in the eye. And she had a very obedient dog who stayed by her side.

Nothing much shocked him, but the fact that Cora Buchanan was blind and had just given him the massage of a lifetime sure as hell left him utterly speechless.

He followed her into the room but remained standing until he saw where she wanted to go. Propping his hands on his hips, Braxton stared down at her where she'd taken a seat on a small accent chair in the corner of what most likely used to be a bedroom. Her dog right at her side.

"Why didn't you tell me you are blind?"

Cora ignored the accusatory tone. "Does my sight change how you felt when you were getting a massage? When you were completely comfortable and talking about the job?"

"No."

His feet shuffled against the wood floors and Cora kept her hand on the back of Heidi's neck. "I asked

Sophie not to tell you. I wanted to be interviewed and judged on my abilities and my professionalism, not my lack of sight."

Because she'd come here to prove she could live alone, she could work and not worry about being judged or discriminated against by those who were supposed to support her the most. Why did her condition disturb so many, when she was the one who lived with it?

She was the one who'd been robbed of her sight, she was the one who'd had to rebuild her life, to rediscover who she was after the accident that ultimately led to a life-altering diagnosis. And damn it, she refused to let any obstacle stand in her way. Independence was hers, she just had to reach out and grab it.

There was a time when she'd been too afraid to grab hold of freedom—a time when she'd reach out and encounter only darkness. She'd had no idea what all she was losing until everyday activities became difficult.

With each passing day her world had grown dimmer and dimmer. She waited for the anxiety, the panic attacks, but they never came. What consumed her had been so much worse. There was an emptiness she couldn't even put into words. There were places she wanted to see in this world, but once the diagnosis hit, her family started to withdraw and Cora feared traveling alone.

"I don't like being manipulated," he told her, pulling her back into the moment. Why did his tone have to be so low, so sexy? And why were her hands still tingling? She'd given countless massages, many of them for men, but there was something about Braxton's taut muscle tone beneath her fingertips that would have them zinging for days.

*Focus. No zinging.*

"I don't manipulate people," she defended with a tilt of her chin. "But I also wanted a fair shot at this position."

The air shifted as Braxton moved. Material slid together in a smooth, quick motion. She pictured him crossing his arms over what she knew was a broad chest. Her heart beat so fast, she had to force herself to take deep, calming breaths. She couldn't let this opportunity pass her by. She needed this position and the women's resort sounded absolutely amazing. Financially she didn't need this at all, but for her sanity, for the life she wanted to have, she wanted this job and she wasn't letting it slip from her hands.

Cora wasn't going to hide behind her lack of sight, wasn't going to use it as a crutch to have people help her through life. Even when she'd been at her lowest point, she'd fought to get back that independence. She'd come so far, and she had no intention of slowing down.

She literally had all the money she could ever want, had a multimillion-dollar company at her disposal . . . but it came with a price, and Cora had to at least try being on her own before deciding what to do with the rest of her life. She wanted—no, needed—to stand on her own two feet, and she damn well would or she'd go down fighting.

"If you need to think about it, or discuss it with your brothers—"

"How would you get to work?" he asked, cutting her off.

Cora pursed her lips. She'd thought of that when first approached by Sophie for the potential job. "If you give me the job, I'll find a way. I know I'm only a couple miles away."

Silence filled the room once again. Braxton wasn't moving, she could barely hear him breathing, but tension filled the room. Cora slid her hand down Heidi's back, taking comfort in her best friend . . . the only being she'd been able to depend on the past three years.

At first Cora had wondered how much a dog could help, but she and Heidi clicked instantly. Cora recalled that moment when she didn't feel so alone. When just the slightest brush of fur reminded her she had a companion who understood and maybe, just maybe, they would get through this together.

"You'll need to see the resort first," he stated, then muttered a curse and shifted again. "Sorry. I wasn't thinking."

Story of her life. Everyone was sorry, which only made her angry. Why was everyone sorry? Had they caused the condition her doctors had overlooked for years? A condition her parents were still in denial about. There was nothing to be sorry about. Her condition was something she'd learned to live with, was still learning to live with. Adjustments came every day, but in the three years since she'd lost her sight, she'd become a stronger woman. Just because life threw her a major curveball, didn't mean she would give up on what she wanted, on what would make her happy.

"Please, from here on out, don't apologize. Don't try to watch your words, don't try to coddle me. I would love to see the house because I can see without my eyes."

"I'm sorry . . . what?"

Cora smiled. Typical reaction from a stranger, and just one more way she could show him that she was not some blind woman who planned to sit on the sidelines and have life pass her by. Yes, she'd had to make some major adjustments, and in the beginning it was easier to feel sorry for herself. But Cora wasn't going to live her life engulfed in self-pity, and she sure as hell didn't want pity from anyone else, either.

"You'd be surprised how much your other senses are heightened when one of them is taken away." Nerves swirled around in her belly, but she pushed forward. She couldn't afford to be nervous now. Strength, independence, and strong will were her new best friends. "I'm guessing you're about six-three. You either work out quite a bit or you're into manual labor. You're nervous since you found out I am blind because you're shifting more now than you did before."

His soft laugh slid all over her. "When you were rubbing on me I was relaxed."

That gravelly voice shouldn't make her body have such a severe response . . . but it did. "Well, I'm not rubbing anymore, and you'll just have to adjust," she retorted. "So. When do I get the tour of this new resort?"

Because backing down wasn't an option. She was good at her job, and that coveted independence was within her reach. Her parents doubted her, her pseudo-fiancé doubted her. The only person with faith in Cora was Cora.

"I'll pick you up tomorrow morning. This afternoon I'm meeting with an inspector to go over all the wiring in the guest cottages."

Shocked he'd just volunteered to be her chauffeur, she concentrated on what else he was saying. "Guest cottages?"

"Besides the main house, there are two small cottages on the grounds." His feet slid across the floor and his breathing grew a touch louder, which meant he'd moved in closer to her. "The main house is done, other than some minor touches. The cottages have a bit more work, but nothing we can't handle in the next couple weeks. Once we tour, I'll need to know how you'll want your space set up and what needs to be ordered for your room. We'll have to get that taken care of first thing."

Cora nodded as she exhaled a breath she'd been holding since they'd walked into this room. Finally, she was getting the break she needed. Being a Buchanan had normally gotten her everything she wanted out of life. She could buy anything at any time . . . except her sight and her freedom. Her parents still didn't understand why she wanted out, why she'd felt trapped in that office day in and day out. But she'd prove to them, and to herself, that she could live on her own, have a job she loved, and be the happiest she'd ever been. It wasn't about money, it never was. It was about finding out who she was, not who she'd been molded to be.

Cora offered him what she hoped was a grateful smile. "Thank you."

"If this works out, I'll be thanking you."

Coming to her feet, she took a step forward. Instantly Braxton's hand gripped her bicep. "There's a towel on the floor. I didn't want you to trip."

"Oh."

His protective hand remained in place, giving her that zing once again. She couldn't afford to zing or tingle or any other verb associated with his touch. That voice alone was enough to have her hormones on high alert. Touching couldn't be added into the mix.

"Did I drop it? Usually I'm good about knowing when something falls."

"I think it was the one I used," he said, removing his hand. "I've put it up on the table. All clear now."

Cora slid her hand to Heidi's head and patted. "You can go ahead. I'll follow you out to the living room."

He didn't move and Cora hated the thought of him studying her. She wasn't self-conscious about her blindness, but she didn't want to be analyzed either.

"You're staring," she accused.

"I won't apologize."

Cora ignored the punch of lust at his soft yet powerful voice. At least he'd listened to her and wasn't saying he was sorry. That was something.

"Do you live here alone?" he asked after a moment. "Not that it's my business. I'm just amazed, I guess."

Amazed? That was a first for her. Her parents certainly hadn't been amazed at her decision to move away and be on her own. Her wannabe fiancé had been stunned speechless . . . so much so he didn't even ask her to stay, which was fine with her since she wouldn't have anyway.

There was just something about the way Braxton delivered such a simple sentence that warmed her. To know a total stranger didn't find her actions ridiculous—her mother's words—was refreshing. The need to be seen as an equal was overwhelming, and she hated that she allowed herself to feel this way. She knew in her heart she would be just fine, but a little encouragement along the way was something she wouldn't turn down.

"I live with Heidi," Cora replied. "She's all I need."

Again, silence settled heavily between them. Uneasiness slid through her. What was he thinking now? Was he staring at her, looking around the small room? Replaying that massage that her hands might never recover from?

"Was there something else?"

"We never did decide how you'd get to work."

Cora shrugged. "Let me worry about that. If I want something, I don't let little things stop me, and I want this job. Are you sure you don't need to talk things over with your brothers?"

"Trust me on this."

Cora thought of the dynamic family who always presented a strong front, but once rough times hit, they were nowhere to be found. Her parents were all about pretenses. Look good on the outside, no matter the turmoil inside. Ignore it and it will go away. "It" was an umbrella term for whatever her parents didn't want to face at that moment. With their money, they'd truly believed they could buy happiness. Unfortunately for their daughter with a health issue, they could toss out any dollar amount and nothing would change her condition.

They ignored the issue once they realized every specialist they'd called in had no cure. So they moved on with their lives, their parties, their business deals and jet-setting, leaving Cora to work everything out on her own. The loneliness had taught her so much. Hard life lessons had made for some deep scars.

Swallowing, she replied, "I don't trust anyone."

Braxton let out an audible sigh. "We all have our own baggage," he muttered, revealing a bit more about the intriguing man. "You'll see, my brothers won't disagree with Sophie's opinion or mine. Actually, Sophie pretty much rules our lives, and we're afraid of her, but don't tell her I said that."

Cora breathed a slight sigh of relief and laughed. "Good to know. Let me walk you and Sophie out, and I'll be ready in the morning for that tour."

# GREAT BOOKS
# GREAT SAVINGS!

When You Visit
## www.kensingtonbooks.com

You Can Save Money Off The Retail Price
Of Any Book You Purchase!

- All Your Favorite Kensington Authors
- New Releases & Timeless Classics
- Overnight Shipping Available
- eBooks Available For Many Titles
- All Major Credit Cards Accepted

Visit Us Today To Start Saving!
## www.kensingtonbooks.com

31901059338147